HUNTED BY THE SKY

TANAZ BHATHENA

Farrar Straus Giroux
New York

Farrar Straus Giroux Books for Young Readers
An imprint of Macmillan Publishing Group, LLC
120 Broadway, New York, NY 10271

Printed in the United States of America
Designed by Michelle Gengaro-Kokmen
First edition, 2020

1   3   5   7   9   10   8   6   4   2

fiercereads.com

ISBN: 978-0-374-31309-8 (hardcover)
ISBN: 978-0-374-31310-4 (ebook)

Library of Congress Cataloging-in-Publication Data

Names: Bhathena, Tanaz, author.
Title: Hunted by the sky / Tanaz Bhathena.
Description: First edition. | New York: Farrar Straus Giroux, 2020. | Audience: Ages 12–18. |
    Audience: Grades 10–12. | Summary: Trained in warrior magic after the murder of her parents, a girl
    with a star-shaped birthmark is prophesied to be the downfall of a tyrant king, but the boy she falls
    in love with owes his loyalty to those hunting her.
Identifiers: LCCN 2019036128 | ISBN 9780374313098 (hardback)
Subjects: CYAC: Fantasy. | Magic—Fiction. | Prophecies—Fiction. | Revenge—Fiction. | Love—Fiction. |
    Orphans—Fiction.
Classification: LCC PZ7.1.B5324 Hu 2020 | DDC [Fic]—dc23
LC record available at https://lccn.loc.gov/2019036128

Our books may be purchased in bulk for promotional, educational, or business use. Please contact
your local bookseller or the Macmillan Corporate and Premium Sales Department at (800) 221-7945
ext. 5442 or by email at MacmillanSpecialMarkets@macmillan.com.

We acknowledge the support of the Canada Council for the Arts.

To my mother—the first warrior I met.
And to the late Russi Lala—
for encouraging me to wield my own weapon: words.

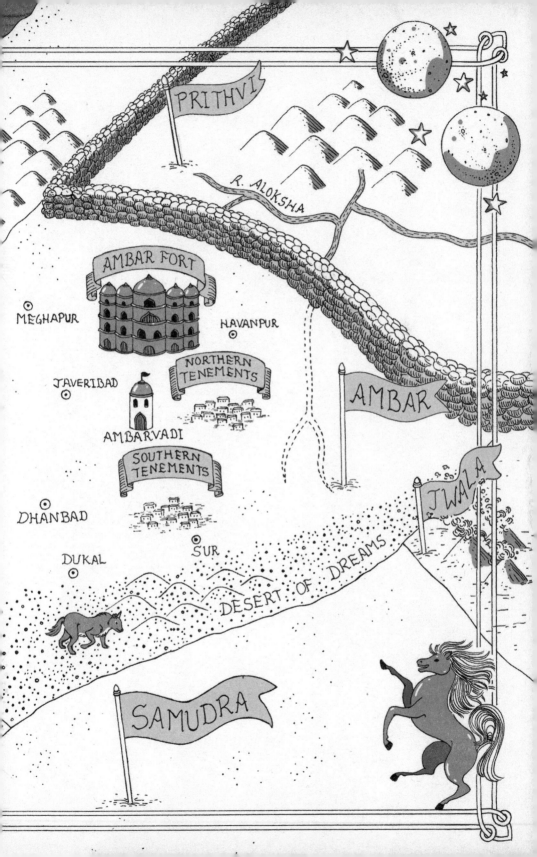

THE STAR

A village in the kingdom of Ambar
2nd day of the Month of Moons
Year 20 of King Lohar's reign

1

GUL

They come for us in the night and shoot my father through the skull. I expect his head to crack open, to burst like the melon my cousin Pesi shot with the old atashban he found outside our village schoolyard when we were twelve.

"See, Gul?" he panted, pointing out the fruit's pulpy yellow carcass. "See what I can do?"

My father's head does not burst open, but it does ooze blood. Red, trickling down his cheek and neck. Into the dark-green collar of his tunic. He falls, his body thudding to the floor.

"Look around for the daughter." The Sky Warrior who killed my father is a woman, her voice musical, oddly dissonant. Unlike Pesi, who used up so much of his magic to shoot the atashban that he had to rest for a whole day afterward, this Warrior shows no sign of exhaustion. Her atashban, a weapon that looks like little more than a golden crossbow with an arrow permanently nocked into place, glows from recent use. It rests casually against the silver armor on one shoulder. Crouched next to the railing that rings the first-floor balcony, I see the tip of the arrow and the top of the woman's silver helmet, the shimmer of sky-blue cloth winding it like a turban. "She must be here somewhere," she says.

"Yes, Major," a man responds, his voice so quiet I wouldn't have heard it if I hadn't been listening closely.

Ears of a shadowlynx, that Gul, Papa used to say with a laugh. *My daughter can catch any sound, anywhere and at any time.*

Kind words for a child whose magic emerges only on rare occasions, a child with nothing to her name except the single star-shaped birthmark on my right arm, a finger's length above the elbow. Twenty years ago, when Lohar, the current king of Ambar, first ascended the throne, his priests prophesied that a magus girl would vanquish him at some point during his reign:

> *The sky will fall, a star will rise*
> *Ambar changed by the king's demise*
> *Her magic untouched and unknown by all*
> *Marked with a star, she'll bring his downfall.*

When I was born, Papa said, my magic surrounded me in a glow of orange light, my skin singeing anyone who tried to touch me. "It wasn't normal," Ma admitted. "There *is* some magic that cloaks a baby when it is born, but your magic was unusually powerful. And then there was that mark on your arm."

But my magic faded within a few hours, to a point that it became nearly nonexistent. Unlike other magi children, who grow into their powers, wielding them with ease by the time they're nine, over the past thirteen years, I have performed magic only unintentionally—during moments of anger or terror—and even then, not always. Among magi, children like me are considered a curse and are usually sent away to the tenements to live with non-magi. While I'm grateful that my parents didn't send me away, I have never understood why my father believed I was the girl from the prophecy.

Because of this prophecy, hundreds of magi girls with star-shaped birthmarks have been taken or killed over the years. A few families try to hide their girls in the tenements by passing them off as non-magi, but that ruse never lasts long. Now even non-magi girls with birthmarks aren't spared, the slightest suspicion of "magical abilities" instantly making them targets.

Because of my birthmark, my parents and I have moved from town to town, village to village, ever since the day I was born. Because of my birthmark, my father, who said I was worth a dozen children, is now dead.

My body has frozen. My scream ties itself in a knot, buries itself somewhere between my throat and my tongue. I know my next move is to find Ma and run, to leave the house the way Papa instructed me to years ago, but I am glued to the scene, eyes burning, turning the tall Sky Warrior into a blur of blue and silver.

"Come." A sharp, familiar voice pricks the inside of my ear. Ma.

My mother herds me up the stairs to the roof terrace my father was going to renovate and plant a garden of roses in. "A garden? Here in Dukal?" Zamindar Moolchand, the richest landowner in the village, laughed when Papa told him about it. "See if your plants survive the desert wind first."

Today, there is nothing except for a raised bed made of wood and, next to it, a gunnysack of dirt.

My mother makes me lie in the raised bed; I'm small enough to just fit in. "Stay still."

"Ma, what are you—"

"Do you trust me?" My mother's pale-gold eyes stand out against brown skin warmed deep by the Ambar sun. She is what Papa said I would have grown up to look like if I hadn't inherited his bone structure. In the moonlight, she looks delicate, as ethereal as a winged peri in a painting. The fingers that grip my wrists, however, feel like stone.

"I trust you with my life." I give her the oath daughters have given to their mothers from generation to generation, before the Great War divided the four kingdoms of Svapnalok—Ambar, Prithvi, Jwala, and Samudra.

"Lie down, little one." Ma rips open the gunnysack with brutal efficiency. Her voice, however, is soft. In the sky overhead, two moons shine full and bright, one yellow and one blue. A beautiful night, Papa said earlier this evening. Perfect for the moon festival. For lovers to unite. For spirits to leave their graves and meet the sky goddess in her cloudy home.

"Am I"—my voice catches—"am I going to meet the goddess tonight, Ma?"

"No, daughter." Ma's hard hands push down my head, rub earth over my face. "You are destined to live long and burn bright. To end all this. You will not let our sacrifice go in vain. Now close your eyes."

In the years to come, I will wish I had listened to her this one final time. But I don't—and so I see everything that happens next.

My mother's hands glow green with magic, scouring the soil from her hands and her dress. A shadow covers the doorway to the terrace.

"Where is she?" the woman with the musical voice asks.

"Gone." Ma's voice brings goose bumps to my skin, even though the night is warm. "You'll never find her."

"Don't play with me, foolish farmer!" The arrow tip of the atashban glows red with magic against the Sky Warrior's shoulder. "Where is she?"

"I am not playing." My mother holds up the sickle that normally hangs on the wall at the back of our house, used to harvest wheat and safflower during the Month of Flowers. Tonight, though, the crescent blade glows faintly pink at the edges when Ma dives in, slicing into the tunic sleeve of the Sky Warrior, who dodges the blow.

"A farmer with the spirit of a fighter." The Sky Warrior sounds mildly intrigued. "A shame that we must meet like this today. A shame your death magic isn't as strong as mine."

Shadows struggle above me. Something clatters to the floor. Then, a scream that could have been a laugh of triumph. The air clouds with the rust-metal smell of blood. My mother drops to the floor between me and the dark shadow of the Sky Warrior, a thin red line curving her neck. The Sky Warrior wipes the bloody dagger with the edge of her long blue tunic. She looks around, kicks at the gunnysack, still half-filled with dirt.

"Are you in there, little witch? Or have you suffocated and made my life easy?"

I bite back a shout when the hammered heel of a boot presses over my palm. Tears bleed out, along with urine: a hot trail inside my woolen leggings. My mouth fills with the taste of brass. The Sky Warrior peers into the ground. She is staring right at me, the lower half of her face covered by the same sort of cloth that winds around her helmet. Her eyes narrow for a brief moment, but she does nothing. For some reason, she does not appear to see me.

A clatter of boots up the stairs. "Major Shayla, we searched the whole house," a woman says. Her face is similarly masked. "No sign of the girl."

The Sky Warrior straightens. "Send Emil ahead of us to look, Alizeh. The little witch couldn't have gone too far."

Her boot rises off my hand. She follows the woman back into the house without another glance at the damp patch of earth she just stood on, or the layer of girl underneath.

When someone dies, even a loved one, grief takes a back seat. Terror reigns in me, instead, for a good hour, the ebony star on my arm aching like a wound.

Ma tried so hard to get rid of my birthmark, even going so far as to try to burn it off my skin when I was five. It was the first time my magic resurfaced: when my fear made the fire ricochet off my skin and race up the long sleeve of Ma's favorite blue tunic. Knives did not seem to do the trick, either, my fear once more shielding me, hardening my skin to the consistency of metal. Armor.

"A protection spell," Ma muttered back then, almost as if it was as big a curse as the birthmark. My mother said the spell was a sign of the magic lying dormant within me, except that I had no control over it, no way of summoning any of its power or harnessing it at will. By the time I turned nine, my parents withdrew me from school because it got too difficult to explain why, out of an entire classroom of reasonably competent magi children, my performance remained the worst.

"Perhaps you should take her to the tenements outside the village," the schoolmaster suggested quietly. "Non-magi children don't have to go to school; they don't have to worry about any of these things."

"You mean non-magi aren't *allowed* in schools with magi anymore," Papa responded in a cold voice.

"Savak," Ma told Papa. "Now is not the time—"

"Where is your honor, schoolmaster?" Papa demanded, ignoring Ma's terrified face. "Why do you still keep this in your school?"

He pointed to a scroll that spelled out the Code of Asha hanging on a nearby wall. A system developed by the first queen of Ambar, the code declared that every human, regardless of gender, or magical heritage, must be treated with honor and respect. Originating first in Ambar, the code spread across Svapnalok before the Great War. It had been our kingdom's greatest contribution to the united empire.

"You go too far, Savak ji!" the schoolmaster exclaimed. "How dare you question my honor!"

Ma finally put an end to what might have been a major shouting match between the two men by fervently apologizing to the schoolmaster and pulling my father out of the classroom.

Later that evening, when she found me crying at home, Ma gave me a warm hug. "Don't be sad, my child. Look at the positive side. This way, you get a reprieve from five more tedious years of school."

"You don't mean that," I said in a thick voice. "You were disappointed. Don't lie to me, Ma."

Ma sighed, not confirming nor denying the statement. "The sky goddess works in mysterious ways. Perhaps she has a reason for keeping your magic hidden."

"Can we pray to Prophet Zaal or Sant Javer instead? How about the earth god from Prithvi or the fire goddess from Jwala? Maybe the sea god from Samudra—"

"Shhhhhh, my girl. We are from Ambar, a land named after the sky itself. Our souls are linked to the goddess who lives up there, the goddess who gave birth to Asha, our first queen. We do not share the same sort of affinity to the gods and the goddess from the other kingdoms, or to human prophets."

"That's not true!" I protest. "Several children at my school pray to the fire goddess. And nearly as many follow the teachings of Prophet Zaal!" The Zaalians, as I knew, didn't believe in the gods at all, but in the raw power of magic alone. I didn't really understand how praying to a prophet would help me, but I was willing to give anything a shot.

"Yes, people *do* pray to other gods and prophets, but *you* are different, my daughter," Ma told me, her eyes bright, more intense than I'd seen them before. "Ten years ago, I prayed to the sky goddess for a child, and she answered my prayers by giving me you. Your connection to her will always be stronger than to any other deity."

Yet, in the months that followed, the sky goddess never spoke to me, never responded to my prayers or pleas to strengthen my magic. By the time I turned ten, I stopped praying to her altogether.

Where are you, Sky Goddess? I think now, looking heavenward. Anger tempers my grief for a brief moment. *Why didn't you protect my parents?*

As expected, there is no answer.

Something crawls over my right arm, bites the tender flesh. A bloodworm. Long-bodied, many-legged. The insect, found all across Ambar, isn't poisonous. But it will feast on my blood until its body turns scarlet,

8

leaving behind a jagged scar on my skin. I have many such scars on my feet and calves from my childhood—from playing barefoot in the sand with my cousin Pesi, before he accidentally saw my birthmark and told his mother about it.

"I didn't push up my sleeves," I cried out to my parents. "I promise!" It was the one promise I never broke, ever since I saw what happened to the only other girl in Sur village who had been cursed with a birthmark like mine. The sound of her screams as the local thanedars dragged her off to prison still rings in my ears at night. No one knows what happened to that girl, and even if they do, no one ever speaks of it.

"I will make sure it never happens to you, Gul," Ma vowed.

We had already moved four times in the twelve years since I was born, but once my aunt and uncle found out, my parents didn't want to take any chances. We packed our belongings and slipped out once more into a starlit night, journeying farther and farther west, until we reached a hamlet at the edge of the desert. Dukal. The smallest and sleepiest of Ambar's villages, where the only newsworthy thing that ever happened was someone breaking wind in the marketplace. Two years have passed since then. A long stretch of boredom punctuated with terror.

My mother's last three fingers are curled inward, the index finger pointing up, as if clutching an invisible weapon. Stiffness has begun to set in, the way it does when a body dies, the magic seeping from the skin and into the air, leeching it of vitality.

I wonder who tipped off the Sky Warriors about our newest location. Any one in the village might have been tempted by the reward King Lohar offers. A hundred swarnas is a lot of gold—enough to feed a family of four for a year. No one would have felt guilty about sending the Sky Warriors our way: a strange man, woman, and girl who kept apart from the rest of the villagers, rarely ever mingling with them.

Why did they report us now, *though?* I wonder. *What tipped them off?* I guess I'll never know.

I rise slowly to my feet, dirt falling off me in clumps, and stagger to my mother's body. My gaze is drawn to her neck—bare of the necklace that Papa had given her only this morning. It lies next to her body now, broken, its silver beads scattered on the ground.

I pick up three of the beads with the foggiest idea of stringing them back together. *Maybe this is a dream. Maybe if I string the beads together, I'll be able to bring Ma back*, I think before nausea sets in.

When my vision clears again, the air around me reeks of vomit. The bloodworm has left behind a red moon-shaped ridge on my arm.

I wonder if it's meant to mock my cursed star.

2
GUL

Shortly after the Sky Warriors leave, villagers from Dukal enter our house, glass lanterns held high above their heads. *Who was it? I wonder. Which of these people reported us to the Sky Warriors?* Fear kicks under my ribs. I remain hidden, crouched near the railing of the first-floor balcony.

From the spot where I watched the Sky Warrior kill my father, I now watch the villagers carry his corpse out of our house, leaving behind nothing except a dark patch of blood staining the floor. A few others troop upstairs toward the roof, forcing me to duck around a corner and press up against the wall. Long moments later, I hear them come back down. I risk a peek and see a pair of women carrying my mother's body down the stairs.

"Both parents are dead. Goddess help them," I hear a woman say out loud. "They were foolish to keep the girl hidden for so long. Did they think we wouldn't find out?"

"How *did* you find out?" another woman asks. "You never said."

"At the market last week. The girl's sleeve ran up by accident, and

11

the mother was terrified. I got suspicious, so I reported them," the first woman says. "If they were innocent, there would have been no harm, would there?"

"Where's the daughter now?" the second woman asks. "No one could find her here in the house. Do you think the Sky Warriors took her with them?"

"If they did, we'll find out tomorrow at the constabulary. One of the thanedars there is my cousin. If not, then one of us will have to capture her and take her in ourselves. It's the only way we'll be able to collect the reward money," the first woman says grimly. "Not something I'm looking forward to, trust me. The last girl we took in put up such a fight! Five years gone and I still have the marks."

"Let's pray that the Sky Warriors took her, then," the other woman says. "What now? Shall we clean the house?"

"No, we must wait until tomorrow morning. Allow any spirits to leave the place."

My fingers curl around three of the silver beads from my mother's necklace. I hold my breath until the villagers are gone, leaving behind nothing except silence and specks of dust floating in the air. Tomorrow they will return and sweep out the rooms, cleanse the house with soap and water and prayers, readying it for another occupant. I saw it happen once before in another village: the girl gone, her parents and brother laid out dead on the front veranda.

Once they're gone, I slip out the door, narrowly avoiding the village guard and the light tap of his stick against the gravel. Sunheri and Neel, the yellow and blue moons, glow in the sky like sentinels, their brightness taunting in the face of my grief.

Magic still appears in traces against the bushes nearby: silver-blue, tinged with blood. Ma told me that magic always comes at a cost—the more you use it, the more it will take out of you. When Ma's hands began glowing green on the roof tonight, I didn't realize how high the cost would be, how much she was willing to bear.

By the time I reach Zamindar Moolchand's stable outside the village's biggest haveli, a mansion twice the size of my former home, my stomach has begun to growl. In the haste of escaping the villagers, I didn't even think to go to the kitchen first.

The smell of discarded food rises from the garbage heap outside the haveli gates. I scrounge through it, coming across a half-eaten portion of yellow lentils and pulao wrapped in a banana leaf. The food appears fresh—the lentils still warm, the rice made my favorite way, with coriander, spices, and bay leaves, interspersed with tiny honeyweed dumplings. It tastes like ash in my mouth.

I avoid the haveli itself, its sandstone walls painted a bright yellow, and instead press a hand lightly against the stable door. To my surprise, it opens with only a slight creak, and for a moment, I freeze, terrified that I'll wake the horses. A grunt rises, followed by a whinny.

Cautiously, I step inside.

The stable is clean, the sweet smell of dried hay filling the cavernous space. The paint on the wooden beams is faded, but not entirely gone: the remnants of an old fight scene between the Sky Warriors and the Pashu, a race of part-human, part-animal beings who were mostly extinguished during the Battle of the Desert seventeen years ago. Overhead, the artist has depicted King Lohar bent in supplication before the sky goddess, who is perched on a cloud, her eyes closed, her right hand raised in blessing.

The squat building must have housed several horses at one time, but now there's only one, a Jwaliyan mare with black eyes, her mane gleaming ruby red in the moonlight pouring in from slats overhead. For a second, I forget myself. Forget everything as the mare and I watch each other, partly awed, partly suspicious.

"You're a beauty," I whisper, breaking the silence. I've only ever heard about horses like this—the sort that run wild in the plains of Jwala, animals that are so difficult to procure that they sell for no less than a hundred swarnas at the flesh market in Ambarvadi. The mare snorts, ears flattening against her magnificent head.

"I won't hurt you," I whisper. "I swear I won't."

I take a step closer and pause again, spotting a carrot on a bale of hay. I hold it out to her: an offering. "Hungry?"

The mare's ears perk up, almost as if she could understand what I said. A wet nose brushes my fingers first, followed by the snap of teeth, which I narrowly avoid. With another snort, the mare turns away, dismissing my presence—I'm clearly not threatening enough to be of any consequence to her. I slip into the stall next to hers and sink into the sweet-smelling hay. For tonight, at least, I have a place to sleep. A place to hide.

As for tomorrow—who knows what will happen? I think of the women who entered our house tonight, the way they talked about my parents. About me. Anger slides through my fear, threads through it like a silver needle. My first instinct is to blame the villagers who tipped off the thanedars about us, who ripped my entire family apart for a bag of coins. But my mind finally settles on two people: the major who killed my parents, and the king who started it all.

Major Shayla. King Lohar.

I repeat their names over and over, memorizing them the way I would a lesson. A prayer.

"Kill Major Shayla," I whisper. "Kill Raja Lohar."

The idea is instinctive, ludicrous. Yet, for the first time since my parents died, my shivering hands grow steady. I wipe the tears off my cheeks. Slowly, under the watchful gaze of the mare, I unearth a bit of string lying on the stable floor and push my mother's beads through it, one by one. Seconds after I tie the cord around my neck, exhaustion creeps up on me, and I fall into an uneasy slumber.

The wealthiest landowner in Dukal has gray hair, a greasy smile, and teeth that shine yellow in the light of the fanas he holds over his head, flames dancing in the lantern's clear glass confines. I peer at

Zamindar Moolchand through the window next to the Jwaliyan mare's stall, watching him talk to three traveling women who have asked to spend the night. The mare, whom I've named Agni for her fiery coat and mane, nudges my shoulder playfully. Over the past four days, we've reached an understanding: I duck out each night to steal food from the zamindar's kitchen, and Agni is awarded carrots for not giving me away. I don't know why Agni has taken a liking to me. Or why I instinctively feel safe in her presence.

"Anandpranam." *The happiest of salutations.* Even with his palms respectfully joined, Zamindar Moolchand makes the ancient greeting sound perverted. "Be my guests for the night, ladies. Sate your hunger with my bread. My home is your home."

"Sau aabhaar, zamindar," says the tallest of the women. *A hundred thank-yous.* Another woman might have added the Common Tongue honorific *ji*, perhaps even delivered the greeting flirtatiously. This woman doesn't, even though she smiles, her deep-brown skin glowing in the moonlight. The pallu of her simple homespun sari slides down her head, revealing streaks of blue in her midnight hair. Ma once told me that it's the sort of blue that can't be covered up with soot or the oil from a jatamansi plant or magic. The mark of someone from the seafaring kingdom of Samudra.

The sight of it makes Zamindar Moolchand's unctuous smile slip. Had the woman been out in daylight with her head uncovered, the very look of her would have raised unspoken questions. The deadly Three-Year War between Samudra and Ambar ended fourteen years ago, but everyone still remembers the bloodshed: the corpses littering Ambari streets, the high screams rising from firepits where soldiers with blue-and-black hair burned Ambari citizens alive.

"My father married a woman from Samudra before the Great War," the woman says now. "She died when I was a baby." She speaks our language perfectly, her Vani smooth, the accent crisp and airy. It holds no trace of the sea. "We are headed back from Sur, where one of my

15

daughters had a baby. The zamindar would do us poor women a big favor by offering us a place in his stable for the night."

The zamindar turns his attention to the other sari-clad figures. One has shielded herself from his gaze, tucking her pallu like a veil over her mouth and nose. The other, a pretty, pale-skinned young woman, looks unperturbed by his leer.

"What's your name, my dear?" he asks her.

"Kali," she says.

"Kuh-lee," he enunciates slowly, as if savoring the sound of the word. "Why don't I offer you and your friends more comfort? My only brother is in the army and no longer lives here. I have five guest bedrooms. It can get lonely in this big old house."

If I could speak to any of these women, I would tell them not to do it. Every female in Dukal—old or young—knows how unwise it is to meet Zamindar Moolchand alone or to accept any favors from him.

"We prefer the stable." A hint of steel cuts through the quiet deference in the older woman's voice. "Our horses are tired; we need to ensure they are well rested. And with so much thieving in Ambar these days, one can never be too sure."

She stares at the zamindar until he averts his head and nods.

"Of course. Of course."

I duck behind a bale of hay in Agni's stall as Moolchand opens the door to the stable, letting in the women.

"Come on, Ajib. Gharib." The women click their tongues gently, guiding their horses into empty stalls on the opposite end.

"What a lech," a voice says. It's the veiled woman—no, a girl—who finally uncovers her face, revealing dark surma-lined eyes and skin like fine copper. Like her companions, the girl's black hair is bound in a braided bun. Unlike the other two, however, she wears a square amulet tied around her upper arm, marking her as a follower of the prophet Zaal. She appears to be a few years older than me. "I thought I'd have to strip him naked and hang him upside down from the roof of his stupid haveli."

The pale girl—Kali—snorts. "Like what you did to that safflower merchant last year for calling you his little flower bouquet? Seriously, Amira."

"Don't give me that look, Kali. You were a few seconds away from slicing that zamindar up like an onion with your daggers."

A pause before they both burst into giggles.

"Enough, you two," the older woman cuts in. "I don't want to have to modify the memories of an entire household again. Sky Warriors were at this village a few days ago; I still see traces of their magic against the trees outside."

As the girls murmur apologies, I think of the stories I heard growing up. Of women with shadowy faces and daggers glinting in their hands. Women who wear their saris like fisherfolk, who knock down doors and slash into enemies with knives and swords and spells. The Sisterhood of the Golden Lotus.

Witches, some men call them. *Thieves.*

Fighters, my mother told me. *Protectors.*

No one is quite sure if the Sisters are legends or common brigands, and no one ever quite remembers what they look like. Appearing and disappearing from villages and towns with a stealth that rivals King Lohar's Sky Warriors, the Sisters have no permanent home, successfully melding into their surroundings like color-changing lizards. I can't tell if these women are from the fabled Sisterhood. But I know it isn't wise to be seen by them before I find out more.

"Look!" one of the girls says, a sound that makes Agni snort angrily, ears flattening again.

I sink into the shadows, the hay behind me pricking my skin like needles.

"How lovely you are." It's Kali, reaching out to touch Agni with a hand. Not a chance. Agni snaps her teeth together, forcing Kali to jerk back.

"Strange. Horses usually aren't this afraid of me."

"Leave the animal alone." The other girl—Amira—says with a yawn.

"She's acting like she's protecting someone. Is there a foal?"

"Let me see." It's the woman again. From the shadows, I can see her face quite clearly: high cheekbones, slender lips, shrewd eyes that are as black as the sky outside the stable window. She must be least forty years old.

She begins murmuring words in an incomprehensible language that makes me think of sand under my feet and wind in my hair. She waves a hand over Agni's head, snapping her fingers once, releasing fine sparks that glow and smell of sandalwood. I feel the tension in the air dissipate. And sure enough, Agni's ears emerge from the back of her head. She dips her head into the feeding trough, nibbling a bit of the hay.

The woman wipes her forehead with the edge of her sari. "Amira, get me some light, will you?" There's a soft sound not unlike marbles rolling across the floor.

"You're scrying with your shells? Again?" Amira places the lantern on a hook near Agni's stall, casting light upon the shadows. I hold my breath, doing my best to blend in. If I had a choice, I would turn invisible. But invisibility is a difficult spell for even the most advanced magi, and I can barely produce a spark. My best hope, I know now, is to slide against the wall toward the girl-size gap behind the wooden partition that splits Agni's stall from the one I normally sleep in. As the woman and Amira argue with one another, I begin inching away from my hiding place.

"Didi, do you think it's wise to do a reading *now*?" Amira is saying.

Didi. The Common Tongue word for "elder sister" gives me pause. The Samudra woman and Amira look nothing alike, are perhaps not even related by blood. But you wouldn't know that from the worry and frustration lacing Amira's voice.

"You know how those shells affect you," she tells the woman. "They misled us today, taking us to that awful moneylender all the way near the edge of the desert. He would have turned us in to the thanedars if I hadn't tied him up!"

"The shells never lie, Amira." The woman's voice, barely louder than a breath, is the only indicator of her exhaustion, of the toll her magic took on her. "That there are indications of Sky Warriors being here confirms this. Someone in this village needed our help. Perhaps they still need our help. The only way to know is by doing another reading."

"But, Didi—"

I'm nearly inside the next stall, so close to freedom that I don't hear the way Amira's voice abruptly cuts off or the shift of her feet as she lunges at me in the darkness, her arm winding around my neck.

"By Zaal!" she screams when I sink my teeth into her skin. But she does not let go. Her arm tightens its grip, so hard that for a moment my vision blurs. In the background, I hear Agni's loud neighs, the sound of her hooves hammering the earth. The stall's wooden beams shudder.

"Immobilize her!" the woman shouts.

"I can't!" Amira's hands are hot with magic. But the birthmark on my arm burns hotter, sends a shock through her body. "Aaah! It . . . it doesn't seem to be working."

I kick backward, the sudden movement nearly making Amira stumble. A hard hand winds through my tangled hair and tugs sharply. It forces me to loosen my teeth and, in the process, feel cold steel pressed sharp against my throat.

"Another sound and you will no longer have a voice." I only have to look into the Samudra woman's cold eyes to know she means every word. "Understand?"

As if I didn't get the point already, the blade at my throat stings. I take a deep breath and force myself to go limp. My unreliable magic may have protected me from Amira's spell, but it will not shield my throat against a dagger.

From the corner of the stable, a horse whinnies. "Someone's outside," Amira mutters.

The blade bites my skin once more: a warning.

Kali is already at the stable door, speaking to someone. "No . . . no, it's all right. One of our horses got spooked by something moving outside. Thank you for your concern. Please tell the zamindar that all is well. Anandpranam."

Once the door is firmly shut, the woman turns to face me again. Her nose wrinkles, and suddenly I'm very aware of the sour smell coming off me. But then her gaze falls on my right arm, bared to the cool night air from my scuffle with Amira. She pushes aside the torn sleeve of my tunic and stares at my birthmark for a long time.

"What's your name?"

3
GUL

"**H**avovi!"

I blurt out the first name that comes to mind, belonging to a girl my cousin Pesi was smitten with.

A finger runs lightly down my cheek. "She's lying. You have both succeeded in terrifying the poor thing." There's a hint of sympathy in Kali's wide gray eyes. Up close, I realize that she's younger than I first thought—perhaps only sixteen or seventeen years old.

"It's true! I'm Havovi!"

"Silence." The woman's knife does not move from my throat. "Kali's gift is seeking out truths, scouring them for lies."

I bite my tongue. So Kali is a truth seeker. I'd seen one before, in a village square, accompanying a thanedar to interrogate a prisoner in the constabulary. But I'd never met one in person.

"Don't worry, girl. I will not force you to tell me your real name. It's not important to me in either case," the woman continues. "Though I must give you some credit for having the guts to lie with a dagger pressed to your throat. For a girl who has barely seen twelve blue moons in her life, that is impressive."

"Thirteen!" I spit out. "I will be fourteen in two months!"

Something shifts within the black depths of the woman's eyes, and for a second, I wonder if I've amused her.

"Truth." Kali laughs softly when I flinch. "She *has* seen thirteen moons. Still a baby, though. Probably just broke her blood barrier."

I feel my face grow hot. I am small for my age; it's something my mother always lamented when she looked at me, worrying over my narrow chest and my narrow hips, wondering if I would ever be strong enough to bear children. "I do not want children," I told her fiercely back then and never understood the weight that settled over her at my response.

"She's old enough," Amira says. Her heart beats like a war drum against my back. Her fingers dig into my shoulders through the cloth of my tunic. I am now beginning to regret the bites I took out of her.

"So you're going to hand me off to the thanedars, then."

The woman tilts her head to the side. "What makes you say that, girl? Why would we do such a thing?"

"To get a hundred swarnas. To gain favor with Raja Lohar." The latter is even more valuable than a hundred gold coins. If Ambar is our world, then King Lohar is its god, able to close shops, burn villages, and drain the most powerful magi of their powers with a snap of his fingers. "Besides, the penalty of hiding someone like me is—"

"We know what the penalty is," the woman interrupts. "Amira, release her."

"But, Didi—"

"Do it."

Amira drops her hand to the side and suddenly, shockingly, I find myself free. I collapse to the ground, air burning my windpipe, and wonder if she was planning to choke me to death.

"You can go," the woman tells me dismissively. "But don't expect to survive. The food you've been filching from the zamindar's kitchen will go unnoticed for only so long."

I no longer bother wondering how she knows this. Perhaps she, too, can read minds like the truth seeker. Or perhaps she simply possesses the one thing that Papa said does not seem to exist among many of our kind: common sense.

"I can take care of myself," I say defiantly.

"What are you going to do?" Amira asks. "Piss again when the Sky Warriors capture you?"

She is close, and I am angry enough to lose my mind with that comment. Like a bull, I charge, ramming my head right into her belly. She grunts but does not fall—probably used to worse blows than mine—but I can tell I have taken her by surprise.

A pair of slender fingers wrap around my arm like a band of newly forged iron. They burn into my skin, and I almost faint from the pain of the sensation. Another hand muffles the scream that emerges from my mouth. In the background, I hear Agni's furious neighs, the sound of her hooves clomping the dirt as she struggles against her bonds, trying to get to me.

". . . control that horse . . ."

The woman's black eyes glow red. Her words stifle the air, make breathing difficult. As I gulp a lungful, my head grows light. *No. No, I can't faint now!*

To remain conscious, I try to focus on something concrete. For some strange reason, a tiny wooden figure pops up in my mind: the statue of the sky goddess at our prayer altar at home. I have not prayed to the goddess in three years, but now I find myself doing so out of desperation: *Goddess of the sky and the air, let your hand guide mine . . .*

The Samudra woman's shouts are followed by the sound of Agni's terrified neighs. Abandoning all attempts at proper prayer, I unleash my fury at the silent sky goddess. *You abandoned my parents when they needed you. You abandoned me. But Agni is innocent. She does not deserve to be ensnared in this fight. If you really do exist, Sky Goddess,* do some-*thing. Help Agni.*

The birthmark on my arm begins to burn. In my mind, the goddess's eyes glow green, and I am suddenly split in two, observing the scene from two vantage points: my own and Agni's.

Even though I am still being restrained by Amira, I feel the bind of the rope around Agni's mouth and head, feel the way her strength is muzzled by the spells woven into it. The air she breathes pricks my insides like ice. *Danger,* I hear her saying over and over. *The little girl is in danger.*

I'm all right, I try to tell Agni. *I'm all right, Agni, I promise.*

Another lungful of air, and suddenly I'm Gul again—only Gul—struggling against Amira, returned to my body. Whole again, I think, until the pain of the woman's spell makes Agni double over, combines it with my own.

My vision clouds over. The world turns black.

When I come to, a pair of gray eyes look worriedly at me. "I'm sorry," Kali says. "I only meant to stop you from hitting Amira, I swear. The spell I used must have been too strong."

Kali reaches out with a hand again, but I crawl back against the wall. "Don't touch me." I force myself to my feet. I now can sense that Kali's powers do not work if she's not touching me. I do not need her probing the layers of my mind, discovering that I somehow momentarily slid into Agni's.

Whispering. That's what they call this kind of magic, where humans can telepathically communicate with animals. Before the Great War, whispering was a rare magic prized by many, including the Ambari royals. But as time went on and wild animals were domesticated, whispering became less and less important. Animal handling is now delegated entirely to non-magi. There are hardly any whisperers left in

Ambar, most having gone to other kingdoms or to lands beyond the Yellow Sea.

For years, I've dreamed of discovering my own magic; as a child, I even prayed for it to the sky goddess. I don't understand why the goddess decided to listen to my prayers *now*, nor do I understand why she chose to give me this particular power.

Whispering isn't flashy or showy like the death magic used by Sky Warriors; in fact, few magi think of whispering as a valuable skill anymore. But I can't help feeling excited by my new ability. If these women try to hurt me . . .

I glance at Agni, who isn't moving anymore, and feel my heart sink. My discovery of my own hidden magic has come at a price.

"It's all right," the Samudra woman tells me. "Kali won't hurt you."

I would laugh, if not for the pain suddenly jabbing the left side of my ribs. Over the past few years, I've been hit by fighting spells at several village schools. Other magi children, who saw that whatever magic I had only came out as dull sparks during our classes, often mocked me for not shooting back a spell of my own. Kali's spell to restrain me was slightly stronger, perhaps, but not much worse.

I hobble to Agni's stall. I need to make sure she's unharmed.

"The mare is fine. She's only sleeping." The woman's lie would be as soothing as balm to anyone who didn't feel the knifeburn of her wicked spell. "Why don't you come with us?" The look in her eyes is an odd mix of both calculation and concern.

"Why should I?" I reach out to touch Agni's nose; she is in pain. I can feel it by the way she shivers. "I don't know you or these girls. How do I know you won't take me to the Sky Warriors? That you won't treat me as badly as you treated this horse?"

Surprise flickers through the woman's eyes. She scrutinizes me, and I'm afraid she can sense what happened to me, the true reason I fainted. But she presses her lips together and says nothing. Instead, she turns to her companions and raises a hand. It is now that I notice the rings: thin, finely wrought marble bands on each finger. Pure white sangemarmar, used to amplify her powers. To my surprise, Kali lifts her sari petticoat up to the knee. Amira turns around, pushing down the shoulder of her blouse. The woman holds up the lantern to each exposed body part, one after the other.

Each girl has a birthmark. A brown one in the shape of a diamond right next to the dagger strapped to Kali's calf; a black one in the shape of a falling star on Amira's shoulder blade.

"My name is Juhi," the black-eyed woman says. "And you must be the girl my shells have been leading me to. The girl from the prophecy."

Instead of making my heart soar with triumph—*Papa was right about me all along*—Juhi's words settle like curdled milk in my belly.

"What makes you think that? *They* have birthmarks as well!" I say, pointing to Amira and Kali. "One of them could easily be the Star Warrior."

"I thought for a time that one of them might be," Juhi admits. "But the shells do not lie. Whenever I asked them to show me the Star Warrior, they led me somewhere else, away from Amira and Kali. According to the prophecy, there is only one Star Warrior, and for a time, I thought she might be from Samudra or another kingdom.

"Yet the shells never lead me outside Ambar. Over the years, I've been to different towns and villages: Meghapur, Dhanbad, Amirgarh, and Sur. I stayed in every place for a few months, looking for her. But eventually the shells would grow cold, and I would lose the Star Warrior's trail all over again. This time, the shells led me to Dukal." Juhi studies my face, as if memorizing it. "And their magic has never felt stronger."

My insides coil tight. *No*, I tell myself. *It's impossible.* So what if my parents and I lived briefly in each of the places that Juhi mentioned? It doesn't mean I'm the Star Warrior.

"The Star Warrior possesses magic unknown to all," I say, recalling the words of the prophecy. "I can barely do any magic!" I've known this since the day I first entered a village schoolroom—and walked right into a battle of spells between two boys. Neither of us was hurt—the magic the boys produced wasn't strong enough—but it wasn't my first experience at feeling powerless. "You might as well take me to the tenements to live with non-magi."

To my surprise, Juhi laughs. "Don't be silly, my girl. The way you resisted Amira's magic—a non-magus isn't capable of doing that. Only another magus is."

The comment elicits a smile from Kali and an eye roll from Amira.

"Kids at a village school called me a dirt licker once," I say quietly. When I asked Papa what that was, he was so angry. He told me never to use that kind of language in the house. Ever. That it was a filthy word made of ignorance and fear of non-magi. After I was forced to leave school for my poor magic, Papa taught me at home from his own scrolls, and when he ran out of them, he would buy used scrolls at the bazaar. *Just because you can't go to school anymore, it doesn't mean you should stop learning,* he told me.

"Children only repeat what their elders say." Juhi's voice is grave. "Years before the Great War, magi and non-magi lived side by side, they bound with each other, they had children. Many things have changed since then, and the time will come when magi children will pay for their parents' sins. When that is, I don't know. The shells do not tell me this.

"But you are not a non-magus, Havovi. You may have suppressed your magic when you were very young, perhaps out of fear of revealing yourself because of your birthmark. Or you may simply be one among the hundreds of other magi girls who aren't prophesied to save Ambar. Only time will tell."

Yes. Only time will tell if I will be anything apart from the girl whose very existence killed her parents. My throat pricks, my ribs growing tight.

"So." I pause, unsure how to phrase my next question to these strange, dangerous women who have offered me an escape route. "Who are you?"

Kali laughs out loud. Even Juhi's lips nudge in the direction of a smile. Only Amira seems unamused, her scowl deepening. In the background, their horses nicker. Agni nudges my shoulder protectively; I stroke her velvety nose.

"People who do not know us think we are ordinary Ambari women. Seamstresses. Midwives. Farmers. Mothers. Daughters. People like your zamindar will offer us food and shelter in exchange for a walk through the fields or a night in their beds." Juhi's eyes harden. "Of course, deceptive appearances are a must in our line of work." She holds up a hand. There, right in the center of her palm, I see a golden tattoo shaped like a lotus.

"Do you know what this is?"

Warriors. My heart skips a beat. *Protectors.* "You're the Sisterhood of the Golden Lotus. But I don't understand. Do the Sisters . . . do you all have birthmarks?"

Juhi lowers her hand. "No. Only Amira and Kali. But I don't limit the Sisterhood to marked girls. There are other women as well who need saving, who need to escape their pasts."

I sense Juhi is now talking about herself, but I don't have the courage to ask her about it.

"Long before I was born, my parents had another child, an elder sister I never got to know," I say instead to fill the silence. "Ava, her name was. One day she came home sick, feverish. On the advice of the village healer, my parents took her to the big hospital in Ambarvadi, to see one of the vaids there. But even he couldn't diagnose the cause of her illness or prescribe a cure." With the exception of the gods, vaids, who train for several years in the art of healing and life magic, are our last barriers between life and death.

"The vaid told my parents that the sky goddess had called Ava back early, that the best of us died young. Ma would not accept it. After Ava died, she fasted for a whole month, praying to the goddess for justice, until she finally collapsed in the temple. When she came to, Ma said she had seen the goddess herself. The goddess had granted Ma a boon: a daughter. I was born ten months later, during the Month of Tears."

People say rain poured from the sky every day of the month that year, infusing the land and the crops with magic. Men danced in the village square until their long white tunics and dhotis were drenched, their mouths open to the sky. Women caught one another by the wrists and twirled in circles outside, in the rain-soaked earth.

"My parents were so happy when Ma got pregnant." My voice catches. "I wish she hadn't. I wish I was never born."

Outside, a pair of dogs begin barking, cutting through the heavy silence that has fallen over the room.

"Every birth has purpose," Juhi says. "And yours is important or the Sky Warriors would not have come to this sleepy little village to look for you."

She walks to a corner where their belongings are heaped together, and from the pile, she pulls out a small, sweet-smelling bundle wrapped in cloth. Even through the layers, I can smell the richness of nutty mawa and honeyweed and ghee, my dry mouth watering almost instantly. I am too hungry to care or be embarrassed by the way I fall upon the moon-shaped kachori, devouring the first one so quickly that Juhi gives me three more in quick succession, saying nothing even when I pick the flakes of fried dough out of my clothes and lick the sugary grease off my fingers. *Slow down*, Ma would have said. *Slow down or you'll be sick.*

Hot tears slide down my cheeks.

None of the three Sisters who watch me eat speak a word of comfort. They quietly turn away when I begin to cry and talk among themselves—Kali making an exception by getting up to fetch a cup of water from the clay pot in the corner when I begin to hiccup. I can see, even through my grief, that this is a move neither Juhi nor Amira approve of. They glare at Kali, who only shakes her head.

"The girl has lost both mother and father," she says. "What do you want me to do? Ignore her?"

"She's already too soft," Amira says. "Useless."

My eyes dry up. Once again, I feel the strong urge to bite Amira. Instead, I wipe my face with the cleanest part of my sleeve.

"Are you from Ambarvadi?" I ask Juhi.

"We live in a village called Javeribad. A few miles west of Ambarvadi."

Ambarvadi, the capital. A city glittering with houses made of marble and sandstone, havelis that make Zamindar Moolchand's mansion look utterly ordinary. It is said that magic is so concentrated in Ambarvadi that the glow of it blots out the stars with its brilliance. A couple of miles from the city, King Lohar lives in a sprawling fortress on a high hill.

"Is Ambarvadi really the way people say it is?" I've always wondered if the stories our teachers told us are true or mere embellishments. More propaganda courtesy of the new Ministry of Truth established by King Lohar—an organization that monitors and controls the publication of all information in Ambar, from royal proclamations to scrolls of children's stories.

"It is exactly that way. Which only makes it more dangerous."

I think of the one and only portrait I saw of the palace—or a part of it, at least. A tall building in the shape of the sky goddess's own crown, its tiered towers clustered together like sweets on a tray, the very tops of it hidden by mist, except for clear, sunlit days, when you could see its gleaming points and grilles and dust-pink domes.

"Does Raja Lohar live there?" I remember asking my father.

"No," Papa said. "Ambar Fort is a giant complex consisting of two big palaces and several other buildings grouped together. The palace you see from the city of Ambarvadi is Rani Mahal, where the queens live. The king lives in Raj Mahal, a palace on the other side of the complex."

Some say that Raj Mahal is a mirror image of Rani Mahal, but built with black marble and rainbow-hued metal called indradhanush. Some say that the king's palace is made of firestones, thunder, and clouds. No one really knows, as no portraits are allowed. Some secrets were paramount to the king's safety. Even then, I had the sense that Papa knew more about those secrets than he was telling me. And now I will never be able to ask him what they are. I swallow against the tickling sensation in my throat, barely holding back a fresh bout of tears.

Useless. My heart burns when I think of what Amira called me. I am not useless. I am not weak.

I recall King Lohar's portrait that hangs in every school, every hospital, every government office, and even some private homes. The king is seated on a cushion, cross-legged, wearing a deep-blue angrakha embroidered with gems, matching narrow trousers and a sash. His cheeks are tinted with gold dust to indicate royal blood; his jootis, crafted by the kingdom's finest shoemakers, are decorated with shimmering threads of indradhanush. Crowning his head is a turban of blue silk, set with a plumed ornament made of an enormous firestone in the shape of a teardrop.

I don't know how I will do it, but one day I will meet Raja Lohar, I vow. *And when I do, I will kill him.*

"What do the Sky Warriors do?" I ask Juhi. "To the girls who are taken? Do they really drain them of their powers?"

For the first time, I glimpse fear on Kali's and Amira's faces.

Juhi frowns. "That is a question for another day. Sleep now, Havovi. It's getting late."

I feel the exhaustion of the past few days creeping up on me, threatening to unravel me like a spool of wool.

"Gul," I tell her. "My name is Gul."

A TWO-MOON NIGHT

The city of Ambarvadi
2nd day of the Month of Moons
Year 22 of King Lohar's reign

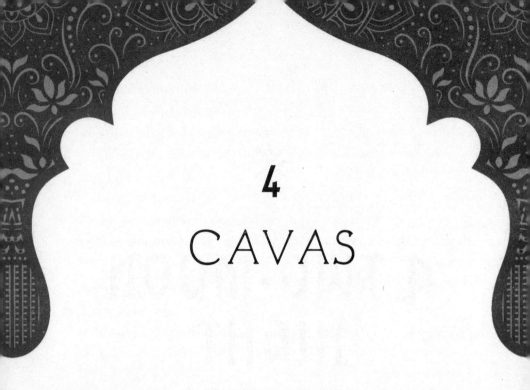

4

CAVAS

The fireflies stop glowing.

It happens for an instant, a faint crack in the brilliant dome of insects magicked over Ambarvadi's bazaar before it reseals, barely noticeable unless you're like me, your face scrubbed clean with sugar oil, your skin prickling from being out in the crowded marketplace, pretending that you belong. It's a sticky night, the day's heat still lingering in the air, compounded by bodies jostling for space, sand feathering the roofs of the tents. The sweat beading on the back of my neck, however, is cold and has little to do with the temperature around me.

When I arrived in the market, the sky was still awash with orange—the exact time Latif asked me to meet him here, behind the bangle seller's stall. The sun is gone now, but Latif is still missing.

"Time flies quickly in my line of work," Latif always says, even though he never mentions what that work is.

A thanedar passes by, glancing at my face first and then at my palace-issued orange turban, with its identification pin in the center. His gaze travels over my white tunic and dhoti, the pointed tips of the worn leather jootis on my feet. I brace myself for the slurs, more out of habit than out of fear. *Dirt licker. Abomination. Get out of my way, filth.* But when he simply nods and moves along, I realize the uniform has done the trick. In the palace, every servant wears a uniform, whether they are magi or not. Here, in this moment, no one knows about who I am or the blood that runs through my veins. Unless the thanedar decides to ask me to identify myself on a whim—to press my thumb into the tip of his lathi, waiting for the wooden staff to change color, the way it would for a magus.

A beat passes. Two. I let go of the breath I'm holding. Overhead, through the shifting veil of glowing insects, two moons hang in the sky. Sunheri, the yellow moon, and Neel, the blue one. According to legend, the moons were both goddesses once. "Friends first and then lovers," Papa told me, "until one of Sunheri's many suitors killed Neel out of jealousy."

But their love was a true one. A moon appeared in the sky one night: blue, like the color of Neel's skin. Pitying her plight, the sky goddess granted Sunheri's wish to join Neel—turning her into a moon as well—a faded yellow orb that waxes and wanes, that grows full, but never brightens to gold except for one night out of every three hundred and sixty. On Chandni Raat—the night of the moon festival—the only night in the year when the blue moon appears in the sky.

There are those who call the story of the two moons a myth. A tale of childish fancy, spun into a clever way of gathering coin for the king's depleted coffers after two successive wars. Out of the story of Neel and Sunheri emerged the moon festival: a night for lovers, revelry, and mischief. A night where it's possible to find your neela chand. In Vani, the words *neela chand* literally translate to "blue moon," a phrase that refers to your mate. Your perfect other half.

A few feet away, I spy a pair of girls, no older than fifteen, holding hands as if preparing to launch into a rain dance spin. But then the girl dressed in yellow rises to her tiptoes and lightly kisses the cheek of the one dressed in blue. The fireflies, drawn by their laughs, glow brighter, several twirling around the girls before rising up to float overhead again.

Bahar, the girl I once thought would be my mate, used to laugh like that, her dark eyes sparkling with mischief, her face full of joy. Yet, on the heels of that image, I recall another one: Bahar, her skin leeched of color, dragged off in a cart by a thanedar, her hands bound behind her back. The charge was magic theft—made by a palace worker who allegedly saw Bahar's hands glow green while helping her mother in the kitchen garden.

That Bahar also had a tiny birthmark on her cheek did not help matters. I remember running after the thanedars' wagon, screaming, "It's not a star!" before one of them hit me in the chest with a spell that knocked me unconscious.

My insides feel raw, like skin singed with hot oil. I am about to turn away from the girls when I see it again. The fireflies flickering. A crack of darkness within the light.

I see the girl's dusty brown feet first: bare of anklets and shoes, skimming the packed earth with such lightness that she barely leaves a footprint. Unlike the bright silks of the other revelers, she's dressed in black, her plain choli leaving most of her back bare and her arms covered to the elbows. If there's a hint of color, it comes from the tiny blue mirrors embedded in the depths of her ghagra, making the wide skirt glimmer like a starry sky.

Her thin dupatta veils most of her face, but even I know what she's up to when her hand lightly brushes the back of a man's tunic belt, when she walks away with a polite apology, a furrow etching her brow.

A pickpocket who didn't hit her mark. Unlike Bahar, this was a real thief, trying to steal gold and silver coins for the tiny bits of magic embedded in them. The magic in the coins itself isn't very powerful. The palace's stable master, Govind, calls the magic in money *dead magic*, limited in the things it can do. "It is true that non-magi can access bits and pieces of the magic embedded in coins; they can even produce a few sparks if they try," he told me once. "But for this sort of magic to have any consequence, a treasure trove of coins would be needed. You'd also need a talented alchemist to distill the magic from the coins and stabilize it. For magic to be truly powerful, it must be *alive*, must be part of the person manipulating it."

Yet I also know that, regardless of the truth, those who have no magic of their own would risk anything—including imprisonment or death—to get their hands on some.

It's perhaps this thought—or maybe some other instinct entirely—that draws me away from the spot where I'm supposed to wait for Latif. I weave through the bodies pouring down the narrow lanes of the bazaar and duck under the jutting beam of a sweets stall, following the girl dressed like the night. Like a shadow.

Except she *isn't* a shadow, and the next person she targets—a young merchant with sharp eyes—catches hold of her wrist.

"What do you think you're doing?" His voice cuts through the surrounding chatter like a cudgel, draws the attention of a nearby thanedar. "Thief!"

The girl's dupatta slides down her head, revealing frizzy hair as black as surma, a cleft on a stubborn chin, and gold eyes as hard as the firestones from Ambar's jewel mines. She gives the merchant a sudden, dazzling smile and tosses her long braid behind one shoulder.

"I apologize," she says. "I thought you were my mate."

In Ambar, a person's looks are often enhanced with glow: shimmery creams, oils, and powders ranging from the pure gold dusting the cheeks of the royal family to the cheap sugar oil used by the poor. A glowing face is an indicator of being blessed by the gods, whether magic flows in your veins or not, and can be traced back to the figures in ancient paintings found in caves in the mountains of Prithvi. Two kings and two queens, four rulers of a then-united Svapnalok who were said to have descended from the gods and goddesses themselves.

My father doesn't believe in these theories about outward appearances. "Inner radiance is more important," he always says. And there must be some truth to this, because even without a trace of artificial shimmer, the girl's brown skin is luminous. It reminds me of another face—one that can still wake me in the middle of the night, her screams ringing in my ears.

"Oh really?" A grain of lust slides into the merchant's angry voice. I've heard that tone before. Seen similar leers on other magi men. It doesn't matter that the girl failed to steal from the merchant. He will not let her go without a price. "Or did you just want a kiss from me on this two-moon night? Where is this so-called mate of yours?"

"Here."

I don't realize I've spoken until the merchant's neck snaps in my direction, along with those of several others. I clear my throat, noting the merchant's furious look as the girl wrests her hand from his grip. "I'm right here."

It's probably a good thing that everyone is now staring at me, because I'm the only one who sees the girl's eyes widening for a fraction of a moment before her features smooth into a mask again. She smiles at me.

"Where were you?" The tone is lighthearted. Flirtatious. The sort that makes heat creep up my ears even though I know it's false. A show put on for an unwanted audience.

"By the bangle stall." I force a trace of impatience in my voice. With the thanedar waiting nearby, I even manage to sound convincing. "Don't you remember?"

Taking advantage of the confusion our little scene is causing, the girl steps out of the merchant's reach and makes her way toward me. There's an expression in her eyes that could range from anything between anger and fear.

"I forgot," she whispers. "Will you forgive me?"

I open my mouth to say yes and lead her away.

She rises on her feet and leans in, cutting off the word with her lips, chasing it away with her tongue. I want to wrench my head away. I want to freeze time.

My kisses with Bahar were gentle. Innocent. They didn't make the fine hairs on the back of my neck stand up, nor did they make my blood simultaneously rush to my cheeks and groin. The girl runs her hand up my jaw and then around my neck, her fingers lightly brushing the curlicues of hair at the nape. Without thinking, I tilt my head slightly, fitting our mouths tighter. Deeper. Where my hand grips her wrist, her flesh burns, feels like stone when I was certain it was soft moments earlier.

Cheers and laughter erupt in the background. The girl breaks the kiss, her mouth wet in the firefly glow. Her golden eyes are wide, oddly curious. On a normal day, the crowd would have shouted at us for being vulgar and told us to get bound for the next three lifetimes. But, on Chandni Raat, kisses are seen as auspicious, are even encouraged to promote future bindings.

I slide my fingers through the girl's. The curiosity in her eyes vanishes, sharpening to something else when she focuses on the king's emblem fastened to the front of my turban.

"Come," I say with a glance at the merchant, who still watches us with suspicion. "Let me take you home."

The people in the crowd laugh again.

"Stole your heart with that kiss, did she, boy?"

"Gave him a little something in return, too!" someone else says, pointing at my dhoti.

The statement makes me grit my teeth. The girl's radiant smile edges on a smirk. For a second, I can almost pretend that the warmth in her eyes is real.

"Keep up the act," she whispers into my ear. "The thanedar is eyeing us like a dustwolf."

I ignore the jolt that goes through me at the brush of her lips and draw her away from the scene, weaving through the crowd that, by some miracle, has decided to indulge us for being young or stupid or perhaps both. A few moments later, the girl lets go of my hand.

"Don't get too attached, pretty boy." Her voice has the texture of gravel and honey. "I might burn you."

I feel my face grow hot with embarrassment. "I have no intention of getting attached," I inform her as coldly as possible. "What possessed you to steal from that merchant anyway?"

"What are you talking about? I wasn't steal—"

"Don't you know how dangerous it can be for people like us?"

The girl frowns. Her mouth opens, as if to say something, then shuts again.

"Which part of the tenements are you from, anyway?" I continue. "I don't remember seeing you before." It's likely I might have missed her. The tenements outside the city of Ambarvadi are spread out over only fifteen square miles of land, but nearly a hundred thousand non-magi live within its boundaries. On the other hand, she may not be from the northern tenements at all, but a villager from the tenements in the southern part of the kingdom.

The girl says nothing. A faint flush colors her cheeks. Unlike the other women at the festival, she wears no jewelry, except for a simple black cord around her neck with three silver beads in the center. I decide to fill the silence. "I'm Cavas. From the west end of the tenements. I work in the stables at the palace."

"Cavas," she says my name out loud, as if testing it on her tongue. "How did you, uh, know I was, uh, from the tenements?"

I smile. "Magi generally don't need to steal coin."

"Is that so?"

"Of course." I've seen it happen before. The king's messengers sounding the news throughout Ambar, thanedars raiding the tenements for possible suspects, making arrests, tightening the rigid laws already in place for non-magi.

"I know it's difficult sometimes," I tell her now. "My father and I

40

have nothing to eat some days. But it's better to earn an honest living than to get arrested for attempted theft."

Unless lies are the only way you can survive, a voice taunts in my head. I push it aside.

She stares at me for a long moment. "You're wrong."

I frown. "About earning an honest living?"

"There *was* no attempt at theft. When I do attempt to steal, I rarely fail—especially in a crowd like this." She's about to add more when her eyes narrow on seeing something—or someone—behind me. "Hide. Now."

"What are you talking—"

She gives me a hard push, nearly knocking me into a nearby stall. That's when I see them—a giant thanedar in white, along with the merchant from before. The latter is pointing at the girl and shouting. "There she is! The girl who tried to steal my purse! Thief! Thief!"

Another thanedar reaches out to catch hold of the girl. He screams in agony as flames lick at his sleeves—a cheap magic trick that can be purchased at any stall—a trick I've seen some non-magi use whenever they want to evade detection by the thanedars, even though it never works for long. The girl skips backward, ducking behind a man with a cane, and lets forth a trill of mocking laughter.

"Thieving girl!"

"Catch her!"

But they cannot. The girl truly is a shadow, weaving around a group of desert musicians and a pair of dancers balancing several clay pots on their heads, before sliding and disappearing into the stall of a Javeri seamstress. The fireflies, I notice, seem to be helping, no longer flickering out, but plunging entire areas of the festival into darkness and chaos. Screams erupt around me. I duck behind a clothing stall, next to several tall rolls of fabric, to avoid being knocked over. A group of thanedars thunder past, the outlines of their white tunics glowing in the dark.

Then light breaks through, a giant orb of it bursting out of a thanedar's lathi, hovering in the air overhead. Other thanedars follow suit, and soon the bazaar is suffused with harsh white beams. I press myself farther into the rolls of fabric when I notice the merchant the girl had pickpocketed again, talking to someone.

". . . a boy, too . . . orange turban . . ." Fragments of the merchant's voice reach my ears, making me freeze in place.

"Which boy?" The thanedar's voice is louder, more impatient. "There are about a hundred boys wearing orange turbans here. Did you get a good look at him?"

My shoulders sag with relief when the merchant shakes his head, frustration etched on each line of his face. The thanedar turns away and raises his fingers to his mouth. A whistle, magnified to four, possibly five times its normal volume by magic, cuts through the noise.

"We ask you to remain calm," he says in a deep voice. "We will have everything in order."

But even as the officers stalk the bazaar, peeking under tables, questioning stallkeepers, and marshaling a group of rowdy city boys out of their way, I can tell they are too late. The fireflies have begun to light up overhead. The girl is gone.

A girl who, if the insects' odd behavior was any indication, has whisper magic in her veins. A girl who, whether she was a thief or not, never needed my help in the first place. The realization is like being doused in ice water and scalded by fire all at once.

How could I have been such a fool?

I wipe a hand roughly across my mouth, but the memory of the kiss remains seared into my skin.

A hand clamps over my shoulder, and for a second, I grow still, thinking someone has recognized me from the scene I caused earlier that evening.

"Well"—a man's voice brushes softly against my ear—"that was quite a show, wasn't it?"

Latif is finally here.

He holds up a cloth-covered box, its edges crusted with sequins. "I got these for you."

If the distinct smell of the rose syrup and ghee rising from the wood did not give away the box's contents, then the burst of moisture at the back of my tongue definitely would have. A box of chandramas. Filigreed dough shaped like full moons, foiled with gold and garnished with rose petals and dried honeyweed seeds, a chandrama is a delicacy made only during the moon festival. I still remember the one and only time I tasted one—or the broken half of one—salvaged from the partly eaten food tossed into the palace garbage heap. An explosion of sherbet and roses in my mouth. A single moment of bliss, followed by an odd sense of loss. Gold eyes flash in my memory. I push aside the thought of the thief's kiss—the only other taste that left me with a similar feeling.

I look into Latif's pale, nearly colorless eyes. "What do you want?" I ask. A single chandrama costs no less than twenty-five silver rupees. Boxes like these are even more expensive, worth more silver than I would be able to save in a year. After a year of dealing with Latif, I know that gifts from him do not come without a price.

"Why must I want something?" he asks mildly. "Can I not bring sweets for my friend?"

If my nerves weren't already frayed by what happened at the festival, I would laugh. Latif is many things. A follower of Prophet Zaal and Sant Javer. A connoisseur of sweets and lateness. A master at invisibility magic. But he is no one's friend.

I study Latif's face now—beard, the blue-black shadows under his eyes, his skin so leached of color that it looks gray in the moonlight. Latif always wears the same clothes when I see him: a long gray tunic with a vest and matching narrow trousers. Gray jootis encase his feet. Unlike most Ambari men, who wear their turbans in tight, practical coils around their heads, Latif wears his gray turban the way the merchants, shopkeepers, and high-ranking servants at the palace do—in elaborate layers, with the edge fanning out from the top left. I wonder at times if Latif's strange appearance is due to the magic he uses to vanish so often. Or if he's averse to bathing. But I hold back my questions.

After all, this man has been paying me ten whole swarnas every month for the past year in exchange for telling him secrets about the palace and its inhabitants—an act that could land me in prison or get me executed if anyone ever found out. But secrets can also be used to buy medicine from the black market and mixed into Papa's morning tea. When you're poor, secrets can very well be the difference between life and death.

"Tell me." Latif's voice takes on the singsongy tone I've grown familiar with. "What news of the palace?"

The palace. Or rather, two specific people within the palace.

"The Spider is supposed to be here in a fortnight," I say.

"What about the Scorpion?"

The Scorpion. General Tahmasp's—or the Spider's—right-hand woman, Major Shayla.

"When I saw her this morning, she was crushing a child's hand under her boot." The serving boy's screams were ringing outside the stables. Apart from their stiff backs, none of the other servants gave any indication of having heard them. It might have continued for longer— Major Shayla has a fondness for sadism—if not for the king, who had sent a messenger summoning her to Raj Mahal. "She's still staying in Ambar Fort."

Latif looks unsurprised by my comments. The only person Latif never asks me about is the king. Perhaps he knows more than I do, or perhaps he's simply not interested. The latter seems unlikely to me, but again, these are secrets I am not privy to. Latif gives me a nod and then, as he always does, drops a bag of coins into my hands. Enough for a month's worth of Papa's medicine. Latif joins his palms in a final farewell.

The first time we met, it happened so quickly that I missed it. But afterward, Latif always made sure I saw him leave. Tonight, he is even slower than usual, the pointed tips of his jootis disappearing first, and then his knees, hips, elbows, and finger joints. He gets creative with the head today, skin disappearing first so that I see the veins and tendons underneath, until even those disappear and all that remain are a skull, eyeballs, and a mouth.

"Remember the girl you saw today," the mouth says before disappearing completely, leaving me with another puzzle that I don't expect to solve anytime soon.

5

GUL

The fireflies failed me tonight.

I felt them flitting around me, burning bright and glorious when I planted that kiss on the boy, and then later when we talked, drawing that awful merchant back to me, along with the burliest thanedar I'd ever seen.

"This is the last time I ask a group of giddy insects to help me find someone during mating season," I mutter to myself.

Had it not been for the fireflies, I would have been quicker to realize that the person I was supposed to meet at the moon festival was a no-show. Had it not been for the fireflies, I would have left the boy behind, without answering his questions.

I ignore the voice in my head that accuses me of not wanting to leave. That I wanted to keep talking to the boy under the bright, flickering lights, to touch the stubble on his rough cheek, taste the salt-sweet flavor of his mouth again. I failed so miserably tonight I can barely stand to think about it. I click my tongue softly and, within seconds, feel the brush of a wet nose at my shoulder.

Agni, at least, does not fail. She knows when she's needed, where she's needed, before even I do—finding her way to Javeribad two years ago, a fortnight after Juhi and the others sneaked me there from Zamindar Moolchand's haveli in Dukal. I reach up, grip Agni's thick red mane, and climb onto her back.

You smell like boy, Agni accuses. *Boy and lust.*

I grimace. Agni lets out an odd, high-pitched neigh—her version of a mocking laugh. It's not like I haven't lusted in the past—or even thought of acting on it at times, when invited to walk through the bajra fields in Javeribad with the farmer's handsome son.

But, in two long years, my lust has never interfered with my goal of finding a way into Raj Mahal and seeing the king—a flame that began burning ever since the day my parents were killed. It would not do, I knew, to be distracted by a boy's touch or to be ensnared by a binding that would mate me to him and his babies, forcing me into a life of complacency and forgetfulness.

I don't want to forget. Or forgive.

You nearly got caught today, Agni scolds. I roll my eyes. I love the magic that allows me to whisper to animals; there are nights when I wake up, terrified of losing it as suddenly as it came. But I do not need a horse playing the role of a nag and my conscience. Agni shifts, forcing me to hold on more tightly so I don't slide off. A warning.

"It wasn't my fault," I say out loud. Not my fault that the merchant whom I touched thought I was a thief when I wasn't planning to steal anything. "I was really there to see someone. I thought they'd be . . . there."

A snort. Agni breaks into a gallop, the sound of her feet so light, I can barely hear them on the ground. Papa told me that the horses of Jwala were thought to have wings, with feathers that sprouted from both sides of their backs, letting them fly in the sky.

I know Agni's right. I took a big risk by sneaking out tonight—only to meet a stranger who'd whispered the following words in my ear at the Javeribad inn last week: *Be at the moon festival in Ambarvadi after sunset for a way into the Walled City.* I had not seen the person's face, seen nothing except shadows in the crush at the inn. But I remembered the brush of their cold lips on my skin. Felt the shift in the air that had come from another presence. *An invisible presence.* Invisibility wasn't unusual at the Javeribad inn during happy hour; the old innkeeper never asked questions as long as enough silver slid across his table in exchange for the drinks. That this unseen person approached me wasn't unusual, either—I'd spent the past hour flirting with a pair of drunken palace guards, not-so-subtly making inquiries about getting into the Walled City.

I wonder now if I had been dreaming. If the words had been a figment of my imagination—the hope of a desperate girl still haunted by her parents' deaths. It's not difficult to imagine ghosts being out on this night, the tops of the thatched roofs of Javeribad lit blue and yellow under the two moons.

Agni slows to a canter; even with quiet feet, sounds can be magnified in sleepy, little villages. Unlike Ambarvadi, where celebrations for the moon festival will continue into the wee hours of the morning, Javeribad is as quiet as a cemetery. Here, festivities begin when the blue moon is first sighted, a little after sunset, at the sky goddess's temple, where a long prayer ceremony takes place, followed by an even longer distribution of prasad—food and fruit made in offering by the worshippers and blessed during the course of the ceremony. Afterward, families head home for quiet celebration; the revelry and mischief so prevalent in Ambarvadi are frowned upon here. "We are not like those promiscuous city people," Kali often says, mimicking the baritone of Javeribad's head thanedar so perfectly that we always burst out laughing.

I suppress a snort at the memory. It will not do to laugh now, not in this silence, when a single barking dog can wake the whole street, when house after mud-brick house is shrouded in darkness except for the white filigree moons painted on the doors.

The Sisters live on the street behind the temple—in a two-story building that once housed the village orphanage. Some of the novices mock the villagers for not guessing that it no longer functions as one, for never questioning why we don't take in boys. Yet I can't entirely blame the villagers for being ignorant. I've seen how their eyes glass over whenever they enter the orphanage, especially when Juhi is in the room. The speed with which Juhi modifies memories is both impressive and frightening. Even the village elders are unable to remember exactly when the orphanage changed hands (*three years ago, with stolen coin*, the novices say). For all they know, Sister Juhi and her orphans have been in Javeribad forever.

The gate is still partly open from when I left it earlier this evening. I heave a sigh of relief and dismount before leading Agni to her stall in the stable. "Anyone still awake?" I whisper.

You'll see, the mare taunts, which means it could be anyone from ornery Cook, who always accuses the novices of stealing from her kitchen, to an angry Amira to Juhi herself.

I sigh, more out of resignation than nerves. Agni was right when she said that I am not supposed to be out tonight. Or any other night, really. Juhi does not trust me with the jobs she gives out to the other Sisters. They are the sort of magi who, unlike me, can cast fighting spells, who are able to wield death magic the way it should be: like a long, sharply gleaming sword instead of a stubby, rusty dagger.

"You are the most useless creature here," Amira has told me countless times, and in my darkest moments, I can't help but agree.

Agni nickers, sensing my thoughts in a way only she can. *It will be all right*, she assures me before shooing me from the stable. It's a warm night, but I still feel the blue moon's chilly, spectral glow. In the courtyard of the Sisterhood's house, I see the shadow of someone waiting: a slender figure still wearing her dueling sari, flipping two daggers round and round. Up close, I know I'll see her namesake—a *kali* or a flower bud—engraved in the pommels.

Kali. Only Kali.

Well, not *only Kali*. Kali is as capable of handing out punishments as Amira and Juhi, but she tends to give them out less often than they do.

"Out for a midnight rendezvous, are we?" she asks, having sensed my presence around the same time I spotted her.

I say nothing. Kali is capable of picking out my lies in an uncanny way, and these days she doesn't even have to touch me for it.

"Come closer, my girl."

I reluctantly do. Kali rises to her feet and circles me with a look that eviscerates from head to toe.

"Let's see." She sniffs the air. "You reek of sugar and horse and sweat—and not the kind that comes after a roll in the fields. You were at the moon festival in the city."

It's an obvious guess. If the moon festival in Ambarvadi is a fire-cracker, then the one in Javeribad is a doused lantern. None of the novices would break curfew for something like that. But the festival wasn't the reason I was really out tonight, and the less Kali knows about *that*, the better.

"So what if I was?" Defensiveness can work sometimes—especially when coupled with round eyes and hurt looks. "So what if I wanted to get out of the house for once on my own in a whole blue moon? It's not like you'd let me out if I asked."

Kali's face is still stern, but her mouth twitches, which means she's at least considering my excuse. "You know you can't go out by yourself. Not to the festival; especially not to Ambarvadi. Not only that—you are still not of age."

"I will be of age soon," I remind her. Right after the Month of Drought blurs into the Month of Tears. Eight more weeks. Sixteen years old.

"And neither Juhi nor I want you to be dead when that happens," Kali says, her voice hard in a way that tells me there will be a punishment, no matter what I say.

"It's not like I did anything!" *I only got mistaken for picking pockets. I only kissed a boy. I only nearly got arrested.*

"And I suppose those bruises on your wrist mean nothing, do they?"

I automatically glance down and, for the first time, notice the fingerprints on my left wrist, left by the merchant who accused me of stealing. My face grows hot. Of course Kali would notice. If I have the ears of a shadowlynx, Kali has the eyes of one, capable of seeing things in the dimmest of light.

"Show them to me."

It's not an order I dare refuse. I hold up my wrist while Kali examines the skin with gentle fingers. "What happened?"

"A merchant thought I was trying to steal from him. I wasn't!" I insist when Kali raises an eyebrow. "I swear!"

Kali nods, accepting the truth she senses by touching me. "You're lucky he didn't break your bones or do further damage. You need to be careful, Gul. Remember what Juhi taught us?"

"*No target is worth a Sister being seen.* I remember that." I withdraw my hand before Kali asks more questions and figures out the real reason I was in Ambarvadi. "But I'm not even a Sister, am I?" I flip over my hands, showing Kali my untattooed palms. "Juhi keeps saying I'm not ready."

I'm unable to keep the envy out of my voice. At mealtimes, some of the Sisters occasionally boast about their exploits. Magically tying up zamindars who deceive farmers into signing over their land—and not releasing the former until the land is restored. Rescuing girls who get harassed by men in marketplaces. Standing up to women who beat their daughters-in-law.

The only real job Juhi has given me so far is picking pockets of rich merchants in Ambarvadi and leaving the stolen coin outside the gateway to the city tenements. And even then, I'm always supervised by another Sister.

A part of me knows I can't exactly blame Juhi for this. Not with my poor performance at Yudhnatam, Juhi's martial art of preference, and during magical training. The one and only time my magic did emerge over the past two years, it injured another novice so badly that she nearly died.

The novice had been criticizing my techniques during our practice fight—something that the other girls usually left to our instructor, Uma Didi. I remember getting annoyed at first and then angry. Then, the girl rose high into the air, her kick knocking me flat on my back, my head hitting the ground so hard that I saw stars. Her bare foot was descending, ready to crush my nose, when a scream rose into the air. Hers, not mine.

It's one of the last things I remember about that fight, along with my hands gripping her foot and the searing pain in my right arm, moments before I blacked out. I've refused to participate in any magical battles since then, despite Kali's encouragement and Amira's shouts.

"Juhi doesn't trust me," I say now.

"It's not about trust," Kali corrects. "It's about samarpan, as Juhi calls it. Juhi doesn't make anyone a Sister unless they're ready for that."

Samarpan. A Common Tongue word synonymous with dedication, submission, and sacrifice. With immersing oneself so completely in the Sisterhood's main mission—*protecting the unprotected*—that everything else ceases to exist. The truth of it doesn't take away the sting of Kali's words.

"Perhaps there is more to your destiny than being a Sister," she tells me. "Have you ever considered that?"

"And what destiny is that? A common pickpocket?" I ask sarcastically. "The way things keep going, I'm probably better off selling myself in the Ambarvadi flesh market—aaah!" I nearly scream when Kali pinches my arm.

"Don't you dare joke about such things. The flesh market is no place for you. For anyone, for that matter. I don't know how you even heard of it."

"Everyone knows, Kali. It's not exactly a secret," I say, even though this time I'm more careful with my tone. "People offering themselves up as servants. Being sold for hundreds, thousands of swarnas at auction. Even Raja Lohar sends buyers there."

My last sentence hangs in the air, spoken without real thought. Words that I would on any other occasion have bitten back.

"The king isn't the only person who buys from the flesh market." Kali's eyes are icy in the moonlight. "There are others as well. Ministers, Sky Warriors, shopkeepers, merchants. They don't care for the rules binding masters to their servants. Even if you do make it into the palace, there's little hope for your survival. The life of an indentured laborer is little better than that of a non-magus living in the tenements. In many cases, it's even worse. You must promise me you'll never take such a step. Promise me, Gul!"

"I"—another pinch—"ow! All right! I promise! I promise!"

Kali stares at me for a long moment and then, as if satisfied with my answer, releases my arm. "Power comes in many shapes and forms. You keep doubting yourself, Gul. *That's* your biggest weakness. When you don't, you can take down men twice your size. Remember that shopkeeper in Ambarvadi last year?"

I'm tempted to tell the truth. That the shopkeeper, though huge, had been distracted by the gold sheen of a swarna I'd planted on his floor. That luck and finely milled glass powder had a lot more to do with his eyes watering than the blow I'd managed to land on his hand when he grabbed at me, freeing my ankle from his grip, before escaping with a sack of his money.

"Come now," Kali says after a pause. "You must be hungry."

Perching on top of the short staircase leading into the courtyard, Kali takes the cloth off a metal plate and hands it to me. I tear off a piece of the thick khoba roti and scoop up the lentils in the container next to it before dipping into the spicy lotus sabzi on the side. I chew slowly, relishing the taste.

"So. Was he handsome?"

I nearly choke on my food. "Wha—who?"

"The boy you kissed," Kali clarifies.

I scowl. She must have scanned my mind when she touched me. "I suppose he was handsome."

Handsome the way a cactus is handsome, the way metal is when shaped to form a mace. Sharp edges. A soft mouth. A neatly trimmed mustache and dark-brown eyes. Warmth unfurls in my belly when I think of the kiss, making my toes curl. My next bite into the roti is savage, a grisly grinding of teeth.

"That good?" A note of amusement has crept into Kali's voice.

"It wasn't that good," I mutter.

Kali laughs. "You can lie to me if you want, but at least don't lie to yourself. We're all allowed a kiss that makes our head spin. Even if it is with a stranger."

"You mean like the one between you and that girl during last year's moon festival?"

"Maybe." Kali gives me a sly smile. "But we're not talking about me right now. We're talking about you."

"My head did not spin." Though I did feel insatiable, reluctant to break away from the boy's kiss, the warmth of hands that were strong but didn't hurt.

While the boy and I were talking, I'd seen something else on the front of his simply wound orange turban: a brass pin with the king's symbol of a warrior wielding an atashban. From eavesdropping on various conversations over the past two years, I know that Ambar Fort is self-sufficient, surrounded by a fortified city with its own small farms and irrigation system, its own clothing shops and libraries. A part of me longed to start interrogating the boy immediately, to flirt my way into more information.

But when he mentioned he was from the tenements, the words had washed over me like a bucket of cold water. As a boy with no magic in his veins, Cavas took a great risk to save me by pretending to be my mate in front of that crowd. I nearly said yes when he asked if I was from the tenements: I didn't want the warmth in those brown eyes to get overshadowed with disappointment. I only hope that he hid when I told him to. That he didn't get caught. Thieves aren't treated kindly in Ambari prisons; non-magi even less so.

"A novice found something interesting when she went in to clean your dormitory today," Kali says, interrupting my thoughts.

"Oh?" I keep my voice casual, unaffected.

"Yes. She found a map of Ambarvadi and Ambar Fort tucked inside the pillow on your cot."

"That old thing? I got it at the village fair last year."

"Indeed." Kali holds up the scroll I designed with slow, painstaking care. "With details about the queens' palace: the entrances and exits, notes on the number of Sky Warriors in Raja Lohar's army down to the number of courtesans he employs. There's also an empty square drawn in for the *king's palace*. Interesting. Where did you hear about that?"

From Papa. From eavesdropping on Kali and Juhi. From the palace guards who occasionally get drunk on orange liquor at the Javeribad inn, blurting out secrets to girls with veiled faces and pretty laughs. It was the first thing Kali taught me when I began to pickpocket: how to laugh pretty.

Though Kali can't read my thoughts unless she's touching me, I am careful not to laugh now or tell her anything of what I know. Not that I know much when it comes to Raj Mahal. The palace guards grew abruptly tight-lipped when asked about that, which made me wonder if there is some kind of magic binding them to secrecy.

"So you found the plot of the story I'm working on," I say with a shrug.

She raises a skeptical eyebrow. "You're writing a story?"

It's such a poor lie that I want to kick myself for it. I've never been the sort to live in dreams. Not when there are days when my own memories fail me and I forget my mother's favorite sweet. Or wonder if there really was a mole on the side of my father's cheek.

Except in the nightmares that shake me awake sweating, my mouth bloody, my cheeks sore from being bitten. In nightmare, at least, I can remember every detail about my parents and the day they died. The silver thread running through the weave of Papa's green tunic. The rabdi Ma made that morning, garnished with fried cashews and raisins. The tale of the two moons that Papa recited every Chandni Raat as carefully as a spell.

Instinctively, I reach for the three silver beads that I always wear around my neck. What if Papa had never answered the door when the Sky Warriors had knocked? Would the three of us have had time to escape? Would I still have my parents with me?

"We always wonder about these things, don't we?" Kali says softly. "The what-ifs?"

I bite my tongue. I must have spoken my last thought out loud, because Kali hasn't touched me at all.

"I'll have to shackle you to the house, you know." There's a hint of regret in Kali's voice. Her hands glow blue.

"I know."

I may have escaped the shackle for breaking the rules to leave the house tonight. Kali could chalk that up to a bored girl wanting to enjoy a festive evening. But the map is another matter altogether. Sneaking out to find a way into Ambar Fort could not only potentially get me arrested, it could reveal the location of the Sisters and endanger them as well. And Kali can't ignore that.

I don't try to run. Or argue. I am no match for Kali in close combat, especially not when she uses magic. I offer her my hands, wrists turned up, and then my feet. The spell burns my skin like a hot splash of oil, even though it leaves no marks. A shackle effectively confines you within a space of the spellcaster's choosing—in this case, the four walls of the orphanage—the magic forming an invisible barrier against every door and window, even against the ground if you try to dig your way out. I know. I've tried.

"You'll tell Juhi about this, won't you?" I ask.

"You know I have to."

I sigh. Juhi's anger is always ten times worse than anyone else's, mostly because of the heavy disappointment she attacks you with first.

"Sleep well, pretty girl." Kali gives me a wry smile.

"I will." I force myself to smile back.

I will sleep well—once I get into the palace, to the demon king, and sink a dagger deep into his heart.

6

CAVAS

I was twelve years old when I first entered the palace stables, when coincidence—or perhaps the sky goddess herself—put me directly in the path of General Tahmasp, unofficially called the Spider in the palace for his intricately spun battle plans. Officially, the general is the commander of the king's army, which also makes him head of the Sky Warriors.

As a young boy, though, I did not know who he was. If I had, I might not have had the courage to do what I did then—to reach out and stop him from brushing against a shrub a few feet away from the stable door and getting bitten by a venomous grass snake protecting her eggs.

I still recall the shocked sound the general made when I touched him, the way he stared at the prints my dirty fingers had left behind on his sleeve, the mud that had splattered the front of his pristine white uniform. I remember the hard grip of my father's hands on my shoulders as he pulled me back, his profuse apologies to the general.

"What in Svapnalok did you do that for, boy?" General Tahmasp asked me in a stern voice. "Did you find it amusing to soil my uniform?"

I swallowed the stone in my throat and explained myself, even though I was sure that I would be imprisoned and that my father, too, would be punished for bringing me with him to work.

Instead, General Tahmasp looked at Papa and said, "Don't you work in the palace stables? Keep this boy there with you, and train him. If he stays out of trouble, perhaps, in a couple of years, he can be your assistant."

My father hasn't stepped into the stables for four years now. But the horses know me. They recognize my smell, the sound of my voice, even the most difficult of Jwaliyan mares, who nuzzle my hand, their rough tongues licking up the lumps of sugar I offer.

"You're late today."

I feel my shoulders stiffen at the sound of stable master Govind's voice. "Papa was ill," I say—not really a lie.

Govind frowns. "It's a marvel he's lived this long through the Fever. Some stable boys have wondered how he's doing so without proper medicine. I deflected them by giving them more work."

"Thank you," I say, grateful for the warning. I know people talk about such things at the palace when they're idle. But I also know I can count on Govind to back me up. Despite being a magus himself, Govind has always been on Papa's side.

"I knew your father as a boy," Govind told me once when I asked why. "Long before non-magi were segregated into tenements, your father and I were neighbors. Friends."

Though they haven't seen each other since Papa was struck by Tenement Fever, Govind always asks after Papa and looks out for us when he can. When Papa's illness took a turn for the worse a year earlier, it was Govind who arranged my first meeting with Latif. "There is a man," Govind said. "His name is Latif. He used to work at the palace before as head gardener. He can help you get medicine for your father in exchange for a price."

"What kind of price?" I asked, feeling uneasy.

"He didn't tell me in his letter." Govind's lips grew thin. "Be careful around him, Cavas. Don't agree to anything that makes you uncomfortable. I would go to the meeting with you, but Latif and I didn't part on good terms. Either way, I know he'd want to meet in private."

To my surprise, Govind pressed a swarna into my hand. A coin no different from any other, except this one was a bright, shimmering green instead of gold. "Rub the green swarna, and whisper Latif's name when you're alone. He will be there."

Govind is aware of my monthly meetings with Latif even though he does not know where we always meet. He's also aware of the herbs I buy with Latif's swarnas, though he doesn't know what I'm offering Latif in exchange for the money.

The medicine isn't a cure, of course, and the woman selling it at the black market warned me as much. There is no cure for Tenement Fever for those who continue to live there, so close to the pits that accumulate the city's wastewater, to the stench and dust from the firestone mines.

"Tell me if you need a day off," Govind tells me now. "I can try and make arrangements."

I nod, even though I know I won't. A day off from work can very well mean a day General Tahmasp returns—a chance lost to give Latif the information he needs and get coin for Papa's medicine.

"How is the new foal?" I ask, changing the subject.

"Running through the pasture outside, nibbling on grass. Happier than his mother, at any rate. She's still not letting anyone near him. She grew agitated last night and then again early this morning when General Tahmasp came in to see his horse."

The mother, a wild Jwaliyan mare, mated with a palace stallion the previous year and birthed a foal a couple of days ago. But it's the other piece of information that makes me grow still. General Tahmasp wasn't supposed to be here for at least a fortnight—according to what I heard the stable boys say. But Govind is definitely a more reliable source of information. If he said the general was at the palace this morning, then it is true.

In the years since I began working in the stables, I've learned to track people's movements by their horses—if they'd been anywhere dry and dusty, or if the journey had been long. The general, however, has always made tracking difficult, appearing and disappearing with a finesse that can rival Latif's.

I've often heard jokes that compare General Tahmasp to a living specter—a spirit that remains chained to our world partly due to an inclination to remain alive and partly due to an unfulfilled wish. Though I laugh at these jokes, my humor is often forced. I don't like to remember how, as a boy of five, I had imagined seeing my mother in the tenements, how I thought she had turned into a living specter just to come and see me.

"You can hear a living specter, but you won't ever see one," Papa said firmly when I asked him about it. "The only people capable of seeing specters are the half magi: people who have both magus and non-magus blood in them. Your mother died a long time ago, Cavas. *If* she were a living specter, she would have tried to contact you long before today. And you would have only heard her."

I didn't believe Papa at first. I even dragged him to the spot where I thought I saw my mother wandering. I called out for her over and over again. But she didn't answer. No one did.

Papa's strong arms held me when I cried.

"There are days when I wish I could see your mother, too," he said softly. "But you're a non-magus, Cavas. You can *not* see the spirits of the dead. In fact, neither can any of the magi. It's why some people turn themselves invisible during the moon festival and play pranks on others by pretending to be specters. It does not help to dwell on dreams, my boy."

I now push aside the memory and force myself to focus on the matter at hand: General Tahmasp.

"Will the general be riding Raat tonight?" I ask Govind casually.

"Not tonight," Govind says. "The stallion needs some rest."

I nod. So the general is staying at Ambar Fort—at least for now.

"Also, Cavas, I could use one of your concoctions on the mare to calm her down. Get her to sleep."

"Of course." It is what I do best, why Govind has kept me here for so long instead of replacing me with another stable hand with magic in their veins. Though, most days, I rarely ever use sleeprose on animals. Not only do they sense it and refuse, but too many doses of the herb can be dangerous in the long run. It was the first thing Papa taught me on the job: *Never do something just because it's convenient.*

"We could have used you last night with the mare," Govind muses, eyeing me. "Remember what I told you, Cavas. Be—"

"—careful with Latif," I finish. "I know. I am."

Govind nods. "You're a good boy."

I push aside the twinge of guilt that sometimes comes from lying to Govind. But the truth is a luxury I can no longer afford. Govind might bend the palace rules here and there, but he will never overlook something as big as leaking palace secrets. And lawbreaker or not, Latif's money is the only thing keeping Papa alive.

I get to work, first by cleaning out a few stalls and then checking in on the mare.

I don't approach Tahmasp's horse until the mare and her foal are calm and settled, and until Govind and the other stable hand are nowhere to be seen.

"Shubhsaver, Raat," I say upon entering the stallion's stall. *Good morning, Night.* The greeting never fails to amuse me. I think Raat finds it funny, too, because he always whinnies when I say the words, as if acknowledging a private joke. He whinnies now, and I grin. "How are you doing today?"

I reach out with a carrot in my hand and get a rough lick in return before Raat nibbles down the offering. The affectionate gesture is a rare one, reserved for General Tahmasp and, over the past five years, me. Most of the other hands are terrified of Raat, a stallion bred for war, powerful muscles rippling in his thighs and haunches, his mane and coat as black as his namesake. Today, when I go through the motions of grooming him, though, I note iridescent white sand on the back of his hooves, mixed in with the red mud of Ambarvadi.

I frown. I scrape off a bit of the sand, lift it close to my nose. A ticklish sensation curls through my belly, and I curb a laugh just in time. *So not sand, then*, I think, carefully wiping my hand with a rag. I don't know why I didn't guess before. During my earliest meetings with Latif, I'd seen enough men and women inhaling lines of the powdery Dream Dust in Ambarvadi's seediest inns. Found only on the southern edges of Ambar, deep in the Desert of Dreams, the dust is so difficult to obtain that a tiny vial of it goes for close to twenty swarnas on the streets.

"So you went to the desert," I murmur into Raat's ear. "Did you see the fabled city of Tavan?"

Raat, of course, does not answer, except with another lick.

As a young boy, on the days when Papa and I had nothing to eat except what we could conjure in dreams, I would imagine our leaving the tenements behind and heading into the desert—to mythical Tavan, a city that began as a pit stop for weary travelers. In Tavan, it was said that firestones grew like fruit on trees, the streets were paved with gold, and the air always smelled like flowers and rain. It was a place where humans and animals wandered the streets and soared the skies unchained, where magic did not divide people the way it did in Ambarvadi.

Outside the stables, I reach into the pocket of my tunic and touch the green swarna lying there. Latif told me to use it whenever I had any information about the general. But before I can do anything with the coin, my ears pick out the sound of approaching footsteps, followed shortly by the word *Ambarnaresh*.

I freeze in place. There is only one person in the kingdom who can be referred to by that title, and that is Ambar's ruler—King Lohar.

"Your *restraint* only led you back here to the Ambarnaresh, empty-handed." The woman's voice is familiar, angry. "If I were there—"

"You'd have had our heads delivered to the king on a platter." It's General Tahmasp. But it's the woman's voice that makes my hands both clammy and chilly at once. There is no way I can escape without either of them noticing, so I kneel to the ground, pretending to clean the dirt on my jooti. "Our western neighbors are not like the Jwaliyans, Shayla. The Brimlanders might be our allies now that Raja Lohar has made their princess one of his queens, but they are still wary of us politically. They will not bow to our every whim. I had to proceed with caution."

His voice is so smooth that I nearly believe the lie myself.

"Some would say your speech is traitorous, General. Even disrespectful of the Ambarnaresh." The threat in Major Shayla's words makes my skin crawl.

"Rest assured that Raja Lohar knows my thoughts," Tahmasp tells her calmly. "You are not privy to our every conversation."

The rivalry between the two isn't that surprising. Major Shayla has never been secretive about her disdain for Tahmasp or her ambition to be general herself. Some say that Shayla's gender is the only barrier that has kept her from being promoted. But I also sense that it's more to do with her cruelty, which, unlike Tahmasp, is not calculated, and the terror she inspires in some of the king's own ministers. You cannot predict what Shayla will do at any point in time.

"You are not—" Shayla's voice breaks off abruptly as she notices me.

I rise to my feet and bow, pressing a hand to my heart.

"Boy. What are you doing here?" Tahmasp's voice is sharp, and there's no hint of recognition on his face. The blank expression is unsettling. Even though the general and I have not really spoken since the day I saved him from the snake five years ago, he knows who I am and has, several times, given me direct instructions to saddle or unsaddle his horse.

"I was only cleaning out my shoe, General." I lower my voice until it's soft, even a little terrified, which isn't entirely difficult in front of the kingdom's two most powerful Sky Warriors.

"A dirt licker." The tip of an atashban raises my chin, forcing me to look directly into Major Shayla's pale-brown eyes. "A handsome one at that."

Major Shayla is nearly as tall as I am, her graying hair cropped to her skull. The hair is the only concession she has made to fit in with the mostly male contingent of Sky Warriors, most of whom she outranks as indicated by the four red atashbans embroidered on the front of her uniform. Unlike the other women, she does not make any attempt to flatten her curves; if anything, Shayla's uniform emphasizes her form, her cheeks bronzed by the sun, her full lips painted the color of blood. My gaze wanders to the top of her left ear, where three tiny firestones blink against the auricle.

"Didn't know you liked rolling in the muck with the filth." General Tahmasp's voice is calm. He looks older than he did when I first saw him—especially around the eyes and the mouth—a weariness that emerges from things other than time. Unlike Shayla, who wears the sky-blue tunic and narrow trousers of a Sky Warrior, Tahmasp has a uniform as white as a cloud in sunlight, a simple lightning bolt threaded in silver over his heart.

He does not look at me, not even when Shayla decides to prick the underside of my chin with the tip of her weapon, drawing blood.

"You're right," Shayla says. The atashban stops short of making a deeper wound and withdraws. "I do despise filth." She points at her dusty boots. "Clean up, boy. Put that tongue to good use."

Bile rises to my throat. Forcing a non-magus to lick the dirt off magi shoes wasn't an unusual punishment a few years before and during the Great War, even though it was banned by the king afterward. A ban, however, will not stop someone like Major Shayla from abusing her power with little or no consequence.

"We don't have time for your antics today, Major." Tahmasp's voice is harder than I've ever heard it.

Shayla stares at him and then laughs. "I'd forgotten how sympathetic you are to these abominations. Don't be mistaken, General. These dirt lickers will do anything—even sell their own mothers—for a bit of coin."

I try not to flinch or express any outward sign of relief under her gaze, which still assesses my body as if it were a slab of cut meat at the bazaar.

"Get back to work," Tahmasp says, and I'm not sure if he's talking to me or to Shayla.

I bow again, careful not to show either of them my back. As I rise again, I see it: the flash of concern in the general's eyes when he looks at me, the slight stiffening of his mouth before he turns around, joining his long stride with Shayla's.

I wait for several long moments after they leave, partly shaken by the encounter, partly relieved at the prospect of finally providing Latif with the information he needs. Ignoring the thin trail of blood seeping down my neck, I reach into my pocket again and rub my thumb hard against the green swarna before whispering Latif's name.

A moment later, grass erupts from the ground surrounding my feet, long and green, growing so fast that it's already up to my shoulders in a few seconds. This is the sort of magic Latif performs whenever he feels we need a shield from prying eyes—or if he feels like showing off. I never get tired of watching the grass, can never stop the growing sense of claustrophobia it causes whenever it surrounds me.

"What news, boy?" Latif's voice is a thousand whispers scraping my inner ears, his gray face growing disembodied from the leaves.

"The Spider is here," I tell him quietly. "With the Scorpion."

Memories rush in: the snake in the grass, stepping in to save the general. Only now, I've become the snake.

Have you, really? the voice in my head asks. *It's not like General Tahmasp is anything to you. He has done nothing for you except offer a single moment of kindness and then chosen to ignore your existence.*

Even now, had it not been for his own aversion to being touched by a non-magus, he would have let Major Shayla have her way with me, would have simply watched as I licked the dirt off her boot. "The Spider's horse has been to the Desert of Dreams. And the Scorpion does not know," I say.

"Interesting," Latif says. "Really interesting. Do you remember what I told you last? At the moon festival?"

"Remember the girl you saw." I repeat Latif's words.

"And do you remember her?"

"Gold eyes. Brown skin. Black hair worn in a braid. Skinny. Short." I am careful to keep my voice detached and aloof, even though I haven't been able to forget the thief. Even now I can picture her with an annoying ease.

But Latif's words also make me wary. The only other time he asked me to remember someone like this was around the same time last year. A boy—General Tahmasp's personal servant—turned up suspiciously dead in the Walled City, his broken body found lying a few feet outside the Sky Warrior barracks.

As irritated as I was with myself for stupidly rushing to the thief's rescue at the moon festival, something within me tightens at the thought of her ending up like that boy, the sparkle faded from her eyes.

"Good," Latif says. "Make sure you don't forget."

"Why? What does she have to do with you? Or me?"

"You'll find out soon enough," Latif tells me before disappearing again, the sort of answer that doesn't bode well for me—or for the girl. I close my eyes and whisper a prayer to Sant Javer. *Keep her out of trouble.* I don't ask myself why I didn't make a simpler wish to keep my own misfortune at bay: one that would involve my never having to see her again.

7
CAVAS

When Govind finally lets me go, the sun has sunk into the hills beyond Javeribad. Sunheri is still full but ashy against the sky, stark and lonely without Neel.

"Follow Sunheri," Papa told me when I was a young boy. "Follow Sunheri and you will never get lost."

Built on Barkha Hill, Ambar Fort can be a maze of buildings to anyone who doesn't know it well. After a princess got lost wandering many years ago, her mother had palace workers discreetly engrave Sunheri's moon in its various phases across the wall bordering the complex. The trail leads to the Moon Door, the palace's rear gate, where two full moons are engraved right next to each other, atop a towering cusped arch. The Moon Door directly faces a window into Rani Mahal's kitchen—which, some say, was one of the princess's favorite haunts.

I follow the engraved Sunheri now, but in waxing order, around the perimeter of the wall, out of the Moon Door, and into the Walled City—a fortified area that surrounds the palace. Built on a steep incline, with stairs connecting the various havelis and ministry offices, the

Walled City is where the higher-ranking royal servants like Govind live, along with the king's ministers, courtiers, and Sky Warriors.

Palace servants hurry up the steps past me, carrying various items—baskets of laundered clothes, pots of cosmetics, bushels of safflower and millet—sweat pouring down their foreheads and darkening the armpits of their clothes. No one takes notice of me. The workers in the Walled City are far too busy, constantly at the royal family's beck and call.

The stairs eventually taper to a smooth road, which ends in a giant outer gate leading to the city of Ambarvadi, a couple of miles away. The guards at the outer gate check everyone who comes into the Walled City by verifying the badges on their saris or the pins on their turbans. They also keep an equally careful eye on who goes out, nodding at me curtly as I walk out the gates. I avoid the temptation to glance up at the watchtower, where a Sky Warrior always stands guard, atashban in hand. Though this doesn't happen often, there have been a few cases where a bystander stood gaping at the watchtower for too long and was shot at—as a warning. *Don't act suspicious*, I remind myself. *Don't draw their attention in any way.*

The knot above my stomach does not loosen until I'm well away from the gate. Instead of heading down the darkened path that leads to the city of Ambarvadi, I turn left, making my way down another smaller path, paved by footprints instead of the city's road builders.

Here, there are no lightorbs, nor is there any of the magic that envelops the palace like a shroud. The air grows thick, smells strongly of tar. Sunheri glows faintly over the gravel and dust, illuminating the path to a cluster of small houses and buildings that form the west end of the tenements.

During the day, smoke from the mines lingers perpetually over the area in a brown haze. It's only during the nights, when the mines shut down, that the homes—and the people living in them—grow visible again. Lanterns hang from poles along the path, moths dancing around the yellow flames. A man plucks an ektara's single string outside a dilapidated haveli, his rich baritone rising in the air without blending into the evening din. Soon enough, a group of enthralled children are drawn in to listen, followed by some weary adults. As tempted as I am to linger, I force myself to keep moving. Past mud-brick buildings patched up with sheets of wood and hammered metal. Past homes where old tent canvases serve as roofs against the rain and the sun. Thin flower garlands made of jasmine and marigold bracket the tops of many doors, some of them so well made that for a moment I forget they're nothing more than temple discards salvaged from the waste pits.

The smell of frying kachoris rises, scenting the air with sugar and grease. After a long day with only khichdi and honeyweed stew for sustenance, my mouth automatically begins to water. As if sensing my approach, a head pokes out from a kitchen window, white hair turning silver in the moonlight. A wrinkled face breaks into a wide, familiar grin. "Come here, boy! Have a kachori!"

"Ruhani Kaki!" I feel the day's invisible load roll off my shoulders and don't even mind the slight burn of the piping hot pastry Ruhani Kaki pops into my mouth. Self-appointed aunt—or kaki—to everyone in the tenements, Ruhani is often said to be over a hundred years old. People say that when she first arrived here, she looked exactly the way I see her now.

"Here." She hands me two large kachoris wrapped in a banana leaf. "Take these to your father."

"But, Kaki—"

"I've put some herbs into these." Unlike many tenement dwellers whose eyes have grown milky with age, her pale-brown eyes are unclouded and far too sharp. "They will help with the night sweats."

I silently accept the package. Feeding Papa has become more and more difficult these days; he throws up most of the food I cook for him. Perhaps something more delicious might stir his appetite.

"Tenement Fever is a curse," Ruhani Kaki says, sensing my thoughts. "The air itself is riddled with disease. But he's a strong man, and you're a good son. You take care of him."

70

I swallow the lump in my throat. "I try."

There are times I wonder if she knows how Papa has survived for so long. If anyone has guessed what I'm doing to keep him alive. If she does, Ruhani Kaki says nothing, her face suddenly breaking into a smile again.

"Tell him that if he complains, he'll have me to contend with," she says. "No one insults my cooking!"

I feel my lips curve into a smile. "I will. Shubhraat, Kaki."

She waves in return—both good night and dismissal—and turns back to her stove.

Mouth still savoring the sweet pastry, I nearly forget where I am until I pass another building—the one Bahar's family lives in. Since Bahar's arrest by the thanedars, her parents have avoided me completely, and today is no exception. Perched on the steps leading into the building, Bahar's mother looks right through me, her eyes dull, listless. Bahar's father, who was recently elected to the tenements' governing council, pretends I don't exist. Leaning against the lathi that marks his elevated status, he talks loudly to a neighbor about the new identification pins and badges the palace issued its workers last month.

". . . one of the sweeper's boys forgot his turban pin at home and was beaten to a pulp by the guards at the Walled City entrance!" Bahar's father spits on the ground. "If he'd had the coin, he could've just paid them off and entered the place. Poor boy! Thank Sant Javer they didn't split him to pieces."

My own turban pin feels like an added weight to my head. The two men glance up as I pass by, both of them glaring at me.

"You watch yourself," Bahar's father says suddenly after three years of silence. "You watch yourself closely, boy, or you'll face the same."

I do not reply. For the longest time, I wondered if Bahar's parents blamed me for her arrest. Papa said back then that I was imagining things.

"My daughter was innocent!" His voice grows loud, drawing more

71

stares. "She had no magic in her. She hadn't even talked to a magus! Not like his whore of a mother!"

It's been a while—several years—since someone has made such a reference to my mother directly in my presence. Death mollifies most people, and after my mother died, many chose not to speak of her and the past out of respect for Papa. Except when they thought I wasn't listening. The damage was already done when I finally put meaning to the words people used for my mother—words Papa slapped me for uttering in his presence.

"You know nothing about your mother or the sacrifices she made," he said, neither accepting nor denying the accusations.

No, I think bitterly now. I don't know my mother. What I do know of her is from whispers and conjecture, from the malice of broken-hearted fathers. The shouting shakes Bahar's mother from her stupor. She pulls her husband back in, leaving me standing there, surrounded by stares.

The tenements outside Ambarvadi are set up like a small town, with wards to the north, south, east, and west, each area populated with a fixed number of houses and buildings, which are little more than ruins of old havelis and temples.

Even though the population of non-magi has doubled over the past couple of decades, the government has done nothing to increase the land allotted to us, ignoring every request and petition we've made. To accommodate the increased inhabitants, larger apartments are now divided with bedsheets and tarps to house two or more families. In some cases, whole other floors were added atop the roofs of existing buildings, the walls a patchwork of mud brick, corrugated metal, and old wood.

Years before the Great War and King Lohar's reign, Papa said, the tenements did not exist. The area that now forms the northern tenements consisted of houses inhabited by both magi and non-magi, of buildings that were an integral part of Ambarvadi itself. Queen Megha wasn't the most egalitarian ruler, but during the earlier part of her reign, non-magi still had a voice and the ability to use it when they wished to challenge a royal edict. But as the queen grew older—and more unstable, some say—things began to change.

Ministers, who envied higher-ranking non-magi for their positions at court and non-magi farmers for their prosperous land, began poisoning the old queen's ears. They eventually convinced her to introduce a set of land taxes on non-magi for "occupying magical soil." My people revolted—and in doing so, played right into the ministers' hands. Non-magi were branded traitors, and people like Papa, who had trained to work at the Ministry of Treasure, were replaced with magi workers without explanation.

The idea of the tenements came from a priestess in the queen's council. She suggested housing us at a distance, ensuring the safety of the magical population from further rebellion, and integrating us back into society through hard, honest work. As for King Lohar—one of his first acts as the new ruler was to make the last remaining non-magus minister on his council lick the dirt off the ground, and then kill him without mercy.

"Because we know how dangerous non-magi are to people with magic in their veins," Papa liked to joke when I was younger and knew little better than to laugh at everything my father deemed funny. I hardly think Papa would find the things people say about Ma funny, either.

But perhaps Papa knows more than he lets on. Even before he fell ill, my father hardly ever talked to the other tenement dwellers, except Ruhani Kaki, which earned him a reputation of being self-contained and aloof. After Bahar was taken away, I became much the same.

People look at you only if you give them a reason to, I remind myself.

So I do what I've always done when faced with unwanted attention. I lower my gaze and hunch my shoulders. I walk away, neither too fast, nor too slow. The farther I move from Bahar's building, the fewer stares I draw. My muscles relax, my feet picking up the pace as I approach our house.

"Papa!" I push open the door and step inside. "Papa, are you awake?"

Formed from the ruins of an old haveli, our house itself is no bigger than a small room. The only light that spills in is from a latticed window near the ceiling. A few pots in the corner and an ashy woodpile function as our kitchen, the flat stone slab in front of it our dining area. A bucket in another corner to be taken outside for bathing and washing—when the only reservoir in the tenements doesn't dry up or get defiled—and a pair of netted cots in another corner where Papa and I sleep.

Only today my father is nowhere in sight.

"Papa!" Panic raises my voice to a shout. "Where are you?"

"I'm here, boy."

I turn to the sound of his voice and find him standing right behind me, hazel eyes alight with curiosity. "You were outside?"

"A man has to relieve himself from time to time," he says mildly and not without a touch of humor.

My heart slowly returns to its normal pace. "I thought something happened. The last time I found you unconscious on the floor, remember?"

The corner of Papa's mouth turns up. "I'm not on the floor now, am I?"

Yet, even as he says the words, his knees knock together, a spasm going through his limbs. I catch hold of him before he falls, ignoring the protests that emerge from his mouth, and guide him to his cot. For a thin, small man, Papa is still heavy, weighed down by his bones, even though the muscles he built working at the palace stables have long since wasted away. I pour out a cup of precious drinking water from the large clay pot and, from a small cloth bundle next to it, withdraw the last of the medicinal herbs I bought in Havanpur. Latif's coins, hidden inside my tunic pocket, arrived in the nick of time.

"I don't know why you make me drink this. You'd be better off saving that coin to bind with a pretty girl."

"Papa, please." I crush the mix gently between my fingers—black sleeprose stamens, dried champak flower petals, the wings of a fire beetle, bits of garlic, and the saints know what else—before adding it to the water.

"Come now, Cavas. Are you telling me you've never had your eye on a girl?"

I expect to feel my heart squeeze out of habit, for Bahar's face to flash in my mind. Instead, I see someone else, her gold eyes startling me enough to reply with a snap.

"No. Drink your medicine."

"Is this how you talk to your father?" His amused smile is replaced quickly by a grimace. "With all that talk about modern medicine and the healing magic of the vaids, can they really do nothing about the taste?"

I watch him drain the last drops of the cup. "At times like this, I really miss your mother," he says, the light slowly fading from his eyes. "She'd laugh at me. She'd say that if it tasted good, it wouldn't be medicine, would it?"

I glance at the binding cord on my father's right wrist, its blue and gold threads frayed, the colors so faded that you can barely see them anymore. He never took it off after my mother first tied it on his wrist, not even after she died. Ma's portrait—sketched inexpertly by Papa—hangs garlanded in our room, right next to the small statuette of Sant Javer and the shriveled incense sticks we occasionally burn during prayers. Papa said that Ma's eyes were the palest green—and that my face looks a little bit like hers. I don't resemble my father at all. Papa's eyes are hazel, not brown like mine, and he's at least half a head shorter than I am.

There are nights when I see Ma's eyes in my dreams, when I imagine her holding my hand, the sand under our bare feet cool, stars pricking a moonless sky overhead. When I tell Papa about these dreams, he says that my mother was born in the tenements in the south of Ambar, near the Desert of Dreams.

Strange, I think now, *how my dreams about Ma took me to the desert, how they always take me there when I think of her. My boy,* she calls me in these dreams. *My precious boy.* The last dream of her had been so vivid that the world I woke up to in the morning didn't feel quite as real.

"I miss her, too," I tell my father. "More than anything else in this world."

8

GUL

Their voices wake me up before the sun does, floating in from the courtyard, through the window to my dormitory.

"... dressed in a black ghagra and choli ... capable of whisper magic, perhaps. The fireflies were acting most strangely." A man's voice. One that's oddly familiar. I bury my head deep in my pillow.

"The thanedars in Ambarvadi must be mistaken. None of my girls were near the city last night." Juhi's low voice reaches my ears as distinctly as a temple bell. "We have a very strict curfew policy here, Thanedar ji."

"If you're sure about it, Juhi ji." There's a shuffling sound, a pause right outside our window. "You know how it is with young boys and girls these days. The things they get up to."

My eyes snap open.

I climb out of my cot and nearly fall to the floor, knocking over the copper mug that I keep for washing on a small trunk next to my bed.

"Queen's curses!" someone swears inside the room. Before the other novices can do more than groan their wakefulness, I'm already up, out of the dormitory, and sliding against the mud-brick walls until I reach the end of the corridor. There, I pause a few feet from Juhi standing at the door, the blue tips of her braid peeking out from behind the crumpled white sari draped around her head.

"Ji. Ji. I am sure, Thanedar ji." I'm pretty sure I haven't heard Juhi use that honorific so many times in one breath. There's a pause, during which the thanedar says something else and Juhi laughs. "Oh no, you are too kind to an old widow."

My palpitations don't ease until she shuts the door, and slowly I begin to make my way back to the dorms. I nearly forget the shackles glowing around my wrists and ankles; the shock going through them makes me nearly take another tumble.

"You." Juhi's quiet voice feels like ice on my spine. "Follow me."

I know better than to argue. I follow Juhi down the corridor to the schoolroom at the back of the house, nearly slamming into her when she suddenly stops.

"What happened?" I say—and then see that we're not alone. "Oh."

A shvetpanchhi is perched on a short desk in the center of the room, a bird the size of a human baby, white-feathered and red-eyed, blinking as I appear at the doorway.

"Gul?" Juhi looks the way some of the other novices do upon finding a dead bloodworm in their soup. "Do you know this bird?"

"Sort of." Birds are a lot more difficult to whisper to, and two months ago, when I'd first tried to whisper to this shvetpanchhi, she'd pulled out some of my hair. These days, she brings me an occasional dead rat as a present. I always politely decline. "Would you like me to—"

"Please," Juhi says, failing to suppress a shudder.

I bite back a smile. Shvetpanchhi aren't dangerous to humans unless provoked; they can also be used to send messages over long distances. But this shvetpanchhi's bloody beak is working against her image today. *Sorry,* I tell the bird. *Can we talk later?*

There's a brief silence. Then the shvetpanchhi whistles softly and rises in the air, black tail feathers fanning as she flies out the window.

Juhi releases a breath. "Sit."

I quietly pull up a cushion from the corner of the room and plop it down next to a short desk, where several cowrie shells are arranged in two perfect circles. Juhi sits next to me, and for the first time, I notice her exhaustion, the veins in her eyes redder than normal.

"You were scrying again," I say. "Weren't you?"

It's not really a question. Juhi is the most powerful magus I've come across. She can modify the memories of several people at once; she's an expert martial artist who mastered death magic at a young age. While all magic is draining in some form or another, everyone's tipping point is different. And no magic takes more out of Juhi than scrying does. There have been a couple of times when I've seen Juhi lying on the floor of her room after a scrying session, Amira and Kali sprinkling water over her face, slapping circulation back into her hands and feet.

"No sleep for the wicked, as the thanedars say." Juhi shrugs now and gives me a sudden smile. "Don't look so worried, my girl."

"I'm not worried." Even though my heart leaps to my throat each time Juhi takes out her shells. Even though I wonder every day about what will happen to us if Juhi dies.

"The shells aren't that bad. They led me to you, remember?"

"I remember." Not that I believe I am the girl Juhi was looking for. I sigh. "I suppose you're going to give me a new punishment, then."

"I should, shouldn't I? For that map. For nearly causing a riot in Ambarvadi. For bringing the head thanedar to our door."

I feel my insides curl. No one piles on guilt better than Juhi.

She pauses briefly. "How long have you been with us, Gul?"

"Three days shy of two years."

If the exact nature of my response surprises her, Juhi doesn't show it. Her dark eyes narrow at the shells, which she now arranges to form a five-point star. "I've scried over and over during this time, looking for the Star Warrior. But the shells are always silent. They've been so ever since the day we found you in that zamindar's stable in Dukal."

I say nothing in response. There are days when I wonder if it could be true. If I really am the Star Warrior. Before I remember who I am. A magus with power that's as unreliable as it is dangerous. *You don't need magic to kill someone*, I remind myself. *A well-placed dagger works; so does poison in a cup. All you need to do is get close.*

"Why *is* finding the Star Warrior so important to you?" It's a question I've asked Juhi many times in the past. "You always say you'll tell me when the time is right. But you never do. Not the real answer anyway."

"And why do you think rebelling against the raja's atrocities isn't a real enough answer?" she asks mildly.

I think back to my own parents, who hid me for years—and lost their lives for it. "People don't rebel against tyrants unless they're affected somehow," I say. "Unless there's a personal reason involved."

It's why I have asked Juhi several times over the past two years—with little success—to help get me into Ambar Fort.

"I can't wait anymore," I tell her now. "When I come of age in two months, I am going to infiltrate Ambar Fort. I am going to find Raja Lohar, and I'm going to kill him." I gather my courage, the question spilling out of me again, for perhaps the twelfth time in two years. "Juhi Didi, please. Will you help me?"

Juhi stares at me, saying nothing for several long moments. Just when I think I'm not going to get any answer, she speaks again: "What do you know about the Great War?"

I frown. *What?* "What does this have to do with the question I asked?"

"Bear with me, please." Juhi points to the mural in front of us. "Come now, we learned this when you first came here."

Spanning the entire front wall of the schoolroom, the painting is a detailed map of the four corners of the known world. Bhoomi, the continent we live on, forms the map's center and its focus: with the Free Lands of the Brim in the northwest and the land of Aman in the northeast. The kingdoms of the empire formerly called Svapnalok form a diamond between the two, flanked by the Yellow Sea in the west and the Bay of Fire in the east.

I bite back a grimace. As much as I hate this, I know I won't get any answers until I answer her question. "Once, there were two kings and two queens, descended from the gods and goddesses," I say quickly. "Each ruler created his or her own land. The son of the earth god established Prithvi in the north. The daughter of the sky goddess built Ambar in the west. The fire goddess's son drew on the power of her flames to carve out Jwala in the east, and the sea god's daughter harnessed the ocean's strength to grow Samudra in the south. Together, they banded and formed an empire called Svapnalok. It was Year 1 of Dev Kal, the first year in the era of the gods.

"For fourteen hundred and eighty years, all was well. Then Rani Megha of Ambar died. Her stepson, Lohar, succeeded her, as she had no children of her own. Raja Lohar, however, was suspected of foul play—some say he poisoned his stepmother. The other rulers of Svapnalok rebelled against his ascension, and a war broke out."

Juhi nods. "Yes, but a suspicious death is not the only reason the rulers rebelled. Why else?"

"A prophecy was made by Lohar's priests shortly before his ascension." I break off. This is the part that always gets to me—a part that I've never liked saying out loud. "It talks about—"

"Recite it," Juhi says quietly. "A prophecy is of no use unless spoken in its entirety. Come on now. You haven't forgotten it."

I should have—the way I've tried to forget every terrible memory. Yet, how could I, when our teachers made us recite it every morning at school? When my parents had moved from village to village, town to town, just because of it? I choke out the words:

"The sky will fall, a star will rise
Ambar changed by the king's demise
Her magic untouched and unknown by all
Marked with a star, she'll bring his downfall."

When I was ten, I asked my parents why the king believed the prophecy. "Prophecies are made by scryers all the time! Not all of them are true!"

"This prophecy was made by Raja Lohar's own priests, who are the best scryers of fortune in the land," Papa told me gently. "Some say they can speak to the sky goddess herself. The king had no choice but to believe them."

My hand tightens around my right arm, around the mark that no weapon can erase, no tattoo can hide.

"Terrified by the prophecy's implications, Lohar began hunting the fabled Star Warrior," I continue. "The prophecy never mentioned if the girl would also be from Ambar, so he decided to hunt for her across Svapnalok, sending his Sky Warriors to the other three kingdoms as well. Naturally, this made the rulers of Jwala, Prithvi, and Samudra furious. They called Lohar's actions a blatant abuse of power. They also feared a rebellion from within their kingdoms as more girls began disappearing.

"The Prithvi king erected a giant magical wall overnight, barricading his entire kingdom from everyone else. Made of Prithvi Stone and ancient earth magic, the wall is so powerful that it cannot be scaled or burrowed under, nor can it be cracked open with a giant atashban. The other rulers, however, had no such option. Internal corruption had financially impoverished Jwala, and shortly after the war began, the queen signed a peace treaty with Ambar, offering Lohar access to her own army and military base. To the marked girls in her kingdom as well.

"The Samudra king continued to fight, allying with Subodh, the ruler of the Pashu kingdom of Aman."

Part-animal and part-human, the Pashu are a race bound by an honor stronger even than the Code of Asha. The Pashu can't tolerate injustice, which gives their magic a unique purity, allowing them access to powers that are rare or unseen among humans. I recall the pictures I saw of some of the Pashu from our history scrolls. The peri, who appear human apart from their golden skin and the giant wings sprouting from their backs. The simurgh, who are part eagle and part peacock, with the faces of women. And then there was King Subodh himself, a rajsingha, with the head of a lion and the torso of a man, his bloody teeth bared against the Ambari troops, his reptilian tail embedded with arrows. Born of the union of a magi human and a lioness, Subodh's lizard-like tail was gifted to him by the gods when he lost his own as a youth in battle.

"Ah yes, Raja Subodh," Juhi says. She smiles slightly, as if recalling an old memory. "You would like the Pashu, Gul. They, like you, are also capable of whisper magic. In fact, the early Pashu taught whispering to our human ancestors. Did you know that?"

"I didn't."

Warmth suffuses my face and, for a moment, I feel exactly the way I did as a child, whenever my parents were proud of me. Then memory intervenes, cold hard facts that I read in history scrolls, reminding me of what ultimately happened to Subodh.

"But there were limits to Pashu magic, weren't there?" I continue, bitterness creeping into my voice. "Lohar developed the atashban, the most powerful weapon in Ambari history, and armed his Sky Warriors with it. Subodh and his army of Pashu were no match for the combined forces of Ambar and Jwala and were defeated brutally in the Battle of the Desert. Subodh died in the battle, and his decapitated head was paraded throughout Ambar in celebration.

"Left without allies, the Samudra king fought for three more years, leading to more bloodshed between the two kingdoms. This was known as the Three-Year War, which eventually came to an end with the king's death. His successor, Rani Yashodhara of Samudra, signed her own treaty with Ambar, offering a form of collateral to ensure the treaty remained in place." I pause. "What *was* the collateral, though? That's never mentioned in the history scrolls."

Come to think of it, Juhi didn't mention it, either, during our lessons over the past couple of years. Juhi gently traces the border between Ambar and Samudra on the map, her fingers lingering over the desert that separates the two. Her lips have grown so thin that I can barely see them.

"This has something to do with you—doesn't it?" I ask hesitantly.

"Yes." Juhi reaches into the folds of her sari and, to my surprise, pulls out a small drawstring purse. Made of blue silk and covered with embroidered golden lotuses, it is the most exquisite thing I've ever seen. "Rani Yashodhara did use a form of collateral. She put up her twenty-five-year-old sister, binding her to Lohar."

She undoes the purse's strings, pouring the contents into her hands. I stare at the gold choker she holds in her palm, the square edges of its pendant encrusted with fat, iridescent pearls. Engraved in the center is a weapon I've seen before only in illustrated scrolls, but one I instantly recognize: a Samudra split whip, embedded with mermaid hair and green waterstones that glow even in the faintest light. It is a symbol every child in Ambar learned to recognize several years ago and eventually associate with fear and bloodshed.

After a long moment, I look up at Juhi's face, at the blue streaks in her hair, and wonder how I didn't guess before. "Do the others know?"

"That I am Juhi, daughter of the late Balram, seventy-second king of Samudra? Amira and Kali do. The others may have guessed; I don't know."

Juhi's voice grows hard. "Yashodhara thought I would be the perfect spy. That I would go into Ambar Fort, win over Lohar, learn his secrets. But Lohar didn't trust me. The night of our binding, he made one of his guards strip me naked and search me in front of the court. 'A security measure,' he called it. I didn't give him the satisfaction of screaming."

My throat tightens, and for a moment, I think I'm going to throw up.

"He eventually tired of me, of course," she continues. "Lohar's obsession always has been with the Star Warrior. Once he began looking for her again, he forgot about torturing me. That was when I began making my move. Gathering power while pretending to be weak."

"Was that where you met Amira and Kali?" I ask.

"Not exactly. And not by intention," another voice says.

Amira stands in the open doorway, paler than I've seen her before. "Are you regaling her with tales of your time at Ambar Fort?" she asks Juhi. "Or did you head straight to the cesspits, where you found us?"

I do my best to keep my face expressionless even though my stomach is still churning from what I've heard.

"Are you afraid, child?" Amira drawls. "Can you handle hearing about what they do to magi girls they drain of their powers? Of how the guards like to play with them when they're bored? I won't even tell you what they did to the one and only non-magus girl over there."

"I am not a child," I say. Even though her words do make me ill.

"At Ambar Fort, without any control over your own powers, you will be far worse than a child. By some miracle, if you do kill the king, have you considered what will happen to you after that? What they'll do to you at the palace? Have you even thought of whom you'll end up putting in his place?"

I evade Amira's gaze and focus on the empty silken purse. It doesn't seem like a good idea to tell her I haven't really thought beyond getting into the palace and killing King Lohar—two tasks that, in themselves, are massive and likely impossible. The idea of killing Major Shayla—the woman who murdered my parents—sometimes hovers in my mind as well, but she still does not take up as much space as the man who gave her those orders.

"Why does it matter *who* replaces Raja Lohar?" I ask. "Once he's dead, the prophecy won't matter anymore. The other king won't bother hunting girls with birthmarks. There'll be no more deaths, no more orphans."

I can feel both of them staring at me now.

"How naive are you?" Amira cries out. "Tyrants always replace other tyrants—hasn't history taught you anything?"

Juhi, on the other hand, is more sympathetic. "I understand your anger. Your need for revenge. But, Gul, even if I ignore everything else Amira said, I can't deny that you need more control over your magic during combat."

"*More* control?" Amira laughs. "She can barely do any magic as is."

"She can whisper to animals," Juhi says in a cool voice. "That's also magic, Amira."

"Yes, but it's not useful if she plans to infiltrate the palace. Whispering doesn't work on humans, so unless she somehow gets an armored leopard or a pack of dustwolves in with her, she's completely helpless."

My nails bite into the fleshy insides of my palms. The birthmark on my right arm begins to burn.

"She had the lowest score during last week's practice fight," Amira continues. "Her posture is poor, her aim weak. Even a spiked mace with poisoned tips would be of little use to her."

Blood rushes to my arms and to my face, my body growing so hot that it feels like I'm on fire. There's a flash of green light, and the silken blue purse before me explodes, ripping into fragments of cloth and lint. Juhi brushes a hand under my nostrils. My blood coats the creamy white pallu of her sari.

"Gul. Gul, look at me."

Juhi's voice breaks whatever trance I'm under. Shivers race down my body, and I wonder if I'm running a fever. Juhi brushes her thumbs up the sides of my nose and presses the bridge. Pain stabs my forehead.

"There," she says. "That should clear up the blood."

"How in the name of Zaal did you do that?" It's Amira who speaks now, her voice sharper than I've ever heard it before.

My mouth opens, trembles. "I don't know. I was angry with you, I guess. I . . . tried to push it out of my system." I don't tell them about how my birthmark began burning a moment before the magic burst out of me. How it always seems to burn whenever I'm afraid or terrifyingly angry.

A dead silence follows. Juhi eyes the fragments of cloth as if they are newly discovered treasure and not the shreds of some of the most expensive silk on the continent.

"She's an anomaly, isn't she?" Calculation has entered Amira's voice.

"Seems so," Juhi murmurs. "All that repressed magic . . . it has to come out somehow."

"I'm an ana—*what?* What does that mean?" I ask.

"You performed death magic without a weapon," Juhi explains. "And, apart from that nosebleed, you seem to be fine."

"So?" My heart is thumping so loudly I'm sure they can hear it. "I bet a lot of magi can do that."

"They can't, princess," Amira says. "Just as not every girl born with a birthmark is capable of magic, let alone death magic. Even the strongest at death magic need some sort of weapon to focus their powers. There are, however, rare instances when a magus represses their powers for so long that when it *does* come out of them, it's almost always explosive."

"Repressed?" I frown. "Why would my magic be repressed?"

"Sometimes trauma or fear can cause repression—for instance, if you badly injured someone with your magic," Amira replies, referring to what happened during the practice fight last year. "In your case, though, the repression has been happening for much longer—since you were very young, right?"

"Since I was a baby," I admit.

"Were you ever punished for using magic as a child?" Amira asks.

"Never. My parents encouraged me to use magic all the time. So did my teachers at school. Some even tried to scare the magic out of me. It didn't always work." I tell them about the few times my magic did emerge—when Ma tried to burn off my birthmark, when I felt like Agni was in danger back in Dukal, the practice fight with the novice here in Javeribad.

"Each of those times, I felt like I was in danger," I say. "Like if something didn't happen, I would die—or that terrible things would happen. Right before my magic erupted, my birthmark would burn. Maybe that's what needs to happen. But why?"

I don't tell Juhi and Amira about how I'd begged the sky goddess for help in the stable in Dukal. How her eyes had glowed green right before my mind slid into Agni's. The goddess coming to my aid—now *that* had to be the anamoly. *Or a figment of my imagination.*

Amira looks as bewildered as I feel. "I don't know, princess. I've never heard of anything like this happening before." She looks at Juhi. "What about you, Didi?"

"I haven't," Juhi says. "But that doesn't mean anything. Human knowledge of magic is not absolute. Only the gods know everything, and they often work in mysterious ways."

Amira rolls her eyes. "Your gods do not exist, Juhi Didi. Only magic does."

Juhi smiles, glancing at the amulet on Amira's arm. "I will not argue theology with a Zaalian."

"Because you know I'm right! The gods never come to our aid when we need them."

That's true, I think. Though I would cut off my tongue before admitting that out loud.

"I imagine our princess would end up with worse than a bloody nose if she tried blowing up anything bigger than that purse," Amira continues. "Not to mention endanger everyone else around her."

"Not if she uses a weapon and not with proper training." Juhi stands and walks over to the map, studying it for a long moment. "There are risks, of course. A well-placed hit or an accident could mean instant death. We'd have to be prepared for that."

Instant death. The words chill my insides, twist into something that oddly feels like guilt.

Juhi murmurs a few words, moving her hand over the purse. The tattered edges glow, float up, and join back into shape.

"Death magic, if done properly, wouldn't have let me do that. I wouldn't have been able to mend the purse. So this is what I'm going to do." She locks gazes with me. "I'm going to start training you in magical combat. If you perform a proper attacking spell at the end of two months, I will see what I can do to help you get into Ambar Fort. If you don't, you will have to find your own way in."

"You can't be serious," Amira protests. "She won't last a moment in that place by herself!"

But Juhi isn't paying attention to Amira.

"You really mean it?" I can't believe my ears. "You'll help me get in?"

Juhi holds up a hand, her lotus tattoo glowing. "I swear by the god of the sea and by the goddess of the sky. Unless you don't want me to. Don't tell me you're nervous all of a sudden."

"Of course not," I say, even though I am nervous. Yet, underneath that, I feel something else awakening. Excitement. Hope. After two years of asking questions and sneaking around, two whole years of trying to figure out a way on my own, I will have someone else—perhaps the best person I know—help me.

"This is a mistake," Amira mutters.

"I can start training you tomorrow," Juhi tells me. "You're a magus, Gul, and it's about time you learned to use the power lying dormant in you. Don't you agree?"

I try to look calm and confident, but from the twinkle in Juhi's eyes and the surly look on Amira's face, I can see I've failed. I'm much too excited.

"I agree," I say.

9
GUL

Mornings for novices are dedicated to stretching and exercises for Yudhnatam. Initially, because of my small size and general agility, Juhi thought I would be good at the martial art's intricate spins and kicks and the high jumps needed to perform said kicks. That she was wrong is an understatement. I grimace, not looking forward to facing the gray-haired Yudhnatam mistress's shouts this morning. Having seen seventy-five blue moons in her lifetime, Uma Didi is the oldest member of the Sisterhood, but you'd not know this from the way she pins down the tallest and sturdiest novices with barely a move of her wrist or a twist of those scrawny hips. Uma Didi suffers no fools, which makes things difficult, as I am considered the biggest fool among the novices.

"Got yourself into trouble again, did you?" Uma Didi says now, eyeing the shackles glowing on my wrists and ankles. "No practice for you this morning. Instead, you'll be helping Cook in the kitchen. You will chop the vegetables, scrub the utensils, and make fuel at the end of the day. Also, no magic is allowed."

I grimace, wondering if she's taunting me with the *no magic is allowed* stipulation. Working with Cook isn't exactly easy, either. Cook's real name is Kalpana Bai, though no one ever calls her that, and she is one of the grumpiest people I know. Not only does she clean her ancient, rust-covered pots with ash and coconut husk, but she also insists on our making fuel out of straw and cow dung instead of using the less disgusting and more convenient grass-oil. She says dung cakes make the food taste better.

I'm about to complain about this when Uma Didi adds: "You will do this for the next two months."

"W-what?" I stutter. "Why?" Two whole months in shackles and working with Cook? "It's not like I'm the only one who has broken curfew before! None of the others has had such a harsh punishment."

"And none of them has brought the head thanedar to our door," Uma Didi points out. Behind her, I spot Amira watching us and suddenly realize who is behind this new addition to my punishment. "Go on," Uma Didi says, dismissing me. "I've wasted enough time on you today."

News about my punishment spreads quickly. Novices smirk at one another while passing by the kitchen, giggle openly when Cook screams at me for tripping and spilling a platter of newly cut vegetables to the ground. My lessons with Juhi are to take place in the evenings in a small room next to the kitchen, once used to store sacks of grain.

A part of me knows that the punishment is simply a ruse to hide my training sessions. The fewer who know about what we're really doing, the better, Juhi explained. And even though the idea is perfectly sound, I cannot help but bristle when I hear the laughs behind my back, some of them right in the open, in the alley behind the kitchen, where a couple of girls spy Cook shouting at me for mixing too much straw in with the dung. I know that the other novices don't mean to be unkind—most of us get along fairly well outside of practice fights—but the Sisterhood's strict rules for secrecy can be difficult. With the monotony of daily chores and training, everyone looks for ways to amuse themselves.

Stars prick the sky when I finally trudge back into the house, stinking, my thighs and back muscles aflame, and make my way to the armory. Juhi suggested picking a real magical weapon in lieu of a sparring sword for these training sessions, which did little good for my peace of mind. *Though, if the punishment goes on the way it did today, it probably won't even matter*, I think dully. Juhi will be sweeping the floor with me instead of the broom.

I brush a hand against the armory wall, feel magic buzzing against my fingertips. Ignoring the uncomfortable sensation that comes with it, I breathe deep and unlock the door with the key I borrowed from Juhi. The moment I step inside, I feel like I'm in a small, stuffy cage, hung with an array of different weapons—most of which have likely been banned by the government.

Sharpened jambiyas encased in iron sheaths. Round Ambari chakras that can be spun in the air and decapitate an enemy. Deadly battle-axes, ball-shaped maces with poisonous spikes, talwars forged of Jwaliyan iron, their long blades curving gently at the end. At the very center of the sword gallery hangs a Samudra split whip: a sword that in its deadliest form splits into four bendable, serrated blades.

No one from the Sisterhood apart from Juhi is capable of wielding the split whip, and no one really wants to. The one time Juhi demonstrated the deadly weapon, she sliced a tree into five chunks with one stroke. Mastering the split whip takes years of practice, and even then, Juhi is uncomfortable using it.

"When you get too comfortable with a weapon, you get overconfident. That is when you—and others—can get seriously hurt," she told me once.

I study the daggers again, drawn to a pair with blades shaped like shadowlynx horns. Unlike the others, these blades are made of glimmering green glass and hilts embedded with seashells and pieces of mammoth tusk. I imagine their sinking into the king's belly, carving new shapes into it with brutal efficiency. My hands reach out and pause breaths away. A pulse begins at my diaphragm, skittering up to my chest cavity.

I draw in a lungful of air. Hold. Release slowly. Without a touch, I can tell that these green daggers will need immense magic to power them. They are much too beautiful and likely too advanced for me. I turn away to listlessly stare at the weapons again, debating between a longsword with a firestone at its hilt—a weapon that's probably too heavy for me to wield—and a lighter variation of the Ambari mace.

"Are you going to stand there all night or are you going to make a choice?"

I spin around, heart racing, only to be greeted by Amira's unamused face. I did not even hear her come in.

"Why are you here?" I demand. "Where's Juhi? I'm supposed to be training with her."

"Juhi is indisposed. You're training with me, instead," Amira says coolly.

"What do you mean, she's *indisposed*?" A memory flashes: Juhi's body lying still on the floor, her pupils white, her hands cold to the touch. "She said she would be here!"

A shock goes through the shackles on my wrists, ending with a throb in my skull. I grit my teeth as Amira clicks her tongue. "Your impertinent questions don't deserve an answer. Now come with me."

I grit my teeth, refusing to budge. Sighing, Amira raises a hand, and another shock goes through me, this time through the shackles on my ankles.

"Pick a weapon. Or two. A shield would probably be of use as well."

As tempted as I am to spit at her, I turn and grab the two green shadowlynx daggers and a belt to sheathe them in. My hand reaches out for a shield, landing on a round one made of metal with a lion engraved at the center. It reminds me of the Pashu king Subodh. Pashu, I recall, are also capable of whispering. Feeling a little better, I slide the shield over one arm.

"Come. We've wasted enough time here already." Amira steps out of the door without another look in my direction.

Under my breath, I call Amira a word so foul that Juhi would skin me alive if she heard me say it. I follow Amira to the room next to the kitchen, the doors now closed, Cook's snores the only sound cutting through the silence. At the threshold of the old storage room—my new training ground—another shock goes through the shackles, making me tumble to the floor, pain shooting through my knee bone.

"That was for your filthy tongue," Amira says before disappearing inside.

The moment the door locks behind us, Amira begins tapping the walls of the room with a finger. The faint, crackling sound of the noise-blocking shield raises tiny bumps on my skin. Apart from a small glass window, the storage room has no natural light. Before I can offer to bring in a lantern or two, a lightorb bursts from Amira's fingers and floats overhead, illuminating the room.

Show-off.

Making light isn't a gift limited to only a few magi, but not everyone is capable of doing it. Ma was the only one in our family who could magic lightorbs. Papa called her his *Little Light*, even though there was really nothing little about my mother—she was slightly taller than Papa, even. I blink away the sudden tears pricking my eyes and focus on Amira's sharp voice.

"Fighting without magic often involves training the body in a series of physical movements," Amira says. "Fighting with magic, however, is largely mental, and not every weapon can withstand the power of the human mind. There *are* substances, of course, that are useful. White

Jwaliyan marble called sangemarmar, mammoth tusks from Prithvi, Ambari firestones, and seaglass from Samudra," she says, pointing to the shimmering green dagger in my hand. "Any of these, when used in a weapon, can amplify magic." She picks up a metal spear leaning against the wall, its sangemarmar tip glowing in the dim fanas light.

"The shield you're holding is reinforced with chips of mammoth tusk, so it will protect you from quite a few spells. But no shield is better than the one you can raise with your own magic. When we fight, you must focus on a single word: *Protect*. Make it the sole object of your meditation, make it your prayer. Now raise your shield!"

It soon becomes clear why.

I barely take two steps forward before a blast of light hits my chest, sending me to the floor, the metal shield nearly clocking my jaw. Amira stands on the other end, unarmed apart from the spear. Her simple white sari is tied like a kaccha, the cloth draped to form pantaloons for ease of movement. I expect her to be sneering at me, but her face is expressionless.

"Up again. Concentrate this time, and try to protect yourself with your own magic instead of the shield."

Another blast of magic. *Protect*, I think, but even though I raise my shield to block it, I simply fall to the floor again.

She clicks her tongue disapprovingly. "Clearly someone hasn't been doing their morning squats. If you can't even withstand a blast of air, how will you last through an actual fight?"

When she sends the next blast, I remain standing—out of sheer stubborn will. But I'm still unable to cast a shield spell.

"Good," Amira says. "Now try to block me. Focus on *protecting* yourself. Use your mind, princess!"

"How—" The question gets lost in the next blast she sends my way—one I narrowly dodge. She has me like that, skipping and ducking, until a blast hits me right in the back, blowing me off my feet.

"Be aware of your surroundings at all times." Amira sends another shock through my shackles. "First rule of fighting, remember? You didn't even hear me come into the armory tonight."

A stitch runs up my side as I try to catch my breath. "I didn't know I had enemies to fear here as well."

In the very next instant, I have to duck and roll across the floor, dodging a jet of light she sends my way, burning away the tail of my braid. Rising back to my feet, I react on instinct, throwing the dagger the way the Yudhnatam mistress once taught us, surprising myself when it misses Amira by a hair, forcing her to spin out of its way.

"Not bad." She picks the dagger off the ground and twirls it. I barely have a moment to dodge the beam of green light she aims at me. "Even though throwing away one of your only two weapons *without* hitting your mark is a stupid thing to do during battle."

My fingers curl around the hilt of the other dagger, feel the ridges and curves of the shells. This time, I let Amira move closer and use every bit of training I remember from the past two years.

Yudhnatam is not a fight, Uma Didi always said. *It is a dance of approach and retreat. If you can remember this, you will be able to defend yourself on the battlefield with or without magic.*

I spin and lunge to one side, then to another, dodging Amira's spells each time. She's initially amused by my moves, almost lazy in the way she shoots at me. But a few moments in, she begins to get frustrated. I feel the next blast of air full on, my teeth knocking together so hard that, for a moment, I think I've broken one. I sit on the floor, clutching my throbbing head.

"What exactly are you trying to do?" Amira's voice is quiet. Furious.

"Tire you out?"

My sarcasm infuriates Amira even more. "Your biggest problem has always been defense. You need to learn to protect yourself if you ever hope to do any real damage to your enemy."

"If you told me how to protect myself, maybe I could!" I have a hard time believing that focusing on a single word will do anything.

"I already told you. *Focus on the word* protect. I don't control your thoughts, princess—you do. Now come on. We don't have much time left before our session ends."

I want to walk out of the storage room and quit. Instead, I think about Juhi's challenge—the strange, hopeful look in her eyes when she issued it. I think about the Sky Warrior who murdered my parents—a woman who was a hundred times more brutal than Amira ever could be. I grit my teeth and rise to my feet again.

10
GUL

"Don't you bathe?" Amira wrinkles her nose when I enter the training room one evening. "You'd think you were rolling in dung, not simply making cakes out of it."

I say nothing in response. Nearly two weeks have passed since Amira replaced Juhi during our training sessions. Thirteen consecutive days during which I've learned to tolerate some of her taunts—when I'm not thinking of ways to sink a dagger into her eye. It took ten evenings of going to Juhi's quarters and repeatedly knocking on her door before a frustrated Uma Didi (who sleeps in a room nearby) admitted that Juhi wasn't in Javeribad at all. Neither was Kali—and that probably explains the sullen expression on Amira's face. She hates being left behind.

"I hope you'll do better accessing your magic this time," Amira says now. "You haven't progressed a bit since our first lesson."

"If you *told* me how to access my magic, then maybe I could make some progress," I bite out, unable to keep the frustration out of my voice.

She sends a gust of air my way, knocking me off my feet. "Haven't you been listening to me? Magic is a *mental* game. And I've already told you several times before to use your mind. Look out, now! You'll be fighting fire next."

She's not joking. I barely have time to raise my shield before she sends an arrow of flames in my direction. My shield, made entirely of metal, makes things even worse, marking my skin with burns.

"Concentrate on protecting yourself!" she instructs. "Use your *mind*, princess!"

If I were a princess, I would have replaced you a long time ago, I think. But since I'm not, I bite my tongue and continue dodging, sometimes managing to throw a dagger, which Amira flicks away with another blast of air, once throwing my shield at her, which, after her initial surprise, makes her roar with fury.

"You think this is a *joke*?" She sends even more flaming arrows my way. "You think you'll survive a battle with Raja Lohar, the most powerful magus in Ambar, with this sort of nonsense?"

I'm barely able to register her words. After a long day, exhaustion has begun creeping in, and the more I dodge her, the more my anger diminishes. I close my eyes for a second and breathe deeply.

"Protect!" Amira shouts. "Protect yourself, fool!"

Fool. The word brings back an old memory I'd forgotten. I was six years old and playing with a group of children in a village. I followed them everywhere, even climbed a tall mango tree with them. On a dare, they all jumped down as one, some magically floating to the ground, others finding their balance without any magic, like cats. I stayed up on my branch, terrified. Unlike my playmates, I had no experience jumping out of trees. And my magic had failed me far too many times in the past. I didn't expect it to cushion my fall.

"Jump!" the kids shouted. "Jump, fool!"

I didn't. By the time my mother finally came to the tree to fetch me, I was in tears.

"Jump, my girl," Ma said. "I will catch you."

After a long time, I jumped, right into Ma's strong arms. However, to my surprise, when Ma let go, I floated in the air for several moments before gently landing on the ground.

"I'm sorry," I told Ma, feeling embarrassed. "The other kids were right. I am a fool."

"You are not. You were simply nervous," Ma said, her voice fierce. "You have magic in you, daughter, and it is strong. Always remember that—even when I am not there to protect you."

Ma is not here now, in this training room. But her words sink in, slowing my movements, an odd calm falling over me. It's similar to what I felt when my mind split for the first time and slid into Agni's, only clearer and more intentional. As if I just understood how to open my eyes underwater. The birthmark on my right arm grows warm. There is no burning sensation this time, only heat. Power.

Protect. The word sinks in, even though my limbs are screaming for a break, an instant of relief. *Protect yourself.*

When Amira sends a ball of flame morphing into an armored leopard, I hold up my hands. Her spell hits my hands, glows for a split second before turning blue. The flames ricochet back at Amira, who instantly douses them with water.

For a long moment, we both stare at each other. Then Amira's mouth hardens, and she gives me a nod. "Again."

Wood shrapnel turning into arrows that shoot my way.

Protect. The arrows turn to powder.

Water shaped into a four-headed sea serpent.

Protect. It disappears into mist.

Fire again, this time with the face of a man: King Lohar.

Anger twists my gut. My hands shake. "Do it! Destroy him!" Amira shouts.

But when I raise my hands, my shield fractures. I scream as steam sizzles my skin, but I continue to stab at the air with my dagger until Amira finally sends a blow my way, knocking me to the ground.

"We'll stop here tonight," she says.

Panting, I slowly rise to my feet.

"So you do have something in you. Let's see if it remains consistent." She points at my face. "And clean that up."

I touch my nose and lips; blood coats my fingers. The surprise that overcame Amira's face when I raised my shield for the first time has been replaced once more by the all-too-familiar contempt.

"Be prepared tomorrow. There will be no room for error."

The next morning, after being yelled at by Cook again for not adding enough salt to the lotus sabzi, I see a familiar figure instructing a pair of sparring novices in the courtyard.

"Kali!"

Kali looks up at my shout and grins. She says something else to the girls before ambling my way. As she comes closer, I notice the thick bandage wrapped around her bare waist, under the blouse of her training sari. The smell surrounding her is astringent and bitter.

"Are you all right? What happened? Where's Juhi? Amira didn't say—"

"The sky goddess has been kind," Kali says. Despite her pallor, Kali's gray eyes are bright and keen when they scan my appearance. "You've done magic, haven't you?"

"Wha—? How did you know that?"

"Amira told me."

"Oh."

"Your training's not going too well, I take it?"

"I hate her." The words float like poison in the air, and for a second, I worry if I've overstepped an invisible line.

Kali laughs and then winces, clutching her bandage. "Don't worry. I would hate Amira, too, if she were training me. She's absolutely terrible at it."

"Why her, then? Why not Juhi? Or you? What *happened* to you? And don't tell me it was nothing!"

Kali sighs. "Why don't we talk later tonight? After your lesson?"

"Swear on the Sisterhood, you will?"

"Gul, I can't—"

"Please! If I am to tolerate six more weeks of Amira, I need to know!"

"Kali!" a voice shouts across the courtyard. "Are you coming?"

She hesitates, but only for a brief moment. "I swear. Tonight. In the courtyard."

Life while shackled to the house turns into a monotony of chores. Eventually there comes a time when I have nothing to do—not even Cook to exchange insults with. I wander to the training room and pause before a sack of rice lying in the corner. The seaglass daggers I use during training have been locked in the armory again, but Amira's sangemarmar-tipped spear is still here. She must have forgotten about it. With a quick glance at the door, I pick it up and take aim.

Attack, I think. I try the same trick I used when producing a shield the day before and recall the memory I had about my mother. Nothing happens. I try over and over again, aiming for the same feeling of calm that fell over me, but instead, I grow frustrated as more time passes and the sack remains as is. As a last resort, I try the only spell I've truly mastered—the shield spell—but all it does is throw me back with such force that I hit the wall of the room, my bones rattling.

Useless. Amira's most recent taunt burns under my skin. *No better than a non-magus.*

The words remind me of Cavas from the moon festival—a boy with aging brown eyes on a still-young face. A heat that has nothing to do with the stuffy room rises to my cheeks. I do not normally think of Cavas when I'm awake. It's only during the night when he sneaks into my thoughts. Once, during a nightmare I was having about my parents, he slipped his hand into mine, holding it tight. There are other dreams, too. Dreams where I relive our kiss at the festival. Where he does a lot more than simply curl a hand around my waist. But in my nightmare, we didn't kiss. He just stayed with me, holding my hand until everything—including the sneering Sky Warrior—faded into blessed black.

"Gul!" Cook's gravelly voice echoes in the corridor. "Arri O Gul! Where is that cursed girl?"

Sighing, I lower the spear, carefully placing it exactly where I found it.

"Don't worry, Cook," I say under my breath. "This cursed girl isn't going anywhere."

Tonight, I fail three times in a row before my shield shatters the phantom King Lohar.

"That will do for now," Amira says. "At least you've stopped with the nosebleeds. Let's see if you can generate any attacking spells. Use your daggers to protect yourself. I'll give you a moment to think and strategize."

How? I want to ask but don't. I have no intention of getting shocked through my shackles again. Goddess knows it has been the longest time I've worn them. Instead, with gritted teeth, I try to think of the ways the other Sisters—including Amira—fight during practice battles.

"All right. Get ready."

Despite her curt words, Amira is being a lot nicer to me than usual, giving me advance warnings and time to think and prepare. It makes me uneasy, and I wonder if this lesson is going to go even worse than usual.

Fire erupts from Amira's hands. I instantly raise a shield, expecting the flames to shoot back at her. They push even harder at my magical barrier, so much so that my hands begin to shake.

"There will come a time when you will encounter someone with more power than your shield is capable of handling." Amira's voice, though loud, reveals no strain. "You must, in that case, *attack* the way I instructed in the first place."

"I would if I knew what to do!" I shout.

It's a bad idea. The energy expended in talking makes my shield collapse, forcing Amira to put out her fire with water. She examines my arms and upper body—apart from the right sleeve, which has been somewhat singed—the skin around my birthmark remains unbroken, only slightly reddened from the heat.

"Thank Zaal it was your right arm, not your left. Of course, even the skin of an armored leopard won't save you from an atashban or a well-placed jambiya in the ribs."

"If you would *tell* me what to do, then maybe I could try to do it!" An unsurprising shock goes through my shackles, but I shake it off and go on talking. "You keep giving me *instructions* that are mostly useless—"

Another shock, this one so sharp it makes my tongue burn. Amira's eyes glitter with anger. "So far you have only produced a shield with some consistency—and with intent. Your other magic has been unstable, has relied on emotions you have no control over. If you don't learn to control your emotions, I have no hope of teaching you anything useful."

She begins to walk out of the room in clear dismissal when I stop her, intending to demand she give me more pointers. Instead, what comes out is: "Why do you hate me so much?"

The flicker of surprise in her dark eyes disappears so quickly that, for a moment, I think I imagined it. She shakes off my hand on her arm. "You're pathetic, little princess. Not everyone in the world has to like you. Least of all me."

She leaves me standing there, openmouthed, simmering with anger, and is already gone by the time I produce a burst of magic: a faint glow of green in my dagger before it flickers out.

"You're in a temper." Kali's voice stops me in my tracks on the way back from the armory. "Did you forget about our meeting?"

"Of course not." I am grateful it's dark, so she can't detect the lie directly from my face. A pair of fingers lightly pinch my cheek.

"A liar who smells like dung." A fanas emerges from the darkness, its flames illuminating Kali's grin.

"Do you even need me to tell you why?" I ask, exasperated.

"Shhhh. You'll wake Juhi." Kali places the lantern on the ledge of the balcony overlooking the courtyard. "She's having one of her headaches."

"What happened to her? To you?" I point to her injury. "You'll tell me, right? You swore you would!"

"That's why we're meeting here, aren't we?" Kali pauses for a moment. "Juhi saw something while scrying her shells. She insisted she had to find someone in the Desert of Dreams. I wouldn't let her go alone, of course. It was probably a good idea I did go with her, because we ended up finding a pack of dustwolves instead."

"Goddess!" I wince. Rabid and ferocious, dustwolves are known to tear fully armed Sky Warriors apart. Juhi and Kali are lucky to have escaped alive. "Who in Svapnalok were you looking for?"

Kali shakes her head. "I've said too much already. Listen, Gul. I know Amira is hard to take, but she's brilliant at death magic—the only one of us apart from Juhi who's capable of wielding an atashban. That's why Juhi picked her to train you over me."

"But she's so difficult to work with! She doesn't want to train me. She hates me!"

"Amira doesn't hate you. Not really." Kali shrugs. "There might be a bit of jealousy involved. Before you came along, Amira was the star of Juhi's eyes, the girl who might have been the One."

The One. The prophesied Star Warrior who is meant to take down the king. Had it been anyone other than Amira, I might have sympathized with her. "I don't know why she's so worried. I can whisper to animals, yes, but I can barely do any death magic—apart from a shield spell. Or two."

"Don't belittle yourself. You *can* do magic," Kali says. "If you didn't get blocked by what happened with that novice, you would've had more control over it sooner."

"That novice nearly died!"

"Death is a risk every trainee faces during magical combat," Kali says firmly. "In any case, I think Amira may be good for you. Her bark has always been worse than her bite—even though her bite is pretty bad. According to her, you haven't suffered enough."

The words take a while to sink in. "Suffered enough? What does that mean?"

Kali gives me a wary look. "Amira and I went through a lot at the labor camp. More than losing our families. We didn't have any saviors until Juhi came along, and by then it was too late for us in some ways. Certain sufferings harden you more than others."

Rape. Torture. I heard the stories through other Sisters when they thought I wasn't listening.

"Amira went through even more than I did," Kali continues. "She resents you for it—which is her problem entirely, not yours. But you need to also start toughening up. Stop taking every little thing to heart."

"I *don't* take every little thing to heart!"

Kali raises an eyebrow.

"All right, so maybe I could be better about it," I admit. "But she imparts nothing except criticism and taunts. I never know what she wants me to do, *how* she expects me to figure things out for myself. What kind of teaching is that?"

"The sort that life gives you. The world you are going into is not going to care for your feelings."

Maybe not, I think. But there are differences in Kali's reprimands and Amira's. Amira's hardness comes from a place of contempt. I may fear Amira, even pity her for her sufferings, but I do not respect her.

"I will try," I say out loud. How, I don't know.

There's a pause before Kali replies. "How did you produce your shield?"

I blink, surprised by the change in subject. "I guess I concentrated on the word *protect*. And . . . I remembered a time my magic had emerged without my knowing, protecting me from harm." I tell Kali about how my mother caught me when I jumped from that tree, how I floated above the ground. "I felt calm because I knew I'd done it before. I felt that even if Ma had not come to catch me, I could have been able to save myself. But what works for the shield spell doesn't seem to for an attacking spell. And I don't understand why."

"The human mind is complex," Kali says, a thoughtful look on her face. "Every magus wields power differently. It's why Amira's instructions may seem useless to you. Amira feels most powerful when she rids herself of emotion and turns her mind to a blank slate. You, on the other hand, seem to get power from tapping into your emotions and into memories that make you feel safe."

I sigh. "I wish I knew what memory I need to do an attacking spell."

"You'll figure it out." Kali speaks with such confidence that even I believe her for a moment. "I have faith in you."

"Thanks."

For now, Kali's faith is all I have.

Later that night, as I'm falling asleep on my cot, a candle lights up the doorway to our shared dormitory.

"Where were you?" a voice whispers.

"Out in the fields with the farmer's boy," another voice says, giggling. In the dim light, I make out two figures: Urvashi and Prerna, a pair of novices I hardly ever speak to even though we share sleeping quarters.

"Amira nearly caught me sneaking in," Prerna whispers. "Can you imagine my punishment? I'd end up smelling of manure like our dear Gul. No boy would ever want to touch me again!"

"Amira is such a witch." Urvashi's voice, though soft, is far more carrying than Prerna's in the silence. "I wonder why Juhi keeps her around. Especially after what happened in Havanpur."

My ears, already alert upon hearing my name, sharpen even further.

"What happened in Havanpur?" Prerna echoes the question in my head.

A smile appears on Urvashi, equal parts beautiful and cruel, before she whispers the secret out loud.

DEATH MAGIC

23rd day of the Month of Drought
Year 22 of King Lohar's reign

11

GUL

"Ready?" Amira asks.

We're seven weeks into training, and my shield spell is now strong enough to repel most of the magic Amira sends my way. But I still haven't been able to retaliate with an attack of my own. Now, with only seven days left before my test, both of our tempers are on edge, Amira's tongue lashing out more and more like a serrated knife.

"Yes," I barely have time to say before Amira sends the first attack my way. Shield raised, I begin to concentrate. *You have magic in you, Gul. You can do this.*

Instead of focusing on anger or fear or any other emotion, I dig deep, looking for a memory that made me feel safe as a child. I remember Papa reading me a bedtime story and focus on that. A feeling similar to the calm I felt while producing the shield rises: like sun-baked earth, like a roti fluffing on the fire. *Attack*, I think, over and over, until the word becomes a mantra evoked by a priest at a temple. The tip of my seaglass dagger glows red, releases hot sparks into the air. I frown. The spell wasn't strong enough. But why?

It's the memory, a voice in my head says. *It needs to be stronger.*

"More!" Amira shouts. "You need more! Concentrate!"

I try. I search for other memories; surely, I have more. But it's hard to think of happy things with Amira sending spell after spell my way, her shouts hammering the inside of my skull. My birthmark begins to burn. Sting. A trail of wet slides down my nostril and onto my lips. Blood. My head feels like a pair of tongs have been clamped around it, but I push.

Past the fear.

Past the anger.

Past the pain.

From where only sparks had emerged, now there is fire, a straight streak of green flame, which bursts from my daggers and hits Amira's shield . . . before rebounding, forcing me to jump out of the way.

"Come on! Focus, princess!"

"I *am* focusing! Didn't you see what I—"

She shoots a stream of arrows at me next that, instead of shielding, I roll away from.

"Pathetic," Amira spits out. "Do you think you're being amusing? That you'll find magic like a swarna lying on the floor?"

Rage, building slowly ever since the lesson started tonight, perhaps ever since Amira and I first met, bursts out of me: "At least *I* didn't whore myself out in Havanpur for a few coins!"

A blast, sharper than ice, hotter than flame, throws me back against the wall of the training room, disorienting me so badly I can barely stand. Amira's face is ashen, sweat matting strands of long hair to her brow. She wipes them away before rising to her feet.

"What did you say?"

My mouth tastes of blood. I don't dare spit it out. "I know about Havanpur. I know what you did there."

Amira stares at me for a long moment. Her eyes grow glassy. She drops her own weapon to the floor with a clatter. "Our training ends here."

For a long time, I sit there on the dirt floor, staring at the space she once occupied. I don't know why, instead of feeling satisfied, I feel sick. Like I've done something irreparably wrong.

I can't bear to go back to my dormitory. Instead, I sit on the stairs leading into the courtyard, my shoulders sagging, my head still hurting from the force of Amira's retaliation. Moments later, a figure approaches, settles down next to me. I smell the amla Juhi oils her hair with. If not for what just happened, I would be overjoyed to see her.

"Amira told me she won't be training you anymore," Juhi says quietly. "And she won't say why. Will you?"

I'm tempted to say nothing. But one look at Juhi's sympathetic face and everything comes pouring out—the training session tonight, Amira's taunts, and what I said in return. There's a long silence. I wait for Juhi to slap me or render a worse punishment than what I already have. She doesn't.

"When I first saw Amira, she was in one of the labor camps near Ambarvadi," she says. "She was perhaps twelve or thirteen, and her teeth had been bloodied from biting one of the guards. He wanted to know what tricks she'd learned in Havanpur. I guess she showed him."

I cover my mouth in an effort not to throw up. Amira was only twelve!

"Back then, I was scheming to get out of the palace," Juhi continues. "I didn't know when that would happen. But I knew it would. On a whim, I asked to see the prisoners alone. No one thought it strange back then. I had a reputation for trying to help whom they considered worthless causes. I was also one of Lohar's queens, and queens had some privileges over the guards. When I reached Amira's cell, I don't know what came over me. I kneeled next to her and said: 'Make sure you can run.' I'm not even sure if she registered the words at the time.

"But the day finally came. I staged my own death and escaped the palace with the help of a few palace workers I trusted. I later found out that the head gardener, Latif, died trying to protect me." Juhi's voice has the flatness of someone forced to relive a nightmare far too many times to count. "I could have escaped then. Gone back to Samudra. But I remembered the bargain my sister had made with Lohar. Their magical contract would have forced her to return me to him. With home no longer an option, I felt lost, even a little hopeless. Then I recalled the girl in the labor camp, the one I begged to stay alive. It took me four days to reach the camp on foot, to knock out one of the guards and steal her uniform.

"Amira was there. Starving, but still alive. And she had Kali with her. So I took them both with me. Sneaked out into the night with no one the wiser. I heard later that the supervisor of that labor camp was transferred somewhere else and that new security measures were put in place. We were lucky to escape when we did."

I'm silent for a long moment. "There's one thing I don't understand," I say. "If Amira's and Kali's magic had been drained, then how can they do magic now?"

"That's something I couldn't quite understand myself. I'd seen girls who had been drained of magic before. Some were little more than husks: creatures without souls. But Amira wasn't. Neither was Kali. My only guess is that whoever was assigned to drain them of magic hadn't done a proper job of it. It took Kali over a year to regain her powers, Amira even longer—around two years.

"Prayer and meditation help in these cases, and so they meditated to the four gods, to Prophet Zaal, to Sant Javer. They practiced magic until they collapsed with exhaustion. And even if they hadn't regained their powers, it wouldn't have mattered to me. The day I rescued them, I vowed that we would be sisters in life and death. And that I would always protect them."

I can't help but feel awed by her story. "Was that how the Sisterhood was formed?"

"Yes. Amira told me that she and Kali would feel like thorns in my side. Kali countered that they were like the gold lotuses of Javeribad, the kind that bloomed in the mud. That's how we came up with the name."

The Sisterhood of the Golden Lotus. As badly as I want that tattoo on my palm, I know now that I am not worthy of it. Not one bit.

"I understand why Amira told Kali I haven't suffered enough," I say. "I haven't. Not like that."

"Suffering is different for different people. The gods never give you more than you can bear at a certain time in your life. Perhaps they have other tests planned for you. Other challenges that they might only reveal in the future."

I shake my head. "That's so arbitrary. As if we're nothing but simply stringed puppets pulled at by the gods on a whim."

"You sound like Amira." Juhi laughs upon seeing the stunned look on my face. "She gave me the same argument when she came of age and became a follower of Prophet Zaal. Zaalians believe in the concept of free will in the face of magic. Amira's determination alone helped her regain her lost magic."

"Well, maybe the Zaalians have the right idea," I say after a long pause. "Maybe it's only magic—unstable and whimsical—that controls the world we live in with no care for humans or their miseries. The sky goddess didn't come to my aid when the Sky Warriors murdered my parents. Neither did she rescue Amira and Kali. You did."

"Perhaps the sky goddess was the one who sent me."

"That's maddening logic."

"You have your beliefs; I have mine."

It's not really a rebuke—Juhi's smiling—but I decide to say nothing further on the subject. I turn back to the courtyard, where, in a few hours, Uma Didi will lead the novices through the stretches that will prepare them for Yudhnatam, hands and toes gripping the dirt, faces turned up to the sun.

"Do you really think that I'm the Star Warrior?" Spoken out loud, it sounds even more foolish than it did in my head.

"Every heart holds a warrior. Some are born, some are made, while some choose to never take up arms. What you are and who you will become will be entirely up to you."

"Do you give straight answers to *anyone?*"

Juhi laughs again. "Don't blame me. You're the one who still has to pass her test, remember?"

"I don't know if I will be able to pass your test without Amira training me."

"Perhaps you don't need Amira. Perhaps you can do it on your own." She taps my nose. "Go on now. Get some rest."

At the end of the hallway, I turn one last time to see Juhi still there, staring up at the stars.

Over the next few days, my attempts to apologize to Amira are met with unsurprising resistance. Every time I try to talk to her, she makes an excuse and leaves the house or pretends she doesn't see me.

I try to recruit Kali's help, but she shakes her head. "This is between you two. I am not going to interfere." Kali's thick bandage is now gone, three upraised scars marring her waist under the band of her sari blouse.

"I'm sorry." The words feel heavy in my mouth.

"I'm not the one you should be apologizing to." Kali's cool voice isn't a reprimand. Not quite. But after hearing the story Juhi told me, I'm not surprised by her reaction. By wielding Amira's terrible secret as a weapon, I've broken Kali's trust as well.

As a last resort, I painstakingly pen a note in my best writing on fresh parchment: *I apologize for the hurt I inflicted on you. Gul.* When it's empty, I slip into the room Amira shares with Kali and place the note on her cot.

I don't see Amira the next day or even the next. Then, one afternoon, as I'm crouched to the ground, sweeping the courtyard as part of my chores, a shadow falls over me. Amira. I start rising to my feet, another apology poised on my tongue, when she holds up the note and slowly tears it in one half. Then another. Bit by bit, allowing the pieces to float to the ground, like a tree shedding leaves during the Month of Drought.

"Sweep that up, will you?" she says before turning on her heel and walking away.

Rain clouds gather in the sky on the night of my test. The light drizzle eventually grows into a steady downpour, and several novices rush into the courtyard, laughing, splashing in the puddles like five-year-olds. Normally, I would be right there with them, but I'm too depressed tonight.

I head to the training room—more out of habit than any willingness to practice—and pull out the map I'd made of Ambar Fort over the past two years. I hold the parchment straight and slowly rip it in half, then in quarters. Moments later, I'm sitting on the ground, surrounded by pieces of paper. Why keep the map when I am never going to get into the palace?

You still have the test, a voice in my head reminds me.

"What's the point?" I say out loud. I feel dull all of a sudden, the anger draining out of me. "I'm going to fail."

The daggers I normally use are now locked up in the armory—along with Amira's spear. I stare at the gunnysack in the corner of the training room—the one I'd tried to destroy six weeks ago. Outside, rain continues to pour, the drops tapping against the room's small window.

Tap tap taptaptap tap. The sound brings forth a memory from my childhood, when we lived in the village of Sur. Rainy afternoons, when I would sneak into my parents' bedroom and lie on my father's side of the bed, reading one of his old scrolls to the sound of a sparrow persistently pecking at the mirror nailed to the door of the old cupboard.

"Why does it do that?" I asked Papa once. "The sparrow?"

"It thinks another sparrow lives in the mirror," Papa said, smiling. "Look at its focus! It does not know it's staring at itself. It's a lesson of sorts, don't you think?"

"A lesson?"

"A reminder really. To step back sometimes and allow yourself to look at the bigger picture."

And that's what I do now. Instead of focusing on a single, simple memory, I step back and recall the sound of my father's voice. I retrace the lines and planes of his face, the scar that he'd grown a beard to hide. I recall the booming way he laughed whenever he found anything funny; I pretend I can feel the sandpaper texture of his hand brush my cheek again. Papa's favorite color was green, like the tunic he wore at the moon festival two years ago. He believed in justice and in the good of the world, and he loved me and Ma unconditionally.

My mind grows still. Warmth skids from the birthmark and across my right hand, which begins glowing like the sun. Sparks erupt from my fingertips, rise and swirl in the air, encircling me in a web of light.

Without thinking, without even understanding why, I use my hand to gather the sparks, buzzing like fireflies against my palm. My head begins to pound. Just when I think I can't bear the pain in my skull any longer, a beam of red light bursts from my hand—and forms a spear that sinks into the sack, rice spilling out like water, turning to dust as it hits the ground.

Moments later, I grow aware of another presence in the room. When I turn, I find Juhi standing by the door, her dark eyes reflecting my still-glowing hands.

"J-Juhi Didi. Did you see what I . . ."

"I saw," she says. "I saw everything." As she moves closer, I see a smile. And something else that I'm too afraid to give a name to.

Slowly, she waves a hand over the ruined sack. I hold my breath, waiting for a long moment. But nothing happens. My magic held true. I have passed the test.

"Wait here," Juhi says abruptly before leaving the room. I wonder if she has gone to fetch Amira and Kali, but a moment later, Juhi returns alone. In her hands she's holding—

"The seaglass daggers you like so much." She gives me a smile. "My father gave them to me when I was sixteen. But, based on what Amira told me, I think they suit you better."

"Juhi Didi!" I protest. "I can't!" But when she presses them into my hands, I find my fingers curling around the hilts, the fit so perfect that they might have been made for me.

"Performing death magic without a weapon is still dangerous," Juhi reminds me. As much as I long to deny this, I know she's right, my head still throbbing from the spell I cast.

"It's time you found your place in the world."

12

CAVAS

There's a saying in Ambar that you aren't truly grown up until you're caring for more than yourself. Until you've found your place in the world.

"As the king's revered acharya likes to say: 'The greater your powers, the better your chances of progress. With the sky goddess's blessings,'" Govind announces one morning to a chorus of laughter from the other stable boys. "This is why the rest of us are so downtrodden, while the high priest convinced the Ministry of Treasure to hire his beloved son—with a cartload of swarnas and rupees, of course."

I slowly trudge by, carrying two full buckets of water from the palace well to fill the trough of water outside. I always act like I'm never listening to these conversations—and Govind always pretends that he never sees me.

"It might be the only way the acharya can keep him out of trouble," one of the stable boys says. "To surround him with gold and silver instead of pretty dirt-licking boys."

Their laughter crawls up my spine. I dump the water into the trough.

By the time I carry the empty buckets back to the stable, my hands are shaking from gripping the handles so tightly.

"Boy." General Tahmasp's curt voice breaks through my reverie.

I carefully place the buckets on the floor and bow. "Shubhsaver, General."

He doesn't wish me a "good morning" in return. His dark eyes narrow, as if in assessment. I try not to squirm. "How are you?" he asks.

I blink. The general has never stopped to chat with me before, our interactions limited to cold and simple instructions about his horse. "I'm well, General."

"You haven't seen Major Shayla again, have you?"

"No, General."

It has been two months since I last saw the general or the major—even in passing. Latif hasn't been too pleased with my reports.

"Good." The general tugs on the stiff collar of his white jacket. "That's good to hear. Be careful, will you? With her."

As if the other boys the Scorpion has preyed upon weren't careful. As if it's care and not a freakish stroke of luck that has prevented Major Shayla from seeking me out so far. I shift my weight from one foot to the other, wondering why I feel the need to assure General Tahmasp that I'm all right.

Tahmasp clears his throat. "How's your father doing?"

"He . . . he's much the same, General. With the Fever . . . sometimes he's better, sometimes worse. We've learned to take things day by day."

"We were born into this life, and we must make the best of it," Papa always says, and though his voice is gentle, I know it's also a reminder of who we are—and who we can never be.

Tahmasp stares at me for a long moment. "There are houses at the other end of the city. On the outskirts, away from the firestone mines. They're reserved for army personnel only, though, and usually in high demand."

I wonder why he's telling me this. Though the king still allows non-magi to enlist in the army, it's generally for the position of load-bearers, who carry equipment and pitch tents. Houses outside the tenements are strictly reserved for army officers, all of them magi.

"Naturally, I can't give you any guarantees, but there have been exceptions made in the past," Tahmasp says. "On rare occasions, non-magi who show immense loyalty to the kingdom are made captains, sometimes even awarded a house. I'm not saying it will be easy. You'll have to start off small—as a loadbearer perhaps. If you work hard over the next year or two and show some aptitude in fighting, perhaps you can move up the ranks as well."

I stare at him, stunned. While a small part of me appreciates that the general thought of me and my father, I can't help but notice how late this offer has come—and what a poor solution it is. How am I supposed to wait a whole year or two when I don't even know if the Fever will let Papa live for the next *month*?

"Your wages increase as well," the general continues, completely un-aware of my thoughts. "That could help, I'm sure, with the medicine. Enlisting takes place every year in the Month of Tears."

Which is this month. Sweat coats the back of my tunic. "I'll have to talk. To my father. I need to make sure . . . that he'll be all right if I go."

"That's not a problem." The general's hard face softens. "I'll be out of the city for the next couple of weeks or so. If you decide to enlist, come find me in the barracks before the month ends. I can put in a word."

I watch him lead his horse away, my mind abuzz with a hundred dif-ferent thoughts. I could have rejected his offer on the spot, could have told him exactly what I thought, punishment be damned. But petty reactions do not have a place in a world where my father's life is at stake. Where any little thing may help him survive.

I pick up the shovel lying in the corner next to the buckets and begin cleaning manure out of a vacated stall. As a child, I would dream of other things at times. Of new clothes, of sweets, of flying on the back of a giant simurgh. The last dream—one of the few vivid ones I had back then—I still remember, but with the wistfulness of a childhood long gone.

When Papa fell sick, I knew that my life would be limited to a simple set of rules: Keep your head down. Work hard. Come home every night, no matter how bruised. In the army, though, there is every likelihood that I may not come home. I've heard more than one person talk about deaths in the army—how more loadbearers die from thirst and starvation in the desert than from any actual fighting.

I wipe the sweat off my forehead with the back of my hand. The sweet smell of freshly raked hay rises in the air. In the background, horses let out low whinnies, the sound nearly as soothing to me as a lullaby. Outside, there is more laughter among the workers. Now they're talking about the new indentured laborer in the king's palace, and how he was recently seen carrying the Scorpion's armor to the Walled City. My lungs fill with a breath of relief.

Better him than me.

The thought is instantly followed by a sick feeling of guilt.

I pick up the shovel again. Yes, the army may not be my first choice of work—but it is still a choice. And that is something I have never been given before.

Later that evening, I nearly walk past Ruhani Kaki's hut in the tenements, not initially hearing the old lady call out my name.

"It does not do to be so lost in your thoughts that you forget the world around you, Cavas!"

"Sorry, Kaki. I really didn't hear you."

"Of course you didn't. Young people these days don't hear anyone except other young people they're interested in." But Ruhani Kaki's eyes are twinkling, so I know she isn't being serious with her scolding. "Wait here. I'll get you something to eat."

She emerges from the hut shortly with a plate of hot onion kachoris in one hand and a scroll in the other.

"Someone came to see your father today. An old friend of his from outside the tenements," Ruhani Kaki says as I eat a pastry.

"What?" The kachori nearly gets stuck in my throat. "Which friend?"

Ever since Papa got the Fever, we've had no visitors apart from Ruhani Kaki. No one from the tenements has come to see us and certainly no one from the magical world.

Ruhani Kaki hesitates before answering. "Her name is Juhi. Your father knew her when he worked at the palace. I knew her as well. I didn't know if your father was up to taking visitors today, so I simply told her he wasn't at home and asked her to leave her letter with me. I said I would make sure it was delivered to him."

Unease muddies my insides. Papa never talks much about his former life working at the palace stables. Whenever a conversation would lead there, he would divert the topic by asking me questions about my day.

"Who was this woman? Did my mother know her as well?" I ask, taking the scroll from Ruhani Kaki. It glows faintly silver in my hands. *With magic.*

"Juhi and your mother never had the chance to meet," Kaki says after a pause. "But she was one of the few people from the magical world whom your father trusted completely. It has been long since I saw Juhi myself. Until today, I thought she was dead."

I frown. "What does she want now? Why try to contact Papa after all this time?"

"She didn't tell me. But perhaps it's in there." Ruhani Kaki gestures to the scroll. "She didn't stay long. Magi in the tenements usually draw unwanted attention. As a Southerner, Juhi would draw even more notice—and that wouldn't be good for your father or for you."

A Southerner. Meaning someone from the kingdom of Samudra.

"What about you, Kaki?" I ask. "Wouldn't you get into trouble if you were seen talking to her?"

Ruhani Kaki gives me a smile reminiscent of the ones she often gives to young children, amusement lining every wrinkle on her face. "I'm too old to be taken much notice of, my boy. I could sing lullabies to a donkey, and people would still ignore me."

I examine the seal on the scroll. Red wax. Plain. Not the kind used by the palace for sending official notices, which has an emblem similar to the one on my uniform.

"Thanks, Kaki," I say finally. "For everything."

"You never need to thank me for anything." Her hand brushes my cheek, the touch paper-soft. "Go home now. And next time, pay attention when I call for you."

I force a grin. After wishing her a quick goodbye, I make my way home, my feet gaining ground now that I'm alone again, the scroll hot in my sweaty hands.

It's not until I'm back at the threshold of our house that I feel safe enough to break the seal and read the first few lines of the letter.

Papa glances up when I step inside, his smile slipping when he sees the scroll in my hand. "What is it? Is it from the palace?"

"No," I say, waiting for the tension in his shoulders to ease. "It's a letter. For you."

"A letter for me?" Papa sounds bemused. "I haven't had a letter in seventeen years. Not since your mother died anyway. Are you sure it isn't a prank by one of the blacksmith's boys?"

"The blacksmith's boys aren't literate." I release a breath. "Ruhani Kaki gave it to me. It's from outside the tenements. From a woman named Juhi."

Papa's eyes, as placid as Sant Javer's pond on a normal day, grow sharp. "Juhi. She's still alive, then. I haven't heard from her since . . ." His voice trails off. "Read it to me."

"Who is this person?" I ask. "How do you know her?"

"Read it, Cavas. It won't do to have you getting rusty."

When I was a boy, people from the tenements came to my father to read their letters for them—usually ministry documents and scrolls they weren't able to comprehend themselves. Schooling for non-magi isn't forbidden, but shortly after we were segregated into the tenements, schools dropped non-magi enrollment by half. As the years went on, by even more. "The work is too advanced for your children," they told our parents. Or, more simply: "You are rebels and traitors to the kingdom. We have no place for your children in our schools." By the time I turned five, not a single school in Ambarvadi accepted non-magi students.

Ruhani Kaki tried to start a school for non-magi children in the tenements a couple of times. I went to her classes once or twice. But Kaki wasn't a great teacher and couldn't control a group of boisterous youngsters. Her attempts at a school fell apart. Eventually, as taxes on non-magi increased further under King Lohar's reign, more and more families were forced to send their children to work. There was no time to spare for school—not with so little food at home and so many hungry mouths to feed.

"You will not remain uneducated," Papa told me firmly. "Not while I'm alive." He spent his days working at the palace and his nights teaching me to read and write Vani. It has been, to date, his only act of rebellion against the kingdom.

Now I begin reading Juhi's letter out loud, my frown deepening as I get further into the contents. *I hope I see you tomorrow, old friend*, Juhi says in the last line of the letter. *I don't trust anyone else.*

Right, I think. *Sure, you don't.*

"What is it?" Papa asks. "Why did you stop reading?"

"It's impossible, what she has asked you for! How dare—"

"It's not impossible." My father's calm reply cuts me off.

"You cannot even step out of the house without falling ill!"

"Which is why you must go in my stead." There is a look in Papa's eyes that reminds me of the time he told me about the importance of learning Vani. "You must do everything you can—everything that is asked for in this letter."

I shake my head angrily. "Why should we care about this? Magi have never done us any favors."

My father pauses before answering, almost as if weighing his words first. "There was a world once," he says finally. "Before the tenements. Before the Great War divided the four kingdoms of Svapnalok and turned friend against friend, neighbor against neighbor. This might be our only hope of seeing something like that world again."

I grow quiet for a long moment and think of the vile words Bahar's father and others spewed about my mother. People Papa once considered his friends and neighbors.

"If there is a world like that"—I rise to my feet again and walk to the door—"it only exists in dreams and in stories for children. We are born into this life, remember? Isn't that what you've told me all along?"

"Son, listen to me. I know I said—"

"General Tahmasp says the army needs new loadbearers," I interrupt. "He asked me to enlist. And I think I might."

The clay cup holding Papa's medicine falls to the floor and shatters. "You cannot! People die thankless deaths in the army every day!"

"And they don't die in other ways?" I hold up the scroll again. "Do you think I'd be any safer if I was discovered doing *this*? At least the government pays fifty swarnas to the families of each deceased soldier."

"If you join the army, Cavas, you'll see me dead." Papa's voice is quiet, his face paler than I've ever seen it before. "By all the gods and the saints, you will."

"I'm going to clean this up," I say, ignoring the empty threat and kneeling to pick up the broken cup's pieces.

Papa doesn't talk to me for the rest of the night. He refuses the boiled vegetables I've cooked for him—harkening back to a form of protest I used when I was a boy of six or seven.

"Fine!" I shout. "Starve, then!"

I storm out and throw myself on top of the battered old cot by the door—one I sometimes use when the weather is good. Stars have appeared next to a lonely yellow moon, and I slowly pick out the shape of the sky goddess constellation, characterized by the triad of stars forming the tips of her trident.

"You're wrong, Papa," I whisper. "There is no such thing as hope."

13

CAVAS

Even though I know I've made the right decision, I can't sleep that night. *Choices* and *hope* are dangerous words. They draw you in like a moth to a torch; they burn you alive if you get too close.

Yet, long before dawn breaks, I find myself slipping into my shoes again. Instead of my usual orange turban, I tie a checkered scarf around my head the way firestone miners do, angling it so it covers my day-old stubble and fully grown mustache. As a final touch, I drape an old blanket over my shoulders. The fewer people who recognize me, the better, even though no one is awake at this time of the day, not even the city sweepers.

Dawn in Ambarvadi breaks slowly. When I leave the tenements, it's still dark, pale-blue light barely edging the sky. Here, the weather isn't as extreme as it is near the Desert of Dreams. But mornings are still cold, and by the time I reach the outskirts of the city, I'm chilled to the bone. The earth is wet with dew and sticks to the thin soles of my jootis as I make my way to the main square, past darkened havelis and boarded-up shops. I circle the perimeter of the enormous marble temple devoted to the sky goddess, offerings of fruit and flowers heaped outside its gilded gates.

Behind the sky goddess's temple there are more havelis, though many have fallen into disrepair. Women hang clothes to dry on lines on balconies; monkeys perch quietly on the rooftops. If a wealthy magus stepped into this quarter at any time of the day, they'd find themselves looted—either by monkeys or by common thieves. But no one bothers me or even looks as I slip into the alley between a boarded-up apothecary and a bicycle shop. No one cares that I am a non-magus headed to the shrine that lies at the alley's end, dedicated to Sant Javer—a man who spent most of his life healing people without asking for anything in return. Javer had followers among magi and non-magi alike. When Svapnalok was still united, Papa said, pilgrims came from the farthest reaches of the continent to offer Sant Javer their respects or to seek cures.

"Sant Javer never turned anyone away," Papa told me. "Rich or poor. Magus or non-magus."

It's the only reason the offerings placed in front of the closed doors of the saint's temple have remained untouched: a box of chandramas wrapped in gold placed right beside a full bowl of betel nuts and safflower seeds. Even thieves consider stealing from Sant Javer inauspicious.

The sky lightens further to a dusty blue by the time two other figures emerge from the alley leading to the temple. A tall woman in a gray sari walks toward me, her face partly veiled with a thick blanket. She's followed by another woman, shorter in stature, similarly garbed. Their jootis, I observe, are not nearly as mud-encrusted as mine; they must have ridden to Ambarvadi. The taller woman pauses a few feet away from me, watching. Sensing her hesitation, I pull away the edge of the blanket covering my face, revealing it to her.

"Are you Juhi ji?" I ask, adding the honorific at the last moment, some old remnant of the manners Papa drilled into me when I was a small boy.

"Yes," the taller woman says, sounding surprised. "But you're not Xerxes."

The blanket covering the lower half of her face drops. Juhi might have passed for another Ambari woman if not for her midnight eyes and the deep-blue tinting of her hair. She looks younger than I expected, or perhaps it only appears that way because of the magic suffusing her blood and the privilege that comes from living in a place that is not the tenements.

"No," I say. "I'm his son, Cavas. My father is ill. Tenement Fever."

Juhi's face tightens slightly. "I didn't know. Ruhani Kaki didn't tell me."

I nod. I'm about to say more—that there is nothing I can do for her—when her companion, who had been silent all this time, gasps.

"You!" she exclaims. The sun has risen by now, light pouring through a crack in the clouds. Its hazy glow reveals the sharp, familiar contours of the girl's face, a thick lock of frizzy, soot-colored hair that she impatiently pushes off her forehead. It's her. The gold-eyed thief from the moon festival.

"*You.*" The word slips out of my mouth without warning, the single syllable holding so much fury that the girl takes a step backward.

"You know each other?" Juhi asks.

"I saw her pickpocketing at the moon festival in Ambarvadi two months ago," I say.

"I was not!" the girl protests before turning to Juhi. "He saved me from a merchant who *thought* I was pickpocketing him."

"I saved you because I thought you needed it. Because I thought you were like me. I never would have stepped in if I'd known you were a privileged brat with magic in her veins."

Silence. Even after turning away from her, I feel the girl's gaze burning the side of my face.

"I am sorry to hear your father is ill," Juhi says finally. "He's a good man. I knew him well."

"How well *did* you know him?" I demand. "Papa wouldn't tell me."

"There was nothing scandalous about our relationship, I assure you." I detect amusement in Juhi's voice. "But if Xerxes didn't tell you how we knew each other, then I'm not sure it's my place to do so."

I push aside the frustration her response brings. Why does it matter how Papa knew this woman? I already know what I'm going to say to her.

"I read your letter to Papa," I tell Juhi. "It's only at his insistence that I came here to see you today. You need to know that there is no way I can get *her* into Ambar Fort." I gesture to the girl, observe the way she stiffens. "As for Raj Mahal—you can forget about it."

"I know what I'm asking for is difficult—" Juhi begins.

"It's not only difficult. It's dangerous. Besides, *I* don't hire the palace servants. I barely have any power as it is," I say bitterly.

"But you know enough to get the clothes and identification she'll need to pass off as a servant," Juhi says, her eyes shrewd. "I can offer you seven swarnas for your trouble. Every month, if you wish."

Her offer brings Major Shayla's words to mind, pricking at a sense of pride I didn't know I possessed. *These dirt lickers will do anything—even sell their own mothers—for a bit of coin.*

"So much to get an ordinary thief into the palace?" I ask coldly. "I may be desperate, Juhi ji. But I am not a fool."

"Name your price, then."

"No price is worth the danger." I force myself to not look at the girl. I haven't forgotten Latif's words. Or the unease I felt when I pictured her lying dead outside the barracks in the Walled City.

Juhi grabs hold of my wrist. Her palm is rough and hardened with calluses. My stomach drops. I am not one to make impulsive moves. But I wonder now if this single moment of spontaneity of coming here to talk to these women will have me blown up by some spell.

"Listen. I know you don't believe me, but Gul isn't an ordinary thief. Show him your right arm, Gul."

"What?" the girl cries out. "Are you mad, Juhi Didi?"

"I don't need to see anything," I begin, but Juhi cuts me off with a squeeze on the wrist. I bite my tongue.

Juhi and the girl—Gul—are having a silent conversation with their eyes. Gul inhales sharply as if bracing herself and moves aside the blanket covering her shoulders. She slowly rolls up the sleeve of her right arm, bit by bit, her eyes trained on me. Four fingers above the thin green veins in the crook of her elbow, I see it: the raised black ridge of a birthmark, shaped into a perfect star. A blink of an eye later, Gul whips it back into the depths of her blanket, but I'm still staring at her, a feeling like ice in my throat.

"I believe she can help us with our fight," Juhi says, her voice quiet, serious. "I believe she may be the One."

The One, whom magi call the Star Warrior. A marked girl destined to bring forth a revolution, leading to a new era of peace in Ambar.

"I don't care for your magi prophecies!" I wrest my hand from Juhi's grip. "For you, perhaps, the current king may be the worst one in an era, but for us non-magi, Raja Lohar is the same as his predecessor. Do you think some Star Warrior will *magically* undo the wrongs that have been inflicted on us one ruler after another? Besides, if she really were the *One*, as you call her, why would she need *my* help to get in?"

"I understand your disinclination," Juhi says. "But—"

"I am *not* the One!" Gul interrupts. "I don't even know why Juhi Didi thinks I might be!"

"No, you're not," I agree. "You're only another magus who thinks she can change the world for those she considers inferior to herself."

"Or maybe"—Gul steps forward until her face is barely a breath away from mine, so close that I can see the flush tinting her dusky cheeks, the tiny freckles scattered over the bridge of her nose—"*maybe* I'm a magus who every night lives with the memory of her parents getting murdered because of the king's obsession with this so-called Star

Warrior. Maybe *I* just want something simple and selfish, like revenge! Ever considered that?"

Her words don't surprise me as much as the conviction she says them with, her rage so palpable that it renders me speechless.

"I'm going." Gul blinks rapidly, and I realize that her eyes are wet. "Clearly, there is no help here."

"Gul! Gul, no, wait—" Juhi cries out.

Gul doesn't. She walks until the edge of the street, then breaks into a run, disappearing into the shadows of the alley. I barely hear the pleas Juhi makes next—pleas that I don't respond to. Finally, she gives up, and I watch her walk away as well.

It's over. I won't have to see either of them again. The thought should be reassuring, but it does nothing to erase the memory of Gul's stricken face from my mind. *She's a fool*, I tell myself firmly. *A fool bent on killing herself.* Privileged magus though she may be, the last thing I want is for her to die.

A cold that has nothing to do with the weather makes goose bumps break over my skin. I shake it off and begin trudging back the way I came, keeping the blanket on even when sunlight floods the blue sky and the air turns hot and oppressive.

14
GUL

*F*ool.

The word enters my mind, echoes there moments after I get to the end of the alley, where our horses are tethered. Hot tears slide down my cheeks. I wipe them away angrily. When Juhi and I left for Ambarvadi this morning, I was feeling buoyant, fueled by my success at passing Juhi's test a couple of nights ago.

I rode Agni, of course, and the mare and I spent the entire ride speaking through our bond. I told Agni about what I did during the two months I was shackled to the house. Agni warned me not to lose my temper today at any cost.

Now, a wet nose nudges my shoulder.

You lost your temper, didn't you? Agni asks. There's no hint of mockery in her voice.

"I did." Oh goddess, I lost it completely. "It was him. The boy from the moon festival."

Did he remember you?

"It would have been better if he hadn't."

Seeing him jarred me initially, my face warming at the memory of our kiss. But that soon went away, escalating to anger as he continued speaking, his words bringing back every little insecurity I feel about my magic. By losing my temper, I failed myself. And I failed Juhi as well.

Juhi, however, doesn't scold me for my behavior or curse me the way I want her to. She arrives a few moments later and begins undoing the rope tethering Gharib to his post. "I tried to convince Cavas," she says simply. "He wouldn't respond."

My throat tightens. "Is there someone else who can . . ." My voice trails off as Juhi shakes her head. "Maybe if I went back and apologized . . ."

"It wouldn't work." Lines bracket the corners of Juhi's lips. She won't meet my gaze. "The boy isn't Xerxes. It wouldn't be fair for us to expect him to respond the way his father would."

In the distance, a temple bell rings. Figures emerge in the alley: shopkeepers, who roll up their gates without sparing us a single glance. I cast a look at the gleaming tip of Sant Javer's temple and instantly feel foolish for doing so. Whatever chance I had with Cavas got lost the moment my pride took over and I burst into that angry tirade. The moment I ran. I climb onto Agni without another word and follow Juhi back out into the city square.

The ride to Javeribad is hot and feels far too long. There's a horrible ache in my ribs that doesn't go away. My unease sharpens by the time we enter the town and hear screams rising from somewhere around the main square. Juhi and I glance at each other only once before launching into a gallop, forcing the crowd to part for us, allowing us to see what's going on.

"No, please!" A woman in her early twenties is kneeling on the ground before the head thanedar, her face streaked with dirt and tears. "Please, Thanedar ji! Please, someone help me!"

No one does. None of the villagers—people who have likely known the woman since birth—say a word.

"You know the law about marked girls!" the head thanedar shouts angrily. From the wooden cart behind him, I hear the sound of wailing: a baby. "Under no circumstances must they be kept or hidden away. For the safety of the land. For the safety of our king!"

Something hot burns inside my chest.

"She's a baby! Only a few months old!" the woman wails, grabbing the pointed toes of the thanedar's shoes. "Thanedar ji, have mercy! She can't even do any magic!"

"Get off me!" The thanedar kicks her away. "Get off, foolish woman, if you don't want to be arrested."

I dismount Agni and push past the crowd. "Leave her!" I shout. "Let her baby go!"

"Gul!" Juhi screams. "Gul, no!"

A sound like thunder rattles through my head. I'm thrown backward into the crowd, stars bursting before my eyes. I hear my name again— once, perhaps twice. The world goes black.

". . . my apologies. She was distraught. It . . . it's been a difficult morning."

"I'm letting her go this time for your sake. But Juhi ji, you must control your ward. Or the next time I'll be forced to arrest her as well."

Their voices seep into my consciousness, float in from somewhere above. Instead of the ground, I feel something softer underneath: the netting of a cot, a pillow—my pillow. My head still feels sore, as if it's been battered continually from the inside.

I slowly rise to a sitting position. Sunlight pours from the courtyard window into the empty dormitory. Outside, Uma Didi's ringing voice lectures the novices on Ambari history—a pretext that is often put up for the benefit of the thanedars: "In the twelfth year of Rani Megha's reign, an ordinance to limit non-magi holdings was introduced. Acharya Bindu, who would go on to write the Tenement Laws, suggested various—" Her voice cuts off abruptly. "Juhi! What's going on? What did the thanedar say?"

"It's all right, Uma. He's gone now. You can resume your usual Yudhnatam lessons. Yes, yes, Gul is fine," Juhi says. "I'm going to see her now."

And she does, a few moments later, entering the dormitory with a wary look on her face.

"Well," she says. "You've had quite a morning, haven't you?"

"What happened?" I ask, my voice hoarse.

"I tried to stop you from moving forward. So did the head thanedar. Our spells must have collided, knocking you out."

"Not to me," I say. Anger seeps in, straightening my spine. "The baby. What happened to the baby?"

Juhi says nothing.

"They took her, didn't they?" I taste something bitter at the back of my tongue. "They took her, and we did nothing!"

"We *couldn't* do anything," she snaps. "It was impossible!"

"You could have intervened! Modified their memories—"

"There were about fifty people in the square," Juhi says sharply. "Even I can't modify so many memories—not at once. Someone would have seen, would have grown suspicious. Saving that child would have meant exposing the rest of us."

"*Protecting the unprotected*," I recite the Sisterhood's motto out loud. "So that only matters when it's convenient, is it? It's the only time your so-called samarpan counts."

"By the gods! Be sensible—"

"I won't. I won't be sensible if it means turning a blind eye every time another girl gets arrested just for having a birthmark! That girl . . . she was a baby, Juhi Didi!"

I dimly grow aware of silence falling in the courtyard; I must have been shouting.

Juhi's body tenses, and for a moment, I think she might smack me or hit me with another spell. But then her shoulders sag, her face looking older than I've ever seen it. "Yes. I know samarpan stands for 'sacrifice.'

But every sacrifice requires a choice, and I had to choose between saving one life and twenty girls who live with me day in and day out. I chose those girls. I chose you."

Instead of making me feel better, her words make me feel worse.

There's a creak as Juhi settles down on an empty cot next to mine. "What happened this morning in the square got me thinking again. Amira was right. It was wrong of me to be so hasty. To push you so hard when you're so young. I got so consumed by my own desire for revenge that . . ." There's a pause followed by a soft hush of breath. "This is my fault. I failed. Not only that child, but also you."

I say nothing. What happened with Cavas this morning feels like a distant memory, an embarrassment I barely feel. I don't know when Juhi leaves the dormitory or when the other novices enter.

"What's up with her?" I hear someone say.

"She and Juhi had a disagreement," I hear Kali say in her cool voice. "Gul? Gul, are you all right?"

I don't answer, and eventually, as the day goes on, they stop asking. The afternoon meal goes by. So does the evening one.

"You have to eat sometime, princess."

I look up from the plate full of lotus sabzi, dal, and rice and into Amira's dark eyes.

"No one cares, do they?" I ask. "About girls like us."

Something shifts in her gaze, something I don't quite understand. "Eat," she says again before leaving the room.

I don't.

I sit there, unmoving, until the lantern is blown out and the other novices' light snores fill the room. They mask the sound of my feet, the darkness shielding my movements, turning me into another shadow moving across the wall.

15

GUL

A hundred yards from the main bazaar at Ambarvadi, a flesh market is held every day during the first week of the month. Sold here, along with horses, bullocks, and landfowl, are humans—Ambari citizens who voluntarily put themselves up for indenture at the palace or elsewhere for a period of ten years, usually to pay off a debt, sometimes even incurred by a previous generation. Prostitution is forbidden—though that doesn't always stop some from forcing indentured boys and girls into it. As the old saying goes: *Everything sells in a market. All you need is a buyer.*

I stand at the edge of a sweets stall with Agni, the thin gray pallu of my sari drawn over my head, shielding my face from the heat and passersby. Was it only a couple of months ago that the moon festival happened and I kissed Cavas? Only a week earlier, I might have blushed at the thought. Now, I feel nothing except hollow in the pit of my stomach.

I turn around, unclipping the bundle hanging from Agni's saddle. "Go home." I stroke her velvety nose. "Quickly. Before the stallkeepers start coming in. *No*, Agni, I can't take you with me. *You promised.*"

Horse theft is not uncommon in Ambarvadi, even though Agni will never accept anyone's touch except mine—and occasionally Juhi's. Agni whinnies irritably, but eventually she turns away, looking mournful. *I will find you again*, she tells me. *No matter what happens.* I watch her walk away, my heart sinking. *She'll be fine*, I tell myself. *She's found her way home many times before.*

A mynah whistles a song from a nearby tree, bringing to mind a lullaby I once heard my mother sing: a song about a lost bird who found branches far into the sky. There are no branches, let alone clouds, in the sky today—even though it's the fourth day of Tears, which is supposedly the wettest of the twelve months of the year. Beyond the market and the sloping incline littered with houses towers Barkha Hill. Rani Mahal glitters on top, an iridescent pink-and-gold gem, fortified by two thick stone boundaries. More than the palace's beauty, though, I can sense its magic, even from here, hundreds of feet away—a slight tingling under my skin, a feeling not unlike being watched.

Juhi doesn't know you're here, I tell myself firmly. *Neither do Amira or Kali. It will still be some time before they wake, perhaps even more before they discover your absence.*

Thoughts of Kali bring forth a twinge of guilt. I promised her I'd never come here. Two months ago, or perhaps in less desperate circumstances, I might have even kept that promise.

"Not anymore," I say under my breath, even though the words feel like pebbles on my tongue. Today, I turn sixteen, the official age of adulthood in Ambar, and, short of shackling me again, there is nothing they could have done to stop me from leaving.

A few feet away from the entrance to the flesh market, I pause, watching a woman drag a small boy toward a guard in a white turban. The stone in my throat loosens only when the guard bars her entry with his lathi—a tall bamboo staff that looks exactly like the ones the thanedars use.

"No, madam," he says, his eyes on the boy. "Your son isn't willing. And you cannot go in with him."

When she argues, he slams the lathi onto the ground, shooting purple sparks into the air. "There are no compromises here, madam! This is Ambarvadi, not Havanpur. As keeper of the flesh market, I am bound to its rules. The very first rule is: *Humans selling themselves must be of age or older.* Your son is not sixteen years old. He is also unwilling, which contradicts the second rule: *Humans selling themselves must do so of their own volition.*"

The smell of pearl millet, spices, and ghee rises from the bundle in my hands, a stack of the bajra roti I'd stolen from the pantry last night. Under the food, there's a brief, reassuring click. The familiar grooves of the seaglass daggers, their engraved hilts growing warm under my touch.

Around me, people are slowly filtering in: stallkeepers, assistants, a few early shoppers grumbling about the rise in safflower prices. A farmer steps out from the entrance to the flesh market, holding a camel by a heavily tasseled bridle. A boy of perhaps eighteen years trails behind him, his eyes lowered to the ground, familiar blue bands of light glowing on his wrists and ankles.

Shackling. At least I've enough practice with that.

I trudge toward the entrance, but my jootis still cover the distance more rapidly than I expect. Steps away from the banner and the colorful flags surrounding the makeshift entrance, I allow the part of the sari covering my face to fall down. The guard at the entrance watches me carefully. My tongue feels gritty, as if coated with sand. In the background, a shout rises, and for a second, I think I've heard my name.

"Gulab! Chameli! Rajnigandha!" a woman cries out. "Fresh flowers for sale!"

I don't look back.

The first thing I see as I step across the threshold of the flesh market is a giant elephant in chains. What's most striking about it is not that it's an elephant—I've seen a few of those already in Ambar—but the length of its tusks, which are nearly twice as long as a normal elephant's, and that it's covered entirely, from head to hooves, in thick brown fur. It also looks exhausted: bent at the knees, head resting on the ground, barely an eye opening when a small man prods it with a whip.

"Up! Up, filthy beast!"

Another sharp prod and the elephant cries out—a horrible rumbling sound that vibrates through me, even though the man seems to feel nothing. I try to whisper to it the way I do to Agni and other animals, but its pain is so intense that the first mental touch scalds, makes me leap back as if I've been burned.

Furious, I can't help but march up to the man and tell him to stop. "Can't you see the elephant is in agony?"

"This is no elephant, stupid girl," the man says, spraying me with spittle. "This is a mammoth from Prithvi. Nearly gored my whisperer to death when we first let it out of its cage. Bloody beast cost me a fortune! And that was without the cost to bring it here!"

"It needs to be cold," I point out angrily. "Don't you have ice or something?"

"Ice! Ice, she tells me!" The man roars with laughter. Our argument must have captured the attention of a few other traders in the flesh market, because they, too, join in with laughs of their own.

"You'd need a block the size of Barkha Hill to cool that beast down," someone else shouts.

"Go home to your mother, girl! This place is not for you!"

The mammoth's eyelid flickers, its long lashes coated with red dust. *Cold*, I think. I need it to be cold. Spying a bucket of water nearby, I douse the edge of my sari's pallu into it, soaking the cloth. When the man's back is turned, I sneak closer to the mammoth, pressing the wet cloth to its furry face, right under its eyes. The water may not be much, but it's the best I have right now.

Another rumble escapes, but this one sounds more relieved.

Are you feeling better? I ask the mammoth.

A single-worded reply: *Yes*.

Whenever I whisper to animals, each one makes a distinct sound of its own. While Agni's voice is whip-smart and snappy, the mammoth's voice is deep, almost fatherly in its gruffness.

"Ayy! Girl!" A whip snaps against my ankle, stinging it. "Get away from there unless you want me to sell you with the beast!"

I dodge the other hit and run, my heart heavy with regret. The man's comment also reminds me of why I'm here.

I force myself to look elsewhere, to ignore the other animals in chains, until I see it in the far corner of the market—the stage where humans put themselves up for auction. The auctioneers, a middle-aged man and woman, sharply assess each candidate, dismissing cases where they suspect foul play or lack of consent. I wonder if anyone ever considered the consent of these captured animals.

A prickling sensation at the back of my neck gives me pause. I turn, expecting to see the mammoth's horrible owner, perhaps even a thanedar. There is no one. Nothing, except a sinking feeling that I might have bitten off more than I can chew.

16

GUL

"Name?" The male auctioneer looks up to assess me.

"Siya." I pick a name commonly found throughout Ambar—a name that will likely be forgotten.

"Parents' names?"

"I'm an orphan."

"Age?"

"Sixteen years today."

He holds out a yellowing scroll so old that I'm afraid it will fall to pieces at a single touch. "Hold the scroll for a moment."

I do—and it turns green in my hands. He nods and takes it away.

"The scroll tells me you are of age, which is why you must listen to what I say carefully. If you are sold today, you will have to sign a contract. Indenture contracts are magical in nature and can bind you to another person for ten years or more. Do you understand this? This is not a joke or something to do because your friends dared you."

I swallow hard. "I understand."

"You have a village girl's accent, but you look healthy and well cared for. Why are you selling yourself today?"

"I lost my position in my mistress's household last week. This was the only way to get work at the palace."

"How did you lose your position?"

"The master died, and they needed to cut expenses. Half the staff was let go."

The story is perfect—so perfect that I expect the auctioneer to challenge it, to find that single thread that will unravel everything and have me tossed out.

"Hurry, Ghayur!" the female auctioneer shouts from the stage area. "We need to begin soon!"

The auctioneer shakes his head and waves a hand in the air. A strip of gold cloth appears.

"Tie this around your wrist. You will wait with the others in the back. When we call your name, you will come out on stage. Understand?"

I nod. I follow a trail of people to the back of the stage; they have gold ribbons tied around their wrists as well. The female auctioneer's thick white bangles click together as she checks over the humans they expect to fetch the most coin: A farmer, built like an ox, muscles bulging like the man on King Lohar's emblem; a wispy young woman with stringy hair, shooting butterflies from her fingertips; and at the very end, a man of unearthly beauty, his skin golden in the sun, his yellow eyes missing nothing.

"You will go first," the auctioneer tells them. "We will take you out as a lot." She then glances at me and two others—a dark-haired girl of my age, wearing a red ghagra and choli, and an elderly man—and grimaces. "The rest of you will be called at the end, one by one."

"I thought they always saved the best for last at these things," the girl in the red ghagra says out loud, commenting to no one in particular.

"Human auctions don't work that way—especially not when Ambar

Fort is buying," the old man says quietly. "The palace buyers don't like to be kept waiting."

My throat tightens.

"What about the rest of us?" The girl sounds as tense as I feel. "Aren't we being sold into the palace, too?"

"Perhaps. The stables, the laundry, and granaries in the Walled City also require workers."

"I didn't leave my position in Ambarvadi to work in the Walled City," the girl mutters under her breath. She turns to me and asks: "What's your story?"

I repeat exactly what I said to the auctioneer named Ghayur.

"You were with Shalini Bai, weren't you?" Without waiting for an answer, the girl continues talking. "Such a kind woman. And what a tragedy! One day her mate was alive, and the next day dead without a word. Everyone in the neighborhood was so devastated."

"Oh, yes!" When I see her staring, I hastily draw my expression into one of sorrow. "It was terrible."

Then, after a pause, I risk a question of my own: "Why wouldn't you want to work in the Walled City? It surrounds Ambar Fort, doesn't it?"

"Yes, but it's not Ambar Fort or the palace itself, is it?" the girl says. "You'll be lucky if you even *see* a royal in the Walled City, let alone get to serve one."

"So you can't get into Ambar Fort if you live in the city?" I ask, feigning innocence. Pretending to be naive has often served me well in such instances, and today is no different.

"Of course not!" the girl responds imperiously. "You need a special badge, which is checked by the guards. I hear they've added more security measures recently—the servants' old badges and turban pins were replaced with new ones."

I nod, digesting the information. I hadn't heard about the new security measures—but then I hadn't had the chance to sneak into the city for the past two months. A moment later, cheers erupt behind the stage, the sound vibrating in my chest.

The yellow-eyed man watches us expressionlessly. Next to him, the farmer fidgets with something in his hands—*a toy?* I wonder, before his eyes connect with mine and he tucks it back into a pocket of his tunic. A moment later, the male auctioneer returns for a final look at us. Except for the old man, the men are asked to remove their tunics—"for inspection purposes," Ghayur says.

"Are they going to ask us to . . ." The girl's voice trails off nervously, and I don't blame her. Are they really going to make us strip for the crowd?

But Ghayur simply asks us to uncover our faces and hair and to stand straight while facing the crowd.

"Show them you are strong, and perhaps you'll find a good owner," he tells us.

Then, Ghayur marches out on stage, pressing his fingers to his throat. His voice reaches us in the back, magically amplified.

"From the edge of the desert, the desert," he chants.

"The desert, the desert!" The crowd—obviously no stranger to this—repeats the final refrain, their sounds vibrating down the wood, into my body.

"From the humblest village, oh, village!"

"Village! Oh, village!" the crowd shouts.

"From cities brighter than the sun and the moons!"

The crowd's chants turn into hooting and clapping.

"You'd think we were at a celebration, not an auction," the girl in the red ghagra comments, and I can't help but agree.

"Some bring magic with them, some skills beyond your imagination!" Ghayur shouts. "First: a farmer from Sur, a woman who magicks everything out of nothing, and a peri with a voice that can put even the rowdiest children to sleep—in a single lot!"

I stare at the gold-skinned man, who is the last to walk out. Not a man, but a Pashu. A peri, without the wings always depicted on their backs in paintings and scrolls. Now, with his back turned, I finally see them—or what's left of them—a mass of thick scars and bony ridges protruding from his shoulder blades and the sides of his spine, ending a handspan above his plain white dhoti.

"Clipping a peri's wings is the worst thing you can do to them," my father told me. "It affects their magic, their music. It's an unforgivable crime."

It was a crime that the king committed without conscience after the Battle of the Desert, a crime that magi continue to commit to this day. I cannot tell if the clipping affects the peri's music. Because when he's asked to sing, the low, haunting notes of the morning raag fill the air, quieting even the rowdiest among the audience.

The male auctioneer starts the opening bid: Four thousand swarnas per person.

The howls that go through the crowd cover the gasp that leaves my mouth on hearing the number. Four thousand swarnas is more coin than what I ever imagine seeing in my lifetime—an amount that could have supported not only me but also my parents for several decades. My head begins to pound as Ghayur shouts out the bids that go up:

"Four five! Five! Five five! Six! Oh, come now! Only six thousand swarnas for such fine flesh? Friends, can we not have a ten?"

The price goes higher and higher, finally stopping at eight thousand swarnas apiece. The winning bid goes to an unnamed person, who the old man next to me says will likely be from the palace.

"How do you know for sure?" I ask.

"No one else has that much coin to spend at once."

It's the last thing he says before he is called out to the stage, leaving me alone with the girl in the red ghagra.

"Whatever is *he* capable of?" she mutters.

The female auctioneer takes over now, binding the crowd with lavish praise for the old man's skill: seeing, a form of magic that allows him to see living specters. I hear the crowd's curious murmurs—"a half magus"—and feel a little fascinated myself. Only the half magi are capable of seeing living specters. Like whisperers, these days, seers are rare—with next to no magi and non-magi bindings taking place. Any half magi who do remain are probably as old as the man now being auctioned off.

"Must be awful to see dead people everywhere," the girl in red mutters. "More of a curse than a gift, I'd say."

I continue to listen to the rapidly escalating bids until the old man is sold for two thousand swarnas.

The girl looks at me. "Well, then. Just you and me. Wonder if they'll call us together. Serving girls go in pairs sometimes."

But they don't. Perhaps they think they can make more if they bring us out one at a time, because the girl is called out next by name, leaving me alone in the back.

The minute she goes out, though, I hear a few whistles and leering voices call out: "Look at us, too, girl! Show us your pretty face!"

I close my eyes, bracing myself for my false name to be called, when someone grabs hold of my arm and claps a hand over my mouth to muffle the scream that emerges. I am about to use my teeth and elbows to do maximum damage when a voice hisses in my ear: "It's me, Cavas! Don't scream!"

I don't. I realize, with a shock, that I would have recognized his voice by its deepness, by the anger in it—even if he did not tell me his name. When I grow calm and he's certain I will make no sound, he releases me, frown lines marring his broad forehead under his palace-issue turban.

"Come with me! Quick!"

Heart thumping against my rib cage, I follow him out of the backstage area, toward a part of the market that is deserted. There, he leans behind a now-shut-up sweets and ghee shop to catch his breath.

"Have you lost your mind?" His voice is low, hard. "You're going to sell yourself?"

I am so shocked by his sudden appearance that for a long while I don't answer, the female auctioneer's voice and the crowd's cheers a distant echo in the background.

"So what if I am?" I finally say. "It's not against the law!"

"Do you even know what it means to be indentured?" The look he gives me makes me want to shrink. "To give up your freedom? They can do anything to you. *Anything* they like. No matter what the law says."

"So what?" My grip on the bundle containing my daggers tightens. "I'm not completely helpless. Why do you care what I do, anyway?"

He opens his mouth as if to say something, then shakes his head. "It doesn't matter."

The words hang between us, making the fine hairs on my skin rise.

"If I have any hope of getting into the palace, I need to go back there." I point toward the auctioneer's stage. "It's not like I have a choice."

I see him register the words, his frown deepening. There's a part of me that wonders for a brief moment if I should try to beg him for help again. But then I shake my head. It would be foolish to try—not after he rejected me so firmly the last time around.

". . . twenty-five hundred!" the auctioneer shouts. "Going once, twice . . ."

"Shubhdivas," I say curtly. I'm nearly halfway back to the stage when I hear Cavas shout a single word: "Wait!"

Don't, I tell myself, even when I hear him jogging to catch up with me. *Keep walking to that stage, Gul.*

He blocks my way, forcing me to stop. "What if you do have a choice?"

We remain hidden until the auction ends—the girl in red going for three thousand swarnas to a minister's household in the Walled City. For some reason, the name I gave Ghayur isn't called out. I see Ghayur's female companion look around before shaking her head.

"Many people change their minds before the auction," Cavas tells me, as if sensing the question. "But more than that, Ghayur and Shirin are good people. They don't magically bind anyone to a contract before the auction itself."

"You know them?" I ask, surprised.

"I've been coming to the market for the past four years," he says. "Once my father fell ill, the stable master, Govind, started bringing me in to handle some of the more aggressive horses. This year, he let me come here on my own to bid on a spare horse for the palace."

He falls silent at that, which makes me ask: "Did you win the bid?"

"No. A zamindar from Amirgarh outbid me today." He speaks the words with an ease that suggests the truth—or a practiced lie. "It doesn't really matter. If the king really wanted a horse, he wouldn't have let Govind or me handle the sale."

Why does it matter if he's lying? I ask myself. He saved me from selling myself. From possible abuse at the hands of some unknown minister for years on end. As ready as I was to be auctioned off, a part of me can't help but feel grateful for his unexpected aid.

"Come," he says quietly once most of the crowd has dispersed. "We still have a lot to do."

The orange-and-yellow ghagra-choli we steal from one of the washing ghats in Ambarvadi has a blouse that's too loose to be a properly fitted choli and a skirt that's much longer than the kind of ghagra I usually wear. Thank the goddess for drawstrings.

"Are you going to have us both arrested after this?" I mutter to Cavas as we slip behind a thick peepul tree.

Cavas silences me with a finger pressed to his lips and gestures to a bare-chested launderer slamming a few soaking wet clothes against a rock several feet away from where we're hidden. I'm not sure if the clothes we stole belong to his pile. They certainly aren't washed, if the smell of sweat in the armpits is any indication. I wrinkle my nose.

Really, the only thing working in favor of this outfit is the king's seal embroidered near the hem of the yellow ghagra in dyed blue thread, identifying the wearer as a palace worker. More specifically, a serving girl in Rani Mahal, or the queens' palace, as Cavas explains.

"See that?" Cavas points out a pattern running throughout the dupatta: an alternating pair of moons. "When it catches the light, it instantly differentiates the queens' serving girls from the laundresses or the cooks. Only the supervisors inside the palace wear saris."

I glance down at the sari I wore early this morning, tied in its usual kaccha style. It's not like I will miss it. I rarely wore saris outside the Sisterhood's house, preferring the ease of a ghagra or a long Jwaliyan tunic and dupatta over leggings.

"Won't someone notice the clothes are gone?" I ask Cavas.

"Probably." He grimaces. "Which is why you should get dressed quickly so we can leave."

Cavas keeps his back turned while I slip into the clothes and toss the matching yellow dupatta over my right shoulder in a practiced motion. A serving girl doesn't have time for styles that require pins and fussy pleats, so I simply draw the flowing front end of the cloth across my chest and tuck it into the back of my ghagra. As a final touch, I pull the flowing back end of the dupatta over my head and around my ears, allowing the rest to hang behind my left shoulder.

"How do I look?" I ask him, and try not to blush when he scrutinizes me from head to toe.

"Acceptable," he says curtly before turning away. We sneak back onto the street behind the ghats, passing three large bonfires where rubbish is being burnt.

"Wait," Cavas says. He grabs hold of my gray novice sari and tosses it into one of the heaps. When he points to my necklace, though, I shake my head, pressing a hand protectively over the three silver beads.

"Not this." *Never this.* I will fight anyone who tries to take my last tangible memory of Ma from me. Perhaps Cavas senses this from my expression, because he simply nods.

"You will need to have a false name there," he says. "A false childhood, a false everything."

"Siya. From Ambarvadi." The rest will come later. When he reaches for the bundle holding my daggers, I pull away. "That's fine."

I expect Cavas to take us through the city again, down the broad road leading to the Walled City gates. But Cavas sticks to the back lanes, mostly used by non-magi, where he says there's a lower chance of our being noticed.

"I'd rather walk where I'm not stared at or called 'dirt-licking filth' for accidentally cutting across a magus's path," he mutters under his breath.

I pause before asking a question: "Does that upset you?"

"What? That people call me a dirt licker?"

I wince. "Will you stop saying that?"

"Get used to it. You'll hear people say it frequently where we're going." He does not sound bitter about this, merely resigned.

"It's said that your people tried to steal magic," I say after a pause, thinking of the scrolls I've read. "Years before the Great War."

"They did," he says simply. "They stole elephant-loads of firestones right out of the jewel mines. They were protesting the new land tithe that Rani Megha imposed on us."

A land tithe? I try to think back to what I read in the history scrolls, but I can't remember anything about such a tax. Then again, the scrolls don't mention Juhi, either. And while firestones *did* contain magic and stealing them *was* considered a crime—

"There were no kidnappings?" I ask. "No rituals to extract power from the magi?"

He laughs. "*Your* people have awfully convenient imaginations. You probably have forgotten or don't even know of the non-magi children who disappeared and were then found decapitated outside temples as a punishment for stealing the firestones."

"They decapitated children for *firestones?*" My stomach twists. For a moment, I wonder if Cavas is exaggerating, but the bleak look in his eyes tells me otherwise. "What happened to the firestones?" I ask finally.

"Some say they were lost. Some say they were sold to traders from distant lands across the Yellow Sea. No one really knows. After the non-magus rebellion was crushed, Rani Megha established the tenements and forced us out of our homes. Those who fought were imprisoned or executed. Those who survived—well, we had to choose between our own lives and history being rewritten for us."

I'm silent for a long moment. "My father said this wasn't how Svapnalok was supposed to be. That before the war, magi and non-magi lived in harmony. The old rulers never would have wanted this!"

"Well, what the old rulers wanted is of no consequence. Now there is no Svapnalok—only Ambar and three other kingdoms that couldn't care less what happens to us here."

My hand automatically goes to clutch the arm where my birthmark is, relieved to find it covered by the somewhat longish sleeves of the blouse. In fact, they cover nearly my entire elbow. The woman this outfit belongs to is clearly taller than I am.

"Make sure no one sees," Cavas says now—and I know he's talking about the birthmark. "If they do—"

"It won't be good. I know." I pause. "My mother buried me in a patch of soil meant for our garden to hide me from them. She was killed right in front of me. So was my father."

We both say nothing for a long time, the scrape of our jootis against the unpaved road the only sound breaking the silence.

"I'm sorry." It's the first time today that he speaks to me without contempt. "There was a girl in the tenements. Her name was Bahar. They accused her of magic theft. But I think they took her away because she was also . . . She was like you."

Meaning, she had a birthmark. My stomach clenches habitually, but instead of saying anything, I find myself staring at Cavas's drawn face. This girl, whoever she was, had been important to him. I march forward, a little ahead of him, my face suffusing with a heat that has nothing to do with the burning sun overhead. Cavas soon catches up with his long stride.

"How do you plan to get me in?" I keep my voice brisk, strictly business again.

Cavas frowns, as if confused by my sudden change in tone. "We'll tell them you lost your identification badge. The guards at the Walled City gates aren't too bright. They're easily swayed by a pretty face."

I blink. *Did he just call me pretty?*

"Also, you will need to be haughtier," he says. "The queens and their serving ladies act like everyone is beneath them. Not that it should be troublesome for you."

"What is *that* supposed to mean?"

He raises an eyebrow. "I mean a magus like you is used to having servants."

"I spent the last two months making fuel out of cow dung. When I wasn't doing that, I was scrubbing pots or sweeping corridors or cleaning smelly toilets. We had chores to do where I lived."

"There we go." His face breaks into a sudden grin. "Act exactly like that in front of the guards."

He surprises me so much with that smile, I forget to watch where I'm going. A trip and a thud, followed by a roar of laughter that floats overhead.

I am going to strangle him. I rise to my feet, ignoring the hand he holds out. *Whenever I get the chance.*

17

CAVAS

The queens' palace looms ahead, nearly a hundred of its windows facing us, stone and glass laced with magic to form intricate lattices that shield its inhabitants and gleam like jewels in the heat. The king's palace, which is on the other side of Ambar Fort, has a throne room unlike any he has ever seen before, Govind said—which is the most the secrecy spell will allow him to tell us about Raj Mahal.

I take his word for it: Govind does not speak in hyperbole. Besides, it's not like I will ever see the inside of either palace. The king might allow the palace to hire non-magi, but no one without magic is allowed to enter the buildings that make up the private residence of the royal family. *Inauspicious*, the high priest calls it. An insult to the gods—even though it was the gods who supposedly made everyone.

As a boy of four, I would ask Papa about Ma and where she had gone after giving birth to me—and my father always said that she went to live with the gods among the stars. Now, at age seventeen, I'm no longer convinced about the existence of deities. Or the stories Papa told me about Ma's laughter and her courage. Fire burns in my gut when I remember what Bahar's father called her. Though I refuse to believe that as well, the word sticks, stains whatever memories I have of her. Beside me, Gul walks quickly, matching my pace, two for one. From time to time, I find myself turning to catch quick glimpses of her: the sharp angles of her face, her small, compact frame. After that meeting with her and Juhi yesterday, I was sure I would never see her again.

But last night, before I went to bed, the green swarna in my pocket grew warm. After checking to make sure Papa was already asleep, I slipped outside our house and found Latif waiting for me.

"Bring her to the palace," Latif said. "That girl you saw this morning."

"Why?" I demanded. "What does she have to do with you?"

"What she has to do with me is not important. What she has to do with *you* is. It's exactly why I told you to remember what she looks like."

I vehemently shook my head. "No amount of swarnas will entice me this time."

"I'm not offering swarnas. I'm offering you a way out of these tenements. For good. Perhaps as early as the end of this month."

A long silence. "That's impossible. General Tahmasp said the only way to get out was to—"

"Join the army, isn't it?" Latif shrugged. "He isn't exactly wrong. You could join. Stay a few years. If you don't break your back loadbearing, the army may let you fight. Perhaps they'll make you a captain. Even give you a house. But a simple *perhaps* isn't enough—and you know it."

"You were spying on me?" I asked furiously.

"I don't need to, boy. The general makes the same pitch to every potential non-magus recruit every year. He's been doing it for two decades."

"Well, I don't see what *you* can do that the commander of the armies can't!"

"I have my ways. You'll have to trust me."

I don't, I wanted to say. Govind implied that I shouldn't trust Latif completely—and I knew he was right. But I thought of Papa sleeping inside. What if Latif *can* get us out? Will saying no mean that I'm throwing away my father's last chance of surviving the Fever? Of getting cured?

"What must I do?" I found myself asking Latif.

"Get the girl into the palace, and I'll get you out of there as well."

"But how do I find her? I don't even know where she lives!"

"Don't worry. You'll know soon enough."

The message came in the midst of saddling one of the royal horses this morning, when Govind told me to drop everything and go to the flesh market to bid on a horse.

"Our usual bidder fell ill this morning. Food poisoning," Govind said, frowning. "You go instead, Cavas. You've been to the market before. You know how it works."

I did not need to talk to Latif to know that he had something to do with the bidder's sudden illness.

Now I steal another quick glance at Gul. She is not Bahar. If Bahar were a gentle breeze, then Gul is a hurricane, a storm constantly brewing in her glorious eyes. I'm quite sure that if I hadn't been there to stop her, she would have sold herself at the flesh market without thinking once of the consequences.

So why did I tell her she reminded me of Bahar?

Gul squints against the morning sun now, as if in deep thought. She's had the same expression ever since she tripped and fell and I laughed at her and she refused to be helped up. I wonder now if I should apologize and then shrug it off. She needs to develop thicker skin. Or a better sense of humor. There's a natural haughtiness in her disposition—meant for queening over people or kingdoms. Or maybe it's not haughtiness at all. Maybe she's just shy.

I snort at the last thought. She glances at me, her frown deepening into a scowl. Well, she isn't wrong about whom I'm laughing at. I wasn't lying when I said I didn't want her sold—to anyone. Unlike non-magi, who are born powerless, indentured magi are bound to their buyers by a deadly magical contract, unable to use any of their own powers to protect themselves, forced to submit to their buyers' every whim. As the old Vani saying goes: *None more wretched than the non-magus, save the indentured.* It's the sort of life I wouldn't wish on an enemy.

I glance at her once more. No, Gul isn't my enemy. What she *is*, however, is a question I won't be answering anytime soon.

The back roads leading up to the palace are rough and unpaved. Gul, to my surprise, does not complain, even when we navigate a patch of sharp stones, one catching the hem of her too-long ghagra, nearly tearing it. She doesn't allow me to carry her bundle for her, either.

"Don't trust me?" I ask.

She scowls and pulls up the cotton dupatta that keeps slipping off her head. "And give you an opportunity to say that I'm another magus who can't carry her own burdens?"

It is exactly what I would say, but I refuse to admit this. "Burdens lessen when they are shared."

"I am not as weak as you think."

We both walk in silence for a long time after that.

"Weakness is not always a terrible thing," I tell her finally. "It can be used as a shield to hide your true strength."

I can tell she doesn't believe me, even though she says nothing in response. It makes me feel . . . disappointed. A part of me wants her to argue back and tell me I'm wrong, do anything to break this strange tension simmering between the two of us.

I focus on the path ahead, where we reach the peak of the steep incline and then begin walking downward again, making the long trek to the gates of the Walled City: Ninety feet of solid teak from the Jwaliyan forests interwoven with iron, with two armed guards to check our identification. Overhead, a Sky Warrior watches from a tower, ready with an atashban in case anyone tries to force their way in.

"Remember what I said," I tell Gul, feeling my shoulders tense as we close the distance with our feet. "You are a queen's serving girl, and you lost your badge while shopping in the bazaar this morning. And when they ask for your name, make sure to add Rani-putri to it. By tradition, the queens' maids must use Rani-putri to replace their own family names, showing full dedication to the queen they have been chosen to serve."

Gul nods curtly, not speaking until we're at the gate. I tuck in my shoulders, trying to look as unobtrusive as possible, while Gul squares hers, an act that thrusts out her breasts.

I feel my face flush.

The guard leers when she approaches, taking her in with his greedy gaze—until it reaches her face—the hard disapproval etched in every muscle, forcing his grin to dissipate.

"Name and identification," he says.

"Rani-putri Siya," Gul replies, her voice cool, the consonants sharp the way they are here in the city, her village accent completely gone. "I lost my badge in the market this morning."

The guard frowns, his brown pupils sharpening in their yellow eye-beds—as if noticing for the first time the too-long sleeves of Gul's blouse, the skirt that drags across the ground ever so slightly. "What do you mean you *lost* it? I can't let you in without a badge!"

"Don't let me in and the rani will hear about it," she replies with a perfect touch of arrogance, cleverly avoiding mention of a specific queen's name. "Ask *him* if I'm lying." Sharply angling her head to the side, she gestures me forward. "You! Come here!"

I wince, not having to pretend the discomfort that creeps up my spine when the guard's attention falls on me.

"What do *you* know about this?" I see him eyeing my turban pin.

"She works for the palace." I am careful to keep my own answer as vague as Gul's. "She lost her badge in the market."

"O ho!" His sneer becomes more pronounced. "Which rani does she work for?"

"You will know that answer once I tell her *you* were the reason I couldn't reach her on time," Gul cuts in.

The guard's face, likely bloated from gorging on kachoris during every break, reddens. "If you went to the market, where are your packages? Show me what's in there!" he demands, grabbing for her bundle.

Gul smartly steps out of reach, giving him a sneer that could rival Major Shayla's. "The rani's packages are her own business. Surely you don't mean to intervene in her private matters?"

"Hold on." Another guard joins the first one and murmurs something in his ear.

While the first guard's expression says he would like to do nothing better than pummel Gul, after talking to his colleague, he briefly inclines his head in her direction. "Forgive me, Siya ji. You may go in this time. But next time, I will not be able to let you in without identification."

Siya *ji*. As if Gul were a senior staff member and not a girl who's probably only just come of age.

"I'm well aware of that." Gul's voice is cold. "You!" she tells me again. "Carry this for me!"

She tosses that precious bundle of hers at me so quickly that I nearly trip over my own feet catching it. I say nothing about how heavy it feels. Instead, I follow her in, through the gates, ignoring the glare we both receive from the guard.

Once inside, Gul turns to me. "I'm sorry."

"For what?"

"For treating you like that in front of that guard." She frowns. "I know you don't think much of me or . . . my kind, but I don't think you are less than me. I never have."

Though I know by *you* she means non-magi, somehow, the way she phrased it makes the declaration seem more personal. More about me. I shrug off the fanciful notion and hold out the bundle. "Here you go. I didn't peek or anything." Even though I'm now wondering what she has in there.

Her brown cheeks flush slightly, and she takes it without a word.

"What do you think of the Walled City?" I ask.

She looks around, her eyes widening as she finally takes everything in for the first time—havelis, houses, and shops built much like the rest of Ambarvadi, stacked in a series of steep inclines and steps, except for the colors, which range from saffron and peacock blue to pistachio green and rose-petal pink.

"They look like boxes from the sweet seller's," Gul says with awe. And though I've never heard them described that way before, I can't help but see the similarities now between the houses and the gift boxes I saw at the sweet seller's stall during the moon festival.

"We'll have to take the blue staircase," I tell her. "The place where you can get yourself a replacement badge is on the way."

Sidestepping a skinny brown dog sleeping by the side of the road, we pass one of the first houses—blue like the color of the steps—a woman sweeping the corridor of dirt. Her eyes sharpen when she spots us, and she instantly shuts the door in our faces.

"Friendly," Gul comments.

"It's how it is here." I try to ignore the numerous eyes that suddenly seem to be on us. "It's how you know you're inside the Walled City."

"They make the grouchy head thanedar in Javeribad look congenial," she says with a laugh.

I wince; the laugh, though not very loud, only attracts more glares. Gul notices as well, her smile fading.

"Are people really so unhappy here?" Her voice is more subdued now.

"Unhappy is probably their version of joy."

She says nothing in response, says nothing at all until we're standing outside a small haveli tucked discreetly into the corner of the street. Outside, in curving Vani letters, shimmer the words THE MINISTRY OF BODIES, and below that, in smaller letters, FOR THE MANAGEMENT OF THE WALLED CITY AND THE ROYAL PALACE.

"No arrogance here," I warn Gul, giving her the same advice Govind gave me before I went to have my pin made. "Keep your apologies ready, and pretend to be young and foolish. I will not be able to come inside with you."

Gul frowns, seeing the sign next to the entryway: NON-MAGI MUST USE THE BACK ENTRANCE.

"Try to get into Rani Janavi's household," I tell her. "Or Rani Farishta's." Two of Lohar's younger—and reputedly more spoiled—queens, they were the least likely to notice any real changes to their servants. Another girl won't make a difference, Latif told me. I wait under a peepul tree while Gul goes inside. To my surprise, she comes out much quicker than expected, a badge gleaming on her left shoulder.

"I was lucky," she says. "The officer had left his assistant in charge, and she didn't even bother asking me how I lost my badge! 'Oh, you must be from Rani Amba's household,' she said before I could even say anything." Gul grins.

I don't grin back. "What did you say afterward?"

"What was there to say? I said nothing. She handed the badge over to me! I know you mentioned those two other queens, but does it even matter? Amba is Lohar's oldest and most powerful queen. She probably has a lot more servants than the other two combined."

"Yes," I say through gritted teeth. "But Amba also keeps track of everything that goes on in the palace, unlike the other queens, who are more concerned with getting the king's attention or power for themselves. The likelihood of her not knowing the names of her serving girls is slimmer than the edge of a sharpened dagger! So, yes, it does matter, and you could not have picked a worse rani to work under." When Amba gets angry, maids get whipped, on and on until their skin peels off along with their clothes. I decide not to mention this when I see Gul's face slowly leeching of color.

A long silence reigns between us, broken only by the cry of a lone crow.

"Let's go." I begin walking again, sharply turning away from the blue stairs to another, rougher path. "May your sky goddess help us all."

18
GUL

May your sky goddess help us all.

I can't help but agree with the sentiment. The closer we get to the queens' palace, the more imposing it appears, its many windows blinking like eyes. The legends are right. The magic in the air of the Walled City is strong. Unlike other parts of Ambar, even arid villages like Dukal, where the magic in the air seeps into the earth and nourishes the crops, here, magic remains in the air itself, leeching it from your lungs if you breathe too loudly. No wonder these people do not laugh.

I glance at Cavas, whom I've once again disappointed without trying. *Let him be*, Kali would say. *You cannot win over everyone.* I turn away, trying to pay attention to the road ahead, but instead, my thoughts wander to Kali and to Juhi, two people who never let me feel unloved. I wonder if they've found and read the letter I left for them on my cot: *It's time I found my place in the world. Please don't look for me.*

I imagine Amira calling the letter maudlin. Telling them it's probably good riddance that I left. Yet, useless though I may seem to her,

I've come this far. The thought gives me courage, and I finally ask Cavas about the detour he took, leading us away from the palace gates and closer to the wall surrounding the city.

"Servants don't enter through the front gate," he says. "We come and go through the rear gate—the Moon Door."

I do my best to recall the map I'd drawn of the palace, cursing myself now for destroying it a few days ago. From what I can remember, the Moon Door is at the east end of the complex. Which means the Raj Mahal lies in the west, on the opposite side.

"The place looks huge from here," I comment, hoping I don't sound as intimidated as I feel. "Do people ever get lost?"

"Some do. If you get lost, just follow the yellow moon, which is painted in various phases all over the fort walls. The closer you get to the Moon Door, the fuller the moon gets."

He tells me that there are a couple of temples within the complex, too, and another, smaller palace, called Chand Mahal.

"In Chand Mahal, there's supposed to be a room full of mirrors that turn blue on the night of the moon festival. There's also a room of miniature paintings, their colors so bright that the figures within the frames look alive. Or that's what the palace workers say." He shakes his head, as if freeing it of the web of wonder he's spun around us.

"I wouldn't know for sure," he continues. "Rani Amba is the only queen with access to Chand Mahal. Her ancestors built it thousands of years ago—along with Rani Mahal itself. Brace yourself now. We're approaching the gate."

The guards at the Moon Door are tall, their skin gleaming green with scales, their fingers long and webbed. They gesture for us to stop and then, with glowing white eyes, assess my badge and Cavas's turban pin. An infinitely long moment later, they nod, letting us through.

"The guards are makara," Cavas says quietly. "Pashu who are part crocodile, part human. You cannot fool them with disguises; their magic is too strong for that."

"What happens if they do discover an impostor?" I ask.

"Supposedly the wearer turns to ash. But I've never witnessed such a thing."

I suppress a shudder. I had read about makara, the way I'd read about other Pashu, but I had never seen one before. I hadn't seen a peri, either, until today at the flesh market. According to our history scrolls, most of the Pashu disappeared after the Battle of the Desert. Juhi said many were killed, many more captured and used as entertainment.

As we make our way into the palace complex, I see the first four rulers of Svapnalok intricately carved into the pillars and arch that make up the inside of the Moon Door, their heads bent in supplication. Overhead, the gods and goddesses perch on clouds, serene smiles on their faces as a Sky Warrior shoots down a peri from the air, his atashban breaking one of her wings. I think of the peri I saw today, the terrible scars on his back, and turn away, slightly sickened.

"Be careful of the magic here," Cavas says. "It can be strong. Tricky."

I'm about to ask what he means when I'm suddenly hit by a cloud of perfume so intense, so delicious that it feels like eating rose-flavored ice shavings or a chandrama on a two-moon night. The scent seeps into my skin, my veins, my very bones. If I let it, it will lift me into the air. My feet move of their own accord, the red gravel path giving way to smooth sangemarmar tiles that feel cool to the touch, even through my jootis. I'm tempted to take them off and walk barefoot, to see if this is the case, when Cavas grips my arm, pulling me harshly to the side.

"Careful," he says before I can snap at him. "Keep to the path's edges."

I look back at the path I'd been forced to abandon and saw something that I'm sure wasn't there before.

A black-tailed shvetpanchhi, similar to the one I knew in Javeribad, an arrow speared through its breast. Flies buzz over the bird's corpse; it looks like it has been freshly killed.

"The princes like to hunt. Sometimes without magic," Cavas says.

I try not to vomit. "I didn't . . . I didn't even *see*—"

"Tricky." His voice is oddly gentle. "Remember?"

I look toward my own feet, at the hem of my borrowed ghagra, which is now caked with the dirt from our journey, and am suddenly grateful for its very ordinariness. When I look up at the palace again, something about its beauty shifts, like a crack in marble, or a scar marring otherwise smooth skin. I force myself to look away. Cavas averts his eyes as well.

"That's the entrance to the royal gardens," he says. The smell of roses—the sort my father always wanted to grow—wafts out from beyond the arch engraved with flowers in different colors. The trees are much greener here, their leaves untouched by the red sand that smears everything in Ambarvadi and the Walled City, including the skin under my clothes.

"And that's Rani Mahal," he says, pointing to the building ahead of us. "The king and the princes live with their servants on the other side of the garden in Raj Mahal."

"What's Raj Mahal like?"

Cavas raises an eyebrow; I must have sounded a little too eager. "Even if I lived there, I wouldn't be able to tell you," he says. "Besides, I rarely ever go to that side of Ambar Fort."

A secrecy spell, then. Just as I'd suspected.

"Do the queens ever get to see the king?" I ask, unable to keep the sarcasm out of my voice. "Or does he prefer hiding from them, too?"

"It's not a bad idea to remain hidden in this palace." The corners of Cavas's mouth turn down in a grimace. "Speaking of which . . . you'll need to be careful. Occasionally, a prince or a Sky Warrior can take a fancy to a servant and force them to do things they don't want."

"It's good that I have my daggers with me, then." By the time the words slip out, it's too late to snatch them back. *Way to open your big mouth, Gul.*

Instead of looking surprised or eyeing the bundle I hold so tightly in my hands, Cavas merely laughs. "Oh, yes. I forgot whom I was talking to. You can take care of yourself."

I am suddenly aware of everything: the sweat matting strands of hair to my cheeks and forehead, the body that my mother always called too sharp, too thin. Too girlish to ever be womanly. But Cavas does not really look at my body. He's staring at my face, his gaze pausing at my lips. *Focus, Gul*, I scold myself. *You haven't come here to roll in the grass with a boy.*

"You mentioned the princes. How many are there?"

A blink. Whatever softness I saw on Cavas's face now disappears behind a scowl. "There are only three—all Rani Amba's sons." He pauses. "You know, you could always bind with a prince if everything else fails. That's one way to meet the king. He'll have to bless the binding."

Was that a joke? With Cavas, I can never tell.

"I? Bind with a rajkumar?" I ask innocently. "I am far too simple for that. I am, as someone once said, more along the lines of an ordinary thief."

There's a long silence, in which Cavas stares at me. Was that a flicker of amusement in his brown eyes? The lightest touch of a smile on his lips? I'm so busy trying to figure out his expressions that I might not have even noticed the footsteps pattering on the ground or felt the sudden change in the air if Cavas's face hadn't hardened in warning, a blur of color appearing right behind him. A small girl dressed in a bright-blue ghagra shot through with threads of indradhanush, the gold dust on her round cheeks making them glow.

"What are you waiting for?" My voice is loud. Sounds cruel to my own ears. "Get back to work!"

"Ji." Cavas is better at hiding his feelings than I am. With a bow, he turns away, walking past the hedges surrounding the palace and disappearing around the bend.

The girl, who appears to be no more than six or seven, is still staring at me. I give her a bright smile. "Rajkumari," I say, hoping that it's the right way to address someone who looks like a small princess. "Are you lost?"

"Why did you shout at him just then?" She tilts her head to one side, an eyebrow raised. "You were smiling at him before."

Was I smiling? I don't know . . . I didn't even feel my mouth move.

"Was he mean to you? Did he do something bad? Because you shouldn't shout at him otherwise," the girl says seriously. "You'll get him into trouble."

It gives me pause that a girl so young—and so royal—would care about someone like Cavas, a person she has probably been told time and again is beneath her.

"You know him?" I ask, avoiding her questions.

She lets out a laugh that is simultaneously airy and mocking. "Of course I know Cavas. He takes care of my pony, Dhoop. He also never laughs at me when I fall off the saddle." Her eyes narrow at me. "I don't know *you*."

Excellent. I've never felt this intimidated by a person half my size. I swallow back the fear and force a smile.

"Are you sure, Rajkumari? Perhaps *you* haven't seen me. You've been so busy with your dolls and Dhoop this week!" Surely even princesses play with dolls. Don't they?

The princess frowns, a hint of doubt on her little face. Before she can respond, though, I hear laughter in the distance.

Her dark eyes widen. "Hide!" she says.

"What? Why?"

But she's already running, so quick on her feet that I wonder if she has wings on them, and disappears behind a tall hedge by Rani Mahal, leaving me standing in place, openmouthed.

Seconds later, the source of the laughter appears in front of me, three men dressed in the sort of clothes I've only seen in paintings: knee-length white-and-gold angrakhas tied at the right shoulder and white hunting breeches stuffed into tall red boots caked with mud. Indradhanush glints on their bows and the feathered arrows of their nearly empty quivers, the weapons hanging from gilded waistbelts. Only one of the men looks relatively clean. Unlike the first two, who have let their hair flow free along with their laughter, his turban is still rigidly tied in place, gold tipping his angular cheeks. I can tell he's younger than the other two—probably around eighteen or nineteen years old—his face growing sour as another joke is made at his expense.

The princes like to hunt.

I make an attempt to slip away, hastily covering my head and face with my dupatta. But I know, even before I take the first step, that they've already seen me.

"There it is!" A voice calls out. "You, there! Serving girl!"

I pause and turn, watching as the tallest and most handsome of the princes gestures to the dead bird lying behind me. "Bring that here!"

I stiffen, not wanting to cause a scene by disobeying a royal, yet unwilling to touch the dead bird. The turbaned prince looks annoyed, but the smirks on the faces of the other two remind me of some of the novices in Javeribad—the ones who enjoyed seeing others punished. A voice that sounds like mine, yet not quite, emerges from my mouth: "Isn't that the gamekeeper's job? To carry your kills?"

A flash of anger lights up the tall prince's eyes. He moves closer, so slowly that for a moment I don't realize he's moving. "What did you say, girl?"

The other princes follow, even though I can tell that the turbaned one is more reluctant. Up close, I see they all have identical eyes—pale yellow, like the firestones glinting on the small hoops piercing their lobes.

"Go on." The tall prince makes a puckering sound with his lips, like an air kiss for a pet. "Go get the bird before I get angry."

"I am not your servant, Rajkumar," I say. I can hear a voice in my head screaming—another Gul who is cursing my folly. "I work for Rani Amba."

"*I work for Rani Amba*," his companion mocks in a falsetto. The two men laugh as if it's the funniest thing they've ever heard. "Stupid witch."

If we were in Javeribad right now, I would have taken one of the tall prince's own arrows and run it through him.

"Is this how the royals treat those who serve them? Where is your honor and respect, Rajkumar?" I demand instead, invoking the Code of Asha.

In response, the tallest prince's hand cracks across my jaw, making my teeth rattle. He sneers at me, and I wonder how I could have ever thought him good-looking. "First of all, I am no ordinary princeling that you can get away with calling me *Rajkumar*. I am the *yuvraj*—the heir apparent to Ambar's throne. When you talk to me again, you will address me accordingly, the way *respect* and royal titles demand. As for honor? You think you can use my own mother's lectures on me, serving girl? You are not a rajkumari or some jumped-up minister's daughter I need to watch myself around. Your honor is of no consequence to me."

"Let it go, Sonar," the turbaned prince cuts in impatiently. "Father's waiting for us, remember?"

"Shut up, Amar," the crown prince—Sonar—says. "Father can wait."

The turbaned prince shoots me a look that is both angry and pitying. Sonar's hand reaches out, wrenching my dupatta off my head. Instinctively, I grab the cloth, my knuckles turning pale.

The prince standing next to Sonar laughs. "Oh look! She's going to put up a fight!"

Sonar laughs as well, his perfect white teeth gleaming, his grip on my dupatta almost lazy. He knows he can rip the cloth from my hands with a single pull. Another step forward and he will reach for my other clothes, tearing into the sleeve of my blouse, revealing the birthmark I've taken such pains to hide.

No. My heart thuds beneath my ribs. *No.*

Light erupts from my hands, hitting Sonar with a *boom*. His eyes widen, and he staggers back, nearly falling over his own feet. The three princes stare at me in astonishment. A calm feeling settles over my mind, heat steaming the palms of my hands. When Sonar grabs my right arm, he screams a curse and and is forced to release me at once. Triumph floods my veins as angry boils bubble over his bare hand, his face turning red with fury.

"Jagat! Grab her!" Sonar shouts.

A kernel of energy forms in my solar plexus, a little seed of heat I had felt only once before—in a storage room, before a gunnysack filled with rice. *Use me*, it seems to say. *Kill them.*

I know I can. I feel it—death magic ready to burst free and wreak havoc—when a blast echoes through the sky, momentarily eliminating all sound. I feel my mouth open in a scream, see my action reflected in the three princes nearby. We fall to the ground, the thud of our bodies making impact with it finally breaking through to my ears.

"What is this?"

The woman who speaks has eyes the same shade of yellow as the princes' and a voice colder than Prithvi ice. The streaks of gray in her braided hair reveal her age, even though her face appears ageless, the gold on her high cheekbones so perfectly applied that it looks like part of her smooth, sun-kissed skin. The firestones on her cream-colored ghagra catch the light when she steps out into the sun, her mere presence seeming to suck the air from around me, rendering the heat even more oppressive.

The princes sink into deferential crouches at the same moment, their heads bowed so low their noses nearly brush the hot tiles. "Rani Ma," they murmur.

Their mother. Even though I've never seen her before, I know this is Queen Amba. I feel it in my bones. No one else can possibly inspire this level of respect or fear. Holding on to the queen's firm hand is none other than the little girl I'd seen earlier, her dark eyes filled with worry. She widens them at me now and grips her little dupatta, which is tucked neatly across her torso, before jerking her chin at me.

My own dupatta lies pooled at my feet like sloughed snakeskin. I quickly grab hold of it and wrap it around me. I look for the bundle containing my daggers and spot it next to a group of bushes right by Rani Mahal, a few feet from the queen herself. It must have been tossed there during my scuffle with the princes. I try not to groan.

"All this fuss over a serving girl?" Queen Amba's eyes focus on me now, sharpen on seeing the gold badge still gleaming on my shoulder. "*My* serving girl?"

"Rani Ma, I told them not to!" the turbaned prince exclaims. "I have nothing to do with this!"

The murderous looks his brothers shoot him are quickly superseded by the utter coldness of Queen Amba's glare.

"Tell me, my sons. What pledge do you make when you become princes?" She lets go of the little girl's hand and walks around the three men, as if inspecting them. The three of them mumble something. "Louder!"

"Valor in the face of fear. Respect for the poor and the elderly. Honor above all else," they say, their voices a perfect chorus.

"Yes. Honor. The one thing I promise each girl I take into my employ—a trait I expect from my sons as well. If you don't have honor, you don't have anything." Her eyes flash. "Rise to your feet."

The princes wince as a beam of light, as thin as a blade, flashes three times, leaving behind the smell of burned flesh. I wince as well, even though I don't pity any of them. Except the one named Amar, who probably didn't deserve the same punishment. When she finally dismisses them, I see it for myself—three thin lines bisecting the center of three different backs, delicate trails of blood beginning to seep into their white tunics.

She watches the princes walk away and then turns to the little girl. "Malti, you can run along now and play in the garden."

Malti glances at me one last time and then nods. "Ji, Rani Ma."

"What are *you* staring at?" Queen Amba asks me. "Come along." She points to the bundle lying by the bushes. "And bring that with you."

I trudge toward the bushes and bend slowly, my body shielding the bundle from her gaze.

"Hurry up," the queen snaps.

The seaglass daggers catch the light for a brief second before I toss them into the bushes. I rise to my feet, the bundle held close to my hammering heart. But Queen Amba doesn't ask me any questions, and I follow her into Rani Mahal without another word.

SPLENDOR AND BLOOD

19

GUL

Tiles, cool under my feet. Swirls of sangemarmar overhead, interlocking in an archway made of shimmering rose-colored stone and
stained glass. If I were another girl, I might be standing there staring at
everything in awe. Only I'm not another girl. I'm an impostor inside
Rani Mahal, following in the footsteps of a queen who may very well
cut short what's left of my life in this gleaming white courtyard. Balconies border us on all sides. A few women stand there, peering at us, their
whispers like leaves rustling in the silence.

It's not until we cross the entire length of the yard and enter the
building that I begin breathing again. A pair of serving girls dressed in
the same outfit I'm wearing, only better fitting, bow for Queen Amba.
One dares to glance at me, an eyebrow raised at my sweaty face and
dirty clothes.

"Don't loiter," Queen Amba says, as if sensing my hesitation. Or
maybe she has eyes in the back of her head. Though she says nothing
else, I'm sure she hears the whispers that break out behind us. I follow
her farther into the palace, down a long passageway lit by fanas after

jewel-toned fanas. The air here smells of frankincense and oil, the sort used in temples to light wick-lamps for the gods.

A sharp left and we enter another passage, the sun pouring in from the glass panes overhead. At the end is a door, inlaid with firestones and pearls, and it is flanked by a pair of armed Sky Warriors, both women. My fingers curl inward as I catch a glimpse of their atashbans, sharpened to glistening points.

The door opens to a spacious chamber flooded with natural light. My jootis sink into cloud-soft carpets, patterned with paisley and Ambari wild roses. The design echoes on the walls, paint foiled into shimmering greens and yellows. A gilded chandelier hangs over a seating area corralled with mattresses and long, velvet-covered pillows.

"This is the gold room," the queen says, and all of a sudden, I find myself under the scrutiny of that yellow gaze. "But you would already know that if you worked for me."

"I beg your forgiveness, Rani Amba, but I am new here."

I avoid looking directly into the queen's eyes and focus somewhere around the region of her chin, where two full moons are tattooed: one blue, one gold. It's said that only the direct descendants of the moon goddess, Sunheri, are allowed such tattoos—though I'm not certain how these descendants have verified their bloodline and connection to a now nonexistent goddess. The moons are so perfectly etched onto Queen Amba's skin that to anyone not looking closely, the tattoos simply blend in with the hoop of her nose ring and elaborate choker—firestones and pearls embedded in a lattice of gold. She raises her hands in a pair of resounding claps. Within a space of two breaths, another serving girl appears.

"Are we expecting any new girls?" the queen asks.

The girl shoots me a sideways glance. "Yes, Rani Amba. We were expecting someone new today. To replace Siya."

"I see. What's your name, girl?" Rani Amba asks me.

"G—S-siya," I stutter.

"One Siya to replace another. Interesting." A finger tilts my chin up, forcing me to meet that yellow gaze. "What you did outside with that shield spell? That was clever," the queen says coolly. "Who taught you?"

"My mother."

Pain, not unlike the slice of a knife, burns across my left side. I bite back a scream. There's a cruel, knowing look on the queen's face, even though she touches me with nothing other than a finger.

"With a touch, I can enter the recesses of your wretched mind and penetrate its every curve and bend. With a touch, I can make your eyes water, your eardrums burst, turn your organs into tar. I am going to say this only once: *Don't lie to me.*"

A truth seeker. It's the first time I've come across one other than Kali. Only Kali never wielded her power like this.

"No one," I blurt out. "No one taught me this."

The truth. I'm suddenly immensely grateful for Amira's refusal to give me any kind of instruction or help during our training.

The smallest of frowns mars the smooth perfection that is Queen Amba's forehead. "And your mother. What happened to her?"

"She's dead." *Give them the truth, but never the whole truth*, Juhi always said when training us to answer suspicious thanedars. I think of my mother's eyes, golden in the moonlight, the life in them suddenly extinguished in a flash of red. "She died two months before my fourteenth birthday."

I wait for another jab in the belly, a nosebleed, something worse. But what I feel is weight: an invisible rock threatening to crush my ribs, a sensation I've always associated with grief. The queen's hand drops back to her side. Breath rushes into my lungs. *Weakness is not always a terrible thing*, Cavas said. And it's only now that I understand why.

"Open the bundle you brought in," she says.

"Rani Amba—" I begin.

"Open it. Unless you have something to hide."

I swallow hard, undoing the knot, allowing the cloth—an old gray sari—to fall to the sides. The bangles on Queen Amba's wrist click together delicately, pausing inches from the contents. Her nose wrinkles, as if presented with dung cakes and not a stack of day-old bajra roti.

When she looks up at me again, I hope I appear sufficiently embarrassed about my poverty. I hope it is enough to evade another interrogation—one that very well might lead to other secrets being brought out in the open. *Like where my daggers are hidden right now. Like my murderous plans for Raja Lohar.*

"This must be your lucky day, *Siya*. I am not going to punish you for using magic against a royal." I don't miss the slight emphasis on my pretend name. Or the warning that rattles somewhere inside my rib cage, along with my heart. The queen's mouth curves up into a shape that would, on any other woman, be a smile.

"Show this girl her quarters," she tells the serving girl. "And get her a ghagra and choli that fit."

"Look at what the tabby dragged in."

"I thought it was Rajkumari Malti who did the dragging. She's fond of strays, that one."

"No, it was the princes! She's probably one of their discards."

The three serving girls in my assigned dormitory talk about me as if I'm not there, even though I can feel them watching, their eyes examining every inch of my body as I fumble with the string ties at the back of my blouse, struggling to get them knotted. It was already a task keeping my birthmark hidden with these girls staring at me, laughing when I pretended shyness and showed them my back while getting dressed.

"What is this?" a voice cuts across the chatter, soft and imperious. "A show at a bawdy house in the Walled City? Get to work, you three!"

Tongues as sharp as daggers soften to the consistency of rose petals.

"Apologies, Yukta Didi."

"We're leaving, Didi."

Slippers brush over the floor, the sounds rising behind me and then fading away.

"Leave that." The same voice, with a touch of impatience. A hand brushes aside mine and does up the tie that was giving me so much difficulty. I keep my gaze lowered to the floor, to the woman's feet, which are encased in jootis made of polished brown leather.

"Look up—Siya, isn't it? Neither of us are royalty here."

I look into eyes that are neither brown nor green but a mix of the two. Wrinkles fan out from their corners like rivers against the woman's deep-brown skin, bracketing the curves of her pursed lips. Not a single strand of her silver braid appears out of place. Unlike the rest of us, she wears a sari made of orange cotton, simple except for the designs of the two moons embedded in the cloth, reflected with her every move. A supervisor.

"At least your hair isn't untidy like some of the other girls'. Goddess knows how many times I've had to undo and redo their plaits during the early days. Use these." The woman—Yukta Didi—holds up a pair of brass hairpins, which I use to fix the dupatta neatly over my head.

"Now listen carefully, Siya, for I will say this only once. There are twenty-five serving girls working in Rani Mahal and five of us supervisors. Rani Amba's girls report either to Jaya Didi or to me—but mostly to me. Your main duties will involve waiting on Rani Amba and Rajkumari Malti and ensuring that their needs are seen to. You are allowed anywhere on this side of Ambar Fort, in the royal stables, and in parts of the garden that are open to the residents of Rani Mahal. On no account must you venture to the west side of the fort, where Raj Mahal lies."

"Why not?" The words slip out of me before I can stop them. How am I supposed to kill the king if I'm forbidden from going where he lives? Though it's not like I'll be able to kill him anytime soon without my daggers.

"Raj Mahal is surrounded by a rekha—a magical line that allows no woman to pass through," she says coolly. "Doing so results in instant death."

"Even for the queens?" I ask, surprised.

"The queens have their own ways of getting to Raj Mahal. Which really is none of your concern. What you must do is avoid the sort of disturbance you created with the princes this morning."

Disturbance? "That wasn't my fault." I feel my voice rising and force myself to lower it when I see her raised eyebrows. "I wasn't anywhere near Raj Mahal!"

"You don't have to be." Her words may be censure or warning or perhaps both. "Any other questions?"

In the corner of the room, right next to my bed, a spider delicately swings from a thread, barely an arm's length from my pillow.

"No," I say. "No other questions."

20
GUL

The servants' quarters—"women only," Yukta Didi says—are on a lower level within Rani Mahal, accessible only by a pair of ramps instead of stairs, the stone rubbed smooth by frequent use.

"Most of the women working inside the palace live here." Yukta Didi walks ahead, navigating the steep ramp with more agility than I expect from someone of her age.

"What about the Sky Warriors?" I ask, thinking of the ones stationed outside the gold room. "I mean, some are women, aren't they? Where do they live?"

"Most live in the barracks in the Walled City, though a few live in Ambar Fort itself."

I press close to the wall, trying not to slip over the stone and fall backward into the dark. The ramp leads into a small, rectangular lobby, which branches off into three corridors.

"Janavi, Farishta, Amba." She points out each corridor. "You are expected to know where each rani stays and, if called, to serve her within reason. Your badge marks you as Rani Amba's personal staff, so your first loyalty will always remain with her."

Before I can ask what "within reason" entails and risk another reprimand, she's already moving to the corridor on the far left—the one that leads to Amba's apartments. The air here changes almost at once to a cloying mix of frankincense and roses.

Yukta Didi pauses outside a green-and-gold door. "You'll be helping me clean the green room today."

To my surprise, a familiar figure steps out: the turbaned prince I'd seen outside Rani Mahal earlier this morning.

"Rajkumar Amar." Yukta Didi drops in a bow. I realize a little late that I'm supposed to mimic her movements, especially when the prince's gaze locks with mine, his eyes narrowing with interest.

In my haste to bow, I nearly trip over my own feet. Yukta Didi glares at me.

"I hope you are well now, Rajkumar," she tells him, her tone shifting to something more personal. Motherly. "The herbs I gave you—"

"Worked wonders," he says, smiling. "Rani Ma wouldn't have really hurt any of us. You always worry too much, Yukta Didi."

"What else am I supposed to do?" she scolds. "It's because of you and your brothers that my hair has turned gray over the last twenty-one years."

"Are you sure? I thought you were aging backward." He gives me a small smile, and, oddly, I find myself wanting to smile back. "Is this your new trainee?"

"Yes. We're supposed to be cleaning the green room—which is barred to everyone else at the moment," she says, stern again. "The cupboard is still infested with blood bats."

A frisson of fear goes through me. *Blood bats?*

"I know. Rani Ma told me." Prince Amar's serious eyes light up. "I wanted to have a look before you cleared them out. When diluted, their venom can heal some of the most complicated magical injuries, did you know? Vaid Roshan said it's a new experimental healing technique."

"Vaid Roshan had better stick to mending bruises and healing bones with his regular magic if he doesn't want to be out of work," Yukta Didi says sharply. "Goddess only knows what kinds of people get hired at the palace these days!"

Heat rushes to my face at the last comment, especially when Amar says: "Speaking of which—may I have a word with your new trainee?"

"Rajkumar, she's new, she didn't really know—"

"It's all right, Didi," he interrupts gently. "I am not going to punish her. I assume Rani Ma has already done so."

There's a long pause. "I'll be waiting inside," Yukta Didi says, a warning in her tone. She leaves the door partly open—probably to eavesdrop.

"I want to apologize to you for what happened earlier this morning," Amar says in a low voice. "You were right to challenge my brothers—to question them about their honor. What they did to you—what I did—wasn't honorable."

I finally recover use of my voice. "It wasn't your fault, Rajkumar. You didn't do anything."

"No, I didn't. And with my silence, I became an accomplice."

The grim tone of his voice both surprises me and fills me with suspicion. "You don't need to apologize to me," I say, fully conscious of the green room's open door. "I am but a serving girl working for your mother."

"We're all servants in a way. The king must serve his subjects and so must the other members of the royal family. The Code of Asha states that to coexist, we must honor and depend on each other, magi and non-magi. It's what the old high priests—the great acharyas of Ambar—called a sandhi or a joining."

"Not all acharyas believe in being joined to non-magi, do they?" The words slip out before I can stop them. "Wasn't it a priest who came up with the idea of the tenements, separating magi and non-magi before the Great War?"

"Unfortunately, yes," Amar admits. There's a curious look in his yellow eyes. "You are very right—again."

You also sound too well-read for a servant who isn't the royal tutor. I curse myself for my runaway tongue.

"Forgive me, Rajkumar," I deflect quickly. "I spoke out of turn. I heard people talking in the city and—"

"You don't need to apologize to me, Siya ji. No one in this world is perfect—me least of all."

I say nothing in response. I'm not even sure what I *can* say to someone this candid about themselves. And that's when I realize—

"Rajkumar . . . I don't remember telling you my name." Well, my false name. With an added honorific. But still.

"You have your sources of knowledge. I have mine."

I should take his words as a warning. As the threat that they probably are. But Amar smiles at me again, his eyes squinting mischievously—so reminiscent of a boy half his age that this time I can't help but smile back.

"Shubhdivas, Siya ji."

"Shubhdivas, Rajkumar Amar."

I step into the green room and close the door behind me. I find Yukta Didi standing by the cupboard, frowning. "About time you came in. Now take this." She thrusts a poker at me, its tips gleaming silver and sharp.

"What's this for?"

"Blood bats, girl. Weren't you listening to me outside?" She gestures to a wooden almari pushed up against the wall—a cupboard that looks completely ordinary, apart from the fact that it's rattling from the inside. A bloodcurdling screech follows, sending shivers down my spine.

"We had an infestation in the servants' quarters last month." Yukta Didi would have appeared completely unperturbed if not for the hard set of her jaw. "Most of them are gone now, but these two escaped into the palace itself. The head of palace maintenance contained them in here, but he nearly lost an eye in the process. He refuses to come near them, and so do the other girls. Rani Amba wants you to have a try. She thinks it'll be an excellent introductory task for you."

The perfect punishment, you mean. I stare at the poker in my hand and then back at the rattling cupboard, dust rising from it in a cloud.

"I could try whispering to them," I say.

Another scream echoes in the otherwise silent room. Yukta Didi grimaces. "Whispering, huh? Didn't think there were any whisperers left in Ambar these days. Certainly, there aren't any left at the palace. Though I suppose even generally redundant magic has its uses if you know what you're doing."

I bite back my irritation at her dismissive tone. "If I fail, it won't matter, will it?" I ask. "I won't open the cupboard unless I'm certain. They'll remain locked in."

Yukta Didi stares at me, her grip on her own poker tightening. "I suppose there's no harm in trying. But mind you, girl, if that lot gets loose again, you'll pay for it."

I'm sure Rani Amba will agree with you, I think grimly before placing the poker on the floor. The almari's doors are latticed with crevices, carved into the wood to form two interlocking moons. The gaps are so tiny that it's impossible for the flying rodents to break through, but large enough to see a shadow moving within, the blink of a glowing red eye.

The first step in whispering is contact. It doesn't have to be physical. But I need to be close enough so that the animal senses me. Senses that I'm different from other magi. I brush my fingers against the door.

My name is Siya, I think, loud and clear in my head. *I want to set you free.*

I repeat the words over and over, until there's a low moan from within. The rattling stops for a brief moment. There are more sounds,

186

but this time I ignore them, picking out the blood bats' scattered thoughts like heartbeats. *One bat, two . . .*

"Five," I tell Yukta Didi. "There are five bats inside. Three are babies. The mother is frightened. She thinks we want to kill them."

"As we *should.* They've caused enough trouble."

"Shhhh! Not so loud." Animals can't understand human speech, but they sense our moods from the tone of our voices. I close my eyes again, listening to the sounds in the cupboard. My mind floats, at ease with whispering in a way it never has—and likely never will be—with death magic, picking out the shapes of the creatures within.

"We need to open the almari." My words make Yukta Didi blanch. "If we do that, I know I can convince them to leave."

The older woman glares at me in disbelief. But, a long moment later, she walks over to the window and opens it. "Get them to fly out this window. If you can't, then . . ." She holds up the poker, and I'm not entirely sure if the threat is meant for the blood bats or for me.

Carefully, I turn the key and leap back as the doors swing open, bats rushing out in a flurry of brown fur and leathery wings. They swing left first, crashing into a vase, toppling it to the floor.

"This way!" I shout, pointing to the window. "By the goddess, *this* way! No, no! You promised!"

A bat swoops down at Yukta Didi, who closes her eyes and screams, stabbing uselessly at the air with her poker. I swear I can hear the bat cackling. *She wants to kill us, does she?* the bat says. *She can't even look at us. Sorry, girl. I couldn't resist.*

With a parting screech, the bats finally fly out the window, black shadows swirling like dried leaves caught up in the wind.

"They're gone," I say, watching them disappear. "Yukta Didi? They're gone. You can open your eyes now."

One eye opens, then another. "They're gone? For certain."

I can't help but smile. "For certain."

"Well, then." Yukta Didi rises to her feet, cool dignity back in place. "Get to work, girl. That silver mirror needs polishing."

I suppress a sigh. What did I expect? A pat on the back? A *well done*?

It doesn't take long for Yukta Didi to realize I'm hopeless at household spells, and it makes her irritable. "You should have told me that before. Wait." She exits the room and reappears a few moments later with a bucket and a rag in hand. She tosses the rag at me. "Use this. And make sure you squeeze out the tamarind juice properly or you'll stain the floor."

"Yes, Yukta Didi."

The work is tedious, smelly, and unforgiving, and soon I'm sweating despite the open window. It's a waste of time when I could be doing something else—like trying to find a way into Raj Mahal. But that is next to impossible—especially with Yukta Didi still present, eyeing me like a predatory bird.

"Your polishing is satisfactory," she says now. "And you aren't afraid of hard work. That's a good thing. So many girls these days think honest labor is beneath them. They absolutely refuse to do anything without the aid of magic."

I dip the rag back into the bucket and squeeze hard. "My, uh, old mistress taught me that there is no shame in working without magic. Even if you are a magus."

I glance into the mirror, spot the older woman's approving nod. "That is what my old mistress, Rani Megha, taught me as well."

I wonder if she thought the same way when she decided to tax the lives out of the non-magi and brand them traitors, I think. Out loud, I say: "You worked under Rani Megha? Goddess! What was that like?"

I must sound appropriately awed, because Yukta Didi gives me a small smile—the first she's directed my way. "Megha was a brilliant rani and an exacting mistress. We were lucky to serve her, and we knew it. Well, some of us did. There were other girls who wanted more. A lot more than they deserved."

The words send a chill down my spine. "What more could they possibly want than to serve their rani?" The question is innocent—too innocent perhaps for the likes of me. But I keep my eyes wide and open, and soon the suspicion drains from Yukta Didi's face.

"When you become a serving girl, you cannot bind with anyone; you are bound to the palace. It's a hard undertaking for anyone—and many don't realize how hard until they come here. You seem like a good girl, Siya, so let me warn you from the beginning—don't be foolish. The girl you replaced—her name was also Siya. She got caught last week with one of the serving boys in the garden. Major Shayla nearly skinned them both alive."

"Aah!" I bite back a scream, stifling it to a gasp. Blood trickles down my finger, cut by a part of the mirror that my hand slipped up against when I heard the name of the woman who murdered my parents. The taste of copper floods my tongue.

"Queen's curses! Did you get blood on the floor?"

"No." I force myself to focus on the mirror again. "Major Shayla. Who is she?"

"Someone you don't want to come up against if you can help it. They call her the Scorpion in the Sky Warriors' barracks. She's one of the few women apart from the queens who can move freely between both palaces. Keep your head down if you see her. With the Scorpion around, you're better off invisible."

"Why do they call her the Scorpion?"

"Because you never know when she'll sting."

Juhi would say that the gods had played a role in arranging this. For the other Siya to be sacked and Cavas's sudden appearance at the flesh market. The altercation with Amba's sons. For the woman who murdered my parents to be so close. I should feel happy—everything seems to be falling in line with my plans—but unease churns my gut. Once again, I have the sensation of being watched, of being listened to.

In the distance, a gong goes off. "That's the servants' lunch bell,"

Yukta Didi informs me. "It always goes off after the queens finish eating. Leave now or you won't get any food until midnight. The work will still be waiting for you."

The serving girls eat in the kitchen courtyard—an open-air space bordered by a wall of pink stone at one end and a water basin to wash utensils at the other. A woman stands next to a table stacked with brass plates at one end and two steaming vats at another. She gives me the same up-and-down look Yukta Didi did earlier, but her brown eyes are kind, and the portion she serves me is the same as the others'.

I find a spot by the water basin, a brief distance from where a group of other girls are already settled. I feel the others glance as I pass them, hear their whispers even after I crouch on the floor behind them.

"That's the new girl?"

"Queen's curses, how skinny! *She's* not going to last!"

I ignore them and focus on the food itself: a spicy affair of smooth, creamy kadhi and khichdi that tastes as delectable as it looks, each yellow grain of rice melting in my mouth. I'm not here to make friends, and soon enough the conversation drifts from me to other happenings at the palace.

"You were at the raj darbar today, Nargis. What happened?"

I grow still at the words *raj darbar*. The king's court in Raj Mahal. I shift around, trying not to seem as if I'm eavesdropping.

"There was a peri there today," a girl, probably Nargis, replies. Her voice is clear and carrying; she knows she has an audience, and she likes it. "He sang like a dream! So handsome, too. All of us, including the two younger queens, kept drooling over him! Rani Amba was most displeased at our behavior. She called us undignified."

The girls laugh, sounding delighted.

"Did he have wings?" someone asks eagerly. "The peri."

"Did he fight in the cage?" someone else adds.

"Of course he didn't fight in the cage!" Nargis scoffs at the last question. "You *know* the spectacles take place only once toward the middle of every month, Sunaina. And he didn't have wings, either. Remember how the peri were when they *had* wings? They attacked us all with that beast of a Pashu king during the Battle of the Desert. No, they're better off clipped, I say."

"I wish I could go to court," one of the girls says. "If only to see all the creatures the raja brings in from the flesh market. And the spectacles in the cage."

"I still remember last month's spectacle," Nargis says gleefully. "Raja Lohar had brought in five prizefighters from the flesh market and pit them all against an armored leopard. The beast just *ripped* them apart. If you want to see something like that, you *need* to get on your rani's good side. That's the only way for girls like us to attend the king's court or even see what Raj Mahal looks like! That, or serve the Scorpion."

No one laughs this time.

"I hear the Scorpion prefers boys serving her," someone else says. "I saw her eyeing that dirt licker from the stables the other day. What's his name? Cavas?"

The morsel of rice and gravy turns sour in my mouth. Anger, sudden and sharp, spikes through me. I breathe deeply, struggle to hold it in.

"Better him than us," another girl says.

When lunch ends a moment later, a shadow falls over my plate. A girl I don't know scowls at me. "Yukta Didi wants you back in the green room. You still have a lot to do."

Having a lot to do seems to be true, because once I return to the green room, Yukta Didi hands me a broom and tells me to get to work before shutting the door behind her. Around the time my arms feel like they're about to fall off, she reenters to inspect my work. She glances around the room, frowning at the polished table, the shining mirror, and the gleaming wooden floor. "I suppose this will do for now. Come on. The toilets need to be cleaned as well."

A gibbous Sunheri glows in the sky when I finally return to my new quarters, sweat and goddess knows what else sticking to me. Even washing afterward with strong lye and honeyweed soap doesn't do much to improve the smell. I expect one or more of the nine girls I share the room with to comment on this, but no one seems to notice my reappearance. The novelty of taunting the new serving girl must have worn off.

Unlike the others, who fall asleep, one by one, lulled by the relative darkness of the room, I remain awake, my mind turning over the various ways and means I can sneak outside to get my daggers. A part of me knows it's foolish to hope that they're still exactly where I hid them— that they haven't been found already.

You wouldn't be here if they were, I reassure myself. After that altercation with the princes, it wouldn't be hard to deduce that I was the one who brought the weapons in. I wouldn't even need a truth seeker in the vicinity to get convicted. The spiderweb on the wall next to my cot glistens in the dim light.

I wait a moment more before shifting, my bare feet lightly pressing the floor. Unlike the royals, serving girls don't wear anklets, only simple jootis made of tough brown leather. Tonight, I leave the shoes behind as well and slip out, the door making no sound when I pull it shut. The corridors are dark, lit intermittently by a fanas or two. To get out, I know I must make my way to the main courtyard and find the gate leading to the marbled walkway Cavas pulled me away from only this morning.

Cavas. It feels as if I haven't seen him for years, even though it has been only half a day. I think once again of what I heard the girls saying about him and Major Shayla before pushing the thought away. I can't afford to be distracted. Not when I'm so close to avenging my parents.

Spurred by that last thought, I force myself to think, recalling every scrap of conversation I heard today, trying to match it to what I already know about the layout of the palace. Two ramps led into the servants' quarters, one of which went to the lobby of the queens' apartments. Where the other ramp goes, I'm not sure. But I know I'll have to take a chance and find out. Heading farther down the long passageway, I finally reach a dead end. I'm about to head back when a mouse scampers across my foot, nearly making my heart stop.

Turning toward the source of the squeaks, I see the small creature scramble up over stone, lit by a faint light from somewhere above. The ramp here isn't as smooth as the other, which probably means it isn't used as much. It makes the climb easier, ending in a vestibule dimly lit by a small window.

I peek out the window and into the darkness below. The drop must be at least two hundred feet to the palace grounds. I instantly take a step back. Glass shards and old daggers stick out from the top of the pink sandstone boundary surrounding Ambar Fort, separating it from the Walled City. Apart from the window and the door leading to the ramp, there is only one other door, with a sign that says STAIRWELL IN DISREPAIR. DO NOT USE TO AVOID INJURY OR DEATH.

Right. Of course. Then again, if I did care about injury or death, I wouldn't be here right now. I wouldn't be in this palace at all.

I push the door open, revealing a steep staircase that disappears into the dark, moonlight pouring in from an overhead window. There aren't any candles or lanterns, so I try magicking a lightorb. After a couple of failed attempts, I give up and make my way down.

As the sign said, the stairs are in bad shape, the stone crumbling in places. There is also no railing to prevent me from falling into the darkness below, only a slippery stone wall on one side. My foot brushes something in the dark—a furry something that squeals as it topples over the edge. I press myself to the wall, blood pounding in my chest and my ears.

Great. At this rate, I'll probably fall to my own death before even seeing the king.

If you fall, you will float. The voice in my head sounds a lot like Ma. *You have magic in you, remember?*

For some reason, the thought calms me, and I slowly make my way down, one step at a time. Long moments later, just when I think the stairs will lead me nowhere, the ground beneath my feet changes textures—from cool stone to warm earth. Moonlight glows at the end of a short passage that leads outward. I duck underneath a stone ledge, squeeze between two hedgerows . . .

And hear birdsong.

A nightingale perches on the branch of a banyan tree, its voice breaking the quiet of the night. Nearby, nightqueens bloom in a shrub, the fragrance growing stronger the farther I step into the palace garden. It must be the garden. Nowhere else in Ambar have I seen trees this green or felt grass like this, a dewy carpet under my feet.

Beyond the trees, a shadow moves. I duck behind a tall hedge, glimpsing briefly the silvery tip of a guard's helmet. Voices murmur, slowly rising in crescendo.

"Queen's curses," one of the women says, "where are Radha and Laila?"

"Probably still sleeping in the barracks. You know how they are."

"Well, I'm not waiting anymore," the first guard replied. "They should have been here when Sunheri first appeared in the sky."

"We'll get into trouble for leaving our posts!"

"If we get into trouble, so will they! They're not Sky Warriors—just ordinary guards like us. I'm reporting them. This is the fourth time they've been late like this."

I hold my breath, feel it ease out only when I hear their footsteps moving away, the creak of the garden gate shutting behind them. My daggers, I know, lie somewhere beyond the garden gate, in the bushes. I hold my breath, hoping the gate isn't locked or magically sealed.

I brush a finger lightly against the gold grille. It creaks open with a slight push, the sound so loud that I freeze, wondering if it will bring the two guards running back. But no one comes. Ahead of me, the marble pathway leads up to Rani Mahal, gleaming in patches where the moonlight hits it from behind the clouds.

I locate the bushes where I tossed the bundle and, to my relief, find the glass daggers, still hidden exactly where I'd left them, a bloodworm crawling across the hilt of one. I brush the insect aside and hold them to my chest, reassured by their presence, even though I know I now have to look for another hiding place.

Keeping them in the servants' quarters is out of the question—apart from my cot, there's only a large cupboard that I share with the other girls, and the floor underneath is tiled. It will have to be somewhere else—a place I can access easily without being caught by a guard. I look both ways and slip back into the garden, closing the gate without further incident.

"Now where to put you?" I whisper.

The nightingale chirps, as if in response. I decide that the banyan tree is as good an option as any; the mud underneath it is dark, untouched by grass. A memory surfaces: my mother covering me with earth on a similar moonlit night.

You will not let our sacrifice go in vain.

No, Ma, I won't. I slowly rise to my feet, throat tightening. It's only a matter of time.

21
CAVAS

I think of Gul in the dark of the night, long after Papa falls asleep. I think of her the day after, upon hearing the other stable boys talk of an altercation between a serving girl and the princes. I wonder how long she'll last—if she will eventually give up her real name, and mine, as the one who helped her sneak in.

It's not the only reason for my worry. Latif has disappeared after our last encounter, not showing up no matter how hard I rub the green swarna. *He'll come*, I try to assure myself. *He'll keep his promise.* Gul, on the other hand, is best forgotten, a girl synonymous with trouble ever since the day we first met. So I don't understand—or perhaps don't want to understand— why the strange tightness in my chest eases when I see her today, a whole week after I sneaked her in, a few paces behind Princess Malti.

I drop to one knee. "Shubhsaver, Rajkumari."

"Shubhsaver, Cavas." I sense amusement in Princess Malti's high voice and find it when I look up, her dark eyes sparkling with mischief.

"I was telling Govind ji that Siya needs a horse of her own if she intends to keep up with me."

Gul. Or Siya, as she's calling herself these days, the sun reflecting in her eyes. Our gazes lock, slide away. I rise to my feet. I'm not thinking about how perfectly her new clothes fit. Or wondering if the skin on her bare waist is as smooth as it looks. Next to us, Malti is arguing with Govind again—an argument that I know she'll lose.

"Rajkumari, you aren't permitted to race Dhoop," Govind is saying patiently. "Your mother's orders, remember? A light canter is occasionally allowed, but a gallop is considered unladylike. Cavas will lead him for you, and your serving girl will accompany you. On foot."

It's against protocol for servants to ride the horses, and Govind conveys this in a voice that is both gentle and firm.

"I wanted to *ride* today! Properly!" Malti's small face puffs up—the beginnings of a royal tantrum.

"A walk will be so much nicer, Rajkumari," Gul cuts in with a smile. "We can enjoy the cool air, breathe in the smell of the rain. The garden is so green today. Certainly, it seems like it will rain again. Perhaps even the River Aloksha will begin flowing."

An optimistic thought. Ambar's only river, which originates in a glacier in Prithvi's mountains, hasn't flowed since the Great War. Unless Prithvi's king lowers his magical wall, I doubt the Aloksha will ever flow again.

Gul isn't wrong when she says the palace grounds and the garden are green—thanks to the magic perpetually infused into the soil by the gardeners. But magic isn't endless, and it always comes at a cost. Govind tells me that more palace gardeners have depleted themselves and retired early during King Lohar's reign than during any other.

Their only relief comes in the form of the rain now scenting the air, brought forth by clouds that can be seen slowly gathering in the west, a patch of gray in a distant blue sky.

"Siiiyaaaaaaaa," Malti complains.

"Rajkumari Maltiiiiiiii," Gul chides in the same singsongy way.

Govind's mouth narrows with disapproval, but Malti bursts out laughing. I feel myself smile.

I sense Gul watching me, but by the time I turn to look, she's already fussing with the princess's small dupatta, tying it around her waist and carefully tucking it in.

Dhoop, like his name, is pure sunshine during the day, his yellow coat gleaming like butter. Foaled by a sturdy Ambari mare, the pony has strong legs and enough enthusiasm to kick up a whole pathway through the grass if we let him. I feel him tugging at the rope when I lead him out, as excited to see Malti as she is to see him. To my surprise, the pony also nuzzles Gul's cheek, and she strokes his nose, smiling.

"You're a funny one," she says under her breath, her voice soft, meant for the pony alone.

I turn away. Only a whisperer and her magic. What difference does that make?

But it does make a difference. Controlling Dhoop can be difficult, and I need to be firm from the outset that this is a walk and not a run. Today, however, he's relatively placid, and part of this, I believe, is due to Gul's presence, walking alongside us, chatting with Princess Malti, her hand brushing the pony's coat from time to time.

The earth gets drier the farther we walk from the stables, cracks visible in the surface. I keep a lookout for snakes as I lead Dhoop up a particularly steep curve and then down, where the path gently descends and then plateaus—a fairly flat patch of land cordoned off by a ring of sharp rocks. Beyond the ring, the thick wall surrounding the palace rises, locking us in.

Here, away from Govind's stern eye, I finally let go of Dhoop's reins. "Please be careful, Rajkumari. No climbing the rocks. Stick to the—"

"—rock circle as much as possible," Malti interrupts. She gives me a wide grin. "I know, Cavas. I promise I won't get you into any trouble."

She makes a clicking sound, and soon enough Dhoop's walk turns into a light canter and then a full gallop.

Gul turns to me, her eyebrows raised. "Whatever happened to her mother's orders?"

"As far as I'm concerned, not being able to ride a horse is a lot worse than being unladylike. Govind agrees with me. He just can't admit it publicly. Besides, Malti is a natural on horseback."

Gul laughs. "Now I see why she likes you so much." For a few moments, we both watch Malti race around the circle formed by the rocks.

"Dhoop seems to like you," I say at last.

"We had horses at ho—where I come from."

"Many magi homes do. Not all magi seem to really like them, though." Even Govind, who can control the wildest of stallions, sees it as more of a duty than a pleasure. "And the horses, too, rarely respond like that to strangers unless they know them well."

She shrugs. "I like animals."

"Fireflies, too?"

Her body stiffens in response, but after a pause, she answers. "Fireflies, too."

A black-tailed shvetpanchhi circles overhead, perching on a stone jutting from the pink sandstone wall. A white feather floats briefly in the sky before settling on a rock a few feet from us.

"My father told me that shvetpanchhi feathers look like snow," she says. "All white and gleaming in the sun."

I watch the feather, try to visualize a thousand more falling from the sky. "I've never seen snow before."

"Neither have I," she says. "But Papa had been to Prithvi as a boy. He said it snows all the time over there and gets especially heavy around this time of the year. Those who hate the snow call it the Month of Dandruff instead of the Month of Tears."

A laugh spills out of me, almost involuntarily. "You mean the way people here call Tears the Month of Piss?" Her horrified face makes me smile. "What? You didn't know?"

"I didn't—and it reminded me of Javeribad's head thanedar singing to himself while urinating against a wall."

I laugh again. "Urinating thanedars aside, it's a nice place. Javeribad.

My papa used to take me there when I was a boy to seek blessings at the Sant Javer temple. We'd tie scraps of cloth around . . ." I pause, suddenly embarrassed by the way I've been talking—even more so by the captivated look on her face.

"Around the branches of the old banyan tree outside," Gul finishes my sentence in a soft, almost wistful voice. "People said that if you had a problem, all you needed to do was whisper it into that scrap of cloth and tie it around the tree. Sant Javer would take some of your troubles for his own. Which"—her eyes gleam with sudden mischief—"is quite a lot of work for one dead man, even if he was a saint. Don't you think? Or maybe he's a living specter."

The joke isn't that funny, but something about the way she says it makes me laugh again.

"If Sant Javer really wanted to help, he could do something about the poor rain we've had in Ambar over the past few years," I say. "I miss eating levta."

"Levta? You mean the black mudfish that breed in rain puddles?" Gul looks repulsed. "They're so slimy!"

"They don't taste bad fried." I grin, remembering what some of the men in the tenements say. "Though you *can* eat them raw for added virility."

"That sounds even more disgusting!"

The conversation leads to what we would eat for the rest of our lives if given a choice. I pick chandramas; Gul picks sohan halwa, a sticky Ambari sweet made of ghee, milk, flour, and sugar. We argue over the best way to ride a horse (Gul: bareback; me: saddled) and agree that the best sighting of the two moons takes place in the villages, where you can also see the stars, unlike the city, where magic can block them out.

Talking to Gul feels almost like talking to Bahar again. Not because they speak about the same things or even in the same way, but because of how light and unfettered I feel during our conversation—like a boy flirting with a pretty girl on an early spring day, the boy I might have been, perhaps, if Papa had not fallen ill.

The more we talk, the more of an excuse I have to look at her, to make note of her long, straight lashes, the tiny freckle in the hollow between her clavicles. I move closer almost by instinct, and it's only the catch in her breath that reminds me of where we are, making me draw back.

"I'm sorry. I'm standing too close to you." My voice emerges gruffer than usual.

"Not that close."

Does she know how breathless she sounds? Does she care? I glance back in Malti's direction, but she's still riding Dhoop and laughing.

"She knows," Gul says flatly. "She knows we're . . . friendly."

Friendly. Is that what we truly are? Is that what this strange buzzing underneath my skin means, now as I stand, less than an arm's length away, close enough to slip a hand into hers?

"We are not friends, Gul."

"Siya, remember?" A note of laughter enters her voice. "Though I don't mind being called by my real name. Even if it is by a nonfriend."

Had she been a simple non-magus girl, I might have smiled. Responded to the flirtation with one of my own. But there is nothing simple about this girl. Or the laws I've broken to get her in here.

"I am no one to you." I turn away from the hurt I see in her eyes. "It's best you remember that, Siya ji."

A little before the sun is vertically overhead, I whistle for Dhoop to come back to me. The whistle is sharp, and, as a pony, Dhoop is trained to obey its call, though this will change as he and Malti grow older and they grow more independent as horse and rider. He trots back to me and licks my face.

The princess, on the other hand, appears put out. "So soon?"

"It will soon be time for your afternoon meal, Rajkumari," I say, smiling. "Aren't you hungry after your ride?"

Malti continues to pout. "I'm not that hungry!"

"Come, Rajkumari. We can't keep Cavas from his work at the stables, can we?" Gul is smiling at Malti as well, but there's a coolness to her tone now that wasn't there before. "Besides, it looks like it is going to rain soon."

She's right. Rain clouds, so far away when the morning began, approach swiftly now, a gentle rumble going through the sky. Malti sighs but doesn't argue anymore. The walk back to the stables is silent, hot despite the approach of the rain. By the time we reach the stables, a light drizzle begins, dampening the back of my tunic along with sweat. Another serving girl waits there, parasol in hand, to escort Malti back to the palace.

I expect Gul to leave with them, but to my surprise, she doesn't move, her gaze fixed somewhere behind me. I turn around to see what she's looking at and spy the three princes walking in the distance: Crown Prince Sonar, his cruel, handsome face laughing at something his brother, Prince Jagat, said. Lagging at the end is Prince Amar, his shoulders stooped from the weight of his thoughts.

I've seen many a serving girl pause at the sight of the princes, stare at them with open longing. Gul's face, however, looks the way it might if a levta in all its slimy glory leaped out of the mud and onto her lap.

A drop of rain slides down her cheek and then another. It has been relatively dry this Month of Tears—though the clouds seem to be making up for that now, soaking through our clothes.

"My supervisor told me that women cannot visit Raj Mahal without the raja's permission. Is that true?" Gul asks me.

"Yes. There is a rekha—a boundary you cannot cross in certain parts of Ambar Fort if you are a woman. There are exceptions, of course. Like the queens. But even the queens don't often go to Raj Mahal unless the king requests their presence."

Gul says nothing. A furrow appears in the space between her brows, making me wonder what she's thinking.

"It wasn't like that before." I recall the story Papa once told me. "Before Raja Lohar took the throne, Rani Mahal was the seat of power. Some say that the old queen, Megha, wanted another heir—a daughter."

Gul looks at me askance. "Rani Megha didn't have children of her own."

"That's the official version. But there were also rumors that she did have a child. An illegitimate female heir. When Megha died, Raja Lohar set out to quash the rumors by drawing every bit of power to himself. This included changing the succession to male heirs only. It's said that on her deathbed, Megha ranted and raved about a queen who would come, who would be the true ruler of Ambar. The palace vaids say that she had gone quite mad by then, of course."

There are other rumors, too—about how the king poisoned his way to the throne, killing every potential threat, including Rani Megha herself. But I don't say any of that out loud.

"Do you want to move out to the rain?" I ask, a few seconds before we get sprayed by more water and wind. We hasten to the shade of the stables, our feet leaving behind tracks in the earth that's now softening to mud, and stand in silence. Gul stares again into the distance, her lower lip caught between her teeth. I am tempted to smooth away the indents with my thumb.

A faint whistle weaves through the wind in a tune that sounds like a children's song—only it's like no children's song I've ever heard:

> *Rooh was born without a heart*
> *Some say without a soul*
> *But when he ripped his chest apart*
> *He found a girl of gold*

Gul frowns. "Did you hear . . ."

Her voice trails off, eyes locking with mine and widening. The wind shifts, spraying the roof—and us—with more fat drops of rain, but all

I can see is how one of them pauses in the parting of her hair before sliding into it like a melting jewel. Behind me, a door opens, followed by a voice:

"Cavas, I need you in here," Govind says. "The storm is making the horses anxious." Even though I can't see the stable master, I hear the disapproval in his voice. Feel it like a touch on my nape.

My hand, which was on its way to Gul's face, curls into a fist. I draw it back.

"Go on, boy," she says coldly with a swift glance behind me. "The stable master is looking for you."

It's the way she would behave if I were a stranger, exactly what I told her to do a little earlier today. I ignore the tightening of my heart, the bitterness I taste at the back of my throat. I give her a quick bow and walk toward Govind, who is waiting for me by the stable doors.

22

CAVAS

The rain grows vicious once I step inside, spewing from the sky like rice grains from a torn gunnysack. The wind howls. Water hammers the wood. Some of the horses whose stalls are closest to the windows get spooked, and it takes a long time for us to calm them down.

"You'd think they'd be used to it by now," a stable boy mutters, then jumps nearly a foot in the air when a flash of lightning splits the sky.

I'm filling a stallion's trough with new hay when I hear a throat clearing behind me.

"Have you thought of getting bound, boy?" Govind asks.

Heat crawls up my neck. I don't dare look into the stable master's shrewd eyes.

"You should find a good non-magus mate for yourself," he continues sternly when I say nothing. "At your age, I was already bound to my Kamala, and we were already on our way to becoming parents. A mated man is harder to distract from his work."

I nod. What girl will bind with someone who earns ten rupees a month, whose money goes entirely into keeping his sick father alive?

"You're a good boy," Govind says, a sudden, surprising pronouncement that makes me look up, even though he's frowning in the way he does before launching into a scold. "I don't want you to lose your way at the sound of a pretty laugh."

"I won't."

Even though my mind tells me it's too late for that. Too late since the time I first clashed eyes, then lips, then words with Gul. Too late since Latif ensnared me in this strange web of sorcery and deceit. But Govind does not know my thoughts. He simply nods and tells me to put more buckets outside to fill with fresh water.

The rain falls through most of the day, tapering off only when night falls, Sunheri a waning crescent in the sky. I squelch across the grass, mud coating the soles of my thin leather shoes. My stomach rumbles—the palace provides lunch to day workers like myself, but no evening meal, and I'm already longing for the onion pakodas Ruhani Kaki makes on rainy days in the tenements, along with moon-shaped rotis that fluff up to the size of a man's face.

I might have not noticed, perhaps not even cared about who else was around, if I hadn't heard the whistling again:

> The golden girl that Rooh found
> She had a heart of stone
> She caught his wrists and had him bound
> She chewed him to the bone

·This time the words are distinct, as clear as if they'd been whispered in my ear. A giggle breaks the haunting melody, and I spin in its direction, squinting against a sudden fog. Trailing the sound of the whistle around the back of the stables, I pause at the front of a small marble edifice near the queens' palace, a pair of moons filigreed over its entrance.

Chand Mahal. A palace forbidden to everyone except Queen Amba and the king—a palace the queen was rumored to use only on very special occasions. Every time I've passed Chand Mahal, the doors have been closed and the windows dark, not a sound emerging from within. Today, however, music floats out from a lit doorway—so loud that I wonder how no one else has heard it so far. Perhaps it's the fog that has obscured things, that now chills me on a night that was merely cool when I first stepped out of the stables.

Another giggle, followed by a finger lightly running down the center of my back. I spin in place and reach out, catching hold of something solid, something that, by the sound of the gasp it makes, might be human. The fog shifts, revealing gold eyes and frizzy black hair, a face whose shock likely reflects my own. Gul.

"What are you doing here?" I demand. "Were you the one singing?" *Did you touch me?*

"Do I look like a peri to you?" Gul's eyes narrow into slits. "I was going back into the palace when a fog appeared in front of me. A voice was coming from it, singing a strange song."

The back of my neck prickles. "I don't believe you."

"Believe what you want. I heard it this morning as well. Along with whistling."

Low-pitched and playful, the sound emerges again as if summoned by her words:

> *They heard Rooh's voice at the mountain bend*
> *They heard it in the bog*
> *They searched and scoured from end to end*
> *They lost him in the fog*

A series of childish giggles follow, and we both stare at the entrance, which glows so brightly the inside might as well hold two full moons.

"We should find someone," I say at last. "A guard."

"We should," she agrees.

But the fog is thick, and no matter where we turn, we end up at the entrance, a light giggle mocking us the whole time, singing bits and pieces of the song. I can't tell if the door is moving or if it's just the fog that's confusing me by turning everything else into a blur. *Tricky*, I remind myself. *This palace is tricky.*

"Looks like we don't have a choice." Gul pushes a strand of hair off her forehead. "Whoever it is wants us to go in."

I'm quiet for a long moment. "I'll go in first. See if it's safe."

Two steps in, a hand reaches out and grabs hold of mine. "No," she says firmly. "There's magic at work here. We'll go in together."

Another girl might have let me go. Might have even sent me in herself. But then I see a dagger blade gleaming green in her hands, the hard glint in her eyes. My mouth grows dry.

"Good thing I went to check on my weapons before dinner," she says. A tiny dimple creases her right cheek, one I'm sure I haven't seen before. "Grabbed one of these right when the fog hit and I heard that creepy song."

The pretty smile doesn't fool me. Gul holds the dagger like it's a part of her, her grip on the weapon relaxed and comfortable. Though I will never admit it out loud, I'm glad she's here with me right now.

"Right," I say. "Let's go in."

The moment we step into Chand Mahal, the lightorb overhead disappears. Moonlight pours in through the beehive windows, throwing shadows like lace over the ground. Mirrors embed the walls and the ceiling in octagons and tiny crescents, darkening only when our reflections fall on them. We are not alone. The singing, though softer now, is still audible. As if the thing that drew us in here is waiting. Watching.

"What do you want?" Gul asks sharply, and I know she can hear it, too. "Why did you bring us here?"

The singing stops abruptly, leaving behind a silence so thick it could choke.

Then, a laugh. Followed by a hand—a child's hand—appearing in thin air.

"Do you see that?" I murmur.

"See what?" Next to me, I hear Gul spinning, her feet squeaking once on the marble floor. "What are you talking about? I don't see anything."

"She will never be able to see what you see," the voice says. "Though she can hear me."

I stare at the hand, which now extends to an elbow and then a full arm. A girl with pigtails, perhaps half my size, appears slowly, wearing a tunic with a slash through the middle, dark liquid staining the edges of the tear. The grayish tinge to her skin is simultaneously familiar and skin-crawling.

"Did Latif send you?" I ask the girl.

She laughs—scornfully this time. "Latif is not my master. Neither is he the only one of us."

"There are *more* of you?" Who—*what*—is Latif?

"More of *who*?" Gul interrupts. Her eyes scan the room, looking past the gray-faced girl and focusing on empty space. "Cavas, what do you see?"

"It's a girl," I say slowly. "She's . . ." My voice trails off as I stare at the stain on her tunic, which is too dark to be anything but blood. "I think she's dead."

"We prefer the term *living specters*," the girl says. "Though, for your purposes, dead is also acceptable."

"That's impossible," Gul responds before I can. "Living specters can't be seen!" She spins around, not seeming to realize that her back is to the girl. "You're playing a trick on us with an invisibility spell! Show yourself before I force you to with my dagger!"

My skin prickles the way it does when warming after a chill. What Gul says makes perfect sense. Living specters are invisible to magi and non-magi, and the little girl's invisibility *should* be because of a spell. But then . . .

"If that is true, then how can *I* see her?" I ask. Invisibilty spells work exactly the same way on magi and non-magi. There is no way I could see someone Gul couldn't.

Gul frowns, opening her mouth to argue, but then shuts it almost at once. I can see realization sinking in, the incredulous look on her face replaced by a strange sort of understanding.

"Cavas, are you a see—"

"No," I cut in. It's not possible. I am not a seer. Or a half magus. Ma had no magical blood in her veins. Papa would have told me if she did.

Right?

I look at the little girl again—the living specter, as she calls herself. There is a strange smile on her small face.

"I'm non-magus," I tell her in a hard voice. "Both of my parents are non-magi."

"*If that is true, then how can I see her?*" she mocks back. Gul winces, covering her ears to muffle the sound of her high-pitched voice.

"I have not come here to go delve into your messy family history, Seer," the living specter tells me. "I have only come to deliver a simple message to you both: Stick together, no matter what happens. *Do you hear me, Savak-putri Gulnaz?*" Her last sentence reverberates, pulses in my ears.

I turn to Gul, who has paled on hearing her full name. "Yes," she whispers. "I hear you."

Around us, the wind howls like a dustwolf. The little girl begins disappearing again, rapidly, her legs fading to her knees. Gul tugs on my arm, her mouth moving, forming my name. But I can't hear her. The young girl's voice is the only one audible in this wind:

> *Rooh the lost, Rooh the loon*
> *You cannot touch his soul*
> *But see him in a bright-blue moon*
> *And a star will turn him whole.*

By the time the last word is sung, the girl is already gone, her mouth the last bit of her to disappear.

"She's gone, isn't she?" Gul breaks the silence, her voice soft, quivering.

"Yes. I can't see her anymore." I shake my head. "Though I don't know *why* exactly I could see her in the first place. And *no*," I snap the last word as Gul opens her mouth again. "I know what you're thinking, but I'm not a seer! I've lived in the tenements my whole life. My parents are non-magi."

"Are you sure about that?" Gul asks quietly.

My hands turn cold, sweat beading the palms. *Whore. Slut. You know nothing about your mother or the sacrifices she made.*

"Don't you dare question me about my family, magus!"

Anger flashes in Gul's eyes for a brief instant and then, almost immediately, dissipates. *Someone's coming*, she mouths before placing a finger to her lips.

A second later, I hear the footsteps.

The light metal tap of a Sky Warrior's boots.

23

GUL

The dagger, sensing the shift in my mood, begins to glow in my hand. Glancing at Cavas, I tilt my head sideways, gesturing to an arched doorway jutting from the wall. I am hoping for an exit, but it merely leads to another room, a gallery full of miniature paintings I might have appreciated had it not been for the blue-and-silver bodies reflected in the arch's tiny mirrors.

Two Sky Warriors. I press into the wall, willing myself to disappear into it. My hand brushes Cavas's arm. He doesn't pull away.

"No one appears to be here," someone says after a pause. A voice, low and musical, embedded in nearly every innocuous dream I've had over the past two years as well as my nightmares. "You better not be mistaken about this."

"I—I swear I saw them, Major," a man responds. A new recruit, I sense, from his stammer.

It's only when Cavas makes a small sound—a grunt of pain—that I realize my nails are digging into his arm. I loosen my grip and glance sideways in apology when I see the expression on his face. Terror. The kind that blanches color from skin and lips, that loosens bladders without warning.

I hear the Scorpion prefers boys serving her.

The words made me angry before, and they make me angry now. The fury helps, slows the racing beat of my own heart. My hand slides down, curls around his.

I will not let her hurt you, I think, and instinctively I know this is true. Somewhere between the moment I first kissed this boy at the moon festival and now, he has become important to me. Even though I don't like thinking about why.

The shield spell I mastered with Amira will be useless in a battle with two fully armed Sky Warriors. As for the attacking spell—even though I performed it during my test, I'm not even sure I could do it right now, or control it effectively if I did. The best thing at this stage would be to disappear—to become a living specter without dying in the process.

Use your mind, Amira always told me while doing magic. So I draw on every kernel of my will, calling on whatever bits of power I have running through my veins.

I want us to disappear, I think. *To vanish from their sight.*

Warmth rushes from the birthmark on my arm to my hands. Cavas must feel the heat as well, because his fingers tighten around mine in a sudden, painful moment. A strange, tingling sensation crawls up my wrist. When I look down, I see that Cavas's hand is glowing white where mine glows gold. The white light pulses, traveling from his hand to mine, then up my arm, up my neck. It pauses at my throat, bright and hot, sealing my breath in my lungs.

"M-major. D-did you hear that?"

"What?" Major Shayla's voice sharpens.

"It's . . . it's coming from this room, M-major."

They step into the room.

And stare right at us.

It's the first time I put a face to the voice of my parents' murderer. Where the major's voice is like disjointed music, her beauty is like flawed marble, cruelty lining the smile of her perfect red mouth, gleaming in her eyes. Her movements, likely due to her training as a Sky Warrior, are precise and economical, as carefully crafted as her closely cropped gray hair and the three firestones glinting in her left ear.

No. This is not a woman to be trifled with.

The other Sky Warrior—a boy who appears no older than Cavas—stays in the major's shadow, his shoulders shrinking even as I widen my stance and raise my dagger exactly the way I would at Yudhnatam practice, the way I did only three weeks ago with Amira. Major Shayla spins on the heel of her steel-toed boot and backhands her companion. Hard.

"First you see things others don't," she says. "Now you hear them, too? Do it another time and I'll be the one who fills in your application at the asylum."

"Major, I swear I saw shadows near the window!"

"Shadows," she scoffs. Her cold, pale-brown eyes stare right through me at the painting on the wall behind. "Next you'll be telling me that you saw the Pashu king Subodh risen from the dead."

She stalks out, her boots tapping the sangemarmar tiles, her blue-and-silver tunic swishing in the air. The other Sky Warrior glances our way one last time before following her out. It's not until the door to Chand Mahal closes that my grip on the magic loosens. My tongue unravels, a strange thickness to it, and my body tingles, as if doused in warm water after being frozen for a long time.

I turn to Cavas. "What happened?"

"I don't know what you're talking about." He lets go of my hand as if burned.

Had we not evaded the most bloodthirsty Sky Warrior I've ever come across, I might have been kinder and left the interrogation for another day. "You turned us invisible."

"That was you." His voice is sharp, as harsh as it had been the morning Juhi and I first went to him for help. "You and your magic tricks. I had nothing to do with it."

"That was no trick," I tell him. "Your being able to see that living specter wasn't a trick, either." Cavas turns away from me, and I know he does not want to believe me. But I know what I heard. I saw the way Cavas's head had moved—his eyes always focusing exactly where the specter's voice came from. I know what I felt when I wished for us to disappear—finding Cavas's magic drawn to mine like sparks, strengthening our combined powers into a flame.

"Something happened between us today," I say. "Something that's far too big to be ignored. As for those living specters—I think I might have heard one of them months ago at an inn in Javeribad. Maybe it was the one you called Latif. Maybe it was someone else. But they led me to the moon festival, saying that someone there would help me get into the palace. I think it was you I was supposed to meet, Cavas. It was you all along." As I speak the words, my confidence grows. I may not have solid proof, but my gut tells me I'm on the right track.

"You're dreaming. I was not at the moon festival to meet you. It was sheer coincidence that I even saw you there." But his fists are clenched, and he doesn't meet my gaze.

"It can't be coincidence that your father is the one Juhi wanted me to see!" I prod. "It can't be coincidence that the specter brought us here together with her singing. There *must* be some reason we keep connecting time and time again."

"There is no connection between us. There is no prophecy, no *jantar-mantar* involved," he says coldly, emphasizing jantar-mantar, a phrase used to describe illusions, cheap tricks that have nothing to do with magic at all. "I don't know what the living specters are up to, but I didn't bring you here because I believe in some fabled Star Warrior. You are no more to me except a means to an end."

If he means to slice into me with those words, he succeeds. Brilliantly. But he underestimates me if he expects me to burst into tears and act wounded. Instead of walking away from him, I move closer, slow enough that he has enough opportunity to get away, to dodge my approach if he wants to.

He doesn't.

A heat that has nothing to do with the weather or with magic simmers under my skin, reflects in his darkening pupils.

I'm not sure who makes the first move. All I know is that in the next moment, I'm pressed into the space between two paintings, his hand flat on my lower back, anger fusing his lips to mine. I welcome the rage, match it with my own: bite for bite, kiss for kiss. Somehow I know no matter how angry he is, Cavas will not hurt me.

Not physically at least.

My mind issues warnings about magi and non-magi, curses and boundaries, staying away and avoiding big mistakes.

My body takes over, ignoring the warnings. It welcomes the unsteady beat of my heart, the liquid heat between my thighs. It grows malleable, anger fading to a background hum. For a long moment, all I can think of is the skin right above my clavicle that he's gently tracing with his tongue.

"Is this a means to an end, too?" The words slip out, my mind winning for the moment.

He raises his head. Anger flashes on his face once more. Underneath that, there's something else. An emotion he shutters with a blink of his eyes before I can put a name to it.

I didn't say anything wrong. Surely, after the things he said, my cruelty is justified.

So why do I feel guilty when he stalks out of Chand Mahal?

Why does it feel as if I've lost?

24
GUL

Somehow, I keep my wits intact and return my dagger to its hiding place in the garden before heading to the palace again.

Rain pours in torrents the next morning, the clouds overhead blacker than Queen Amba's mood. Before the end of the afternoon, a serving girl leaves the queen's chambers in tears, blood trickling down both nostrils.

"Whoever said things look better in the morning was lying through their teeth," I hear another servant mutter while sweeping the lobby floor, and I can't help but agree. The morning also does nothing to improve my guilt over what happened with Cavas in Chand Mahal.

Cavas isn't wrong when he says we aren't friends. Though the living specter specifically told us to stick together, being around me can only get Cavas into trouble. As selfish as I am in many ways, trouble is the last thing I want for this boy. It's why, when the weather clears up the next day, I make it a point to keep my eyes averted from his when we head out with Princess Malti for her usual pony ride, saying nothing other than a curt "Shubhdivas" at the end.

The stormy weather makes nighttime wanderings impossible. As tempted as I am to go check on my daggers, I know it will be difficult to explain the mud I drag in from the garden and into the servants' quarters. When I'm not thinking about my daggers or Cavas, my thoughts wander to the rekha that divides Ambar Fort in two, separating Raj Mahal from the women. Over the next couple of days, I strike up a rapport with one of the serving girls, attempt a few of the same questions I asked Yukta Didi before getting shut down.

"The rekha? It's supposed to begin in the middle of the garden, I think," she tells me. "I can't say exactly where, though."

"Wouldn't someone be in danger of crossing it by accident, then? If it was invisible?" I ask.

"Oh no!" She laughs. "As a barrier, the rekha is far too strong. Its magic will burn you if you attempt it, so I wouldn't even try. Why are you so interested, anyway?"

"She probably wants Yuvraj Sonar's attention again," another serving girl says before I can answer. "Probably thinks she can be made the crown princess if she tries hard enough. Don't hold your breath, girl. If you're lucky, you might be made the yuvraj's concubine. If Rani Amba doesn't kill you first."

As puke-inducing as her comments are, I keep quiet, hoping she'll equate my silence with embarrassment. Her laughter follows me out of the room, echoes in my ears, as I lead Malti to the stable for her usual ride.

"You don't look too happy this morning," a male voice says, sounding amused.

My heart skips a beat and then sinks when I realize it's not Cavas.

"Rajkumar Amar." I bow. "I apologize. I didn't see you."

"She has been in a bad mood for the past two days," Malti informs her brother. I scowl at her, but she simply widens her eyes, unperturbed. "You *are*, Siya. You didn't even laugh at my joke about the acharya, the fishmonger, and the Zaalian innkeeper."

"Where did you hear that joke?" Amar asks sternly, even though the corners of his mouth twitch under his mustache.

218

"The stable boys." Malti grins. "Though I didn't understand the part about the fishmonger's eel—"

"That's enough!" The alarm on his face nearly makes me smile. "Wait. How about . . . this?"

To my surprise, he kneels and picks up a dried blade of grass. He spins it until it transforms into a pale-pink flower I've never seen before. "An orchid from Jwala," he says, presenting it to a delighted Malti, who insists that he give me a flower as well.

"There's no need," I begin, but Amar is already bending, picking up a handful of dried earth this time, his hands glowing orange. Buds sprout from it, the bright orange of a sunset, the gold of newly hammered swarnas. Ambari roses burst into bloom before my very eyes. I don't know why I flush when he hands them to me or why I'm suddenly aware of the stable boys whispering behind us. What makes me even more self-conscious is what—or who—I see behind Amar: Cavas, leading Malti's pony out of the stable.

"Thank you, Rajkumar," I say finally. "That is the finest bit of conjuring I've seen in a while." I stare at the flowers, unsure if I'm supposed to take them and the dirt right out of his hands, when Amar smoothly deposits them into a pot, which has appeared out of thin air.

"You needn't flatter me, Siya ji. There are better conjurers out there."

"No, there aren't!" Malti tells Amar. "Bhaiyya, you're the best conjurer in the world! You can make things appear out of nothing!"

Her words make me strangely uncomfortable. In this proper, pretentious world of titles, where a queen's own children don't forget to add the word *rani* before *Ma*, it's almost jarring to hear the affection in Malti's voice, to hear her call Amar *bhaiyya* the way any other girl would her brother.

It doesn't matter, I tell myself. *They are still royals. The children of a man who has ripped hundreds of siblings apart with his atrocities.*

"I'm not the best conjurer in the world." Amar gives me an embarrassed grin. "There are things I'm not good at, magic I haven't quite perfected even in the realm of conjuring." Behind us, Dhoop whinnies. "And if I continue talking, you won't be able to go on your ride," he continues. "Be good, Malti. Siya ji, I'll have the flowers delivered to your room."

"That's not necessary," I say. Goddess knows what the other serving girls will say when they see flowers arriving for me!

"They will be for everyone to enjoy," he says, as if sensing my thoughts. "Shubhdivas, Siya ji."

"Shubhdivas, Rajkumar." I bow, feeling the heat of Cavas's gaze.

"Siya, your face is red," Malti comments.

"It's the sun."

"But—"

"Come along now. We've made Dhoop wait long enough," I say hastily before she can point out that the sun hasn't even made an appearance today and that the weather itself is quite pleasant, if not cool. Amar's interest in me also makes me uneasy. Yes, there's interest here. Something I should take advantage of. That I *would* take advantage of—if not for the figure in white walking ahead of me, the king's seal embedded in his orange turban.

I'm so busy watching Cavas that I don't pay attention to where I'm going and trip over my own foot, landing face-first in a puddle left by the recent rain. I don't know what's worse: the mud dripping down my chin when I finally rise to my feet, Malti's bell-like laughs, or Cavas's hovering over me, amusement battling with concern on his face.

"Laugh more, will you?" I don't bother hiding the irritation in my voice. "The rest of the palace hasn't heard."

Malti stuffs her fists into her mouth.

"Do you want to go back and clean up?" Cavas asks quietly. It's the first time in three days that he's spoken to me in a tone that isn't dismissive, and I'm annoyed by how happy it makes me.

"I'd better not." I lower my voice so that Malti doesn't hear. "Rani Amba is on the warpath this week. She might send me to prison for muddying her precious sangemarmar floors."

A laugh booms out of him, surprising both of us. My heart, stupid thing, begins to thrum—even more so when he pulls the checkered cloth off his shoulder and offers it to me. "It's clean. Washed it this morning."

"Thanks." The cloth smells of lye, honeyweed, and horses. I try not to bury my face in the scent.

We walk the remaining way in silence, but it doesn't feel as strained as it was the day before. It's not until Malti begins galloping with Dhoop that I speak again.

"I'm sorry. For what happened in Chand Mahal."

"For the kiss?" he asks quietly.

"Yes—I mean, no!" I flush when his gaze locks with mine. "Are *you* sorry?"

"No." He doesn't look away, though I think I see red creeping up his neck. "I'm sorry for what I said to you, though. About being a means to an end. I was . . . frustrated, I suppose. I took it out on you."

If it leads to more kisses, I don't mind so much. I don't voice the thought out loud, but something about my expression must have tipped him off, because he smiles again.

"You should smile more," I say. "It improves your face."

He laughs.

"Why were you frustrated?" I ask after a pause.

He frowns, turning away to watch Malti and Dhoop for a while. "There is a . . . man—or at least I thought he was a man—whom I meet up with from time to time. You heard me mention his name at Chand Mahal the other night: Latif. He looks a bit like the girl who spoke to us there. Gray eyes. Gray skin. Strangely . . . colorless. Latif was the one who convinced me to bring you to the palace. After what happened at Chand Mahal, I wanted answers. But Latif hasn't answered me the way he usually does when we communicate. Come to think of it, he was ignoring me before that as well."

A living specter. The words hover unspoken in the air, a mammoth in a tiny room. I can't help but feel queasy. *What do the living specters want with* me? As for this Latif. Now that Cavas mentions him again, his name sounds familiar, as if I've heard it somewhere, spoken by someone else before.

Queen's curses, why can't I remember? No wonder Amira calls me useless.

"That must have taken some convincing," I tell Cavas. "You hated me."

"I never hated you, Gul." A slight smile. "But yes, Latif promised me something if I got you in here. Usually he lives up to his promises fairly quickly, but I haven't been able to get hold of him again." Cavas pauses, his smile fading. "I haven't been able to stop thinking about what that girl said. About how she is a living specter. There's a part of me that wants to ask Papa directly, but he's been so ill lately, so tired. I just . . . couldn't."

My mind races, picking out something that I remember Cavas mentioning before. "You told Juhi that your father has Tenement Fever. Is there no cure for it?"

"No. Tenement Fever doesn't go away—unless you leave the tenements. If my contact doesn't live up to his promise, then I'll have no choice but to join the army. It's the only way I can get out. Get Papa to a safer place."

My elbows tighten painfully; I realize I've been gripping them hard with my hands. The army. "Cavas, that's—"

"I know what you're thinking. My father doesn't approve, either. He promised I'd see him dead if I ever joined." He gives me another smile, but this one doesn't reach his eyes. "I don't know what's worse—that, or to see him die little by little every day."

I say nothing for a long moment. That Cavas would be willing to pledge his loyalty to a ruler who has done nothing for non-magi except torture them baffles me.

Or does it?

I try to imagine myself in Cavas's shoes. Imagine what it would have been like if my parents were still alive, but desperately ill.

"I don't like it, but I understand why you'd make that choice," I say finally, meaning the words. "It's always easier to defy someone when you have nothing to lose."

Cavas says nothing in response, but a moment later, I feel the back of his hand brushing mine.

Push it away, Gul, a voice in my head warns. *Push his hand away before someone sees and reports you to Yukta Didi.*

But then Cavas's thumb brushes my wrist, and I stop thinking of everything except for the warmth of his skin, of my own quickening pulse. It's how we stand, for several long moments, until Malti and Dhoop slow down to a trot, and we're forced again to break apart.

Queen Amba summons me to her chambers the next morning. I pause outside the ornately carved door—this one with designs of a river, a sunlit orchard, and a lion—and lightly knock.

"Enter."

Amba sits on cushions next to a large mirror, wearing a ghagra-choli of the palest pink. Right behind her, a servant pulls up sections of her wet hair, holding a fragrant pot of burning incense underneath. If the queen was planning an interrogation, she certainly isn't dressed for it. Heartbeat slowly steadying, I bow low.

"Yes, yes, enough of that," Amba says impatiently. "You'll accompany Rajkumari Malti in the garden today. She's had enough riding this week. You'll find her in the gold room with her tutor."

"Yes, Rani Amba." My jaw unclenches. She doesn't know about me and Cavas. No one knows. Except perhaps Princess Malti.

As Queen Amba said, I find Malti waiting for me in the gold room with her doll. A tall woman wearing the long saffron robes of a scholar stands next to her, holding several scrolls in her hands.

"Are you ready for your walk, Rajkumari?" The tutor's smile does not reach her eyes.

"Yes, ma'am," the princess answers demurely.

Today, Malti is dressed in yellow and white, tiny daisies embellishing her blouse and ghagra and the ends of her two braids. Her eyes glint with mischief when she sees me, and I force myself to suppress a smile.

"Here." The tutor hands me a yellow-and-white parasol. Her mouth looks like it has been perpetually sucking on sour grapes. "Make sure the rajkumari does not get a sunburn."

She does not see Princess Malti's scowl or hear the groan she makes later when we are left alone.

"I hate that thing," she says, pointing to the parasol. "It doesn't let me play!"

"We'll have to take it with us to the garden, Rajkumari. Perhaps you can play under a shady tree?" I suggest. The last serving girl who let Malti play without a parasol had left Queen Amba's room in blood and tears.

She grimaces, unconvinced.

I glance around uneasily before quietly saying: "I don't want to get into trouble." *Not before I kill your father at least.*

My stomach twists. *I should not feel guilty,* I tell myself. King Lohar is a murderer. A man responsible for the destruction of so many families, including my own. The royal family, from what I've seen of them, are little better.

Except Amar. And Malti.

Malti reminds me of the girl I was. The girl who had to learn what it's like to lose a father. I push away the last thought. A pair of female guards discreetly flank the main entrance to the garden. The moment we step inside, one of them leaves her position and shadows us from about six feet away. Malti leans over to sniff an Ambari rose.

"Siya! Look here!"

As I crouch down, she whispers: "Do you want to lose her? The guard?"

I am careful to keep my body relaxed, even though my senses are suddenly on high alert. I lean over and sniff the flower lightly, my nose brushing its yellow-red petals. Losing the guard would allow me to look around the garden more closely, perhaps even spot where the rekha is.

"How?" My voice is little more than a breath, released softly in the air.

Malti grins. "Watch me."

She lets go of my hand and begins twirling on glowing feet. I leap back to avoid being hit by the shower of gravel she kicks up, along with grass and dirt—so much of it and so high in the air that she's completely obscured. And then, the dirt collapses, and Malti is gone, leaving behind a hole in the ground—one in which I instinctively knew she would never hide. The guard—a woman with gray streaks in her hair—races in my direction.

"You fool!" she says. "Why did you let go of the rajkumari's hand? Now we'll have to spend hours searching for her again!"

I say nothing, even though I suddenly spot Malti perched on a high tree branch, holding her finger to her lips.

"Have you lost your tongue?" the guard demands. She curses under her breath. "Check the west end. I will look in the east end and also outside, in case she's slipped out again."

Once the guard is out of sight, I look up at the tree and nod.

Malti lightly drops to the ground and grins.

"Nice trick," I say. "Where did you learn that?"

"I've always been able to do it. It's why Rani Ma makes me wear these." She holds up a pair of simple ankle bands set with tiny polished gray pebbles. "They hold in my magic. Here—you can touch."

I run a finger over the smooth links of metal, the mirror like polish on the pebbles. My mind slows the way it does on drinking a sleep draught, limbs tiring so rapidly that I'm forced to drop my hand and draw in a breath. Even a light touch makes me feel as if something vital within me is being drawn out, reined in. But Malti doesn't seem to notice my discomfort.

She puts the anklets back on and smiles. "Can we play now?"

I lean the parasol against the tree. "Of course we can."

Malti chooses hide-and-seek, a game I've always been terrible at when it comes to the seeking. I think I spot a glimpse of yellow in a tree, but on closer observation, note it's only a small bird on a branch nearly level with my eyes. Instead of flying away, it tilts its head, staring at me with its black-black eyes.

"Aren't you pretty?" I whisper.

It whistles, and I am tempted to believe it understands me. Birds are harder to establish a connection with than other animals, and unlike insects, they cannot be easily controlled with whisper magic.

"Do you know where Rajkumari Malti is?"

It whistles again and suddenly takes off, startling me. I'm about to follow when a voice from the other side of the hedge behind me stops me in my tracks.

"The general is in the Brim again, isn't he?" Major Shayla asks, her voice careless, lazy. "I could take advantage of that, I suppose. Find that dirt-licking stable boy he's so fond of . . ."

Another voice murmurs in response: a man.

All thoughts of the bird and the princess have evaporated from my head. As silently as possible, I head in the opposite direction, alongside the hedge, trying to keep track of the voices moving on the other side. A few moments later, I find myself before a doorway with a pointed arch carved into the hedge—apparently, the entrance to a maze. There are no guards in sight.

Tricky, Cavas called the palace and its magic. The kind that makes you slip up. The kind that betrays. Then again, when has my own magic not betrayed me? I step forward, brushing aside the strange ticklish sensation that comes with crossing the threshold—a disturbance in the air that vanishes the moment I step onto the other side.

226

A KING AND A CAGE

25
GUL

This is not a maze. This is not even an extension of the garden.

While Rani Mahal is a blushing sunset pink, this palace reflects every color, every shift in the sky's mood, its towers, domes, and finials made entirely of glass. I glimpse a figure running down a corridor when the light in the sky shifts, turning the window into a mirror. Though I haven't seen it before, I know it's the king's palace. Heart racing, I spin around, only to find the hedge sealed over, the doorway I came through gone.

"Well, well. What do we have here?"

A hand grabs me by the arm. My wrists and ankles are shackled before I have time to take another breath.

"I thought I heard a trespasser." Major Shayla's voice is soft, almost amused. "What's your name, girl?"

When I don't answer, she holds my jaw in a painful grip. "I asked what your name was."

"S-siya," I force out.

Behind her, I see another familiar face: Prince Amar, whose eyes widen on seeing me.

"What are you doing here, girl?" His voice is so stern that, for a moment, I wonder if he even recognizes me. "Don't you know it's forbidden to cross the rekha? Who let you through?"

"N-no one. I d-didn't know that *was* the rekha," I finally stutter. I think back to the doorway, wonder at why it sealed off again. "I was looking for Rajkumari Malti and thought she might be here."

"A common girl with a common name, sliding through a magical barrier as if it's air. Strange, isn't it, Rajkumar?" Major Shayla says. "Someone might think there is a security breach."

"Palace security is *your* jurisdiction, Major," Prince Amar reminds her, his voice cold.

Shayla ignores him and stares at me, as if trying to whittle out my secrets.

Cavas would advise me to act meek. To plead for my life and hide any strength I have. But I stare right back at the major, years of anger burning through. My fingers itch for my daggers. Or anything remotely sharp.

She turns around and nods at someone else, a gray-haired Sky Warrior accompanying the prince. "Put her in confinement. Let her fight for her freedom in the cage tomorrow."

"The cage?" Prince Amar glances at me quickly. "Is that really necessary? Perhaps Rajkumari Malti—"

"As you rightly said, palace security is *my* jurisdiction," Major Shayla interrupts with a sneer. "Hence, I must treat her the way I would any trespasser."

"You can't put her through the cage for a foolish mistake!" Prince Amar sounds angry now, even a little afraid. "She won't survive it!"

"That remains to be seen, doesn't it?"

Major Shayla's fingers slide down to my throat and tighten in a way that I know will leave bruises. I force myself to stay still and not wince.

She smiles. "Ah, yes. This one will be good for entertainment."

The gray-haired Sky Warrior leads me away from Raj Mahal to another building in the distance, red dust layered over its rough stone surface.

"Come," he says, and my body turns of its own accord, drawn by the magic in the shackles Major Shayla placed on my wrists. Shackles can be used in varying ways: to shock, to tame, to control. I've read that in prisons, the slightest movement can set off a shackle, turning a prisoner into a mess of nerves. I've also read that shackles can be broken if you try hard enough. The only problem: When I was living with the Sisters, I never tried breaking a shackle. Never thought my magic strong enough.

A few feet from the building, the Sky Warrior pauses. "Go in."

I frown. The building, shaped roughly like a square, has an open door and no guards. The queasy sensation I had on touching Princess Malti's anklet returns. *No*, my body rebels. *Don't go in.* A shock—both familiar and painful—goes through my wrists and ankles.

"It will be worse if you don't get in before dark." The Sky Warrior's face is serious, a map of hard lines. "Go on."

The shackles force me to step forward one foot at a time. When I try to resist the shackles' command, a blade of pain burns down my torso. It's not until I'm inside the building's threshold that the pain eases, a moment of sheer relief followed by sudden, unexpected exhaustion. In a moment or two, I'm on my knees, longing to lie on the tiled floor. *Why am I so tired? What's going on?* The more I try to focus on my surroundings, the more my vision blurs. *It's this building*, I realize. Confinement, as they call it. A place that drains you of energy, that prevents you from moving or using magic.

Better designed than any prison cell.

"I will be back for you at dawn," the Sky Warrior says a second before I slide to the floor in a deep sleep.

In my dreams that night, I see many things:

A woman with my mother's voice, stroking my hair, telling me a story about the beginnings of the universe.

The sky goddess on a throne made of air and clouds, spinning a sunlit chakra on a forefinger.

A boy in a plumed turban, firestones gleaming at his ears, the mustache stark on his pale face. *Wake up*, he says. *Wake up, Siya ji.*

I am in a room of starlight and shadow. *Gul*, a boy's voice says. I turn and reach for his hand, but all I feel against my fingers is stone.

When the morning comes, the Sky Warrior returns for me. A shock runs through the shackles, rousing me from my stupor.

"Come," he says. Another shock. "Quickly now."

I cling to his voice, to the stinging sensation on my wrists, and force myself to move out of the stone building.

"Here." A kachori appears before my eyes, and suddenly my mouth begins to water. I grab hold of the pastry and stuff it into my mouth. Onions burst on my tongue, sweet and savory at the same time. Once I finish, the Sky Warrior gives me another kachori. And then another. When he hands me a fourth kachori, I raise a hand. *No more.*

"Do you plan to die in the cage?"

The sharp words make me look up, focus on his face again, the rugged planes of it, silver tinting parts of his shaggy black brows. Papa would have had brows like that, I think, if he had lived long enough.

I take the kachori. "Sau aabhaar."

"There's no need to thank me. You are to be the entertainment today, remember? And there's no entertainment without a fight."

The words are an echo of Major Shayla's, but they do not have the same effect. Perhaps it's because of the look on his face—the subtle tightening of his lips right before he turns away. There is a gentle tug at my shackles, forcing me to move sideways, like a wayward pet brought to heel.

"The cage," I say, suddenly remembering the conversation I overheard between the serving girls on my very first day here. "The palace buys prizefighters at the flesh market, doesn't it? To fight us in the cage?"

The Sky Warrior glances at me but says nothing.

Who am I fighting? I wonder. *Or what?*

The glass palace rises before us, teasing with glimpses of what could be inside: a throne, a king, a crown of firestones and pearls, imminent death. The Sky Warrior makes a sharp left, the magical bond between us pulling me along. He nods at a burly guard posted by the side entrance.

"Any more coming in today, Captain Emil?" the guard asks without even glancing at me.

"No," the Sky Warrior says. "She's the last of today's lot."

I might have missed what he said to me next had I not been following him close enough, might have mistaken the frown on his face for indifference.

"Win the crowd, girl. It's the only way you'll win your freedom."

26
GUL

The inside of the king's palace makes Rani Mahal look like a relic from Svapnalok's past. Reflecting Ambar's desert heritage, enormous, iridescent palm trees form the pillars of a long tunnel, their false fronds curving overhead, weaving together to scatter bits of sunlight filtering in through the web of indradhanush and glass. The marble floor, though flat, looks like sand, glitters the way the desert might in the sunlight, with shifting dunelike patterns across the ground. At the very end of the tunnel is a giant metal box with bars surrounding every side, except the top and bottom.

"Steady," Captain Emil says, before ushering me in and shutting the door. He raises his head upward and cries out: "Lift!"

Barely a moment later, the box gives a sudden jerk as if tipping to the side. I grab onto one of the bars and hold tight. The box rises in the air, Captain Emil's legs disappearing first from sight, then his torso, then his head. I look above, but the roof is a mirror. I see only myself: my hair matted in strands around my terrified face.

A few moments later, the box rises into a room larger than any I've ever seen before.

This is not just a room, I realize. *This is the throne room.* The raj darbar, where the king holds his court.

Lightorbs glow overhead, brighter than the real sun, which is also warming the room. Rows upon rows of courtiers sit on elevated cushions, their eyes focused on me. My gaze, however, is drawn to the very center of the room's end, to a giant glass dome affixed with moons and suns and hundreds of planets.

Underneath, I spot a man dressed in a deep-green angrakha and narrow trousers, raised on a gilded throne over everyone else, perched cross-legged on a set of giant red cushions. Gold dusts his high cheekbones over a pure-white mustache and beard. Pink conch pearls adorn his neck and ears and hang in tassels from his waistbelt. Tucked into the center of his emerald turban is an ornament I've only seen in paintings before: an enormous teardrop firestone set in gold and plumed with ostrich feathers, flames leaping within the gem's many brilliant facets. Though I can't make out his eyes at this distance, I feel them watching as a guard rolls open the doors of the box.

King Lohar. Seventy-fifth ruler of Ambar and the Desert of Dreams. He's a man I've killed in a hundred different ways in my imagination over the past two years. A slit throat. A poisoned cup. An atashban blasted through the heart.

A shock goes through my shackles.

"Move!" the guard says.

I step out of the box and into the throne room. In person, the king does not look as imposing as he does in paintings, his cheeks hollow where they should be round, his limbs bony and weak where they should be muscled. Long fingers curl around the armrests of his throne like claws; indeed, with the beaked nose, he looks less like a man and more like a decrepit bird. Only his dark-brown eyes are the same, small and cruel as they take me in from head to toe, then he waves a hand, dismissing me entirely. The guard ushers me to the side, next to a man who is similarly shackled.

"Is that everything, Acharya?" the king asks.

"Yes, Ambarnaresh." The voice belongs to the high priest: a tall man with shoulder-length black hair. Unlike acharyas in temples, who wear plain cotton robes and no jewelry, the king's high priest wears a floor-length white tunic made of silk, gold hoops in his ears, and a priceless necklace of pale-green jade.

"Let's begin," the king commands. "We've waited long enough."

The acharya bows deeply and then turns to face the audience.

"Lords and ladies of the court. Thank you for attending the spectacle. This month's contenders include a thief who stole bread from the royal kitchens, a soldier accused of treason, and a serving girl who overstepped her boundaries by crossing the rekha."

I break out in a cold sweat, hoping my shock doesn't show itself. Are stealing bread and treason punished in the same way now? What kind of justice *is* this?

Applause rings through the court. A few men bay like dustwolves, the loudest among them the crown prince and his brother. Prince Amar sits next to them, a blue jewel gleaming in his turban. He's the only one who shows no sign of excitement. To avoid their gazes, I glance upward, spotting a gallery where a group of women stands. Even from this distance, I can make out Queen Amba's rigid stance, feel the chill of her gaze on me.

"Today, these challengers will fight with a preselected opponent in the cage," the high priest continues once the noise dies down. "Losing will mean death. *Winning*, on the other hand, will mean freedom."

A few men jeer from the audience. My gaze falls on a figure on the periphery of the crowd, right next to Major Shayla. Captain Emil, his face stern.

Win the crowd, girl.

Ministers and courtiers are placing bets with a servant holding a long scroll of parchment. A hundred swarnas. Two hundred. Six hundred.

The numbers blur in my head, lose meaning, when the acharya raises his arms in the air, parting the floor several feet from the king.

My skin crawls at the sound: a hiss followed by the screech of metal against metal. It reminds me of being trapped in the box again, except what emerges from the ground is even bigger. A giant golden cage, wrought out of bars more elaborate than the one that brought me into court.

Inside the cage is an animal I'd seen only once before as a child, its teeth gleaming at me in the moonlight, moments before my mother snatched me back into our house. A shadowlynx, with eyes the color of sand. Horns emerge from the top of its skull, two pointed spirals that rise in the air from behind its ears. They are exactly the shape of my seaglass dagger blades. My heart sinks, and I desperately wish I had my weapons with me. The giant feline bares its teeth at its opponent: the man who was standing next to me only a moment earlier, his shackles nowhere in sight, his hands gripping a spear and shield. A doorway opens—barely big enough to let him squeeze into the cage.

"You may want to close your eyes, serving girl," someone shouts at me from the audience.

I keep them open and watch the man raise the spear in the air. The shadowlynx bares its teeth and then suddenly disappears from sight, except for its shadow, which shows up against the bars when the light falls over it. The man tenses but does not lower the spear. He lunges to the side. A yowl rends the air.

The man screams next, and it's only when he turns his back that I see the three long scratches marring it. He lunges again, but this time, the shadowlynx is too quick. His spear hits only the bars. In the next moment or two, I wish I'd listened to the person who warned me to close my eyes. A few groans erupt behind me when the man's throat twists sideways, fresh blood running down it. I know he's dead before he even falls to the ground, before the shadowlynx appears before us again, licking its paws clean. The cage disappears into the ground once more.

King Lohar's mouth purses. "Not very entertaining, was he? Bring out the next one, Acharya."

"Yes, Ambarnaresh."

The cage rises again, this time holding a much smaller creature. I feel myself stiffen. It's the young woman I saw at the flesh market in Ambarvadi—the one who made butterflies emerge from her fingertips. Her opponent is a man twice her size, his body marked with knife scars. The type who could crush her neck with one hand.

There's a grim look on his face. For a moment, I think he isn't going to fight her, but then he raises his spiked mace high in the air. As if from a distance, I hear Juhi's voice the way it was in the schoolroom, going over the different weapons used in the Three-Year War—"Ambari mace. Heavier than an atashban, but easier to wield. The spikes, if poisoned with snake venom, are even more effective."

Not so much against this woman. Tiny creatures erupt from her fingers, and for a second, I think they're butterflies again. The buzzing sound, however, tells me differently. *Bees.* Which she points at the man right after dodging his blow. Bees that cover his howling face, his arms, and his legs. This time, I can't bear it. I look away, knowing he has died when the cage gets lowered into the ground again. A hand clamps around my arm, and I feel the shackles disappear from my wrists.

"You're next," the guard tells me.

This time, when the cage rises, I am not even surprised by what I see inside. Twelve feet in height, the biggest of any animal I've ever seen. The mammoth's fur and tusks are caked with blood, and its eyes are veined red. I trudge ahead in a daze. My vision blurs around the edges. I pause several steps away from the cage and close my eyes for a split second, concentrating on the sounds, the smells. The mammoth raises its trunk and roars, and even from this distance, I can sense its agony, feel its anger.

I take off my dupatta with shaking hands and tie it around my torso like a sash.

"Pick a weapon," the guard says.

I scan the table outside the cage, lined with an array of different weapons. Daggers and kitchen knives, swords and maces. I can't tell if any of them have been enhanced with amplifiers or if they can be used in magical combat.

"Be quick about it!"

I grab the closest weapon at hand: a plain dagger that, though not fancy, looks serviceable. If I can get close enough to the mammoth's eyes. The doors shut behind me with a clang. The cage, which looked enormous from the outside, seems to shrink now that I'm locked in it with a giant animal. A part of me hesitates, still petrified by the idea of having to kill something so big.

"No target is ever too big," Kali's voice comes to me—a memory from when I first began learning how to pick pockets. "No target is ever too strong."

It helps me take a step back. To detach from my surroundings and scan my enemy for any exploitable weaknesses. The mammoth's size contributes to its brutal strength. But it does not have my speed. It cannot scale the bars of the cage the way I can—the way I do when a trunk swings my way, the dagger held between my teeth, its edges pricking the sides of my mouth. Great. Now I'll probably slice off my tongue.

The mammoth trumpets and slams its body against the bars. The hit vibrates through my body, makes my teeth ache. Out of desperation, I reach out to the mammoth with my mind: *Can you hear me?*

"What did you bring for us, Acharya?" someone shouts. "A girl or a monkey?"

More shouting, followed by jeers. Then: another voice. A sound that only I can hear in my head.

. . . *pain, pain, pain* . . . The mammoth's words sink in before it lets forth a howl that feels like it might shatter my eardrums. Only barely holding on to the fragile bond I've created, I focus on a series of images—the mammoth's memories now flashing through my head:

238

*A snow-covered mountain, wind howling in my
ears. Men with stone armor, pricking me with their little
thorns. I roar my fury. Red light colors the sky. I fall . . .*

*This place is hot. Far too hot for a body like mine.
Someone splashes me with water, a temporary relief. "This
is no elephant, stupid girl," says an awful voice. Small, wet
hands touch my hot face. Cold, blessed cold. A kind voice
asks me if I'm all right . . .*

I see the mammoth's trunk approaching from a distance, feel it hit
my side before I fall to the cage floor, tears burning my eyes.

. . . kill the girl, kill the girl . . .

The taste of copper floods my tongue. It would be easy to be crushed
under the mammoth's foot. Perhaps I wouldn't even feel the pain for
long. Not the way I do now, hollow sounds echoing in my head, my
body aching so badly I wonder if I've broken my ribs. Somehow, I rise
up and look into the mammoth's angry eyes.

I don't want to kill you, I whisper through our bond, hoping the mammoth can hear me. *I know how hot it was in that market. I know you.*

A blink. I see the images that flicker through the mammoth's mind
as if it were my own: the whip flying, stinging, taking away the relief
wet, cool hands brought.

"I don't want to add to your pain," I say out loud. The buzzing in
my ears intensifies.

A voice from the audience breaks through: "Why is she talking to
the animal? Is she a whispe—"

I focus again on the mammoth. *I saw that man whipping you. I tried
to stop him. Remember?*

Another blink.

My heart leaps to my throat. I kneel, placing my dagger on the floor.
The mammoth cries out again and charges at me. I grit my teeth. I could
use death magic. Could aim an attacking spell right at the mammoth's

eyes—even without a magical weapon. Not doing so could be the biggest mistake of my life. The earth around me trembles. The mammoth's trunk winds around my body and raises me into the air.

. . . kill. Crush her skull and be free . . .

Use your mind, Gul, I tell myself. Held tight in the mammoth's grip, I force myself to think of cold things—of the candied ice I once ate at the moon festival, of chilly desert nights spent laughing with my parents by a bonfire in a village.

My birthmark grows warm and then cool. My fingers turn to ice. Cold seeps from my hands, which I curl around the mammoth's trunk, his hot fur. "Do you remember me?" I ask, praying that my magic has worked and that my chilly hands aren't simply a byproduct of my fear.

For a moment, I'm not sure if my words register through the red haze of pain the mammoth's feeling. Then, a hairbreadth from the ceiling of the cage, it pauses.

The girl. You're the girl from the flesh market . . .

"Yes." I gasp for air. *Yes, it's me. We met before.*

For a moment, the trunk sways, and I think it's going to drop me. Instead, it places me gently on the ground, keeping its trunk curled around my body to hide my trembling.

One kindness for another, the mammoth tells me as I cling to it. *You did not let me die in the market; I will not let you fall.*

I dig my hands into its fur, pouring my thanks into the cold spell. I don't need to talk to the mammoth to feel its relief. In the background, a chant goes up: "Siya! Siya! Siya!" Some of the men are even calling for my freedom. They seem to have completely forgotten that moments earlier they wanted me dead. From behind the gold bars, I watch the king stand and raise a hand in the air. The gesture earns him dead silence.

"It seems the trespasser has earned her freedom."

Cheers erupt, Ambari bugles filling the raj darbar with the sound of celebration. Only I can see the look in the king's eyes. A look that tells me everything his false smile doesn't.

27

CAVAS

Every month, the king holds a spectacle at Raj Mahal—an event that is talked about and discussed at length until the next one happens. It's the sort of conversation that you can't avoid, that you often become an unwitting listener to.

"Who was there this time?" Govind asks one of the stable boys.

"I heard there were only three this time. A thief, who got chewed up by a shadowlynx, then there was this giant ox of a man who was battling a little girl—I think she was a conjurer. Turned the dust in the air into a hive of bees and killed him with those."

"What about the last one?"

"That's the one everyone's been talking about! There was this serving girl—you know, the one who accompanies Rajkumari Malti? She crossed the rekha to the other side!"

My heart sinks to somewhere around the region of my toes. I feel Govind watching me from the other end.

"She fought a mammoth from Prithvi! And get this—"

"I'm going to fill Raat's trough with water," I say.

I don't want to listen to more. I don't want to hear how the mammoth gored Gul with its tusks or crushed her underfoot. I don't want to remember her laughter or the empathy shimmering in her eyes when I told her about joining the army.

I shouldn't be thinking about Gul.

Not when she's probably the reason behind the dreams I've been having since we both turned invisible in Chand Mahal. They're strange dreams, filled with spirits of people I do not know, clawing at my arms and legs, begging me to listen. Last night's dream had been even more chilling. I saw my mother again; only this time, instead of walking with me in the Desert of Dreams, she was at the center of a storm, surrounded by dustwolves. The closer I got to her, the more her body changed, fur sprouting from her skin, her hands and feet turning into paws. Long canines gleamed as she roared, her pale-green eyes the only part of her that remained on a terrible feline face. *Save us*, she cried out. *Save us, Cavas.* I woke, sweat soaking my tunic, a scream locked in my throat.

I'm still thinking of the dream this morning. It's perhaps because of it that I find myself headed past the garden, toward Raj Mahal. I'm not a woman, so the magic of the rekha has no effect on me, feels like nothing except a slight disturbance in the air. A pair of serving boys rush past, none paying attention as I make my way across the too-green lawn, toward the crowd gathered outside the shimmering palace. I am not sure what I'm expecting upon reaching Raj Mahal—a funeral procession? Bodies wrapped in shrouds to be buried in unmarked graves outside the city?

I don't expect to find two courtiers lying on the grass nearby, giggling and smelling strongly of honeyed madira, their cups lying forgotten nearby. I don't expect to hear cheering up ahead, as Acharya Damak attempts unsuccessfully to dodge a group of rowdy men showering him with blue flowers conjured from thin air. There is no wake here, I realize. Only a celebration, which, from the sounds of it, has been going on for some time. I spot the king watching the unfortunate acharya, with a bored expression on his face and a jade wine cup in his hand. Next to the king stands a girl with a trail of blood running down her temple, but otherwise unharmed. Gul. Or Siya, as the bejeweled courtiers call her over and over again, her name a victory chant in their mouths.

She survived. By some miracle, the way she helped us both survive Chand Mahal.

Or perhaps it was no miracle, I think. *Perhaps this is what she was always meant to do.*

Gul, with her too-thin face and far-too-sharp eyes. Eyes that continuously scan her surroundings, that pause and widen when they fall on me. I might be invisible to a crowd of magi, but Gul has always been able to see me. The way I've always been able to see her.

What she has to do with me is not important, Latif had told me. *What she has to do with you is.*

And it's about time I found out exactly what he meant.

The trouble with Latif: He hasn't appeared in nearly two weeks.

Even after constant rubbing, the green swarna in my hand remains cold—which it never has in the past.

"What are you doing?"

I look up to find Papa standing overhead, staring at me. "N-nothing." I put the green swarna aside nonchalantly. "Found this on the road on the way home tonight. Looks like it's a fake, though."

"Hmm."

"Did you take your medicine today?"

He grimaces. "I'm feeling fine."

"That's because you took your medicine on time for the past week." I try not to sound impatient. It was the way this medicine worked. With lots of doses and lots of rest. The moment Papa began exerting himself with more than the most basic of chores around the house, things began falling apart.

"I'll make you some tea."

"It tastes like poison."

"If it *were* poison, I wouldn't be arguing with you right now," I say dryly. "Go rest."

The cot creaks behind me with his weight. Flames lick up the wood on our small stove. I put the kettle on. When the water is steaming, I pour it into a brass cup and stir in the herbs.

"Your ma used to do this, you know," Papa says suddenly. "Make tea. Scold me for letting it get cold."

An image appears in my mind: the strangely familiar woman I saw as a five-year-old, a woman who looked startlingly like the portrait of Ma hanging in our house. Papa called that moment a figment of my imagination, and for the longest time, I accepted his answer. Never questioning it except for the past five nights.

I sit on his cot and grip my knees with shaking hands before speaking. "I saw a little girl five nights ago at the palace. She said she was a living specter."

Papa frowns. "You didn't see a living specter, Cavas. I told you this when you were a boy."

"I know what you told me." I feel my jaw grow taut. "I also know that I was the only one who could see her. There was a magus in the room with me, and she couldn't see the girl. Besides, that girl wasn't the only living specter I've seen. There's another, whom I've been meeting every month now. For a whole year."

Papa falls silent.

"There's something you're not telling me." My voice comes out hard, accusing. "I can tell from the look on your face."

Papa averts his gaze from mine and takes a deep breath. "You said there's another specter you've been meeting with for the past year. Who is it?"

What?

"That's it?" I demand. "You're not even going to deny that you were lying to me this whole time?"

"Cavas, please. I don't claim innocence here, but you need to tell me now—whom have you been seeing? And why?"

It isn't Ma, if you're wondering, I think spitefully. But the sight of Papa's trembling hands stanches my anger somewhat, and I force myself to tell him the truth:

"The specter's name is Latif. I've been telling him palace secrets in exchange for the coin it takes to buy your medicine. He has small eyes, a hooked nose, a beard. He ties his turban like a merchant."

"Or the high-ranking palace servant he used to be." My father puts aside his cup, the tea completely forgotten.

The inside of my mouth feels like sandpaper. "So you know Latif."

"I did know him. Back when he was still alive. He was head gardener at the palace," Papa says slowly, his gaze focused somewhere in the past. "Brilliant at earth magic, but more than that, a good man. He never thought himself greater than anyone else—magus or non-magus. Of course, that got him into trouble from time to time. He had been a favorite of Rani Megha's, but once Lohar became king, things went . . . awry. Latif was arrested and then killed. The Sky Warriors made sure to hang his body in the square of the Walled City."

Questions pour out of my mouth: *What happened? Why was Latif killed? What does he have to do with Gul and Juhi? What—*

"That is a story for another day," Papa's soft voice cuts me off. His face has taken on a pallor I don't like. "Please, my son. I will tell you about this one day, I promise."

I force myself to breathe deeply. Angry as I am, I still can't find it in myself to push him as hard as I want to. "Fine, then. Another day. But I have one important question."

I wait until Papa nods before asking: "You told me that only half magi can see living specters. Is that still true?"

Papa stares at me for a long moment. "Yes, it's still true."

"Papa." My voice trembles. "Papa, was Ma a magus? Is that why the people in the tenements don't like her?"

He closes his eyes. A tear slides down his cheek. "Your mother wasn't a magus."

"Are *you* a magus, then?"

When my father opens his eyes again, they're sad. "No, son, I am not."

My blood runs cold.

"My wife was your mother, yes," Papa says. "But your father was—is—magi."

A pair of strays begin barking outside.

"So he's alive, then," I say after a pause. "My . . . the man who . . ." My voice trails off.

"Yes."

I want him to deny this. To claim that I belong to only him and Ma. But there are other things that don't add up—that have never added up. Like how my eyes are dark brown, while Papa's are hazel and Ma's were pale green.

A part of me wants to know, wants to demand, who my real father is. But then another part wonders about the circumstances under which my mother came to know him. If there was a reason he left me with her instead of coming to claim me for his own.

"Was my mother . . . was she what the people in the tenements say she was?"

"People have tongues that wag far too often and minds that don't think as much. Your mother didn't have much choice about some of the things she had to do. Your father . . . I don't think he was cruel to her. I think she even liked him."

"Stop!" My voice makes him wince.

Outside, a lone stray howls into the night, reminding me of the dustwolves from my dreams.

"Cavas—"

"You told me that I've been living a lie for most of my life. *Forgive me* if it takes me some time to process that I'm not even your son!"

"Cavas, listen to me—"

I don't. I can't. I stalk out the door and into the muggy night air.

28

CAVAS

Half a mile from our house lies the ruins of an old temple, most of its engravings lost to time and the Great War. The inner sanctum, which once housed statues of the gods, now stands empty except for a rusty metal pitcher, a broken fanas, and a tray. Overhead, an old bell still hangs precariously from a fraying rope.

"Ring the bell and the gods will come," the priest in the tenements always says. Only no one else—not even the priest—visits this temple, and the bell never rings except on the days when the wind blows. Sometimes I hear it clanging on my way home, and I imagine the dead returning, demanding why the gods left us here in this place.

Today, however, instead of ringing the bell, I call for my mother. "Ma, are you there?" I shout. "I know what you are—what *I* am now. Papa told me everything. You don't need to hide from me anymore!"

I say the words over and over, perhaps in a dozen different ways. In desperation, I also pull out the green swarna Latif gave me and rub it hard as I call for her. It's only when my throat begins to hurt that I realize Ma isn't coming. That perhaps she never would.

"Well, that was dramatic. It reminded me of the plays put on every year at the moon festival." Latif's voice appears before his face does, which would ordinarily startle me.

"I should have known *you* would come," I say, unable to keep the sarcasm out of my voice. "Are you here to finally tell me that you're a living specter?"

"I would have told you sooner. But neither of your parents would let me."

My parents? "You've seen my mother?"

Evading the question, Latif points to the bell hanging precariously over my head. "Maybe you should move out of the way first before that falls and kills you."

"Why do you care if I live or die?" *My own father didn't.*

Latif makes a sound that might be irritation. "Your father cares for you, boy. And no, I'm not talking about the man who sired you, but the one who raised you. Your mother cares for you, too."

"So she's still a specter, then."

Latif nods. "She hasn't faded yet."

I frown. "Faded? What does that mean?"

"Living specters remain chained to this earth only until their deepest desire remains unfulfilled," Latif says simply. "Once that happens, we vanish, never to be seen again—even by half magi."

While a part of me wonders what still keeps my mother chained to the living world, the thought is superseded by another, bigger question.

"If my mother is a living specter, why didn't she come see me now?" I ask Latif. "She didn't answer even when I rubbed the green swarna. Does it work only for you?"

"No, the swarna doesn't work only for me." Latif hesitates. "Your mother has her reasons for not coming to see you right now."

Silence falls between us, thick and uncomfortable, broken only by the distant barking of dogs.

"She doesn't care about me anymore," I say.

"Don't be a fool, boy."

"But you already think I'm a fool, don't you? Calling me to the moon festival on unknown pretexts, luring me with false promises so that I bring a strange girl into the palace, sending your ten-year-old minion to me in a fog that nearly gets me killed."

"Indu isn't a minion. She would be offended if she heard you call her that. Besides, you wouldn't have been killed. Gul was with you."

"Why?"

"What do you mean, *why?*"

"I mean, why was Gul with me? Why is she so important?"

"She's not the only one who is important. You both are. It's why Indu told you to stick together. It's probably why you're drawn to each other in other ways, too."

"Will you answer the question?" I feel my voice growing louder.

"I would if you were ready to know the truth. But I think you've had enough truths for one night."

I take a deep breath that does little to suppress my anger. What does it matter what Gul is to me, anyway? My interactions with Latif have always been about business. Which reminds me . . .

"You said you'd get us out of the tenements if I got Gul in," I say. "Well, she's in the palace now."

"Change of plans." His voice is so smooth it's almost as if he's expecting this. "Get her out and I'll make sure you and your father are safely out of the tenements."

He barely blinks when I throw my jooti at his head—it goes right through without hurting him. "We had a deal!" I shout. "I've been trying and trying to contact you, but you kept ignoring me. Why don't you admit that you lied? That there *is* no way out of the tenements."

Except by joining the army. As General Tahmasp said all along.

"I didn't lie to you," he says calmly. "I still fully intend to fulfill my promise. But you need to get the girl out of the palace now. There are other forces at work, and she's in serious danger."

"She doesn't need my help! She's a magus. A powerful one, considering she survived a mammoth in the cage!"

"Exactly. She has drawn too much attention to herself." Latif's voice grows dim, the way it always does in the moment before he disappears. "Help her if you can, boy. If that girl dies, nothing else matters."

That night, I dream of my mother again. I follow her right into the storm, to a valley littered with bones. Beyond the valley, shadows rise: the rooftops of havelis, the spires of temples, a winged creature flying overhead.

"Ma!" I cry out. "Ma, where are you?"

The wind carries her words away before I can hear the answer.

"Name?"

"Xerxes-putra Cavas."

"Occupation?"

"I work at the stables in the palace."

The Ministry of War has several branches across the kingdom, including one right next to the Ministry of Bodies here, in the Walled City. The officer in charge at this branch has a bald head and fleshy lips stained red from chewing on betel leaves. He eyes me beadily from head to toe. "Why the sudden change of profession?" he asks abruptly before reaching out to spit in a small steel pot on his table.

I focus my gaze at a point on his chin. "I could use the coin." A partial truth. "Also, General Tahmasp suggested that I join."

"Does your family know you're here?" the officer asks.

I think of the devastation on Papa's face when I told him last night about my decision, a look that told me I'd betrayed him in the worst way possible. "Neither I nor your mother wanted this for you," he told me.

"Yes," I say now. "My family knows."

After another long look, during which I do my best not to flinch, the officer reaches for a scroll behind the table, along with a small bottle of ink. "Thumbprint and signature on the line," he says, voice turning almost indifferent now that I've been deemed worthy of enlisting in the army. "Or—in your case—just a thumbprint is fine. You'll have to go through a medical examination in a week. Make sure you're up to the task. You'll get details on that in a letter once you enlist."

"Do you have a quill I could use?" I ask politely after pressing my thumb to the scroll.

The officer stares at me for a long moment. His teeth, I note with revulsion, are nearly as stained as his lips. "Hey! Hey, Pramod! Get me a quill, will you!"

I quietly sign my name with a quill that Pramod digs out of a drawer. The ink glows green for a brief moment before turning black again.

"Amazing!" The officer is still staring at me. "A dirt licker who can write. I thought you lot didn't go to school anymore."

I can feel his gaze as I walk out the way I came in—from the back of the building and into the courtyard, where another non-magus has been quietly waiting his turn under the branches of a wide banyan tree. It's only when the other man leaves that I realize how hard I'm gritting my teeth. Exhaling, I lean back, my turban resting against the ropy bark.

A year ago—or even a month—I would have seen the officer's surprise as a triumph of sorts, the rest of his words barely even registering. But when he called me a dirt licker . . .

I take a deep breath. *Am I acting superior?* I wonder uncomfortably. Has the knowledge of my true heritage made me feel that I'm better than other non-magi? I think of Papa, forced to give up his job at the Ministry of Treasure twenty years ago. I think of the unnamed non-magi captains General Tahmasp told me about, of the many other non-magi who had built temples and roads, run businesses, advised kings and queens before the Great War.

No. The voice comes from somewhere deep within, fills me with an acute sense of relief. *I will never think myself better than them.* But after what happened at Chand Mahal, I'm only more aware of things I had seen before but chose to not look at closely, simply because they were too painful. Like the mix of surprise and derision in the officer's voice. Like the color of my eyes.

General Tahmasp's grim face flashes through my mind, and I shake my head hard, pushing away the thought. Dark eyes aren't exactly uncommon in Ambar; nearly half the Sky Warriors have them. As angry as Papa made me by keeping the real story of my birth a secret, he's the only real father I've known. The only man whom I would give my life for.

My body stiffens moments later on hearing the sound of boots and the low murmur of voices behind the tree. Instinctively, I move sideways, where the branches are lower, the shadows deeper. I hold in a breath, praying they don't notice me.

"He's gone, then?" Major Shayla's cold voice is unmistakable. "You're certain."

"Decapitated and buried in the Desert of Dreams," a woman replies in a low voice that I'm certain I wouldn't have heard if she hadn't paused by the tree. "The dustwolves did most of the work. I didn't even need to use magic."

"The general thought himself so clever." Major Shayla makes a clicking sound with her tongue. "Evading every question, always on some secret mission. Well, it's only a matter of time until the raja announces a new commander of the armies."

"*You*, you mean." The other woman's laughter crawls down my spine. A blister forms in my mouth; I realize I've bitten the inside of my cheek.

"Listen. We don't have much time. I want you to keep an eye on that girl. That Siya. I checked at the Ministry of Bodies and found nothing. No papers, not a single thumbprint."

"I could take care of her—"

"I don't want her *dead*, Alizeh," the Scorpion snarls. "Not yet, at any rate." There's a pause, during which neither speaks. "Now go. Before someone comes and sees us."

Footsteps crunch against the dried leaves, fade into the distance. A moment later, Major Shayla strides toward the ministry building and disappears around the bend, sunlight beaming off her silver armor. She doesn't look sideways or back, doesn't see me standing among the branches of the tree. Neither do four other Sky Warriors who walk by long moments later, the sound of their laughter echoing in my ears.

General Tahmasp—dead. Eaten alive by dustwolves. As for Gul . . . it seems like Latif's warning about her wasn't wrong, either.

If I had any sense, I would ignore Latif, who hasn't even told me *how* I can help Gul, let alone explained what his plans are to get me and Papa out of the tenements. Only Papa matters, I remind myself. Papa, who raised me like his own son, even when I wasn't, the only person for whom I would have ever considered joining the army of a king I detest. That I successfully sneaked Gul in without getting caught is a miracle in itself. I don't owe her—or Latif—anything else.

So why does it feel like I'm doing something wrong?

I fumble through the Walled City, not realizing I'm in the wrong place until I'm nearly at the palace's front entrance: a pair of large, imposing doors made of sangemarmar and gold that open only to the royals and their entourage of ministers, courtiers, and guards. Today, a crowd of servants gathers outside the gates, as if anticipating a spectacle.

The makara guards hiss and step forward with a swish of their reptilian tails. Within seconds, the crowd parts, making way for a palanquin carrying Lohar's youngest queen, Farishta, in a ghagra-choli of deep turquoise, her eyes gleaming like agates. Behind the palanquin, human guards escort a pair of women dressed in brown tunics and billowing brown trousers, their bald heads marking them as holy women from the south of Ambar. It's odd to see outsiders in the Walled City and, on a normal day, I would have also stood with the crowd and watched them march in.

Not today, though.

Today, I make my way to the Moon Door at the palace's rear, barely registering the guard who checks my turban pin and waves me inside.

I'm careful to keep to the shadows as I make my way to the stables, away from Rani Mahal. I force my mind away from what may be happening there. From Gul, wherever she may be.

29
GUL

The night I win at the cage, I see the sky goddess in my dreams again. Or how I imagine the sky goddess must be, based on the paintings I've seen of her and the statues in her temples: a beautiful woman with pale-blue skin, on a throne of cloud and air, her black hair flowing behind her, the locks speckled with stars. She spins a chakra on one finger: a metal discus with serrated edges, so bright it might have held the sun itself.

"It is good to see you, my daughter," she says. "For years, I wondered how you would turn out."

"Are you talking to me, Goddess?" I ask, surprised. *Or have I been mistaken for someone else?*

The goddess smiles. "Many years ago, a woman lost her daughter to an illness. In protest, she came to my temple every day for a month. She fasted; she prayed. She cursed me for taking her daughter away from her and claiming her too early for my own. She surprised me with her dedication, pleased me with her spirit. And so I granted her a boon: a daughter for a daughter. My child for hers."

I know, without being told directly, that she's talking about my mother. About me. My hands curl into fists.

"Your daughter, am I?" Sarcasm is probably not the best tone to adopt in front of a goddess, but right now I'm too angry to care. "If I'm really your child, then why didn't you ever come to see me? Why didn't you help us when the Sky Warriors came into our home?"

The goddess's eyes are sad, even though her smile does not falter. "Your mortal heart must think me cruel. For staying away from you all these years. For stoppering your magic since the day you were born."

"*You* curbed my magic?" I ask, stunned. I recall the years of insecurity and taunts, the deep shame I'd always felt at not being able to access a power that seemed to hum in my veins. "Why would you do such a thing to me?"

"I had to, my child. So much power in a newborn . . . you would have drawn attention from the get-go. And then there was your birthmark to contend with. To survive and fulfill the prophecy I revealed to Raja Lohar's priests, you had to grow up first. You had to remain undetected until your mind matured, capable of distinguishing good from bad, right from wrong. I did not want you to take your power for granted or use it irresponsibly.

"So I forced your magic back inside your body, not allowing it to emerge except when you were in desperate need or felt like you were in danger. Two years ago, you begged me for help in the stable. It was the first time you called on me—not for yourself, but to help a mare in need. I allowed you to open your mind and whisper to Agni, to all other animals.

"Also, you had just lost your parents. I knew that if I didn't help you then, I would lose you. I needed you to have some hope in magic, to keep going. In Javeribad, I watched you from time to time. As a neighbor, as a beggar, sometimes as an animal. Earlier this year, I turned into a shvetpanchhi and watched the way you kept trying to whisper to me and form a bond, even when I plucked out your hair."

"That was *you*?" I recall the red-eyed bird in the schoolroom at the Sisterhood's house and try to ward off a chill.

The goddess smiles again, which I take as a *yes*.

"I listened to your talk with Juhi in the schoolroom. I realized that you would go to the palace, regardless of the strength of your magic. That's when I knew you were ready. Bit by bit, I relaxed my hold on your powers. My real goal was to see you use death magic with care and intention, which you have learned to do. You can now perform these spells whenever your mind is still, in a perfect state of calm."

My mind, for now, spins like a top, each revelation more dizzying than the next. "I'm dreaming," I say. "All this can't possibly be true."

"Not all dreams are true," she accedes. "But not all are false, either. Think back to everything that has happened till now, daughter. Judge for yourself what is true and what isn't."

I take a deep breath. *Fine*, I think. *So maybe this isn't really a dream. Maybe I* am *really seeing the sky goddess, and what she said is true. But then* . . .

"What about that time in Chand Mahal?" I ask. "When Cavas and I turned invisible? How did that happen?"

The sky goddess's face lights up, her laughter as brilliant as raindrops. "*That* wasn't something I had planned for. That was all you, my girl. And the boy you've chosen for your mate."

My mate? *What in Svapnalok* . . . Heat rushes through my cheeks. "Hold on. *You* didn't send Cavas to me?"

"Not everything that happens in this world is written by the gods. We meddle at times, of course," the goddess admits. "But I had nothing to do with Cavas's entering your life. That happened through chance and circumstance. His fate became inextricably linked with yours when you chose to protect him in Chand Mahal and combine his magic with your own. You must, as that living specter said, stick together if you want to survive."

Her words do little to ease the torrent of questions in my mind, though I limit myself to one more. For now. "Cavas wants nothing to do with magi. He wants nothing to do with *me*. What makes you say that we're mates?"

"You must not judge him too hastily for words spoken out of anger or mistrust. Neither humans nor the gods behave the same at all times. Duality rules the world you live in. Illness walks hand in hand with health, evil hand in hand with the good. Injustice has a similar journey; wherever it goes, justice must follow. It's a perfect circle, you see? Like this chakra I spin in my hand.

"The other gods and I agree that Ambar is where injustice first tipped the scales—beginning with Rani Megha's edict against non-magi, followed with Raja Lohar's escalating brutalities against his citizens. As the mother of Ambar's first queen, I took responsibility for this and made a prophecy to the king's own priests. A revolution is needed, and it will be an Ambari girl who will sow the seeds of that revolution."

"So the prophecy is true, then," I say, wishing my voice didn't shake so much.

"It is true. But no prophecy is ever complete, daughter. Even the gods aren't sure about what will happen once the current Ambarnaresh dies."

"What do you mean?" I demand. "How can you not know? Don't the gods plan for the future?"

"Yes, we do, but the future can go in many directions, child. This is why you must listen carefully to what I say now."

The goddess's voice magnifies as she speaks the last sentence, echoes within itself, until it's a chorus of many other voices. "Raja Lohar's rule is coming to an end. What will follow will be more terrible than you can imagine—if you don't accept your destiny. The king's death will not save Ambar from destruction. Only you will. You must be a leader when all hope is lost, lighting paths that have been left in the dark. Cast your pride aside, for it can lead to your downfall. Ask for help when you need it. Accept love, no matter how barbed it may look. It is the only way to restore balance in the world. Raise your hands, my daughter. Accept my boon."

With a single flick of her wrist, she sends the chakra spinning toward me in a spectacular golden arc.

I jerk into wakefulness. The cot's netting pokes through the sheet, scratching the skin of my arm. The girl sleeping in the cot next to mine grunts, and slowly, the events of the previous day sink in again.

The cage. The mammoth. King Lohar staring at me with murder in his eyes.

Winning at the cage means that I am free to come and go between the Rani and Raj Mahals, to continue living in Ambar Fort or leave it, if I wish. Or so the king said, right after I was released from the cage.

As he spoke the words, I spotted Prince Amar, his eyes widening ever so slightly. For some reason, the expression on the prince's face reminded me of Cavas's, standing outside the palace, watching as I stepped out with the king.

"The Ambarnaresh is kind," I replied with a lowered gaze. "But I am only a serving girl. My duty is to my rani and to you, Raja Lohar. I have nowhere to go."

The last part, at least, is true.

Though my answer seemed to please most of the court, four faces stood out: the king, Crown Prince Sonar, Prince Amar, and Major Shayla. The king and crown prince looked like they had been force-fed cow dung. Amar gave me a smile and a quick nod, and this, for some reason, relieved me. Major Shayla was the only one whose expression I couldn't understand—her initial bloodlust replaced with calculation.

I force myself off the cot and head out of the servants' quarters, to the washing area near the kitchens. After long days in the Ambari heat, the well water is lukewarm, but I still shiver after splashing my face.

What now?

Pickpockets and assassins work best unseen. Winning at the cage may have saved my life, but it has also brought me unwanted attention. *Did you think this was going to be easy?* I ask myself. *That you were going to stroll in, stick a dagger through the king's throat, and stroll out?*

The king's death will not save Ambar from destruction, the sky goddess said in my dream. If that really *was* the sky goddess. There are stories of humans' seeing the gods after years of meditation or having visions of them after inhaling lines and lines of Dream Dust. But I'm no holy woman, nor was I drugged. What I saw had to be nothing more than a vision concocted by my overwrought mind.

Then why did it feel so real?

I wish Juhi or Kali were here now to give me advice. I even miss Amira and her sharp tongue. I'm so lost in my thoughts that it's only when she's standing in front of me that I realize I'm not alone.

"Good. You're up early." Yukta Didi looks as polished as she always does, even though it's dawn, her braided hair perfectly in place. "I was just coming to fetch you."

I frown. It's still far too early to begin chores, but who knows? *Maybe the blood bats are back.* "I'll get dressed—"

"There's no need." Yukta Didi's eyes scan me from head to toe. "I'll be dressing you myself today. It's not every day that a girl—even a freed one—gets to join the king and queens for an afternoon meal at Raj Mahal."

The brass mug I was using to wash myself falls to the ground with a metallic clang. I bend quickly, hoping Yukta Didi didn't see the shock on my face.

But the old supervisor misses nothing. "Yes, it's not every day that a girl gets an opportunity like this. I hope you realize how lucky you are."

Her tone says: *I hope you realize how quickly your luck can change.*

"Goddess be praised," I say.

"Goddess be praised." Yukta Didi nods. "You are wise to keep your position here at the palace, Siya. If you work hard, perhaps someday you will be where I am today. Yes," she goes on after witnessing my surprise. "I won my own freedom at the cage many years ago. At the time, Rani Megha was reigning, of course."

"The cage was there at that time, too? I thought Raja Lohar . . . I thought it was more of a recent thing."

"The cage was there since before I was born, since before the current Ambarnaresh was born. It has always been there to resolve crime, to pass judgment. I came to the palace as an indentured laborer, bought at the flesh market for the things I could do."

She bends down to pick up a stray feather lying on the ground. When she waves it in the air, birds erupt from it, flutter into the sky above us. "Rani Megha found me amusing," she says coolly. "She indulged me more than she did her other pets. So one day I asked to be a challenger at the cage. My opponent was a beast of a man, used to crushing heads twice my size. I conjured, I outwitted, I survived. For my reward, I asked to serve my rani for life."

Tyrants always replace other tyrants. I recall Amira's words, wonder why they make me feel so uneasy now.

"But you had your freedom," I point out. "Why did you give it up?"

"Freedom is relative, child. I am free to bind or remain unbound if I wish; I am free to come and go between the palaces. For me, that is enough—as it should be for most people." I don't miss the warning in her voice or the frown that appears on her face. "Come now. There's a lot to be done. Starting with your hair."

As a servant, my meals at Ambar Fort have been fairly simple: bajra rotis or rice, a bowl of black lentils or creamy white kadhi with freshly cooked vegetables. Sometimes, if we are lucky, we'd get a few honeyweed dumplings in our lentils. The food, though delicious, isn't very different from the meals I ate growing up.

The royal family dines differently. Along a low table, gold dishes brim over with different vegetables and paneer, with curried lamb and spiced rabbit. Steam gently rises from rock crystal tureens filled with lentils in different colors. At the center, there's a goat, which has been roasting on a spit for the past two days, the chef informs the king. The goat's legs are folded over as if in a sitting position, its head rising over a tray of rice garnished with nuts and rose petals.

I enter the room behind Yukta Didi, who points to the king seated at the head of the table on a plush carpet surrounded by silk cushions. She leaves with a bow, while I stand in place, waiting, unsure of where to sit.

"Come here, child," the king says, gesturing to a cushion on his right, between him and the crown prince. He sounds almost paternal. "Sit."

The seat to the right of a king or queen is usually for a favored spouse—or an honored guest, Yukta Didi told me this morning. I glance at Queen Amba, but her face is impassive. I settle down, cross-legged like the others, grateful no one can see my knees shaking.

"When Subodh was still larking around here trying to broker deals for that foolish Samudra king, I told him, 'Do you know, Subodh—I eat your subjects!'" the king says, laughing.

There's a roar of answering laughter at this, though more dispersed than I expect it to be. Queen Amba and Prince Amar, the only two royals with no meat on their plates, do not laugh.

"I don't know what the fuss is about, Ambarnaresh," Queen Farishta says, sounding bored. "In the Brim, we eat meat all the time. Sometimes, the meat eats us. It's a part of life. Besides, Subodh wasn't some innocent. He was a lion, by the goddess!"

"Pashu," Amba says shortly. It's the first time she has spoken throughout the afternoon meal. "He was Pashu. A rajsingha, if you want to get specific."

"*Psh.* Who cares about all that? The point I'm making is that he ate meat," Farishta retorts. "The first four kings and queens of Svapnalok ate every animal—lion and lamb alike."

"We must praise the goddess that the Four Blessed drew the line at eating each other," Amba replies. "It has spared me the indigestion that would surely come from having to eat you, Farishta."

More laughter this time, while Queen Farishta fumes.

"Looks like our newly freed bird doesn't eat meat, either," Sonar says. I feel him eyeing the serving of vegetables, roti, and lentils on my plate. "Squeamish, are we?"

"My needs are simple," I say. I may not eat meat, but if he expects my stomach to turn at the sight of it—the way it does for some other Sisters—he is in for a disappointment.

The king smiles at me, but the look in his eyes is shrewd. "Indeed, you have been most humble in your win, Rani-putri Siya. It is a trait we value most in our servants. In those whom we bind with."

Across from me, I sense Queen Amba stiffening. I place the partly torn roti aside and take a sip of water from a small golden tumbler to moisten my dry mouth.

"Which is why, Siya, I will give you a reward today. You will bind with Yuvraj Sonar on the twenty-fifth day of the month, a week before the Month of Tears turns into the Month of Flowers. A most auspicious time."

The shock that comes with the king's announcement must show vividly on my face. But it does not matter, for the others are shocked as well—the queens most particularly. Queen Amba looks furious, even though she says nothing. Only Sonar looks unperturbed; the king must have already discussed my so-called reward with him. My limbs feel numb. I barely even sense the finger lightly running down my neck, pausing right at the collarbone.

"Now let's see how much of a fuss you make," Sonar whispers in my ear.

30
GUL

After lunch, Yukta Didi arrives again to escort me back to my quarters. In Ambar, once a binding is announced, the two mates do not see each other until the day of the ceremony.

A week, I think. *I'm to be bound in a week.*

As a young girl, I never wanted to bind. It drove Ma up the wall whenever I said it, made her wild with anger. "Do you plan to live with us forever?" she always demanded.

The memory slides through me, leaves behind more grief than bitterness. To my surprise, instead of taking me back to the servants' quarters, Yukta Didi leads me to a door next to the green room that I'd helped clean only a few days earlier, the wood embellished with gold Ambari roses.

"Raja Lohar has said that this will be your room for now. After your binding, it will be accessible by the yuvraj, of course."

I resist the urge to vomit.

My daggers. I need my daggers.

I wait for Yukta Didi to leave the room before slipping out again, this time to the ramp leading into the servants' quarters and then down the corridor and rickety staircase, into the garden, next to the bush of nightqueens. Heat beats down on my head. Peeking both ways, I wait before heading to the banyan tree where I hid the daggers and, to my relief, still find them there.

I've just retrieved the first when I hear the scrape of a jooti against the ground.

"Siya ji." Prince Amar watches me with curious yellow eyes, a half smile playing on his lips. "I was hoping I could find you here."

"Rajkumar!" Heart racing, I bow—a quick jerk of the head—holding my dirty hands behind my back, along with the dagger I've unearthed, the scabbard pressing hard into my skin.

Prince Amar glances at the dug-up earth and then back up at me. "Looks like the gardeners forgot to smooth out this patch of soil," he says mildly.

"You said you were looking for me, Rajkumar Amar." I force a smile, hoping I can distract him, even though a part of me wonders about how much he saw. If he will tell the king.

"Yes," he continues. "I wanted to congratulate you in person for your remarkable duel with the mammoth. Especially after being confined by Prithvi Stone."

I frown. "Prithvi Stone?"

"Confinement," he says, as a way of explanation. "The small building you were kept in before the cage duel is made of Prithvi Stone. The material, when mixed with a clever bit of magic, can drain your energy by a considerable amount, can even lead to hallucinations."

I frown, remembering the tiny anklets Malti wears. "Do Rajkumari Malti's anklets have Prithvi Stone in them, too?"

"Ah, so you noticed." He seems oddly pleased by this. "Yes, they have the tiniest slivers of the stone in them—enough to keep her magic in check, but certainly not enough to cause any visions. Malti's earth magic is too powerful; it needs to be contained until she has more control over it."

I study Amar's face: his firestone-yellow eyes, his thin nose, his perfectly cut mustache. "You came to see me, didn't you? In confinement. You kept telling me to *wake up*."

There's a long pause. For a moment, I think he's going to deny this, but then he says, "I didn't think you'd remember."

"I thought I was dreaming," I admit. "Or having a hallucination, as you called it. But I don't understand. If the Prithvi Stone drained my energy, why didn't it drain yours?"

"I was wearing a tunic made of firestones under my clothes." He shifts aside the collar of his white tunic. Underneath, I spot chain mail, embedded with yellow and red gems. "It isn't perfect, but it does the job."

A spotted dove flutters past, perches on a branch overhead. I feel it staring at us and wonder, for a wild moment, if it's the sky goddess again, come to watch over me.

"Why did you come see me?" I ask Amar, ignoring the bird.

"I wanted to warn you about what you might face in the cage." He bites his lip, as if nervous. "I couldn't overrule Major Shayla, not for a security breach, but I didn't want to sit on my hands and do nothing. Unfortunately, that Prithvi Stone worked too well on you."

"It did," I acknowledge wryly. What am I supposed to tell him? That it was the thought that counts when it really doesn't?

Prince Amar is silent for a long moment. Then, to my surprise, he raises his hands and snaps his fingers. A buzzing sound fills my ears, the kind that tells me a sound shield is now in place.

"I can still help you," he says now. "I've been looking through our library of law scrolls in Raj Mahal. There is an old custom in Ambar, where a citizen—any citizen—is allowed to challenge an unwanted binding, even one commanded by the throne. If my father tries to force your hand, you can challenge him to a death duel. Did you know that?"

A death duel. I vaguely recall the words mentioned once at a school

I went to. *A death duel is the only kind of fight where murder isn't punishable by the law.*

The unease I'd felt upon seeing Amar in the garden a moment earlier triples. Why is he telling me this? Is he testing me? Could Amar possibly know why I'm really here? Who I am?

I curb my instinct to cover my right arm with a hand. Prince Amar has no way of knowing about my birthmark.

"Who told you I don't want to bind with the yuvraj?" I barely keep the quiver out of my voice.

"You don't have to say anything to show displeasure," he says gently. "You have a most expressive face, Siya ji."

"You want me to challenge the king, the most powerful magus in Ambar, to a death duel," I say slowly, not believing his words. "Why in Svapnalok would you want me to do that?"

"You are powerful, too, Siya ji. You crossed the rekha. No other woman, in all these years, has been able to do so."

"Major Shayla has!"

"Major Shayla has a token the maker of the rekha gave her, which allows her to pass through. Her magic isn't powerful enough to let her through without its aid."

"Who is the maker of the rekha?" I ask.

"I am."

"You're lying." But he isn't. From the sick sensation in my stomach, I realize I believe him. He's telling the truth.

"I'm not," he says now, a sad smile on his face. "And you know it. I'm not lying to you, Siya. I . . . I never have wanted to lie to you."

Siya. Not Siya ji. There's a warmth in his eyes that I haven't seen before. *No*, I correct myself. *Maybe I have seen it.* When we met outside the green room. When he conjured those flowers for me. Amar isn't like his two brothers. Instead of cruelty, he possesses many of the qualities that the old stories say princes should have: charm, intelligence, a sense of fairness and justice.

But he's not Cavas. Unscrupulous as I have been this whole time, I cannot bring myself to fake affection for one of the few people who have shown me kindness in this deceptive place.

"Yet, to you, I may very well be Sonar," Amar says, forcing a smile. "Isn't that right?"

"Rajkumar Amar, it's not that. It's . . ." My voice trails off. What do I say? That I like him—but can't imagine kissing him?

"We cannot help who we want. Or who we love. I'm attracted to you, Siya; I'll admit that. But I also know when to step back. I don't like taking what isn't freely given."

I'm sure he can see me blushing. "But surely Raja Lohar would release me from the binding if I asked him to. I've won my freedom at the cage. Why the need for a death duel?" I demand. "Do you want the king to die?"

"Of course I don't!" he says. His head turns this way and that, as if scanning our surroundings, and for the first time during this conversation, I realize he looks afraid. "Under ideal circumstances, I don't want the king to die. But I also know my father.

"As a boy of five, I asked him for a toy—the model of an Ambari foot soldier that could walk and talk. My father had the best conjurers in the land make it out of gold and firestones. It was beautiful, as big as a kitten. Then, he had me and my brothers brought before him. He smiled at me and then tossed the toy onto the paisley rug in front of him. 'Win it,' he said.

"Sonar got to the toy first, as always. I watched him break off the soldier's arms and legs as my father and his courtiers laughed in the background."

Amar's face is taut with memory. "So you see, Siya, he is not the sort of king who will let you go if you simply ask him to. He relishes combat, thrills in it. As I've grown older, I've seen the damage my father has done to this kingdom and his people. For all the power I supposedly have as a prince, I have done nothing except play the role of a useless bystander."

His voice grows bitter now and, for the first time, I sense the undercurrent of an anger that's years old. "You were the one who reminded me again of the Code of Asha. Of what it means to be honorable. My mother considers dishonor to be worse than death. So did the kings and queens of old. If my father dies in the duel, then he dies. You will not be blamed for it."

"What about Raja Lohar's successor?" I ask. "Yuvraj Sonar will never pardon me."

Amar shakes his head. "Sonar may be the least honorable person I know, after my father, but as Ambarnaresh, he will be forced to uphold the law. The law on death duels is pretty clear."

Yes, but laws can change, I think. Before Lohar came to power, no girls were hunted for their birthmarks. It wasn't lawful to kidnap anyone or kill entire families.

The sky goddess's warning echoes in my head again, mingles with what Amira said about tyrants. For years, I didn't want to think or consider what would happen once I killed the king—if I even came close to it. If I did succeed, I didn't expect to survive.

You must be a leader when all hope is lost.

But I have never wanted to be a leader. I have never wanted anything except to avenge my parents and stop the king's senseless kidnapping of marked girls.

"I don't need to challenge the Ambarnaresh to stop him from binding me with the yuvraj," I tell Amar finally. "I won my freedom at the cage. I can leave the palace right now, and no one can stop me."

"Yes, you can leave," he agrees. "But my father and brother can be determined. They will track you down, and also track down the people you love. Have you no family to speak of?"

I picture them in my mind—my parents, Juhi, Kali, Amira—and

am grateful that they are nowhere near this place. "None whatsoever," I say.

"What about that stable boy?"

"What stable boy?"

The buzzing in my ears recedes. Overhead the dove hoots, a strange gurgling that sounds like someone being strangled. Amar's eyes never move from my face, which I struggle to keep straight and unaffected.

"Be careful, Siya ji," he says finally, his tone formal again. "The palace has eyes everywhere. And I am not the only one who notices things."

31
GUL

Moving around the palace as a free woman should be a lot easier than it was as Queen Amba's serving girl. Yet, after the king's pronouncement about my binding to Sonar, I am suddenly surrounded by more people than I want, including the girls I once shared a room with in the servants' quarters. Girls who taunted me now push one another out of the way to curry favor: offering to braid my hair, wash my feet, scent my bathwater with jasmine oil.

The morning after my encounter with Amar in the garden, I find a package waiting for me in my new room. Inside it: my second dagger, along with a brief note that says: *You might need this.*

I feel my skin flush hot and then go cold. There's no doubt in my mind about who sent the package. Prince Amar: the most honorable man in Ambar or the best liar I've ever met. I still don't fully believe in his intentions. Yet, if what he said about the old law and death duels is true, then I have the perfect excuse to commit regicide—and not be blamed for it.

For now, I'm grateful for the reassuring weight of the daggers in my hands, relieved to see them glow green in response to my thoughts. It's dangerous to keep them hidden anywhere in the room, so I strap them tightly to my thighs.

Unlike yesterday afternoon, which was an exception, I learn that the royal family rarely sits down for their meals together and that I can take my meals in my room if I choose. This would be a relief, except that I'm now constantly watched by an attendant over an otherwise delicious breakfast of sweet halwa, methi bajra puri, and fried onion kachoris. The attendant, a fragile-looking girl around my age, is overwhelming in her solicitousness. I pick up a bajra puri and crunch into the deep-fried bread to hide my frustration, the scent of spices and fenugreek rising in the air.

"I was wondering . . ." I begin, carefully watching the way my attendant's slender fingers clutch at the front of the dupatta covering her hair. There's an anxious look on her face, and it makes me soften despite my annoyance. "Does the kitchen have any rose sherbet? Or chaas?" I ask, naming two cool drinks that weren't normally served during the Month of Tears. "If it's too much trouble—"

"No! Of course not!" The girl's face brightens. "It may take the cooks some time, but I'm sure they can make either of the drinks for you. Shall I bring both, Siya ji?"

"That would be wonderful."

I wait until her footsteps have faded down the corridor and then slip out in the opposite direction: across the courtyard and out of the palace, toward the stables. I'm hoping Cavas will be there alone, even though I'm not exactly sure what I'm going to tell him. That Amar—and possibly someone else—knows about us? That there's this vague sense of danger that has been haunting me ever since I won my freedom at the cage, or perhaps even earlier—when I heard Major Shayla talking about Cavas across the rekha.

A pair of voices argue in my head:

You owe Cavas no explanations. You are here to kill the king, and that is it.

But if he's in danger, shouldn't he know? Don't you owe him a warning, at least?

I'm still debating this when Cavas steps out of the building, an empty bucket in hand. For a long moment, we both freeze in place, staring at each other. Every thought I've had disappears as he gazes at my freshly scrubbed and painted face. He frowns when he sees what I'm wearing: a blue choli and matching ghagra intricately embroidered with flowers and leaping silver gazelles. It's one of the many outfits the crown prince had delivered to my room last night. The blouse is so snug that it's nearly suffocating, tied in crisscross strings at the back, the sleeves ending at the elbows—as is the fashion these days. My attendant found me odd for wanting to dress myself, even though she marked it up to shyness this time around. She refused to let me do my own hair, and I know it's only a matter of time before someone sees my birthmark, before this whole charade blows up in my face.

But right now, I can think of only Cavas, the way his brown eyes narrow at the sight of my borrowed finery, the taut set of his jaw. He gives me a stiff bow. "Siya ji. How may I be of service?"

I hate the formality of his voice, the cool, subservient tone that he usually reserves for the royal family. *I am not bound to the crown prince yet*, I want to tell him. *And I never will be*. But I bite back the words. We might be watched, perhaps even be listened to, right in this moment. But it may be my only chance to warn him. "Cavas, I need to talk to you. It's important—"

Before I can finish, a shout goes up behind me: "Siya ji! Siya ji!" Feet pound the earth, followed by the sound of my attendant's gasps. "I was looking everywhere for you! Please don't leave the palace unattended again! You'll get into so much trouble!"

"Can it wait?" I ask impatiently. "I need to—"

"It can't," she interrupts, even more anxious than before. "Rani Amba wants you. Immediately."

My heart sinks. Whatever my new position in the palace, even I can't dare evade a summons like that.

"Shubhdivas, Siya ji." Cavas's deep voice is filled with a warmth that doesn't reach his eyes. I want to tell him to stop. To wait. But all I can do is listen to my attendant's reprimands and watch helplessly as he walks away, a lonely figure in white carrying a bucket to the trough.

My attendant forces me to put on new shoes when we enter Rani Mahal—"Your old ones are muddied from being outside!"—and then escorts me directly to the gold room, where I find the three queens seated next to one another, straight-backed and unsmiling, on red velvet cushions.

"There you are, Siya." Queen Amba's voice is cool, her eyes hard and assessing as they go over my attire. I force myself to stand straight and not wince. Shortly afterward, Amba nods; I must have passed the inspection. "I believe everyone is now here, Farishta—every woman of childbearing age, as your, er, guests requested."

I wonder if I'm supposed to remain standing, but then my attendant ushers me to a cushion on the side, a little away from the queens. I settle down, doing my best to adjust the daggers strapped to my thighs without drawing attention to myself. Farishta murmurs something to a serving girl standing quietly beside her. The girl leaves the room and then reappears a few moments later, followed by a pair of bald figures. Sadhvis, I realize. Holy women garbed in loose brown garments, their faces smeared with vertical lines of blue-gray ash. They pause a couple of feet from us and bow low, their voices rising and falling in perfect rhythm:

"Our greetings to the queens and the future crown princess."

A shock goes through me as I get a closer look at them, and for a moment, I wonder if I'm wearing shackles again.

Kali's long, glossy black braid is gone, her lovely gray eyes almost obscured among the lines of ash. Amira, on the other hand, looks far less recognizable because of the many wrinkles around her mouth and her eyes—wrinkles that I'm certain she didn't have a few months ago. Indeed, I wouldn't have known her if not for her dark eyes and expression—a look of disdain that I'm far too familiar with. She gives the queens the same look now—and while Amba remains un-flappable, I'm secretly impressed by the way it makes the other two cringe.

"I hope your accommodations are adequate, Sadhvi ji," Queen Far-ishta says. "As I mentioned, we have more than enough rooms—"

"And as *I* mentioned before, we require nothing more than the earth under our feet and the goddess overhead. One room is adequate." Amira's voice is cold. "My rani, coins do not move us. Neither does luxury."

"Forgive Rani Farishta for her ignorance, Sadhvi ji," Amba cuts in smoothly. "She comes from the Brimlands. They know nothing about austerity."

"As if *you* know anything about it!" Farishta snaps, no doubt refer-ring to the fine jewels and the expensive green silk sari Amba herself is wearing today.

"I wonder," Kali says, "if the queens have brought us here to solve their troubles or to listen to them engage in petty rivalries."

A chill that has nothing to do with the temperature permeates the room. Queen Janavi, the only queen who hasn't spoken during this ex-change, hides a smile behind her hand.

"We shall begin the cleansing ceremony now," Kali goes on, pretend-ing that she isn't being sent death glares by the first and third of Lohar's queens. "Let the lamps be lit. By the blessings of Asha, the first queen of Ambar, and the sky goddess, who bore her . . ."

"By the blessings of Asha, the first queen of Ambar, and the sky goddess, who bore her," we repeat, launching into the first verse of the Sky Scroll. The ceremony is long and rather boring. Neither Amira nor Kali spare me a single glance, and I have to catch myself from dozing once. Queen Janavi winces often, her hands reaching out to massage her knees. What surprises me most is how well both Amira and Kali stay in character, reciting enormous chunks of the scroll without even looking at it.

At the end of the ceremony, they rise to their feet. First, they approach Farishta, to whom Amira gives a bottle filled with yellow liquid: "Drink this and you should have a son within the year." Next to Amba, whom Kali offers a single flower: "Blessings for healthy grandchildren." Next to Janavi, who is given a handful of tulsi leaves: "Mix these into your morning tea and your joint pains will ease."

By the time they come to me, my heart is hammering. Amira gives me a cool look. "Come closer, girl. Let me see your face."

Her hands cup my cheeks, draw me close, then she murmurs so softly that only I can hear: "The green room."

The room right next to mine. My heart leaps. I give her the tiniest of nods.

"May your binding be long and happy," Amira says out loud before releasing me. "Rise, my queens. Rise, future crown princess. Let us now offer prayers to the sky goddess at her temple."

The prayer at the temple, which is on the grounds outside Rani Mahal, takes a surprisingly short time. Or maybe it only feels that way because I'm thinking of ways to get to the green room without being followed by my too-watchful attendant. It's not until it's time for the afternoon meal, when Amira and Kali finally take their leave, that I have an answer.

"Rani Amba."

The queen turns in my direction—the closest she'll come to dignifying me with a *Yes?*

"I'm not feeling very well." It's not a lie. There has been a sick feeling in my stomach ever since my encounter with Cavas this morning. "I . . . I think it's something I ate for breakfast."

To my relief, the queen doesn't touch me or question the lie. "Go, then. The evening meal will be sent to your chambers later in the day."

"Feel better, Siya ji," Queen Janavi says. There's a kind look in her eyes, and I have a sense that, under other circumstances, I might have even liked her.

I bow, careful not to turn my back to them, then slowly make my way to Rani Mahal, clutching my stomach the whole time.

"Rest, Siya ji," my attendant says softly. She places the cups of rose sherbet and frothy chaas I'd asked for on my bedside table. "You can drink this once you feel better. I will be in the gold room, cleaning. If you need anything, ring the bell." She gestures to a heavily embroidered sash hanging right by my giant four-poster bed. I simulate a weak nod. I wait for long moments, listening to the sounds in the corridor, waiting for them to subside completely. Then, slowly, I slip out of my room. My attendant is nowhere in sight. I look both ways again before quietly pushing open the door to the green room.

Amira and Kali are seated cross-legged on the floor, their eyes closed, hands pressed together in meditation.

"It's me," I say quietly.

Their eyes snap open at once. "Thank Zaal," Amira mutters, rising to her feet. "I've had enough of queens and serving girls barging in here, asking for solutions to their troubled love lives."

"It's only been one night, Amira," Kali admonishes before wrapping me in a warm hug. "I'm so glad you're safe, Gul. We're going to get you out of here."

I stiffen in her arms, but she doesn't seem to notice. "Get me out?" I say.

"I suppose there must be another reason we've shaved our hair off and infiltrated the palace," Amira says sarcastically.

"We were so afraid when you disappeared," Kali says, releasing me. "Juhi was beside herself when she found your note. It was only thanks to Agni that we were able to track you to the flesh market and later the palace. That mare of yours is better than a hound. Tell me quickly—did you sign any contracts? Put any thumbprints anywhere?"

"No. I wasn't sold at the flesh market." I tell them about Cavas and how he helped me get in.

"Cavas?" Kali frowns. "But wasn't he the one who refused to help you and Juhi in the first place?"

I avoid looking into her eyes. "I guess he changed his mind."

"Desperation makes people do things they wouldn't otherwise do," Amira says without a trace of her usual mockery, and I wonder if she's thinking about her own parents, who sold her for money in Havanpur. "Well, the one good thing that came out of it is that you haven't been magically bound to any contracts. It'll make tracking you a lot more difficult. It was Juhi's greatest worry."

My throat tightens. "Juhi. Where is she now?"

"She isn't here at the moment," Kali says cryptically. "But she has a plan to get you out. Now that we've found you—"

"I'm not leaving," I interrupt. It's not until the words leave my mouth that I realize they're true.

"Right." Amira snorts. "And Sunheri and Neel lived happily ever after."

"You can't be serious, Gul." Kali, for the first time, sounds angry and a little afraid. "You can't possibly think you'll be able to kill the king!"

"Maybe I can. There's an old law." I fill them in on what Prince Amar told me, notice nearly simultaneous expressions of distaste cross their faces.

"Challenging the king to a death duel over a *binding*? I've never even heard of such a law!"

Amira shushes Kali, whose voice has grown alarmingly loud, and turns to me, frowning. "Whether the law exists or not, it's still much too dangerous, princess. Lohar is the most powerful magus in Ambar. He could kill you before you take a step into the dueling arena."

I know what she says makes perfect sense. It's not like I haven't thought of the same thing myself. But her assessment still infuriates me.

"If you still believe in that ridiculous prophecy—" Kali begins.

"That prophecy is why my parents died!" I snap. "It's why you both were tortured in that labor camp, why that woman in Javeribad lost her baby. Raja Lohar will be coming for me anyway, so isn't it better if I meet him head-on? Maybe I'll die in the process, but that's better than coming so close and doing nothing!"

"This is not what Juhi wanted." Amira shakes her head. "As much as she believed—still believes—in that prophecy, she never meant for you to die because of it. Use your mind, Gul. Allow yourself to think rationally. *If*, by some miracle, you win this so-called duel and the king dies, he'll be succeeded by Yuvraj Sonar, who is known throughout Ambar for his cruelty. Sonar will leave no stone unturned in trying to avenge his father. Also, if you think Ambar under Lohar's rule is bad, then try imagining a reign of the crown prince."

Maybe it's because Amira called me Gul and not *princess*. Or maybe it's simply because of the horrible ring of truth in her words—one that even I can't deny.

"If I leave with you, then I need to warn Cavas first," I say finally. "I don't want him getting caught unawares."

"Now isn't the time to be noble," Kali says impatiently. "If by chance something goes wrong or someone else discovers our plan to get you out—"

"It's not about being noble! More than one person has seen me talking to him." Malti. Amar. The stable master, Govind. "Tell me, Kali. Who do you think they will turn to when I'm gone?"

Amira glances warily between me and a furious Kali. Neither of them responds.

"If I disappear, the first people they'll come for are Cavas and his father. I can't . . ." My voice trails off. I think of the grim resignation I saw on Cavas's face, his fierce love for his only parent. If either of them gets hurt because of me, I'll never be able to forgive myself.

There's a long silence.

"You have tonight," Amira speaks this time, her voice calm.

My stomach swoops.

"What?" Kali's head turns so quickly I hear the bones in her neck snap. "Amira, you can't be serious!"

"Tonight," Amira repeats. "Figure out a way to tell him, princess. Decide what you want to do. Because tomorrow, we leave, regardless of whether or not you've succeeded. Whether you want to come with us is up to you."

There's a flicker of emotion in her eyes—an understanding I saw only once before, the night I ran away from the Sisters' house in Javeribad.

"Our plan involved rescuing Gul, not taking her with us by force," Amira tells Kali. "She isn't our ward anymore. She made the choice to come here. Let her decide if she wants to leave."

I realize that deep down, Amira probably knows what my decision will be, what it has been since the day I saw the head thanedar snatch an infant from her mother in Javeribad, since a group of Sky Warriors entered my world and ripped it apart.

32

CAVAS

"You did the right thing."

Govind's soft voice startles me, nearly making me drop Dhoop's saddle to the floor. Catching myself in time, I place the saddle carefully over the blanket on the pony's back and adjust its position before kneeling to tighten the girth.

I don't need to ask the stable master what he's referring to. Govind was inside the building, only steps away, listening when Gul came to see me earlier this morning, dressed in royal finery—a princess in every way except in name. It should have been easy to remain cold and detached, to raise a wall between myself and a girl who was little more than a beautiful stranger, her lips rouged and shiny, her eyes painted in jeweled tones, not a single black hair out of place. But then she scowled at me for calling her *Siya ji*, throwing me back to another time, another girl whose eyes burned fire, whose hand I had trouble letting go of.

"Knew she was trouble, that girl," Govind continues. "From the moment I saw her."

"Latif doesn't seem to think so." My words, though quiet, wipe away Govind's tentative smile.

"Speaking of Latif, we need to get certain things clear," he whispers harshly. "You need to stop communicating with him."

I frown. "Why?"

"He's dangerous! He will get you and your father into trouble."

"If that's true, why did you introduce me to him?" I turn around, looking him straight in the eye. "Why did you put us in danger?"

"I did that to help your father." Govind grits his teeth for a moment and then lowers his voice. "I wanted to save Xerxes's life. And I *told* you to be careful around Latif. Do you think I'm a fool? I know what you've been doing to earn Latif's help. I overheard you feeding him information about the palace. I didn't say anything at first, because I knew how desperate you were.

"But that girl being here and trying to talk to you is another story altogether. I am not entirely certain how she got into the palace, but I have a feeling Latif is involved. Isn't he?"

I say nothing in response, and Govind takes my silence as affirmation.

He exhales. "Listen, Cavas. There is something about Latif that you need to know. He's a—"

"—a living specter. I know," I say in a tired voice as Govind's face tightens with shock. "I understand why I can see him and others can't."

"Then you must also know that his spirit is bound to this world out of a single, desperate wish," Govind says flatly. "Latif was executed by the Ambarnaresh for treason, Cavas. After he died, he came to meet me. I didn't see him, but I heard his voice. I knew he had turned into a specter. He wanted me to join him in his quest to dethrone Raja Lohar and to restore Ambar to its former glory, by installing a better ruler in his place. When I refused, we fought terribly. He called me a traitor. I told him I still had a mate and children to take care of. Latif will not rest until his wish is fulfilled, even if you are destroyed in the process."

So that explains a *few* things. "What did Latif do that was so treasonous? Why should I stop seeing him?" If Papa won't tell me this, then perhaps Govind will.

But the stable master simply shakes his head, his brown skin turning ashy. "I can't tell you. Not here. Not now."

"Then you have no right to tell me what to do." I've never been rude to Govind before, but the events of the past two weeks are finally taking their toll. "I'm tired of you and Latif bossing me around, pulling at the strings you both seem to think I'm attached to."

"I could stop you," Govind threatens. "I could report you to the Ambarnaresh."

Two weeks ago, I might have frozen at his words, perhaps even apologized. But today I feel nothing except a vague sort of sadness. "If you wanted to give me up to the king, you would have done so ages ago. But you haven't. If you get me into trouble, I can do the same to you. I can tell Raja Lohar that you were the one who introduced me to Latif, that you were the one who gave me the green swarna."

Govind doesn't answer. Whatever emotion I saw on his face has disappeared again under a blank mask. "Get to work, boy. Rajkumari Malti will be here soon."

The rajkumari, however, does not appear, and a few moments later, Govind sends me to inquire if she has been delayed. I walk toward the garden, where the princess usually plays when not riding, when a pair of voices give me pause.

"I told you, I don't know how she crossed the rekha!" Malti's voice is high, irritable. "Unhand me! I want to go ride my pony."

"Don't be foolish, little girl." A chill skitters down my spine. It's the woman who was talking to Major Shayla in the Walled City. The one who killed General Tahmasp. "If you let Siya past the barrier with your token, it's imperative that you tell me about it now."

"Let go! You're hurting me!" Now, Malti sounds terrified, and it's that, more than anything else, that breaks me out of my own frozen state.

"Rajkumari?" I shout. "Rajkumari Malti, is that you?"

"Cavas! Over here!"

I turn the bend and find Malti standing next to a tall Sky Warrior. A terrified serving girl stands a few steps away, a bruise blooming on her cheek. The Sky Warrior glares at me, her gray eyes flashing contemptuously. "Leave us," she commands.

"Apologies . . . Captain," I say, spotting a single red atashban embroidered on her uniform. "But it's time for the rajkumari's morning ride."

The Sky Warrior sneers at me. "The rajkumari will not be riding today."

"Does Rani Amba know?" My voice is so calm I can hardly believe it belongs to me. "I don't want any trouble later in the day when she asks about the lesson and the princess's progress. I think I should go and confirm with—"

"Stop!" A tic goes off in the side of the captain's face. She grits her teeth. "Go, then! I will make my inquiries later."

You will pay for your boldness, her tone suggests. I can tell from the look in those gray eyes. Her inquiries will involve me as well. Malti races to me, relief etched over her little face. The serving girl hurries behind, not even bothering to scold the princess for running the way she normally would.

"Are you all right, Rajkumari Malti?" I ask quietly when the captain is out of earshot.

"She was asking me questions about Siya. All sorts of things." The little girl grimaces. "She thinks I gave my token to Siya and let her cross the rekha. But I didn't! I swear I didn't, Cavas!"

"I know you didn't," I tell her reassuringly. My stomach, already uneasy from my conversation with Govind, lurches again. I help the princess onto Dhoop and begin walking down our usual route, the serving girl trailing behind.

"I will complain to Rani Ma about this," Malti continues, her voice trembling. "That Sky Warrior should be punished for hurting me. Imprisoned at the very least!"

I say nothing. I don't want Malti to see how disturbed I am by the captain's brazen questioning. In the five years I've worked at the palace, I've never seen members of the king's most elite force treat the royals with anything other than deference. I wonder if General Tahmasp's death has emboldened the captain—and the thought does not sit well with me.

"Cavas?" Malti's voice is soft. Her eyes widen ever so slightly, and I realize she wants to tell me something in private. I glance back, but the serving girl, now separated from imminent danger, appears more concerned about her bruise, examining her face in a puddle on the ground.

"What is it, Rajkumari Malti?"

"You like Siya, don't you?"

My jaw tightens. "I can't say I dislike her."

"Does it matter to you if she lives or dies?"

I glance up sharply. "What's that supposed to mean?"

"I overheard my brothers Sonar and Jagat talking to the palace vaid about how they met Siya for the first time," the little girl says quietly. "They say that she fought them with death magic, that she was so strong she might have killed them if Rani Ma hadn't interfered. The vaid said he could test Siya's magic by cutting her up and drawing her blood out in little vials. He did that to me when I was three, before he gave me these." Malti points to the anklets she always wears. "Sonar wants to bind with Siya, but I know he wants to find out more about her magic as well. I . . . I'm afraid for her, Cavas."

There's a long pause. "Rajkumari, I don't know what I can—"

"You can help her," she interrupts. "You're her friend, aren't you?"

Warmth floods my face. I glance up at the sky, pretending to check the clouds. "Looks like a storm's coming. We'd better end the ride now, before you get soaked."

Malti's mouth trembles, but she does not argue when I change course and lead her back to the stable, ignoring the serving girl's annoyed questions.

Time passes quickly when you're troubled. As a boy, whenever my problems got too overwhelming for me, I buried myself in work. This is what I do now, feeding horses, cleaning stalls, moving the feed, sawdust, and hay. By the time I look up again, most of the stable boys are gone. Sunheri has gone dark as well, the first day of a new moon cycle.

"Lock up," Govind tells me. "Give the key to the night guard."

He pauses for a moment, and I think he's going to say something else. But Govind simply frowns and leaves without another word. I continue working, washing out the trough—my final duty of the day. Even the sound of anklets rustling behind me doesn't give me pause, and it's not until a hand lightly brushes my shoulder that I finally turn with a start.

"What are *you* doing here?" I ask.

The sight of Gul, still in the ghagra-choli she was wearing that morning, different only for the coarse blanket covering the top of her head and shoulders, nearly makes me forget that I've been trying to avoid her. Nearly.

"I told you before. I need to talk to you." The faint light of the overhead fanas outlines the angles of her thin face, glows in her wide eyes. "I don't have much time. Someone might discover that I'm gone and come looking for me again."

"Then you should leave," I say coldly. "We have nothing to say to each other, Siya ji."

"Will you stop calling me that?" she says angrily. "Listen, Cavas. You need to get out of here. Tonight, if possible."

Something about her tone slides like a hook under my skin, scatters my already unsteady heartbeat. "What for?"

"People have noticed us. Together. You can't stay here if I end up finally doing what I came here to do. You'll be in danger."

I struggle to remember Latif's and Malti's warnings again, but they fade away at the sight of Gul's face: perfectly royal except for the gold that will dust her cheeks once she binds with Sonar. *She won her freedom at the cage*, a voice in my head reminds me. *She's safe. What can you give her except a lifetime of hiding and misery?*

"You can still be a princess, Gul," I force myself to say. "I'm not going to tell the yuvraj about a few kisses."

"What in Svapnalok—I didn't come to the palace to get bound! You know that!"

I don't know anything anymore, I think bitterly.

The silence that falls between us might have lasted for a second, perhaps even a day.

"I came here for one reason and one reason alone," she says, a slight tremor entering her voice. "That hasn't changed. But I can't do it while you're here. If something goes wrong, they'll find and punish you, Cavas. Maybe even your father. I won't ever be able to forgive myself if that happens."

"Why? I'm not important to you. I have nothing to do with your mission!"

"Maybe you weren't important at first. But things have changed since then."

"Oh really? *What* has changed?" I demand.

My question hangs in the air, makes her shrink back slightly.

"In Chand Mahal, the living specter said we need to stick together," she says after a pause. "It . . . I feel that's important."

There's a sour taste at the back of my mouth. *Specters and prophecies and missions. Why did I expect any more from the fabled Star Warrior?*

"Or perhaps there was no reason at all," I say. "It doesn't matter. I enlisted for the army yesterday. I'll be gone soon enough."

Gul's mouth tightens. "The army. I see. Cavas, I hope you haven't given them a thumbprint or anything of that sort. It's the worst thing you possibly could have done."

This warning is even more jarring than her earlier one about my being in danger. "Worry about yourself, Siya ji," I spit out. "It shouldn't matter to you whether I live or die."

Heat bursts out of her hands, magic that glows orange, hitting me in the chest with the force of a blow. I bite back a cry even though pain laces through my ribs, nearly making me fall backward.

"You're right. It shouldn't matter to me. But, for some reason, it *does*. If there's a choice between saving your life and taking the king's, goddess knows I will always choose to save yours."

A ringing silence. I still feel the heat of her magic, her anger vibrating in the air.

"But you don't want to hear that, do you? You don't want to believe in the possibility of anything except hate between a magus and a non-magus. Well, you'll get your wish. This is the last you'll ever hear from me."

THE STAR
WARRIOR

33

GUL

The next morning, Yukta Didi comes to see me after breakfast.

"You look sallow," she says critically. "And your eyes are puffy." I'm wondering if she's going to interrogate me about what happened last night, but she claps her hands, calling forth a serving girl into the room.

"Raja Lohar wishes to see you," Yukta Didi tells me. "Alone."

"Now?" The bajra puri and potatoes I downed earlier threaten to make a reappearance. "What does he—"

But Yukta Didi is already talking to my attendant. "Get her into something that complements her hair and those eyes. No, not yellow! Yes, the pink is perfect."

I step behind the dressing screen and put on a loose, flowing pink blouse tied with crisscross strings at the back and a dusty-pink ghagra embroidered with roses in pale-gold thread. This isn't the Ambari rose, which is Queen Amba's signature, but the common rose found all over Svapnalok.

"Come on," Yukta Didi says. "We haven't got all day."

"Only another moment, Didi," I call out. Underneath the petticoat, I carefully adjust the daggers strapped to my thighs.

While my attendant braids my hair, weaving gold beads and chameli flowers into it, I hold on to my emotions, suffocating them in a relentless grip. It will not do to get weepy now. Especially since this outfit weighs at least twice as much as the blue ghagra I wore yesterday. Not exactly the best to run or fight in. Which is probably why they're making me wear it.

I could always pretend it is battle armor. Though we never really did learn to fight with armor during Yudhnatam practice at the Sisterhood. Juhi found this frustrating, but she could hardly place an order at the armorer without drawing massive attention to us.

This is not what Juhi wanted.

But Juhi isn't here. And by now, Amira and Kali must be gone as well. I told them to leave last night—without me—right after my disaster of a conversation with Cavas. *I will stay*, I mentally repeat what I told them. *I will try to challenge the king to a death duel.* For Papa. For Ma. It's the only chance at revenge that I have now.

"There." Yukta Didi adds the final touch: a gold-and-pearl-encrusted maang-teeka in the part of my hair, the ornament ending right over the center of my forehead. "Now you look like a princess."

Delicate and ethereal, my eyes rimmed with surma, my lips stained deep pink with a paste that tastes like honeyweed and beetroot. Only my cheeks remain untouched, bare of the gold dust that will be applied to them every morning after I bind with Sonar. My clean skin reminds me of the girl I was, the girl I still am under this suffocating finery. So do Ma's silver beads, which rest between my clavicles, above the heavy gold-and-pearl necklace. After brushing my anklet, my attendant's fingers rise higher under the petticoat to adjust a stray fold of cloth.

"Enough," I say sharply. "It's not my binding night yet."

The girl's hands drop at once, seconds before they brush the sheaths of the daggers strapped to my thighs. I turn away from her stammered apologies.

"I'm ready," I tell Yukta Didi.

The king's chambers are at the very top of Raj Mahal, in the tallest tower of the palace, which is so reflective that no outsider can look inside, and so heavily guarded by Sky Warriors that getting in would have been impossible without an invitation. Yukta Didi leaves me with a guard in a lobby downstairs, right under a chandelier made of swords, thin longblades jutting out of the floating crystal orb like spikes from a poisoned mace.

Over the chandelier, the glass shifts color, revealing the outlines of a portrait—the sky goddess perfectly etched into the surface, her enormous eyes holding the sun and the two moons, shifting rain clouds and stars.

I breathe deeply, forcing myself to remain outwardly calm, to look happy even though I feel like I might vomit. Walking with a dagger strapped to each thigh, coupled with the heavy ghagra, is awkward, but somehow I climb the flight of glass stairs leading to the king's apartments without tripping over my own feet and tumbling to an early death.

Outside the king's door, I find a familiar face. Major Shayla. To my surprise, she doesn't look at me, only moving aside to allow me entrance before closing the door. You'd think that being surrounded by glass would make the room feel open and full of sunlight at this time in the morning, but it is oddly dark, the air damp instead of dry.

Magic, I think, feeling its suffocating presence. And eucalyptus oil. The room reeks of it: a pungent smell that my mother surrounded me with whenever I was ill. A large, pillared bed dominates the room's center, while the walls are decorated with scenes from battle, much like the portraits that often hung in our village schoolroom, only the colors here are so vivid that the figures on elephant and horseback look alive. In each panel, the king cuts the tallest and most handsome figure—even though he looks nothing like the paintings in real life.

"The Three-Year War between Ambar and Samudra," a voice says from behind, and I nearly fall over. I hadn't heard him sneak up on me. He must have jootis cushioned with rabbit fur. A weathered brown hand traces a picture of a woman being dragged by her hair, a streak of blue running through it. "A fine victory, don't you think?"

I bite back my fury and greet him with a bow. "Raja Lohar."

His hands clamp onto my shoulders, push me upright. "Come now, Siya. Why the formality? You are going to be my daughter now. And we are alone."

His eyes narrow when I move back slightly, nauseated by his closeness.

"You are a fascinating girl, you know. A simple peasant from goddess knows where, controlling a savage Prithvi mammoth that needed to be dosed with sleeprose most of the time. That required a whisperer *and* three other magi to contain it at the flesh market."

"Luck favored me, Ambarnaresh."

"Luck? Luck, my dear, has nothing to do with it. My father, the old fool, believed in it. Believed in the gods. But I know better. There is no luck. There are no gods." He smiles at me. "So why don't you get along with what you've wanted to do and challenge me about your binding?"

The blood drains from my cheeks, leaving them cold. "I don't know what you're talking about."

"Don't you? After everything my son said about challenging me to a death duel?" He laughs. "Did you really think I would allow such an antiquated rule to remain after I came into power? Regicide is regicide, regardless of how it happens."

The back of my throat tastes sour. Amar played me. How could I have been such a fool? "You're mistaken, Raja Lohar."

"Mistaken, am I? But then perhaps there are other ways to make you talk." The king claps his hands twice, and the door bursts open.

Major Shayla comes in, pulling along with her—to my shock—my attendant. "You called, Ambarnaresh?"

"Tell me, girl. What did you see?" he asks my attendant. "Quickly now."

Shayla pulls out a small dagger and presses it into my attendant's neck. The serving girl's eyes are wide, terrified. "It's on her right arm, the birthmark! I accidentally saw it yesterday morning when she was getting dressed. I swear I'm loyal, Raja Lo—" Her voice cuts off as Shayla presses the dagger harder against her skin, drawing blood.

My heart rises, feels like a stone in my throat. He knows. Knew about my birthmark before he called me to him today.

"*Are* you loyal, girl?" There's a cruel smile on the king's face. "Perhaps not loyal enough. You see, you waited a whole day to tell one of your supervisors about the cursed mark, when you should have gone to her at once. Shayla." He nods at the Sky Warrior.

"Ambarnaresh, please," the girl pleads. Tears run down her face, and I can't help but pity her, even though she just threw me to a pair of dustwolves.

"Let her go, Raja Lohar," I say, forcing myself out of my own stupor. Why does it matter that she told the king? So what if he knows I'm here to kill him? I curse myself for my lack of foresight, wishing I had strapped my daggers to my calves instead of my thighs. "You have me, now. So why don't you—"

My voice dies. The girl's mouth opens, sputters blood. With another twist of the dagger, Major Shayla sighs, and the girl falls to the floor with a thud. Her body jerks for a moment, her eyes on me, and then goes still. I didn't even know what her name was. A buzzing sound fills my ears. I don't know if it's from their laughter or if I'm simply going to faint.

"Arrest this fool and have her tossed into the dungeons!" I hear the king say, as if from a distance. "I will relish seeing the magic drained out of her."

"Ambarnaresh," Major Shayla says.

It happens in a matter of eyeblinks.

The major grabs me by the hair and throws me to the floor. A shadow rises over me, followed by a loud cry. King Lohar looks even more surprised than I do by the blood seeping from the cut in his throat. He sways in place for a brief moment and then collapses after the second thrust of the dagger in Shayla's hand.

"You killed him," I sputter, my voice a wheeze instead of a shout. "Y-you—"

"Don't bore me, stupid girl." Major Shayla turns to me, tossing the dagger aside. "No one can hear us. For now."

The buzzing in my ears. That must be the sound barrier she put up. There's no guarantee that I will be quick enough to grab the daggers strapped to my thighs—not with the major eyeing my every move.

"Look at you," she says now, her voice as soft, as melodious as I heard it the first time. "A girl who is both fool and simpleton, yet was so close to stealing away everything I've worked for. My legacy. My birthright."

Birthright?

I stare at her face: the cropped gray hair, the angular features, the full cruel lips. It doesn't seem possible. There is no similarity between the two, but . . .

"You're the king's daughter?"

"I? Lohar's daughter?" She laughs. "I am *Megha*-putri Shayla, the only daughter and heir of Ambar's last and greatest queen. Lohar was no more than a usurper, the son of the fool my mother bound with, a man whose blood was no more royal than a dirt licker's. My mother would have wanted me if she had known I was a girl. She always wanted a female heir. She would have raised me at the raj darbar itself. But my father had other ideas. He didn't want me under my mother's influence. Called her cruel. He paid the vaid to lie to her, to tell her I'd been born a boy. She wasn't interested in male heirs, so she let him have me without looking at my face even once."

She smiles bitterly. "I've learned since then that it's the nature of men to look upon powerful women with suspicion. It took me years to find out who my mother was. By the time I did, she was already dead. But it no longer matters, does it? It will only be a matter of time before I have what I want—before the people see who the true heir is and this nonsense about the Star Warrior is put to rest."

I'm bending, reaching for the daggers bound to my thighs. But Shayla is quicker. A red web erupts from her atashban, binding my hands together. My birthmark begins burning. A pain unlike any other climbs up my limbs. Worse than a dagger, a hundred daggers, it makes my bones ache and my vision blur. There's screaming in the distance; I realize it's me. Shayla raises my body into the air and slams me against the wall a couple of times before dropping me to the floor.

"Do you feel that, girl?" Shayla asks softly. "I don't even need to break your limbs, extract your nails, or peel away your skin. It is worse than anything you have imagined because this is what it feels like to have your magic drained from you, what we do to the girls we take to the labor camps. A pity that I must do the same to you, but sacrifices must be made when fools become kings. Perhaps you will still be useful after I'm done with you. Perhaps not. Come now, Star Warrior. Fight me, if you can."

I barely raise my head before the pain strikes again, going all the way to my eardrums. I can no longer hear my voice, even though my throat burns from screaming.

I'm going to die, I think. *Oh Goddess, let me die.* For a brief moment, I think I get my wish. Everything gets wiped away. There is no pain. No feeling. Nothing except endless waves of black and, within that, a floating golden egg. Voices, at once familiar and not, whisper in the darkness.

Am I going to meet the goddess tonight, Ma?

No, daughter. You will not let our sacrifice go in vain.

You must be a leader when all hope is lost.

The egg glows, brighter and brighter, spilling light over the darkened water. Over me. In the distance, a shadow raises an atashban in the air.

Use your mind, princess, a voice says.

So I raise my right arm and do exactly that.

A crack. A burst of light. Air rushes back into my lungs, my bones snapping back into place. My vision clears for the first time, and I see Major Shayla's gritted teeth, a strange sort of fear in her pale-brown eyes. Her silver armor reflects the light coming from me. All of me. She presses harder and harder; even through the shield, I feel the force of the atashban's spell. My feet tremble, pain creeping up the toes. Any moment now and I'll lose my balance . . . I need to push. I grit my teeth. *Harder.*

Fire erupts. Shayla is blasted off her feet. The smell of burning flesh rises in the air, and I realize it's the king's corpse. Shayla's anguished scream rings in my ears.

"Regicide!" she cries out. "The sky has fallen!"

34

CAVAS

I wake up with a start.

It's a little before dawn in the tenements—the night has barely passed since Gul came to see me in the stables, her words haunting my thoughts even though I want nothing to do with them. I couldn't escape her even in dreams, surrounded by gray spirits, my eyes seeking out the sharp angles of her face, the determined jut of her dented chin. Without really thinking, I reach out to feel the space between my ribs, the spot where Gul's spell hit me last night, leaving a round red bruise. Forcing myself off the cot, I pick up our empty bucket and head off to fill it at the reservoir—an enormous, oblong body of water made by the tenement dwellers, with cleverly designed catchments to channel rainwater during the Month of Tears. With careful rationing, the water lasts for nearly a year, except during periods of drought, when we rely on the government's mercy—and its magic—for replenishment.

A light fog has settled over the houses. Most people are still asleep and will not venture out until daybreak, which is exactly why I choose to go out now. I place my lantern on the reservoir's edge, dipping my bucket carefully into the calm water. To my surprise, I see something solid floating near the top of the reservoir and nearly gag when I realize what it is: the bloated corpse of a stray dog.

I empty my bucket at once. It will be contaminated now, the tenements' only source of safe drinking water. It will be days before someone from the Ministry of Health comes in, even more days before whatever medicine they sprinkle in to clean the water takes effect. Until then, we will be forced to trek around two miles north to bring water from the reservoir next to the firestone mines.

To be poisoned by a dog or to be poisoned by mine waste?

I think again about what Gul said. What if she's right? What if she *isn't* mistaken, and the Sky Warriors come for me and Papa? What if, after all my efforts to keep him alive, Papa doesn't die from disease but gets killed because I was seen with the wrong person?

A part of me wants to blame Gul for the latter—she's the reason I got dragged into this whole mess. Yet a larger, more honest part admits that she wouldn't have been here if not for me in the first place. If I hadn't stopped her from selling herself at the flesh market. If I hadn't sneaked her into the palace. If I hadn't . . . I stop myself right there. I don't want to think about what happened between us inside Chand Mahal. The tug of her magic, the power that seeped out of me and into her.

Half magus. The phrase sends a chill down my spine. Half magus thanks to my real father. A tall figure in white appears in my mind, disappearing before I can identify who it is.

I tamp down my rising anxiety and head back home. It is too late to go to the reservoir now if I intend to get to the stables on time. We must make do with the water we already have.

When I step into our house, I find Papa sitting upright on his cot, quenching his thirst with nearly half of it.

He wipes his mouth. "What happened?"

I put the empty bucket to the side. "Dead dog in the tenement reservoir."

Papa grimaces. "I shouldn't have drunk our water."

"You should have," I say more forcefully than normal. "I'll head to the reservoir near the mines this evening."

Papa is silent for a long moment. "You shouldn't have to do this. If only I wasn't ill."

"I'll be in the army soon. I'll work hard. Send you coin." Spoken out loud, the words sound hollower than they did in my head.

"So you'll let Gul die, then."

I suddenly feel the way I do whenever I sit in one position for too long, my legs growing numb. Only this time, the feeling seems to have crept over my entire body—including my tongue. I shake it off. "What do you mean? What do you know about Gul?"

Papa holds up a scroll and, with it, a green swarna. "You think your old papa knows nothing about what you're doing or whom you're talking to outside the house."

"You mean, Latif told you," I say, staring at the swarna. "Have you been talking to him this whole time?"

"No. I spoke to him for the first time yesterday, after many years. The last time I met him was a couple of years after you were born; he was already a specter by then, so I only heard his voice. Govind was the one who put us in touch again. He wrote to me yesterday after you both argued." Papa holds up the green swarna, which looks like a jewel even in the dim light of our house. "Govind is the only person I know who can make these swarnas. Ruhani Kaki brought it to me last night after you fell asleep, along with his letter."

So Ruhani Kaki probably knows about Latif as well. Yet, for some reason, I can't quite direct my anger the same way at her as I can at the man sitting before me. A man who should have told me the truth about myself. About everything.

"Did you and Latif have a good laugh about how little I know?" I ask. "About how Latif can, with a little vow, make me dance like a puppet on strings?"

"Cavas, we never—"

"Did Latif tell you what he promised me if I could get Gul into the palace? How he took advantage of our desperation and lied?"

"Did he really lie, Cavas? Or did you simply choose not to believe him when he asked you to wait a little longer to get us out of here?"

"You don't understand!" I snap. "If I try to save Gul, then the Sky Warriors will come after me. After *you*. I don't care about myself, but if anything happens to you—"

"Then what? Will you stop living? You can't let your fear for me shackle you into this position, son. I am your father, not your jailer."

I want to argue back, tell him how wrong he is, but every retort that comes to my mind feels weak, fades before the compassion in his eyes.

"In this scroll, Govind described the argument you both had," Papa continues. "He wrote about how he couldn't tell you more about why Latif died. But don't blame Govind, my son. He has a family, and he's afraid. Don't blame Latif, either. Blame me. I'm the one who remains at fault for your ignorance—I made Govind and Latif promise not to tell you."

I hold my breath as Papa pauses for a moment.

"Govind, Latif, and I—we worked at the palace together for several years," my father begins. "I worked under Govind, who had been promoted to stable master. Latif was the head gardener, of course; earth magic had run in his family for generations.

"We were close, the three of us—all outcasts in some way. I was a non-magus. Govind had a mother from Samudra, which made the others suspicious of him during the Three-Year War and even afterward when it was over. As for Latif—well, Latif had opinions about everything, including the new king. Old Rani Megha had ignored Latif—I think his insults amused her—but Raja Lohar was different. He didn't like criticism or want any dissent from his subjects. Latif got into trouble once for calling Lohar the tyrant stepson of a tyrant queen."

"Was that why he was arrested?" I ask, feeling uneasy. "Why he was killed?"

"Oh no. That happened later." Papa's face grows hard. "After the Three-Year War came to an end, Lohar brought in a new queen—Rajkumari Juhi from Samudra."

Juhi? "Surely you don't mean . . ."

"Yes, the very same Juhi who wrote that letter to us," Papa says. "She was different from Lohar's other queens; she didn't act like the servants were beneath her notice—even if they were non-magi. She became friends with Govind because of his Samudra connection, and later with Latif. She was the only royal who willingly took my hand to climb onto her horse—not because she needed the help but because she hated how the other queens treated me. Over time, she won our loyalty and our trust. We knew we had to get her out, help her escape.

"We made a plan and staged a diversion—Latif, Govind, and I. We set fire to the garden, while Juhi was supposedly there and faked her death. In the chaos, we sneaked her out through the Way of the Guard—a secret underground passage within Ambar Fort. Security at the time wasn't as stringent as it is today. Since the fire happened in the garden, Latif was the one who got interrogated by the Sky Warriors. He didn't give any of us away." He gives me a small smile. "I see that I've shocked you."

He has. In all these years, I never imagined that the mild-mannered man sitting before me could have anything to do with something as crazy as an escape.

"So Latif died then. But how . . . ?" I frown. "Not everyone who dies becomes a living specter, do they?"

"No," Papa says. "A specter is only born out of the desperate wish of a dying person to continue to live, a wish so strong that it hinders the spirit's departure from the world, chaining them to it. There is immense willpower or rage involved in the creation of a living specter. Death by torture—as in Latif's case—is one way that I suspect this happens.

"In any case, without Latif's confession, the Sky Warriors could do nothing. General Tahmasp was one of the few people to suspect that

Juhi didn't really die in the fire. They didn't find a body. But there was so much ash, so much destruction . . . He couldn't be sure."

My stomach lurches. A part of me is tempted to question Papa about Tahmasp, about Ma. And perhaps I would have—if I had the courage.

"Papa, I don't understand. Why go through all that to help Juhi escape?"

Papa grows subdued again. "For a time, I thought Juhi was the girl from the prophecy. The one who would change things, uniting magi and non-magi again under a better ruler. But Juhi told me she has no special birthmarks, not even a tiny mole on her body. The Star Warrior has to be a marked girl."

I nod. "But the prophecy also talks about a girl with unusual magic."

"*Magic untouched and unknown by all,*" Papa corrects. "Though the kind of magic she is capable of may certainly be unusual. Tell me, son. Have you seen Gul do magic?"

"I have." The fine hairs on my back rise. "She made us both invisible by . . . I'm not really sure, drawing onto something from me." *My magic.* I still can't say the words out loud.

Papa frowns. "You mean, she used you as an amplifier? That's interesting."

"An amplifier? You don't mean those objects that magi use to increase their powers."

"*Objects*, yes. People, no. Even when I worked among magi, I never heard of anyone using another person to amplify their magic. It's most unusual. Though, perhaps it might also speak to a certain level of trust between you two. I can't say. There are realms of magic that even magi don't know of."

The fine hairs on the back of my neck rise. I can't deny the strange pull between Gul and me, an odd feeling that goes beyond magic, one that tells me I can trust her with my life if necessary.

Then how can you abandon her? How can you let her die?

"We must get her out," Papa says after a pause.

"We?" I ask sharply. "What do you mean *we*? Papa, it's too risky to go back there. Especially for you! In any case, she's supposed to bind with the yuvraj in less than a week."

"Cavas, I told you how important that girl is to our world—"

"Will you stop it, Papa? The world you idealize—the one your ancestors lived in—is a myth. It doesn't exist anymore."

"You aren't wrong." Papa gently touches the binding cord on his right wrist. "It doesn't. But it once did, my son. If we don't fight, how will it change for the better again?"

I shake my head. "Once you get out of the tenements—"

"My boy, leaving the tenements will not cure me." His voice, though quiet, hits me harder than it would have had he shouted. "Perhaps it might have helped when I'd first caught the Fever. But now it's too late. I am dying, son. I have always been dying. By the time you collect the resources to get me out, I will already be gone."

"I don't believe you," I say stubbornly. "I don't believe you at all."

He raises a hand to brush my face. His fingers come up wet.

"There are times I wonder about your mother. Wonder what would have happened if she had been able to say no to the guards who came to escort her to the Sky Warrior barracks in the Walled City for the very first time."

I feel my mouth grow dry. Until now, Papa had never said anything about what happened to Ma, never addressed the truth in those rumors about her.

"I was afraid to say no as well," Papa says softly. "Your ma and I—we both knew what happened to non-magi who caught the eye of a Sky Warrior, the . . . things that were expected of them. Yet we also knew that refusing a Sky Warrior's interest meant instant death. I've wondered so many times what it would have been like if your mother had escaped somehow. In my more outlandish fantasies, I'm the one who saves her. Foolish, isn't it?" he says softly. "Because even after we bound, I said nothing. I never spoke up, never tried to fight the guards. Our regrets are scars we live with, day in and day out. If you don't go to help Gul today, you are going to be filled with the same sort of regret."

Dawn sunlight seeps into the room from the door, yellow and dif-fused. I hear the cry of a shvetpanchhi. Some say they're birds of death, hovering close whenever it's near. "You are not going to die." I slowly rise to my feet. "And neither is Gul."

35

GUL

The sky has fallen. Major Shayla's voice, magnified to ten times its normal volume, echoes over and over, resounding through the glass palace.

The message is unmistakable. If the people of Ambar represent the kingdom's feet, legs, torso, arms, and hands, then the king is Ambar's head. In schoolrooms and books, paintings always depict the head brushing the clouds and the stars—closest to the sky goddess. To every bit of power that surrounds the land. The sky falling means that the king is dead. And, based on the prophecy, there is only one reason he could have died.

Anytime over the last two years, I would have relished the thought of having killed the king. Now, as smoke rises around us, fear grips my insides. I watch the atashban gleaming in Major Shayla's hand, a strange, insane smile on her face.

"Your daggers won't save you, little girl," she snarls when she sees me holding them, her armor glowing green in their reflected light. "No one can deny what caused the fire here—or whose spell killed the Ambarnaresh."

The smile fades abruptly when I dodge the red streak of the atashban's fire and aim a spell in return.

Attack. Warmth suffuses my arms. I have the oddest feeling that if my blood had a voice, I would hear it singing, thrilling in the magic coursing through it. The green light turns into a beam, forcing Shayla to duck, shattering the chair behind her, chunks of wood flying in the air.

I spin away from another jet of red fire and raise a shield, the combined impact of our spells breaking a giant vase of flowers.

"Come on now, Star Warrior," Shayla shouts. "Don't make this difficult for yourself."

I fight off a wave of nausea. I'm not an innocent. I planned for two years to infiltrate the palace and kill the king. Why does it matter if Shayla does the killing and shifts the blame to me? Why does it matter if I die?

But even as the last thought comes to me, I duck to dodge another spell. Amira's training, along with some sense of self-preservation, keeps me fighting back. Keeps me dodging, shielding, aiming attacks at Shayla, though the light from my daggers is infinitely weaker than the red flames she shoots my way—flames that form into arrowheads, which I narrowly dodge. My heart pounds, roars in my ears.

I recall the time I was in the training room with Amira, the peace that had settled over me right before I put up my first-ever shield. I think of the mirror in my parents' old bedroom, visualize a sparrow pecking at its reflection there. The light from the seaglass splits, changes shape. Before I can see what my spell has become, it finds a home in the major's already-wounded shoulder.

Shayla's enraged scream follows me down the staircase. I slash at the band of my heavy skirt, letting it fall to the floor. In my haste, I trip over my petticoat, hitting the ground with a thud, a shaft of pain rattling my jaw.

When I lift my head, atashbans point at me from all sides. Luck may have favored me against Major Shayla, but even with two magical daggers in hand, I know I have no hope of defeating four Sky Warriors.

"You are under arrest for murdering the Ambarnaresh." The Sky Warrior who speaks is nearly twice my size. "Rise to your feet, and drop your weapons. Do it now!"

Heart in throat, I follow his instructions. My right arm burns, and I instinctively long to cover my birthmark. But why does it matter now?

It matters because the king's death will not save Ambar from destruction, a voice in my head reminds me, one that oddly sounds like the sky goddess from my dream. *Your death will simply serve as an example of what happens to rebels. It will do nothing.*

"Move aside," a voice says.

The Sky Warriors suddenly straighten, letting Major Shayla through. She tilts up my head with the tip of her atashban. "There is no need for an arrest. Or a trial. I saw her murder the king with my very own eyes."

"But, Major—" someone protests.

"Let us kill her and be done with it. A murderess running away after killing the Ambarnaresh—what more evidence do we need?" Underneath Shayla's furious exterior, I glimpse something else. Fear.

"Father!" a voice shouts. "*Father!*"

The crown prince bursts out of the corridor, closely followed by his two brothers. Of the three, only Amar looks pale and uncertain. I want to spit on him. I can't believe I fell for his act—that he's *still* acting.

"She's here, Yuvraj," Major Shayla says. "I saw her murder the Ambarnaresh with my own eyes."

Sonar's face, a perfect picture of grief and fury, turns to me. "I should have killed you sooner," he says softly. "My father wanted to wait. Wanted it to look like an accident after I bound with you. But I knew better. I knew what a witch you were from the beginning."

Nothing he says truly surprises me. What does surprise me is how open he is about sharing his plans in front of the Sky Warriors and Major Shayla. As if he doesn't care for the consequences. Or the law. Have they ever cared—these rulers? Ambar is hardly a utopia, but I remember my father talking about a time before the Great War. A happier time, when non-magi weren't driven out of their homes, when girls weren't hunted for marks that were accidents of birth.

Out loud, I say: "I did not murder the king. Major Shayla did."

I expect the major to laugh, to instantly deny the accusation. I don't expect the sob or the tears streaking down her face.

"I?" Shayla says. "Kill the person I'd pledged my life and loyalty to?" Her voice suddenly grows stronger. "Don't be swayed by her lies or her trickery. Remember how she broke through the rekha with her magic. How she broke the beast in the cage. Remember that she sneaked these daggers into the palace. *Seaglass daggers.*" She points to where they lie on the floor. "It's clear to me that she's nothing more than an assassin sent by the ruler of Samudra. A spy like that blue-haired Samudravasi witch."

The allusion to Juhi—and Shayla's distaste for her—gives me the courage to speak up again. "You're a liar! You're the one who killed Raja Lohar. You—"

A hard hand grips me by the chin, cutting off speech. "Witch," Sonar's voice is low, guttural. "We've heard enough of your lies."

"Rani Amba is a truth seeker," I tell him. From the corner of my eyes, I see Shayla move closer to us, her atashban raised. "Why don't you let *her* do the questioning? Then you'll know who's a liar and who isn't."

A small frown appears between Sonar's brows. Before he can answer, a pair of Sky Warriors troop in, drawing everyone's attention.

"Major! Major Shayla!"

My heart sinks when I see who's with them—Cavas, held by a pale-skinned woman with gray eyes, followed by another tall Sky Warrior in full armor, helmet, mask, and all, gripping the arms of an older man with graying hair. Cavas's father.

"Found these two trying to sneak in past the rekha. Probably trying to steal some valuable magical object!"

"Well, well." Shayla's smile sharpens. "This gets even more interesting. Thank you, Alizeh. You are most resourceful."

"Anything for you, Major." Alizeh's eyes glint with the sort of madness I've only seen among some of the sky goddess's devotees and worshippers at Sant Javer's shrine.

"Look at the way she's looking at her," I say quietly, careful so that my voice reaches no one except the crown prince. "Look at the way they *all* look at her for their next instruction. You may kill me, but you'll be a fool if you think you'll have any control over these Sky Warriors."

Sonar's grip on my hand tightens, making me long for my daggers. But right now, my words are my only weapon, and if they can be used to cast suspicion on Shayla, the better.

"What's the little murderess whispering about?" Jagat asks, leering at me. "Probably offering herself up to save her lover. Sonar will share with us, won't you, Bhaiyya?"

"Shut up!" Sonar's snarl startles him into silence. "Shut up, all of you!"

"Let me handle this, Yuvraj." Shayla's smooth voice belies her tense posture. "You don't have to worry yourself about these petty matters."

"No." Sonar studies me with cold eyes. "I am going to deal with her and these two dirt lickers in my own way."

"If you are, then you better deal with this, too," a familiar voice says.

Kali! I nearly scream her name. *What is she still doing here?*

Sonar's head snaps sideways, his death grip on me loosening. Even if I didn't feel numbed by everything that has transpired so far, I would have to pinch myself to believe what is happening now.

Amar's yellow eyes are wide, and his mouth is parted ever so slightly, over the steel glint of a jambiya, its hilt embellished with a single flower bud. Even though Amar is taller than Kali, and most certainly broader in the shoulders, he is no match for her killer instincts. Perhaps Sonar can see the same from the deadly smile on her pretty face or the grip she has on his brother, because, for the first time, he sounds a little worried when he shouts: "By the goddess! Who in Svapnalok are you?"

"Doesn't matter who *she* is, does it?" another voice says. I spin around to find Amira pointing an atashban at Major Shayla's head. "It should matter to you that I'm about to blow your precious major's brains out."

"Tahmasp!" Sonar shouts. "Where is he? Where's the general?"

"In the Brim," Shayla says, her eyes still on the atashban Amira aims at her. "Raja Lohar sent him there three days ago."

"Lies!" Cavas shouts suddenly. "The general's dead! Major Shayla had him killed in the Desert of Dreams!"

"Silence!" Captain Alizeh tightens her grip around his neck.

Before I can move or scream, the armored Sky Warrior holding Cavas's father lets go of him and spins, catching Alizeh in the eye with an elbow, making her yelp in pain. Alizeh claws out at the Sky Warrior's mask, loosening it, revealing someone I thought I'd never see again.

"Juhi!" Three screams ring in the air: mine, Kali's, and Amira's. Hope buoys under my ribs, strengthens into resolve when I feel Sonar's grip on me tighten.

"Kali! Amira!" Juhi steps in front of Cavas and his father, her voice ringing in the air: "Remember our plan."

She spins once more, dodging a red flame of light. The helmet—which must have been too large—falls off her head and clatters to the floor, her braid spilling out of it like onyx and sapphires.

"What happened, Samudra witch?" Alizeh shouts. "Too scared to fight?"

A moment later, Alizeh loses her sneer as she's forced to put up a shield, dodging something silver lashing out at her like a snake—no, a whip. A Samudra split whip, its four blades slicing the air over Juhi's head with a deadly ringing sound.

Unlike Alizeh, Juhi is utterly calm as she deflects spell after spell after spell—and I suddenly know what she's doing. What all three of the Sisters are doing.

They're buying me time.

I slam my head backward, knocking with Sonar's. He curses, calling me a foul name. Taking advantage of his momentary pain, I use my elbows next and then my feet, spinning out of his grip. I grab hold of the daggers I'd dropped onto the floor moments earlier.

"You little—"

I slash a dagger upward. The scent of copper fills the air. I ignore the blood spurting from Sonar's now-torn cheek, the howl of pain, and roll away from a jet of red light, which nearly burns off my hair. Death magic fills my veins, and I shoot green light at the Sky Warrior who had attacked me.

Everywhere is chaos. Amira and Shayla are on the staircase, shooting spells at each other with atashbans. Kali is fighting another Sky Warrior. Amar is nowhere in sight.

On the other side, Cavas struggles against the hold of another Sky Warrior, whose eyes meet mine. Captain Emil. The man who showed me a moment of kindness during confinement. The man who reminded me of my own father.

Please, I plead with my eyes. *Let them go.* I don't want to kill Captain Emil, but if it comes down to him and Cavas, there are no doubts in my mind about whom I'll save. I see the hesitation on the Sky Warrior's face, his grip on Cavas faltering, when a snarling Alizeh shoots another jet of red light at them—only to be stopped by a shadow.

"No!" Cavas's scream almost gets lost in the melee. A streak of silver lashes out at them, and Captain Emil lets go.

Cavas's father drops like a rag doll, his eyes closed.

I hit Alizeh with one spell and then another. I furiously keep sending spells her way, determined to kill her, when a hard nudge knocks me to the side, out of range of another spell—this one aimed at me by Captain Emil.

"Run!" It's Juhi, who has taken over my place to fight both Alizeh and Emil. "Take the boy and *run*, Gul!"

It's a command that brooks no argument. A choice that may result in Juhi herself being captured or killed. The ultimate samarpan.

I'm shaking so badly that it takes a moment for her words to register. Cavas, on the other hand, appears ashen, still crouched by his father's body.

I reach for Cavas's now-clammy hand. "Cavas," I whisper. "Cavas, we have to go."

In the distance, Shayla's shouting for more reinforcements. I scan my surroundings, spotting a way out of the hall. My grip on Cavas's hand tightens. To my relief, he does not resist, does nothing, even though his eyes are still on his father.

Invisible, I think. *We need to be invisible.*

It's easier this time, the magic in Cavas's blood responding more readily to mine.

"She's gone!" someone screams. "She's gone!"

"She's here, all right." Sonar holds a rag to his wounded face, his eyes scanning the floor. He holds an atashban in his other hand. "I can see her bloody footprints."

I send up a shield, narrowly blocking the red beam of light aimed our way. The spell, unfortunately, turns us visible, making us targets once more. My head tilts up, and I lock gazes with the portrait of the sky goddess overhead.

Help, I plead. *Help us.*

The sun and moons in her eyes begin spinning at a dizzying rate. Time slows, and I grow detached from the fight around me. No one else, however, seems to notice the goddess's eyes. Or how they glow the exact green of my seaglass daggers and then turn red.

"Get out of my way," I tell Sonar. The voice that emerges from my mouth sounds like mine, yet not quite. My head begins to pound.

"Kill her!" Sonar screams. "Kill her!" He aims the atashban at me again.

Raise your hands, my daughter. Accept my boon.

Fire burns in my eyes and under my solar plexus. I raise my hands and spin the seaglass daggers in a way I never could before. Twin red chakras erupt from my hands, slice across the throats of Crown Prince Sonar and his brother, Jagat, before the men can so much as aim a spell or cast a shield, their bodies thudding to the floor.

Pain knifes across my temples. I feel my nose bleeding again. A strong hand grips my elbow, anchoring me when I would have fallen. Cavas's face is paler than I've ever seen it. His mouth moves, speaking words I can't hear. A minute later, he throws us both to the ground; we've narrowly missed another wayward spell.

Gul. I read my name on Cavas's lips. He points to another figure beside us. Kali, her mouth moving, telling us to hurry.

I think I speak. Say something about Amira, Juhi—

"*Now*, Gul!" Kali's shout finally breaks through my haze.

In the distance, I hear a scream. A woman.

Before I can put a name to the voice, a beam of red light hits the chandelier overhead. Kali pulls us out of its way seconds before it thunders over the dead princes, shrouding them with bits of glass and metal, firestones, and blood.

36

GUL

"Hurry!" Kali whispers. "Before someone notices we're gone."

We race down a long passage that's oddly empty, glass rising around us. Major Shayla's voice continues to hum in the walls, reminding everyone that the king is dead. The glass corridor leads to stone walls: a room shaped like an octagon with doorways on all sides.

"Juhi said there was a secret passage that began here. Somewhere," Kali murmurs to herself. "It goes right under the palace garden and ends in the tenements outside Ambarvadi."

"We can go back and see if she and Amira are—"

"No! The plan was to get you out. And you," Kali adds, glancing at Cavas. "Juhi saw more than one person in the shells. I wasn't willing to believe her at first, but it seems—duck!" she shouts.

Over a dozen daggers slice through the air, sinking into the wall above us. I raise my head, glimpsing a brilliant yellow jewel and a plume of peacock feathers emerging from the same, over a red silk turban.

Prince Amar.

Fury rises within me. I get to my feet. Amar aims another spell at us before I can attack: a swarming cloud of bees.

Turn, I whisper to them. *Kill him.*

And that's exactly what they try to do, only to turn into dust when Amar holds up a heavy-looking shield, blocking his own rebounded spell. However, the impact causes him to stumble, and Kali and I take advantage of this, casting our own spells at him in return. My spell knocks the shield out of the way, and a flaming streak of blue shackles Amar's wrists and ankles.

"Hasn't anyone told you to never pick a weapon you can't handle?" I snarl.

He looks up at me, a few odd curls of hair sticking to his sweaty forehead under his turban, his yellow eyes oddly calm. "Go on, then. Finish what you came to do, Siya. If that's really your name."

"I *will* finish you off, you liar!" I cry out. "I thought you were on my side!"

"I *was* on your side." Red flushes his cheeks. "I wanted to save you from binding with my brother. I thought you were an innocent caught in a trap. I was such a fool. You are clearly more ambitious than I thought. You killed my father, both of my brothers!"

"I did *not* kill your father! But you? You *told* your father I was going to challenge him about the binding!" I press my glass dagger under his chin, relish his wince, the thin line of blood marring his skin. "He knew about it when he called me this morning. He was going to have my magic drained." I bite back a wild laugh. "Well, Major Shayla beat me to the killing, didn't she? Or did you both plan the whole thing together? Some twisted idea to rid yourself of your father and your brothers and get the throne for yourself?"

"Major Shayla?" Confusion flickers across his features. "What in Svapnalok are you talking about?"

"Stop lying! I will not be tricked by you again!"

The seaglass's green glow brightens and then, all of a sudden, grows dull. That is when I register Cavas's presence, his hand gripping mine, the tug of his magic on mine like talons, holding it back.

"Gul," Cavas whispers urgently. "Gul, don't. We need to get out of here, and he's the only one who can tell us how."

I wrench my hand out of his grasp. "Don't!" I say. I still feel the grip of his magic on mine, feel it choking me. "Don't ever do that again!"

Pain flickers over Cavas's face. "So it's all right when you draw magic out of me?"

"This isn't the best place for a quarrel," Kali interrupts, looking warily between the two of us. "Cavas is right. We need to get out, and Juhi didn't exactly explain which of these eight doors to go through." She grabs Amar by the shoulders, pulls him into a sitting position. "Show us the Way of the Guard."

"It's gone," Amar says flatly. "My father had that tunnel sealed many years ago, shortly after a fire broke out in the garden."

"He's lying!" I say.

"He's not," Kali replies, her eyes narrowing. "Yes, Rajkumar Amar, I see your truths and your lies. Tell us. Is there another way? Come now. Don't make me finish what Gul started."

Amar stares at her for a long moment. "There is another way. But you'll have to undo the shackles on my feet."

"Truth?" I ask.

"Truth," Kali says. "Is there a trap? Answer me!"

"There isn't," he replies. "Not that I know of, at any rate. Only two people know of this particular passage." He glances at me. "One of them is dead."

Kali rises abruptly to her feet. The shackles around Amar's ankles vanish. "Show us the way, then, Rajkumar. And none of those conjuring tricks."

"I can't exactly conjure with my hands shackled, can I?"

A fair point. Kali nods at Cavas, who pulls Amar to his feet.

"This way," Amar says. Without another glance at us, he disappears through a doorway. Cavas shoots me and Kali one final look before following. Cursing under my breath, I go after them, Cavas's white tunic barely visible in the dim lights of the corridor, which, unlike the rest of the palace, is made of stone and not glass.

"Quickly." Amar's voice is loud in the silence. We follow him through a door that leads into a richly decorated chamber, nearly every bit of the walls covered with shelves of books and scrolls. If not for the canopied bed in the corner, I might have mistaken the room for a library.

"Close the door," he tells Kali. "And throw up a shield while you're at it."

He strides to the shelf opposite the bed, carefully pulling out one of the books with his fingers. From behind the wall, I hear a groan that isn't quite human, followed by the scrape of wood against metal. The shelf revolves, revealing space for a thin person to pass through. Or perhaps two.

"This tunnel will lead you away from Ambar Fort and Ambarvadi. It'll take you a couple of days, but you will emerge somewhere near the end of Aloksha's dried riverbed," Amar says. "Maybe you can escape from there into the desert. I don't know. You don't have much time, in any case. The Sky Warriors will be here soon."

"How do we know this isn't another trick?" I ask sharply. "That we won't find a battalion of soldiers waiting for us at the other end?"

"The workers who built this secret tunnel had their tongues cut off." Amar raises his shackled hands. "And I am at your mercy. Tell her, truth seeker."

"It's true," Kali says, touching his hand. "All of it."

I pause. "I still don't trust you."

"Well, you don't have a choice."

Silence.

Amar stares at me. "You really didn't kill my father?"

I nod at Kali, who places a hand on my shoulder. "I didn't," I tell Amar. "Major Shayla did."

"Truth," Kali says softly.

Amar stares at Kali, whose hand is still on my shoulder, confirming my truth. His face falls. "My brothers—"

"They would have killed us," Cavas interrupts in a hard voice. "Or they would have captured us and used us as playthings. You know this. You know their sense of honor better than anyone else."

Amar's mouth trembles. He does not deny Cavas's words.

A knock slams the door, makes it rattle in its hinges. "Rajkumar Amar!" Major Shayla shouts. "Raise your shield and open the door!"

Amar inhales deeply and stiffens his shoulders. "Go on, then. Once you're all inside the tunnel, your friend's shield won't hold up anymore. *Go*, if you don't want everyone to die!"

The door thunders again. This time the impact is worse.

"Come on," Cavas tells me quietly. He has already slipped through the opening and into the tunnel. He holds out a hand. I take it, and he pulls me through. Kali is the last one to go through, a moment before Amar slams the shelf shut behind us, plunging us into the dark.

Voices rise on the other end. "I don't know where they are!" Amar screams, his voice a high whimper. "I was hiding from everyone!"

I don't know what Major Shayla says in response, or understand the terrible crashing noise that follows. All I hear is the sound of my own heart and the slap of my bare feet against uneven ground, Cavas's hand clasped tightly in mine.

37

CAVAS

The tunnel is as black as pitch, endless. It allows my thoughts to run away with me for the first time, registering Papa's absence.

"Take me with you," Papa had insisted. "Use me as a distraction while you bring Gul out of the palace."

I never should have listened. Should have insisted he stay at home. Safe. Away from magi and the murderous fire of their atashbans. I suppress the voice that insists they would have come for us later, that they would have killed him anyway.

It's my fault. All mine.

I release a sharp breath. It turns into a sob.

Gul places a hand on my shoulder, but I shrug it off.

"Cavas," she whispers, sounding equally tearful. "Cavas, I'm so sorry—"

I pause, spinning around, forcing her to crash into me. Though I can't see her in the darkness, I can feel the scrape of her heavily embroidered blouse against my fingers, hear her rapid, uneven breaths.

"I wanted to run," I spit out. "But Papa insisted *you* were in danger. That's why we were even in that palace of horrors, why we weren't halfway to Havanpur by now. But now Papa's gone, and you and your friend are here, and I don't even know why I'm still alive!"

My last sentence is a shout that echoes horribly in the silence. Ahead of us, I hear the other woman—Kali—stop in her tracks. I know she's waiting, listening to our conversation in the dark.

I turn away from Gul, even though her answering sob cuts through me like a blade. Deep down, I know I'm being unfair. That it isn't Gul's fault Papa died. Papa *wanted* me to be here—to save her.

Use me as a distraction, he'd said.

Well, I did that, didn't I? I think bitterly. *I did that so well.*

"It's my fault," I whisper.

If I'd only chosen not to listen to him, he'd still be alive.

The air smells of decay and rats.

I feel one race over my feet, and I jerk back, swallowing the vomit rising to my throat. A bloodbath and my father's death didn't make me throw up, but somehow a rat in the dark nearly does. Perhaps it's the effect of the adrenaline wearing off, our run slowing down to a crawling trudge.

I'm tired, I think. *So tired.*

"I think we should rest here for a bit," Kali finally says, speaking for the first time in the tunnel. "As far as I can tell, no one's following us."

Fingers snap in the silence. A small lightorb rises up from Kali's hands and floats overhead, illuminating a tiny part of the dark tunnel. Kali pulls up the hem of her long tunic to reveal pockets in her flowing trousers. She unbuttons one and pulls out a small bundle . . . that turns out to contain food. A mix of dried yellow grams with cracked brown shells, moong dal, puffed rice, and fried sev—the sort that people carry on pilgrimages or other long journeys. She offers the bag to each of us in turn, and I take a handful, my stomach growling.

The mix is dry, and there is no water to wash it down. But it tastes good, and before I know it, my handful is gone. I close my eyes and lean back, pretending to ignore Gul and Kali's conversation.

"Crossing the rekha was the most difficult part," Kali is saying. "We didn't know what to do—or how. But a little princess helped us. Dark eyes, beautiful clothes, haughty little voice."

"Rajkumari Malti?" Gul says.

My eyes open of their own accord.

"Probably. She never told us her name," Kali says. "She was following us—had been following me and Amira since we arrived, apparently. Tried to bury us in the ground at one point—I've never seen such strong earth magic before. Somehow we convinced her that we were on your side and that we wanted to help you." Kali pulls out a little gold chain with an elephant hanging from it. "She gave us this token and said it would help us cross the rekha unharmed. Don't know where she got it from."

"She got it from her brother," Gul says, frowning. "Rajkumar Amar. He designed the rekha."

"The conjurer who tried to kill us?" Kali sounds more interested than angry. "You two seemed to have had some sort of . . . understanding."

I hate how my every fiber is now focused into hearing Gul's answer. But all she does is scowl at Kali and says, "*Had* is the key word here. He will likely be king now that his father and brothers . . ." She wraps her arms around herself, and I notice she's shaking. Her lower lip is indented from being bitten.

"We'll worry about that later," Kali says abruptly. She turns to me. "A couple of days after Gul left for the palace, Juhi managed to get in touch with a living specter named Latif. She says you know him as well. That you'll be able to summon him."

My back stiffens of its own accord. "Why?"

"Juhi said our next destination would be a city that only the living specters know of. Latif has promised that the specters will guide us and show us the way."

The green swarna feels heavy in my pocket. The thought of summoning Latif, who promised to get me and Papa out of the tenements, who got me into this mess in the first place, is too much to stomach in this moment.

"Does it have to be Latif?" Gul speaks my thoughts out loud. "You said the specters know the way, so it can be anyone, right?"

"Do you know *more* than one living specter?" Kali asks, astonished. "What are they like?"

Gul doesn't answer. She simply watches me with her clear gold eyes, and I have the uncanny feeling that she understands the thoughts running through my head—exactly the way she did when I first told her about my plans to join the army. I try not to think about how the very same army has my signature now. How it'll allow them to start tracking us, if they aren't already.

"There are many living specters. They can touch things and even people if they want to. Latif used to bring me coin, sometimes sweets," I say, remembering. Gul and Kali are listening to me with rapt expressions.

"I can see living specters clearly in my dreams, but not all of them will show themselves to me when I'm awake. They can choose to remain invisible in front of half magi as well. Latif told me that if a specter's deepest desire is fulfilled, then nothing remains to bind them to the living world. If that happens, the specter fades, never to be seen again. So there is no guarantee that one will answer, even if I call for them."

Like my mother, for instance.

"That said, there *is* another specter I know of. Gul heard her voice, too, in Chand Mahal," I add, and see Gul's eyes widen with understanding.

I pull out the swarna from my pocket and rub it, picturing the specter's young face in my mind. Somehow, I recall the name Latif had mentioned only once before:

"Indu, are you there?"

The coin in my hand grows warm, glows bright green. Indu appears as I pictured her in my mind, face first, one body part after another. I know I'm not imagining things when the lightorb above the specter starts flickering. Gul and Kali grow quiet, their eyes on the space where the girl specter now stands, sensing her presence.

"You called for me, Xerxes-putra Cavas," Indu says.

My father's name feels like pincers on my skin. I speak quickly through the pain of it: "Indu? Kali here thinks the specters can help us. You have to take us to a city that—"

"Yes, I know. It's called the City of Shadows." Indu sounds bored. "I can't guarantee they will let you in, though."

"What is this place?" Gul asks. "A city of shadows? Is it some sort of place the spirits live in?"

Her words spark sudden hope within me. Spirits. A city full of them. Perhaps I'll find Papa there. Perhaps—

"Specters, yes. Spirits, no." Indu continues watching me expressionlessly, but there is a hint of sympathy in her voice.

"Is there a difference?" Kali asks.

"Of course there's a difference. Living specters are chained to the living world in a way that spirits aren't—though there are few who have the gift to see us, either. The living world calls them seers—and you are lucky you have one among you."

My face flushes. I know Gul and Kali are watching me now, but I can't bear their fascination or their interest in this so-called gift of mine. "This city, then. It's for the living."

"For the living and those of us still chained to the living world. Magi have mostly forgotten it, of course, the way they always do things that are inconvenient. It is called—"

"Tavan." The word leaves my mouth by instinct, a fable and a hope, hanging crystalline in the air.

"Tavan?" Kali sounds incredulous. "But that's a myth. A tale for children."

"And there's the amnesia I was referring to," Indu says sarcastically.

324

Gul bites her lip—I have a feeling she's trying to suppress a laugh. Despite everything, I want to do so as well.

"I will let them know you are here. That *she* is still alive." Indu gestures to Gul. "Get to the end of the tunnel. I'll meet you there."

"Hold on," Kali says. "Juhi told us Latif was supposed to tip off Ruhani Kaki, an old woman in the tenements. She has our horses. I don't know where this tunnel ends, so—"

"Wait, Ruhani Kaki?" I interrupt. *Horses?* "What does Ruhani Kaki have to do with this?" I glance at Gul, but she seems equally confused. How many people are involved in Juhi's escape plan?

Indu doesn't seem perturbed by Kali's instructions. "I'll take care of everything. I suppose you'll want them saddled." She sounds so much older than her age that, for a moment, I am disoriented. *She's a living specter*, I remind myself. *Dead for the saints know how long.*

"Yes," Kali continues, as if I haven't spoken. "Now tell us about Tavan. Who's living there? What—"

"No time. You'll find out soon enough."

And with those final words, Indu disappears, the flickering lightorb above us announcing her absence.

"She's gone, then?" Kali asks me.

"Yes," I say quietly, staring at the empty space where Indu's body stood.

"What's this talk about horses?" Gul asks sharply. "And who is Ruhani Kaki?"

"She's an old lady who lives in the tenements," I answer before Kali can. "She's been living there for years. She . . . she always helped me and Papa, when no one else would. She knew Juhi as well," I say, suddenly remembering.

"She did," Kali agrees. "The Way of the Guard, which Juhi had used to escape the palace years ago, ended in the tenements itself—behind Ruhani Kaki's hut. She was part of the old resistance against Raja Lohar. That was all I was told by Juhi. She said nothing about Tavan, though."

"You and Juhi went to the desert looking for someone," Gul speaks slowly as if thinking out loud, her voice growing angrier as she went on. "And you got injured by dustwolves. Were you headed to a city? Was it Tavan?"

"Maybe. I can't be sure." Kali sounds uneasy now. "Look, Gul—"

"She should have told you! She should have let you know what she was leading you into!"

"Or maybe she didn't know about Tavan," I interrupt. I have my own doubts about this, but I don't want to listen to them argue. "The specters don't always reveal everything." I think back to my encounters with Latif, my mother's silence, and swallow back bitterness. "Either we trust them or we don't."

Neither of us speaks for several moments. Kali sighs. "Well, I suppose we should get some sleep. Or at least you two should. I'll keep watch."

"I can do that," I say. Underneath the streaks of ash, I see that there are bags under Kali's eyes. "I won't be sleeping anytime soon."

I try not to look at Gul, who is still watching me, and settle into a crouch against the wall. Cold seeps through the stone—it must be nightfall now. We congregate under the heat of the lightorb, Gul ending up next to me, barely a hand's width away. Despite what I said, my eyes flicker shut with my next breath, the smells of sweat, eucalyptus, roses, and girl surrounding me.

A muffled cry of pain startles me awake.

Instinctively, I turn to Gul, whose back is slick with sweat—the sort that coats your skin when you're having a nightmare. For a moment, I forget what I said to her earlier. I do what Papa often did for me when I was in the throes of a bad dream and wrap my arms around her, rocking her in place, whispering in her ear.

"You're safe," I tell Gul. "You're safe."

The refrain does for her exactly what it used to do for me: It quiets her sobs, turning them to deep breaths. I only register how close we are when wet lashes brush my cheek.

"Thank you," she whispers. "I'm all right now."

The words break the spell. I scramble to my feet. "We should go," I say, my voice raw.

Gul says nothing. I hear her gently waking Kali, and then afterward, their footsteps shuffle behind me: the only sound that prevails as we continue walking through the dark. Hours pass by. Perhaps even another day. Our food is nearly gone. Just when I think we're going to collapse of exhaustion or thirst, Kali lets forth a startled gasp.

"Do you see?"

I frown. I'm about to ask if she's imagining things when I see it. Initially a pinprick, then a beacon. An overhead light that's almost painful to the eyes when we get close.

"A ladder." Gul's hand brushes its rough stone edges. "Thank the goddess."

More like thank the person who had the foresight to have it made, I think. Only that person might be Prince Amar—and for some reason I don't like thinking of him at all. Or remembering the way he looked at Gul.

Kali goes up the ladder first. "Come on. It appears safe."

Gul goes up next and then I follow.

My eyes squint against the sun, directly overhead us, marking the middle of the day. Though which day it is, I'm not entirely sure. As Amar said, we're a couple of miles from the Aloksha riverbed, dry save for the tiny puddles of water left behind by the few rain spells this month. Rocks jut out everywhere like teeth. My mouth burns. Just my luck to realize how starved we are for water in the midst of land so dry it might as well be a desert—even though the real Desert of Dreams is still probably several miles away.

"I don't think we're too far from Sur," Kali says. "Perhaps we can—" Her voice cuts off abruptly, and she presses a finger to her lips.

A moment later, I hear it as well. The sound of hooves, followed by a horse's sharp neigh. Without another word, we race toward a rock, which we duck behind, squinting at the dust rising from a distance. Kali and Gul unsheathe their daggers. I, on the other hand, look around and pick up the largest rock I can find. It could be Indu, bringing the horses Kali talked about. But it also could be a group of Sky Warriors out hunting for us.

A high-pitched voice rings in my ears:

> *Rooh was born without a heart*
> *Some say without a soul*
> *But when he ripped his chest apart*
> *He found a girl of gold*

Gul and I rise to our feet as one, racing toward the cloud of dust. A pair of Ambari stallions pause a few feet from us, but the third horse keeps cantering forward, its coat glistening like rubies in the afternoon light. Gul throws her arms around the red horse and begins sobbing—a mare, I realize, from Jwala. Kali isn't as weepy, but she races to meet the stallions, stroking their noses and calling them by their names.

The rock I picked up earlier clatters to the ground. For the first time that week, I feel something that could be close to relief.

38
GUL

"I thought I'd never see you again," I tell Agni now, stroking her mane.

You will always see me, foolish girl. Even if you don't want to.

I laugh, though at this moment it must sound more like another sob, because Cavas looks at me again, alarmed. Kali on the other hand is checking on Ajib and Gharib, examining their hooves and their eyes. She unties a bag from one of their saddles—a waterskin that she offers to Cavas and then to me. I gulp down the fresh, cool water and then hand the skin to Kali, who does the same.

"Bless Ruhani Kaki," Cavas says, opening another bag. "There's food here as well."

We tear into cloth bundles containing khoba roti and bottles of mango preserves—once Kali rations them out. No meal has felt so filling, has tasted so good. Guilt twists my insides. Regardless of the secrets she kept from us, Juhi *did* care. Juhi, who, along with Amira, has probably been captured by the Sky Warriors by now, if not outright killed.

I glance at Cavas, who is offering a bit of his own roti to Agni. He has unwrapped his turban, and I see his hair for the first time: black and straight, the fringe falling over his eyes. I study the hollowed planes of his face, his aquiline nose, the shadow of a beard over his chin. As if sensing my gaze, he looks up, but I turn away before my eyes meet his. It's my fault Cavas's father died. My fault that Cavas is here now, on a path he never would have chosen for himself.

You are too hard on yourself, Agni says through the bond that connects us. You *didn't bring the boy or his father to the king's palace.*

Perhaps. But I still feel responsible. Just as I do for the power that had burst out of me like fire in Raj Mahal, killing both the crown prince and his brother. With shaking fingers, I pull one of my seaglass daggers from its sheath. The blade instantly glows green, showing no hint of the scarlet it did two days earlier.

Raise your hands, my daughter. Accept my boon.

In accepting the sky goddess's boon, I allowed her magic to enter my body and gave her full control of my powers, unable to stop what happened next, even if I wanted to. *Did you, really?* a voice in my head taunts. *Did you really want to stop?*

"Hurry up," Indu's disembodied voice cuts through my thoughts. "We haven't got all day."

"I agree," Kali says. "I don't like the look of this place."

I understand what she means. Even though there isn't anyone around—the nearest settlement must be at least a day's ride away—we're too exposed here in the open, too easily seen. As for the horses—I don't even know how the three of them successfully made it here without getting noticed.

Kali offers Gharib's reins to Cavas and takes Ajib's reins for herself. I force myself to focus on the task at hand—reaching Tavan—and climb onto Agni's back. A keening erupts in the distance, followed by a series of howls. My skin crawls at the sound. Agni's ears flatten.

"Dustwolves," Kali says grimly. "Indu, where do we go?"

"This way," Cavas says, watching the space somewhere behind Kali. Though he's still pale, his brown eyes are alert now. We turn our horses around and begin following Cavas. By nightfall, we make it to the edge of the Desert of Dreams without incident, and we camp next to a nearly dried-out pond, the water browning with mud. Indu whistles the Rooh song again while the horses pause to drink and nibble on the clumps of wild desert grass growing nearby. Cavas leans against a dhulvriksh, its rootlike branches jutting into the sky.

"We'll need to keep moving," Kali tells me. "There's no saying what might be happening at the palace now. Or who's already on your tra— *Queen's curses!*" She's staring somewhere behind me.

I turn around to see a rising cloud of white dust, the sort that might be caused by a battalion of soldiers or—

"A dust storm," I say out loud.

My mother often warned me about the Desert of Dreams—especially about the diamond-bright Dream Dust that swirls through its center like powder. "It glitters," Ma said. "It stings your eyes and your face. It creeps into the crevices of your clothes and body. It does its worst when you accidentally catch a whiff of it."

"Perhaps we better stay here," Kali says, staring at the white cloud of dust. "Wait for the storm to subside."

"Bad idea." Indu's voice, her cold breath so close to my ear that it makes me stumble.

"By the goddess! Will you stop that?" I shout.

"You'll be jumping at more than my voice when the dustwolves get here."

We hear howls again, as if summoned—only this time they're louder, closer.

Dustwolves or a dust storm. I'm not sure which option is worse. Next to the dhulvriksh, I notice that Cavas is breaking off a long stick— likely to ward off the wolves. I find myself walking toward him, pausing less than an arm's length away, a dagger in my hand.

"Do you want this instead?" I ask.

His eyes widen as he stares at the hilt of the seaglass blade, then narrow as he vehemently shakes his head. "I want nothing to do with all that."

All that. As if it's something repulsive. As if I am the same. I swallow back a retort. I know Cavas is grieving for his father. That he's justified in his response after years of being ill-treated by magi like myself. Underneath the hurt, I feel something else: anger, simmering under my skin. I hold on to it, let it fuel my limbs into action by reaching out to climb onto Agni, who nudges Cavas with a sharp snort. His eyes soften infinitesimally, and after a pause, he heads to Gharib.

"Follow my voice," Indu says. "Follow the sound of my voice and I'll do my best to keep them off your scent."

She begins whistling again—though this time, instead of getting annoyed by it, I clutch onto the sound like a lifeline. We gallop toward the column of rising dust in the distance, Agni lightly churning the sand under her hooves, putting up a veil between me and any possible predators.

Behind me, Cavas lets out a curse, followed by my name. That's when I feel it—the brush of a paw, of *something*, on my bare foot—and then I hear a yelp as I kick out. A long howl claws up my spine. Agni spurs faster, the road growing bumpy the farther we go into the desert. I can't see Kali, even though I hear her cry out somewhere to my left. A shadow rises amid the dust, nearly invisible, if not for the telltale eyes glowing red with hunger. This time, however, I'm ready, my dagger sending a beam of green light directly into the dustwolf's eyes. The spell isn't strong enough to kill it, but from the yowls I hear, there must have been enough damage to push it back.

I hear Cavas curse again. "I lost my stick! And there are more of them!"

I raise my dagger again and aim another spell—this one much weaker than the one before. I see the dustwolf outlined in the green light, bigger than the biggest dog I've ever seen, stubby horns growing out of its skull. It dodges the spell this time around and reaches out with a slash, catching Agni with its claws. The mare screams, nearly bucking me off in her efforts to dodge the wolf. The sky darkens in this part of the desert, the air around us turning a murky yellow.

"Aim for the rising dust!" Indu shouts. "And try not to inhale anything!"

"Kali? Cavas?" I shout. "Are you there? Did you hear Indu?"

"Here!" Kali appears ahead of me, heading right into the storm. "I heard her!"

But there's no answer from Cavas—not even a shout. Each of my senses screams that something is wrong. Without really thinking about it, I turn Agni around.

What are you doing? she demands.

"He's in trouble!" I shout at her. "We can't lose him!"

If we lose Cavas in the storm, the Sky Warriors will find him. And when they do . . . I shake off the awful thought, keeping my daggers out and my eyes narrowed for any signs of a horse. Then, through a part in the clouds of dust, I see him—struggling against the grip of a dustwolf that's trying to drag him along the sand. There's no sign of Gharib. I hesitate. Attacking the dustwolf could easily hurt Cavas as well. But doing nothing would be worse.

Attack, I think, and take careful aim. The dustwolf's howl of pain is my only answer.

"Cavas!" I cry out. "Cavas, are you hurt? Can you climb on?"

A long scratch mars Cavas's face. His calf is bleeding profusely. By a miracle, or maybe the grit that has kept him going for so long, he grabs my hand and manages to climb onto Agni's back. More howls behind us. We don't have a choice. We'll have to make a run for it.

"Hold on to me," I shout, hoping he can hear. "And don't let go!"

It is a dangerous move. I have never ridden double before on a gallop, and I doubt that Cavas has, either. If Cavas falls off Agni, so will I. But, after a brief hesitation, I feel Cavas's arms wrap around my waist, holding tight, and we dive into the rising dust.

In the storm, I imagine I am alone, sleeping on a cot in the courtyard of our old house in Dukal. My mother sits on the ground next to me, holding my hand, twisting my fingers, breaking them one by one.

The cot rocks gently from side to side, and now I am floating on a raft on the lotus pond in Javeribad. The water looks like mermaid hair and has the texture of husk when I touch it. Flies buzz overhead, and the flowers turn into parts of bodies I once knew.

A spasm of pain goes through me, and the dream shifts again. I am on a horse now, tossed upon the dunes like a boat on the high seas. Rain falls from the sky, cuts into my skin like glass. Overhead, shadows loom: the roofs of havelis, the spires of temples, a giant bird with hollow eyes. Gold bars surround me, and for a moment, I think I'm back in the cage facing the mammoth, a flimsy dagger in hand.

A young girl in pigtails and a ragged tunic grips my wrist. Her eyes are gray, and so is her face. "Show them your mark!" Her voice is oddly familiar. "Show it or they won't believe us!"

I pull up the sleeve of my blouse and raise my right arm high in the air. Light pours out of me, banishing the shadows. The cage disappears. Sand shifts, revealing a path encrusted with rock so old it looks skeletal, bleached remains rising from the dust. I hold on to my horse's slippery mane, fall off when I realize the rain isn't rain, but sand, and that the sweat coating the horse's neck is blood.

A CITY OF
SHADOWS

39

CAVAS

*W**ake up.* The woman in my dream is chasing away monsters, beasts with the sort of fangs that can cut through stone. *Wake up, son.*

I see my mother's face: hollow-cheeked and gray-eyed in specter form, her hair whipping across it in long, silvery strands. As a boy, I'd seen her a few times in my dreams, veiled by shadow and moonlight. I did not expect to see her again. To appear when Gul and I plunged into the dust storm and draw me out of my dust-addled nightmares.

"Ma?" I whisper now, reaching out to take her hand.

"He's waking up, thank the goddess," a distant voice. "It's all right, boy. You're safe now."

Like smoke, my mother's hand fades, and my eyes flutter open to light. The soft yellow of morning pours in through a window overhead, casting shadows and starry patterns across the white sheet covering my legs. The air around me smells of flour and herbs, a shaft of pain going through my calf when I try to move.

"Easy, there." It's the voice again. "That was no ordinary animal bite."

I sag into the mattress underneath—a real *mattress* cushioning my body instead of the bare net of my cot, and a real pillow under my head instead of an old turban. The feel—the very luxury of it—seems wrong. Like I'm still in some kind of vague dream. Yet the voice speaking to me doesn't sound dreamlike.

I force my eyes open again. The woman looking at me must be in her midthirties, with deep-brown eyes that curve ever so slightly at the corners. A mole the shape of a falling star marks her left cheek. There are other stars: silver-and-black tattoos that curve over her eyebrows like constellations, and a small gold one etched carefully above the very center of her chin.

"Is he up yet, Esther?" another voice asks. One that I might have heard before.

"He is," the tattooed woman says. "His fever broke sometime this morning—*no*, boy, not now!" She holds me down when I try to get up, and a moment later, searing pain shoots through my calf. "I told you your leg isn't up to it yet!"

Memories unravel: Papa falling, his body lit red. The tunnel. Indu. The storm. I remember falling off my horse and then—

"Gul." My throat feels raw, like I haven't spoken in ages. "Where's Gul?"

"She's still asleep. The dust seems to have hit her worse than you two," the woman named Esther says.

You two. "Kali. Is she all right?"

"No worse than usual," Kali says. I slowly turn around, seeing Gul's friend for the first time without ash marring her features. Bald head, pretty face, bright-gray eyes. I raise a hand to shield my eyes from the shaft of light pouring in through an overhead window and see that my skin is covered with brown scratches.

"That's from the dustwolf that attacked you," Kali explains when she sees me looking. "We're lucky that we had Esther. She got the poison out before it could do much damage. I swear she was better than a vaid!"

"Hardly!" Esther laughs. "Don't be excessive in your praise, Kali. You know that only magi gifted in life magic are trained to heal and become vaids. Good vaids can work their magic and fully heal wounds like Cavas's in perhaps an hour. I'm but a half magus with some knowledge of healing."

I glance up sharply. *Another half magus? A seer?* Esther smiles and nods at me, as if sensing my questions.

"I was lucky that the old vaid at this labor camp needed help and agreed to show me how to mix herbs and make salves and potions," Esther says. "I could have worked much faster if not for the dust that you all inhaled. Kali had been knocked out for a whole week."

A *week*? "How is that even possible?" I croak out. "How long have we been here? Where *are* we?"

"So many questions this one asks!" Esther turns to retrieve a small vial from a table next to us and mixes a drop of it into a steaming copper mug.

"Wait until the other one wakes up," Kali says. "She'll ask about ten times as many."

"Don't worry; it isn't a criticism," Esther says before I can open my mouth to retort. Her brown eyes look at me kindly, and despite my confusion, I find myself relaxing under her touch. "To answer your first question, it's the Dream Dust that puts you to sleep, though you may have guessed that already. Some people can go into a permanent sleep state; it drives many mad. Second, you've been sleeping for around ten days. Third, you are in Tavan, which was a city for weary desert travelers once and later a labor camp where marked girls were held captive until the Battle of the Desert."

Tavan, a labor camp? "But all those stories—"

"Hush! You can ask your questions later," Esther scolds. She hands me the copper mug, which is smoking now.

"What's in there?" I ask suspiciously.

"Chai, mostly. And diluted blood bat venom. Don't look so alarmed—I've been feeding you a drop of it every day. It helps leech out the poison from your leg."

I take a sip, grimace at the taste. Is this what Papa felt like when I gave him his medicine? I glance up and find Kali looking blankly out the window. A sound not unlike hooves clatters outside, reminding me of—

"Your horse," I say, making Kali turn around. "I'm sorry."

"It's all right," she says gently, even though pain flashes through her eyes. "We saved Agni and Ajib at least."

"Thank the goddess that you had Indu and Latif with you," Esther says. "They guided the horses, protected you from the worst of the storm."

"Latif?" The name tastes sour on my tongue. "He was there with us?"

"He didn't show himself because he knew you were angry at him," Esther says. "But he wasn't willing to leave you behind. Not after what happened at the palace."

The words claw at my insides, dig deep. It would be easy to give in, to sink along with the strange weight crushing my chest. I breathe deeply, search for a distraction, a lifeline. "So, Gul—"

"Will be all right. I was in to see her earlier, before I came to see you."

I say nothing. I don't miss the glance Kali exchanges with Esther or the fact that neither of them looked at me while talking about Gul.

"How about having a look outside your window?" Kali asks me brightly. "He can do that, can't he, Esther?"

Esther frowns. "As long as he doesn't overexert himself."

With their help, I climb off the bed and hobble to the window, its curtains drawn open to let in the morning light. The room we're in looks over a courtyard overgrown with desert grass, thhor plants, and honeyweed bushes, interspersed with odd little wooden posts. A narrow path connects the building we're in to another one: a house built in the style of an old haveli, dark figures dancing across the roof.

I squint.

No. Not dancing.

Fighting.

Braids flying in the air, their long wooden staffs making a noise that, over here, sounds like a gentle *clack*.

"Lathi practice," Esther comments softly. "We've been training for the past twenty years. Waiting. We couldn't believe it when Indu brought her here."

Her. I know, without asking, that she's talking about Gul.

The faded letters on the building across from us spell out SOLITARY CONFINEMENT. DANGEROUS. I narrow my eyes at the posts in the courtyard, at the broken chains hanging off them, blackened with rust and time.

"We call this courtyard Freed Land," Esther says. "The posts are a reminder of our former captivity. Twenty-two years ago, at least two girls, if not more, were continuously chained here to the stocks for what the guards deemed misbehavior. The building we're in formed the barracks. It took me a long time to see how afraid the guards were of our dying—of turning into living specters—because of the way they tortured us. Few did, though. By the time most of the girls had their magic drained, they wanted to die anyway. Not everyone was as angry or as strong-willed." She points into the distance. "Look. Beyond the building. Do you see them?"

For a few seconds, I don't. Then, slowly, they begin materializing before my eyes: golden bars as tall as mountains. One bar after another, as far as the eye can see. Small gray figures circle the air around the bars. Without being told, I know they are living specters.

"It's like a cage," I murmur.

"Yes. As long as we can see the bars, it means Tavan remains invisible. It's how we've lasted for so long over here. Not that the Sky Warriors haven't come looking. Raja Lohar's general used to come once every month to look for ways to infiltrate the city." Esther's lips flatten. "It has been difficult keeping our security measures in place. The specters don't like playing guard for long amounts of time. They left a part of the barrier unguarded at one point. But we were lucky. The general didn't find us. Instead, we saw him from behind our barrier, stabbed in the back by one of his own Sky Warriors and left for the dustwolves."

"Raja Lohar is dead now," I say slowly. "Doesn't it mean you're free to leave?"

"Not if we're hiding the two most wanted people in Ambar," Esther says. Kali clears her throat. "Three, rather," Esther corrects.

"Why are you hiding us when you could easily hand us in?" I ask. "You would probably be rewarded for it."

"Yes, it would be easy to turn you in," Esther says. "And we would have if we hadn't been praying for this—for the Star Warrior—for two decades. We're hoping we can negotiate a deal with the new king. Bargain for your safety."

"Rajkumar Amar was crowned Ambarnaresh three days after Lohar died," Kali tells me. "We're hoping he might be sympathetic once he learns the truth about what happened at the palace."

"You're facing an uphill battle there," I say, thinking of the fury on Prince Amar's face, the hatred in his eyes. Even if we were pardoned for regicide, he could still punish us for his brothers' deaths. Imprison us for life if he so chooses.

"But—" Kali stops abruptly at the sound of pattering feet. Another girl bursts into the room, her eyes bright with excitement. She must be in her twenties or so, her face tattooed exactly like Esther's. She pauses to stare at me for a moment, as if marveling at my wakefulness. She grins. "Brilliant. He's awake."

"Yes, Sami." Esther's voice is calm, holds only a trace of impatience. "Did you come specifically to see that?"

Sami shakes her head. "Oh no, Didi! I wanted to let you know that the Star Warrior is awake, too!"

"Where are *you* going?" Esther's stern voice makes me realize I've been making a move to follow them out of the room.

"I'm only going—"

"Nowhere," Kali cuts me off, and with a hand gently, but firmly, steers me back inside. "Come on, Cavas. You'll get to see Gul soon. We need to make sure you're fed a proper meal before you can move around again."

"I'm not hungry." My stomach growls a split second later, traitorous thing.

"Sami will get you some food." Kali smiles. "We won't keep you caged in here. I promise."

Perhaps they wouldn't. But this city is a prison itself. Defeated, I sag back onto the bed. *Gul's all right*, I tell myself. *She's alive.* The crushing weight on my ribs lessens somewhat. Cool air wafts in through the window, and I suddenly remember what Indu said a few days ago about specters living here, in the city of shadows.

"Papa?" I whisper into the air around me. "Are you there?"

In the distance, there are more *clack*ing sounds. But no answering whisper. No Papa.

"Papa?" I say again, loudly this time.

"He won't be here."

I stiffen at the sound of the voice. "Show yourself."

He does, at once, appearing right next to the window where I stood only moments earlier, his gray body almost translucent in the sunlight.

"Don't ever do that again." My words feel like an echo, a reminder of something I'd heard once before—from Gul, I realize. She'd said the same thing to me when I'd held on to her hand, had somehow stopped her from killing Prince Amar with her magic.

"I'm sorry, boy," Latif says, a strange sheen to his gray eyes. "I know I failed your father. Failed to keep my promise to you. But he isn't here with us now. He never will be."

"How can you know?" I demand. "He'll come if I call for him! Papa! Papa!"

My voice echoes in the small room, but there is no answer. Latif's expression is oddly sympathetic.

"Why, then," I ask, "are you still here?"

Why you and not him?

"Your father was ready to die," Latif says. "I wasn't. If your father wanted to stay, you would have seen him emerge from his body in specter form right after he died."

The words splinter something inside me. But I do not cry. Not a tear emerges as Latif continues staring at me in silence. What use are tears? When have they ever been of use?

"You'll have to cry sometime, boy. It's never any good keeping grief bottled up."

I don't scold him for reading my thoughts. All I know is that I won't be crying.

Not today. Never again.

"Not even when you see your mother?" Latif's voice is quiet.

"Don't you dare play games with me."

"I'm not playing games. Your mother is here. She is a specter as well."

"I know she's a specter. But she doesn't want to see me, remember?" I point out in a hard voice. "She never came when I called for her. You confirmed it."

"Why she did not come and see you is her story to tell," Latif says. "But she does want to see you, boy. She hasn't forgotten her only son."

"Oh really? Where is she, then?"

But Latif refuses to tell me where my mother is in this moment. "Apart from you, Esther is the only other seer in Tavan. I don't want her getting angry with me for disturbing your rest," he tells me. "Your mother will come to you tonight. Right now, she's on guard duty at the city's boundary with the other specters."

"Guard duty?"

"How else do you think Tavan has remained safe all these years? The specters circle the golden bars and make sure the city remains invisible."

Before I can respond, Latif disappears again, and I'm left to stare into the space he leaves behind.

The hours go by slow when you have nothing to do. Even slower when you're desperately waiting for someone who also happens to be your mother. But my injuries make movement difficult, and Esther's medicine is strong. I doze intermittently, finally falling into a deep sleep. When I wake again, Sunheri is a full moon outside my window. I force myself to rise up into a sitting position.

I feel my mother's presence before I see her standing by the window: a shadow among the many others cleaving to the wall. Like Latif, my mother's skin and hair are gray, and so is her worn sari. In the yellow moonlight, I can almost pretend that her eyes are green the way Papa said they were when she was alive. For the first time, I see bits and pieces of myself in another person—in the slant of her jaw, the protruding tip of her nose, in the smile that now curves her lips. My stupid eyes want to brim over. I blink them dry.

"My precious boy." Unlike Latif, who strides with the grounded gait of a man still alive, my mother doesn't walk as much as she floats, her fingers brushing me as lightly as butterfly wings. "At last. At long last I can show myself to you."

"Why?" I don't attempt to soften my tone. "Why now?"

Her hand drops from my cheek. "You have every right to be angry with me. I abandoned you, didn't I? Or it certainly seems like it. But what you don't know, my son, is that I did stay for a while. After giving birth to you, my body died. But my soul didn't. It still languished, longing to brush your face with a hand, to see you happy and safe. So I came back. Weekly at first and then daily when I realized you could see me. You always smiled when I appeared, did you know?"

The sadness in her voice tempers my rage. I will myself to remain silent.

"Your father saw you trying to talk to me when you were very small. You must have been about two years old. *Ma*, you kept saying over and over again. And then he knew. He understood what I'd become. He urged me to leave. To not show myself to you. 'What will I tell him when he starts asking more questions?' your papa demanded. 'When he asks how he can see living specters, but I cannot?'

"Now, wait," she interrupts before I can express my outrage. "Before you judge your father, think carefully. His hold on you was precarious. If the government discovered that you weren't his son—or that you were a seer—it would have done its best to make him give you up. Seers are that rare and valuable. To the world, you had to appear non-magus. You *needed* to be Xerxes's son. I agreed with him. Three years went by. My longing to see you increased. When you were five, I came to see you again. You'd grown so much. I wanted to touch you so badly, I reached out, forgetting that I wasn't supposed to. That you could see me.

"You were amazed, of course, and shocked. You went and told your father that you saw me, even brought him to the place where I revealed myself to you. The moment I saw Xerxes's face, I knew what a mistake I'd made. It took everything in me not to reveal myself to you then—to stay away."

My head spins, unable to process the enormity of what I'm hearing. "But you didn't come even when I found out the truth about my blood. When I called for you at the temple in the tenements. Why did you stay away then?"

"I thought you'd see me differently," she admits. "You were so angry, Cavas. I was afraid you wouldn't love me anymore."

"You are my mother. I can't *not* love you!" I force myself to breathe deeply. "I was angry with Papa. He was wrong to keep you away from me."

"He didn't keep me away. I chose to keep myself hidden. To make sure you were safe. Cavas!" she cries out when I slowly rise to my feet. "Cavas, you'll hurt your leg!"

"It doesn't hurt as much as what you've already told me," I say bitterly. Grief presses down, crushing the breath out of me. "Everything hurts."

"I know, my son," my mother says. Her cool arms wrap around my shoulders, pulling me close. Angry as I am, I can't bear to pull away.

"Ma," I say after a pause. "Who was he? My . . . the man who . . ." My voice trails off. I'm unable to use the phrase *my real father* or even *the man who sired me.*

But my mother understands.

I sense it from her tightening fingers, from the growing coldness of her embrace. I'm not entirely surprised when I open my eyes a moment later and find that she's gone, and that I'm alone once more in a darkened room.

40
GUL

They won't let me leave my room except to use the toilet. And even there, I'm accompanied by someone—usually Kali or the woman named Esther, her starry face so striking that it makes me speechless the first time I see it. I try to step out on my own—to see where I am, to find Cavas, who Esther said was in a room a few doors away from mine—but my head spins so much that I fall to the floor.

"If you move again, I'll shackle you," Kali threatens. "Neither of you are ready to step out of your rooms. It's a miracle you both woke up after inhaling all that dust."

"Cavash." My voice slurs. "Hish leg . . . Is it . . . ?"

"Esther says it's healing well." She hesitates, as if wanting to say something else, but then simply says, "Sami will bring in your lunch for you."

I grab her wrist. "Kali, w-wait—what about Juhi . . . Am-mira?"

"Imprisoned, from what we know, but still alive." Kali forces a smile. "You know how stubborn they both are. They're probably giving their interrogators hell."

My empty stomach turns over. I'm not fooled by Kali's bravado. "H-how . . . Who t-told you—"

"You'll find out everything soon," Kali says, gently withdrawing from my grip. Her face looks like it has aged several years. "Rest now, my girl, or Esther will have my head."

I call out Kali's name again, but my voice echoes in the empty room. I fall back against pillows that are nearly as soft as those in Rani Mahal. They make me forget where I am, my body shocked into a state of semiwakefulness that is nearly as awful as sleep. Now that I'm awake, all I can do is relive what happened at the palace. Shayla killing my attendant and King Lohar. Cavas's father dying. Juhi fighting with Alizeh, giving us time to run. Amira's scream of pain.

A soft knock on the door makes me look up. A tall, muscular girl of perhaps Amira and Kali's age stands at the threshold, a plate of food in her hands. Her fine black curls are held back in a bun, her bronze skin tattooed exactly like Esther's, with silver-and-black stars over the forehead. She's dressed like the older woman as well—in a short blue tunic and billowing trousers that cinch at the ankles.

"You're awake," she says, and I'm surprised by how soft her voice is. "I can't tell you how long I've waited—how long we've all waited—for you."

"What d-do you mean?"

She walks into the room slowly, holds up the plate like an offering. "You're the One. The girl the prophecy foretold."

I want to deny this. To tell her that I'm no Star Warrior and that I didn't even kill the king. But something about her expression gives me pause. It has been so long since someone has looked at me without any calculation or dislike. I take the plate from her hands. Warm, fragrant roti. Small bowls of cool yogurt and steaming black lentils. A whole pink onion, the outer shell removed.

"I know it isn't much," she says, sounding embarrassed. "Not like what you're probably used to—"

"It's m-more than what I'm used t-to," I say slowly, carefully enunciating each word. And I'm not just talking about the food. I rip into the roti and shovel a morsel of the lentils into my mouth. Without even thinking about it, I take a bite out of the onion and then grimace at the sweet and pungent taste. My disgust makes the girl laugh. I find myself smiling back.

"I'm Sami," she says.

"I'm Gul."

She grins again, and I realize she probably already knows who I am. "He's handsome. Your neela chand."

Neela chand. The Vani phrase for blue moon. Or mate. I begin sputtering. "C-cavas? He's not m-my neela—he's not my mate."

In fact, I'm pretty sure he regrets that I'm still alive. From the startled look on Sami's face, I realize I've spoken that thought out loud.

"Sami!" a voice calls from outside the room. Esther. "Where are you?"

"Coming, Esther Didi!" Sami looks guilty, as if she has been caught doing something she shouldn't be. She clasps my left wrist and gives it a squeeze. "I don't know much about love and things like that. They brought me here shortly after I was born. But he called for you when he was asleep. When I told Esther Didi you had woken from your dust dream, he tried to follow her outside."

She leaves me there, staring into space, with a hope that I have no right to feel blooming in my chest.

It takes three more days before the grogginess subsides and Esther declares I'm fit to leave the room.

Sami holds out her hand to help, but I shake my head. I don't want to appear weaker than I already am.

"Burdens lessen when shared, Gul ji," Sami says softly.

"I wish you'd call me Gul," I tell her. I don't deserve any honorific after my name. In fact, Sami's words remind me so much of Cavas, it's painful. My heart races with the knowledge that I will see him today. Esther said she wants to speak to both of us first in the courtyard outside.

Though my room has windows, there's a vast difference between looking out at the courtyard from here and stepping into the open and feeling the ground under my sandaled feet. A pair of girls dressed in blue tunics and trousers pass us by. Their foreheads are tattooed like Sami's, and they gape when they see me dressed exactly the way they are, except with a bare face.

"Move on!" Sami's voice, so soft while speaking to me, sharpens while addressing them. "Get to training!"

After the girls leave, I turn to Sami again and finally ask the question I'd been too hesitant to over the past three days. "Sami, your tattoos. What do they mean?"

Sami smiles with a touch of pride. "The tattoos mean we are the Legion of the Star Warrior. It was Esther Didi's idea. We've been training for the past twenty years. Well, I've only been training for fourteen. We all knew you would come someday."

"The Legion of the Star Warrior?" The words make me feel queasy. *Does she mean what I think she means?* "Are you an army?"

"Yes," Sami says patiently. "But we're not just any army. We're *your* army. Ready to fight at your command."

Overhead, I hear voices rising and falling in a chant: *The sky has fallen! A star will rise!* The familiar clack of sticks rattles the air, making my skin break out in goose bumps.

I wonder what Sami will say if I tell her that I didn't kill the king. Or that the king's death has only unleashed the sort of chaos I didn't even imagine. But before I can open my mouth and reveal any of this, a pair of figures emerges from the building behind us. Kali, followed by Cavas, who walks with a slight limp. My eyes take in everything: the dark-red angrakha that fits him like a glove, the loose white trousers, his head bare of its usual orange turban, silky black locks falling over his forehead. My hands itch to push them aside. The scar on his face has healed well; in a few days, barely a trace will remain.

Cavas is studying me in a similar fashion. A faint flush rises up his neck, over his jaw, which holds traces of a patchy beard. There are purple shadows under his brown eyes—as if he's been sleeping as badly as I have.

"You look well," he says, and I wonder if there's a trace of bitterness there, mingled with the obvious relief in his voice.

"I, uh, need to check on Esther and see where she is," Sami says before rushing off somewhere. Kali murmurs something in response. Cavas's eyes widen, and a moment later, I realize why: I've moved several steps forward, hands reaching out for him. I drop them, blushing.

"You . . . you're all right? Your leg . . ." I curse myself for my own inept mutterings.

His lips, I realize, appear a lot fuller when he smiles. "I've been better." He blinks as if remembering something, and his expression shutters.

"Cavas, I'm sorry for—"

"Don't." His breath rushes out as if he's been holding it in. "I can't. Not now."

I nod. I can't expect him to forgive me for what happened at the palace. Not in this moment. Perhaps never.

"Do you know why Esther wants to see us?" I force myself to change the subject.

"I think she wants us to meet someone. Though I'm not sure who. I've asked," he adds, when he sees me raise an eyebrow.

A gust of air curls around us, bringing tears to my eyes. For a moment, I think it's the dust again, but Cavas suddenly moves forward and pulls me away from the wind with a frown. "That was a—"

"Living specter," I finish. I can feel its presence now, hear the malevolent cackle. A girl.

"They're all over this place," Cavas says quietly. "Some are women. Some are little girls like Indu. They probably died while their magic was being drained out of them."

My stomach turns over. Indu was simply another girl who had been taken from her family, who had been tortured until she became a specter. "All these specters . . . they're from Tavan?"

"Most, but not all. Latif didn't die here." Cavas pauses for a moment. "And I officially met my mother. She's a living specter as well."

The words take a moment to register. "By the goddess! Cavas, you must be . . ." My voice trails off when I see his expression. *Uh-oh.* "Did your meeting not go well?"

He lets forth a bitter laugh. "To say the least."

I'm deliberating on how to respond to this when the sound of footsteps makes me turn. Esther has emerged from the building. "Oh good. Everyone's here now. Well, almost everyone."

I look around her but see no one else. "Who is it that we're supposed to be meeting? Where are they?"

"It's only one person," Esther says, hesitating slightly. "I would have brought him here, but Kali believes I should prepare you first, give you both a bit of background."

I glance at Kali apprehensively, but she simply shakes her head. *Listen*, her eyes tell me.

"In a few minutes, you'll be meeting with our savior," Esther says. "The Pashu king, Subodh."

Cavas is frowning—as puzzled as I am. I wonder for a moment if it's a joke. But from the grim expressions on Kali's and Esther's faces, I can tell it isn't. "But Raja Subodh's dead. He's supposed to have died during the Battle of the Desert. There are portraits of Sky Warriors parading his head around the city of Ambarvadi!"

"That was an ordinary lion's head," Esther says quietly. "Lohar wanted people to think he killed the Pashu king, but he really hadn't, not even with a giant atashban that took ten Sky Warriors to power it. When the Pashu armies perished or retreated, Subodh was one of the few left fighting. But he was also injured. Badly. Lohar managed to shoot a spell chaining him to Tavan. But Lohar hadn't anticipated what Subodh had done before. Subodh and the Pashu had killed the guards at the labor camp and freed the rest of us girls."

Her voice rises, gaining strength. "We rose as one to fight—the living and the dead. The living fought off the Sky Warriors. The dead—well, most of them were living specters, really—turned us and the whole city invisible. When Subodh woke, he helped the specters reinforce the city's invisibility by raising a magical gate. As long as the specters remain on guard, the gate cannot be breached. It's why, whenever the Sky Warriors returned, they couldn't find us, their spells shooting into nothingness."

"Why is Subodh still here, though?" Cavas asks. "Why didn't he break his chains and leave?"

"Lohar's magic was too strong. The chains burned whenever Subodh tried to break them. Nearly killed him at one time. It's only now that the king has died, they've been broken and—"

"—I've finally been freed."

His voice reminds me of rainfall, of thunder rumbling in the sky.

Even being told of his existence beforehand doesn't prepare me for the sight of the rajsingha standing behind us: nearly twice as tall as a tall man, his torso and legs the only parts of him that resemble a human, though these, too, are covered in a coat of tan fur. A thick mane surrounds a heavily scarred face, some wounds healed, some fresh, right around the whiskers. His eyes are like liquid suns, glowing even from this distance. I have the oddest feeling he can look right into me, can read my mind without a touch. I'm not sure I like it.

It seems both strange and perfectly natural for him to slink into a crouch and walk to us on all fours, reptilian tail swaying behind him—though I'm certain he could, if he wished, walk to us the way a human would. Or someone who is both lion and human. King Subodh of the

Pashu. Neither Cavas nor I move as he pauses before us and scans our faces.

"Welcome," Subodh says in perfect Vani. "We've been waiting for you, Star Warrior. And you, Seer."

I'm no Star Warrior, I want to tell him. *I don't deserve your hopes. Or your dreams.*

Bite your tongue, girl. A chill goes through me. It's Subodh's voice in my head. Whispering to me. *Don't speak your mind. Not yet.* Though Juhi had told me that it was the Pashu who taught humans whispering in the first place, it's still shocking to hear Subodh's voice, to realize that his magic was so swift, so smooth that I didn't even feel him attempting to create a bond with me.

"Come with me," Subodh says out loud to the four of us. "The birds will bring news, I hope. Nearly two weeks have passed."

"Yes, Raja Subodh." Esther bows.

Subodh lightly brushes his forehead against hers. "Bless you, little sister. But I am not a king anymore."

He leads us out of the courtyard and down a road paved with cobblestones that glitter whenever the sun falls on them. Small, mud-brick houses rise on both sides, their roofs flat instead of thatched with hay. Beyond that, a city—or the ruins of what once must have been one— dust lining broken pillars of stone and marble, gilded rags fluttering from the flagpoles of abandoned temples.

"Tavan used to be beautiful a long time ago," Subodh says. "Autonomous in many ways and self-sufficient. A city made for the desert. Its people were brave enough to rebel against Lohar's ascent to the throne. Lohar crushed the rebellion brutally, executed the Tavani governor, and turned the city into a labor camp." He gestures to the walls of the houses, some of which are marked with red atashbans. "We can't get the marks out. No matter what we do."

Two girls are drying dates on one side, a sheet of brown pebbles on a blanket on the ground. When Subodh passes by, they call out greetings, which he returns. I feel them watching me as well; unlike Esther, they're frowning, as if they can't quite believe my presence.

Intruder, their body language suggests. *Impostor.*

"How many people live here?" Cavas asks. He's looking at the girls as well.

"Of those who have survived these twenty years in the desert, about fifty. There used to be thrice as many before," Subodh says. "There were about fourteen labor camps when I was imprisoned. I don't know how many are left now."

"Still far too many." Kali is the one who responds. Her lips are ashen, and I suddenly remember that she was at a camp as well. That Juhi helped her and Amira escape.

"Perhaps there won't be any left by the end of the year," Subodh says gently. "We've sent the new king a message by shvetpanchhi, asking for his pardon. My sources tell me he's different from his father. More malleable."

I think of Amar, the confusion I saw in his eyes when I accused him of colluding with Shayla. Was I wrong? Did he really want to help me avoid binding with Sonar? I hesitate before asking Subodh the next question. "Why are you doing this? You're free now. You could . . . leave."

"I can and I will. Once I'm assured that Esther and her girls are safe. That they can return home. After all they did to keep me alive and well, it's the least I can do."

His words feel like a gut punch. I think of Juhi, who rescued me. Of Amira, who infiltrated the palace despite the awful things I said to her. I might have talked about avenging my parents, but in truth I was only thinking of one person: myself.

Do not judge yourself too harshly, Savak-putri Gulnaz. Subodh's voice feels like a gentle breeze in my mind. *I am older than you are and have made mistakes that are even bigger. There are always ways to make amends.*

Moments later, we've left the houses behind and are approaching a copse of date palms and other trees. *A mirage*, I think, when I see the water, but when Subodh pauses before it, I realize it's a rectangular reservoir, the surface so flat and clear that it might be a mirror reflecting the clear blue sky.

"Hundreds of years ago, the rulers of Ambar learned that they would need a more consistent supply of water apart from the rain that fell every Month of Tears to sustain their land-locked kingdom," Subodh tells us. "They built a series of underground aqueducts to supply their towns and cities from the River Aloksha and from the Prithvi mountains. During the Great War, though, Prithvi raised its wall, and many of the underground channels dried up, along with the Aloksha itself. Raja Lohar was forced to build new underground channels from the Jwaliyan mountains to supply the kingdom's cities and villages."

"How does this reservoir survive?" Cavas asks. "Raja Lohar might have not been able to get into Tavan because it was invisible, but he still could block your supply of water."

A shiver goes through me as Subodh turns his great yellow eyes in Cavas's direction. But maybe meeting his mother changed things, because Cavas stares back at the Pashu king fearlessly, completely different from the cowed boy I'd seen before.

"You're right," Subodh says, and I think I hear a smile in his voice. "After the Battle of the Desert, Lohar *did* block our water supply. Luckily, this reservoir wasn't empty. With the help of a little magic, I keep replenishing its water and make sure it never dips below a certain level. It's the only reason we've survived this long."

"What about the food?" Cavas asks. "Surely you can't grow everything here. The soil isn't fertile enough."

"Right again," Subodh says. "Let me show you. Esther, would you please . . ."

Without a word, Esther walks to the edge of the water and quietly adds a drop of clear liquid from a vial.

"That is drishti jal from the waterfalls of Aman," Subodh explains.

"The Pashu use it to scour the truth and communicate with one another. To travel and bring provisions—if necessary. It's how we have been getting food that is harder to grow in the desert, even with magic. It will not work as well for a human."

"I've tried," Esther admits, a little sheepishly. "I thought I could go out and get us some food. But the water tossed me out."

Subodh places a paw against the water: It glows, turning for a brief moment into a human hand, then a hoof, then a bird's foot with talons. He raises his head and makes a terrible shrieking sound. The surface of the water turns silver. For a long moment, there's utter silence. Then:

A hum in the air, which sends a shiver down my spine.

The water begins to churn, concentric and swirling, sinking deeper and deeper to allow a figure to rise from within. My breath catches.

It's a simurgh. A Pashu with a woman's face and an eagle's beak and wings. Peacock feathers curl around her, gleaming like jewels, fanning out like a cloud. If Subodh's eyes are suns, hers are the night sky: black and deep, glittering with infinite stars. A small crown rests on her head. Not only a simurgh, but also a queen. Over twenty gunnysacks are clutched in her beak and her claws. She rises in the air above us and then drops them gently onto the ground.

"Food. To last you for the next three months," the simurgh says, perching before Subodh. She is nearly as large as he is, and her voice sounds like several birds singing at once.

"Rani Sarayu," Subodh says, bowing. "You honor us with your presence and your gifts."

Without even thinking, I sink into a bow as well. Beside me, I see Kali, Cavas, and Esther doing the same.

"Raja Subodh." Sarayu bows in front of him and tilts her magnificent head to acknowledge the rest of us. "I am only a regent. The land of Aman and the Pashu still await their true king."

"I have never been a good ruler, Rani Sarayu." Subodh's voice is grave. "But I do hope to return home. You said you have news."

Sarayu says nothing for a long moment. "We do have . . . news. The message was delivered by one of my birds, three days ago, shortly after the new king, Amar, was crowned. There was a meeting going on between the new king and the palace vaid. My bird overheard the vaid telling Raja Amar about how he found traces of poison in the old king's body. The poison was likely being fed to him over years at a time. The vaid mentioned that the new general, Shayla, had been responsible for overseeing Raja Lohar's security, including his food. The information made Raja Amar furious."

There's a crawling sensation in my belly.

"Later, when my bird delivered the letter, she ensured that Raja Amar read the whole scroll. He sent back a letter in return, asking if he could meet you." She holds up a scroll but does not hand it over.

"What happened to him, Sarayu?" Subodh growls. "What are you not telling me?"

"There was a coup that night. I found out through my other birds only this morning."

I don't want to hear what Sarayu says next. But I can't make myself walk away.

"The Sky Warriors, led by General Shayla, ambushed the new king when he came to see his mother in Rani Mahal. The chase led to the servants' quarters in the palace, to a hidden passage. The Sky Warriors were shooting atashbans at him. Raja Amar jumped out of the window, over two hundred feet to the palace grounds."

My heart sinks. Next to me, Cavas curses out loud.

"Did he survive?" Subodh asks urgently. "Did you check?"

"My birds saw no traces of blood in the area. But a funeral was held for Raja Amar the next day. Perhaps the Sky Warriors found his body before we did. Or perhaps they used a false body in his place. We don't know for sure."

A drop of over two hundred feet. Amar could have floated above the ground, the way some magi children in my village did when I was younger. The way I finally did, after I dropped into my mother's arms.

Or perhaps he couldn't.

Magic doesn't work the same way for everyone. I think back to how Amar could conjure daggers and bees but not a shield to protect himself. And falling from that height, at that speed . . . As much as I want Amar to be alive, I know the possibilities of his surviving that fall are slim to none.

"General Shayla declared Raja Amar's death a suicide—the unfortunate aftermath of his father's and brothers' murders," Sarayu says. "She has also declared a bounty of five thousand swarnas for the heads of the new leaders of the rebellion."

Sarayu raises her wings, revealing two faces within: Cavas's and mine.

It's my fault, I think, feeling nauseous. *I made up my mind to kill the king. I infiltrated the palace without thinking of the consequences of what would happen after he died.*

Others have paid the price for my thoughtless actions. Juhi and Amira, who are now being tortured in captivity. The marked girls, who are still locked up in labor camps. Amar, who is now dead. I don't dare look at Cavas, who is now part of a war he never wanted to fight.

A pair of voices echo in my head:

You must be a leader when all hope is lost.
We're your army. Ready to fight at your command.

A small, selfish part of me longs to go back into hiding. To forget everything I've done.

But you are not that girl anymore, a voice in my head reminds me— my own. *Even if you hide from other people, you will never be able to hide from yourself.*

The knot in my chest unravels.

My reprieve here in Tavan is temporary. The time will come when I will have to go back to Ambarvadi. When I will have no choice but to face Shayla, regardless of what happens next.

As if sensing my thoughts, Queen Sarayu's beautiful, terrible eyes find mine again before she makes her final pronouncement:

"The Sky Warriors, the army, the ministers, the courtiers, and Lohar's three queens have unanimously accepted General Shayla as the protector of Ambar and sworn fealty to her.

"She was crowned queen by the head priest this morning."

A QUEEN AND A HOUND

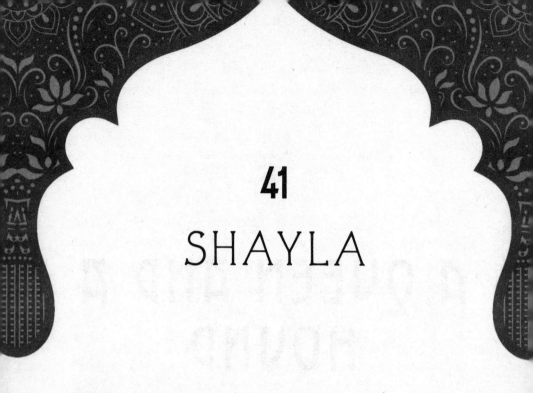

41

SHAYLA

"No news yet, Rani Shayla."

The messenger speaks in Paras, the language of Jwala. He's young, perhaps in his late teens, his skin sun-browned, his copper hair shining under the bright lightorb in my private chambers in Raj Mahal.

Black flames tattoo the muscles of his bare arms, the way they do all the Jwaliyan queen's precious hounds, the best trackers and messengers on the continent. He gives me a smile—wide, toothy, and dimpled. A boy used to the effects of his own charm. I tilt my head sideways, scan his dirty brown vest and orange dhoti, the red dust caking the pointed tips of his shoes.

"Did you travel from Jwala by foot?" I ask in Paras, my accent perfect, my voice like silk.

The boy's smile slips. "I did. H-her M-majesty, the rani of Jwala, c-couldn't spare any horses."

"Interesting. A kingdom known for its horsepower unable to spare *one* to reply to an urgent message." My lips curl into something that might outwardly resemble a smile.

Some ally the Jwaliyan rani was. Then again, she had been acting up even when Lohar was still alive. Cutting off the water supply for first one, then two, then four Ambari reservoirs. Slowly reducing the number of Jwaliyan horses gifted to the king every year. Using *old age* as an excuse for the past few years to avoid diplomatic visits to our kingdom.

The boy's knees knock together, bone audibly hitting bone. Behind him, Alizeh's gray eyes meet mine. She is the only one who watches me without fear. The only one whose loyalty I can count on. It's why I made her my general. Gave her a uniform of pristine white and silver.

"Lohar-putra Amar, the conjurer king, is gone," I say. "His body vanished into thin air. And you tell me that no one can find it. Not even you, one of the continent's best hounds."

It had been easy to fake the conjurer's death. To kill a non-magus palace worker, deface his corpse, dress it in royal finery, and place it in the casket before it was buried. The sound of Queen Amba's sobs made things better. Sweeter.

Finding the conjurer's *real* body was another story altogether. He wasn't lying broken on the palace grounds after his fall. Nor did we find him in any of the palace's secret tunnels. I know. I had my own hounds look everywhere.

The messenger's soft mouth trembles. "M-my queen, I—"

"I am not your queen, messenger. *Your* queen is in Jwala," I cut in. "*Your* queen did not have the courtesy to congratulate me on my ascension. *Your* queen ignored the urgency of my message and took *two whole weeks* to send me a useless boy with a worthless answer."

"Kabzedar," the conjurer king had called me before leaping from the window in Rani Mahal. Usurper in the Common Tongue. "You will never be accepted in Ambar. You will never be its true queen."

Amar thought himself so smart. Thought he could imprison me based on a fool vaid's simple testimony about the poison berries they found in Lohar's body. In the drink that I pretended to sip for him every day.

363

Silly boy. Naive king. Did Amar really think it was easy to defeat the most powerful magus in Ambar without weakening him a little? Had he forgotten how his own father had poisoned my mother?

My newly forged gold crown fits like second skin, tapers to a point with a teardrop-shaped firestone in the center. I watch the messenger's eyes flicker to it from time to time, as if mesmerized by the lights dancing in the jewel's many facets. Is he thinking now about how I'd ripped the stone from the *real* kabzedar's turban, shortly after I'd sliced his throat?

Unlike the rulers of old, who dressed for politics in colorful, resplendent silks, I dress for battle: my tunic and trousers made of lightweight black silk, my armor and boots made of matching leather. As far as ornaments go, however, a queen's crown isn't a bad thing. It's the only jewelry I wear now, along with the three firestones studding my left ear. My mother's firestones, three of her tiniest jewels that I'd stolen years ago from the usurper's Ministry of Treasure—*my* Ministry of Treasure.

"Do you know what I do to men who lie to me?" I ask the messenger now. "Do you know what I did to my own father?"

My Sky Warrior father thought he was protecting me when he told me that my mother had never wanted a daughter. He thought he was doing right when he enrolled me in the academy for the kingdom's most elite soldiers the year I turned five—just to keep me out of the queen's sight. Back then, I was one of two girls among twenty boys. Over the next twelve years, only three of our batch survived the training necessary to become Sky Warriors: Alizeh, Emil, and me. Twelve years had been more than enough time to learn how a woman's body could be used and abused at the academy, how little her tears mattered in this world.

My mother would have never let them hurt me. She would have never let me cry.

Yet your mother never tried seeking you out, did she? The thought hovers at the edges of my mind, has Lohar's serpentine voice. *She never even looked at your face.*

I rise from my chair and make my way to where the messenger stands, his scattered breath brushing my cheek. "I crept up on my father while he was sleeping," I whisper. "I sank the tip of my atashban between his ribs and carved out his heart, the organ still pumping blood in my hands."

As if to demonstrate, I withdraw my obsidian and firestone atashban, a weapon newly forged to be more powerful than Lohar's original design. The boy's throat bobs, but my arrow tip is sharp. The line I'm carving into his flesh doesn't falter.

Hiss. A trickle of water. No, *piss* soiling the Jwaliyan messenger's bright-orange dhoti. A sour smell rises in the air.

My laugh breaks the quiet of the room, is echoed by Alizeh.

"Poor child," I say lazily. "I branded him with only half of the royal seal." A new seal made of my mother's trident crossed with a Sky Warrior's atashban. A symbol that I wear stitched over my black silk tunic in scarlet.

The trident I've carved into the messenger's skin gleams wet and red. He whimpers.

So young. So pitiful. So *boring.*

"Toss him into the dungeons," I tell Alizeh, setting my atashban aside. "The shadowlynx needs to be fed. Any leftovers can be boxed up for our dear ally, the queen in Jwala."

"Wait!" The messenger's voice is barely more than a squeak. "Wait, Rani Shayla! I can tell you more. I saw living specters on my way here. They're all over the city. Singing, rejoicing!" He trembles when I turn to face him. "I . . . I'm a seer, my queen. I swear I'm telling the truth!"

He is. I have seen enough liars to know the difference. *A seer.* Half magus. Half dirt licker.

I raise a finger. Alizeh lets go of the boy's arms.

"What were they singing, messenger?" My voice is as soft as a mother's. Nearly as kind.

The messenger releases a shaky breath. The voice that emerges from his throat, however, high and oddly pure:

> *The sky has fallen, a star will rise*
> *Ambar changed by a king's demise*
> *A girl with a mark, a boy with her soul*
> *Their fates intertwined, two halves of a whole*
> *Usurpers have come, usurpers will go*
> *The true king waits for justice to flow.*

Fury rises, burning my neck and my ears. That stupid Star Warrior and her worthless dirt licker lover. Hindering me all over again. I breathe deeply. No matter. I would deal with them both the way I dealt with the kabzedar king. The way I dealt with the dirt-licking maids whom my father had bribed to lie to my mother, telling her I was a boy.

I rest a hip against my desk and clap my hands once. A wooden chair slides forward, knocking into the back of the Jwaliyan messenger's thighs. He collapses into a sitting position, his lips chapped and dry. He no longer attempts to woo me with stupid smiles.

"You have my attention, messenger," I say. "Now tell me more about these living specters."

Glossary

Note: *You will find many of the terms below common to our world and the former empire of Svapnalok. However, there are a few words that differ slightly in meaning and/or are used specifically in the context of Svapnalok. These have been marked with an asterisk (*) wherever possible.*

acharya: A scholar and religious leader

almari: A cupboard

*Ambarnaresh: A title for the king of Ambar

*Anandpranam: The happiest of salutations

angrakha: A long tunic that is tied at the left or right shoulder

*atashban: A powerful magical weapon resembling a crossbow

bajra roti: A flatbread made with pearl millet

bhaiyya: Brother

chaas: A cold drink made of yogurt

chakra: A disc-shaped weapon with sharp edges

chameli: Jasmine

champak: An evergreen tree with fragrant orange flowers

*Chandni Raat: The night of the moon festival; native to Svapnalok

*chandrama: A sweet, circular pastry, garnished with edible foil and rose petals

choli: A short blouse; worn with a sari or *ghagra*

*Dev Kal: The era of the gods

dhoti: A garment wrapped around the lower half of the body, passed between the legs, and tucked into the waistband

*dhulvriksh: A desert tree with rootlike branches; native to the kingdom of Ambar and the Brimlands

didi: Elder sister

*drishti jal: A magical elixir used by *Pashu* to travel and communicate with each other; native to the kingdom of Aman

dupatta: A shawl-like scarf

ektara: A drone lute with a single string

fanas: Lantern

ghagra: A full-length skirt; worn by women with a *choli* and *dupatta*

ghat: A set of steps along a riverbank

ghee: Clarified butter

gulab: Rose

haveli: A mansion

*indradhanush: A rainbow-hued metal; native to the Brimlands

jambiya: A short, double-edged dagger

*jantar-mantar: An illusion; derogatory term for false magic tricks in Svapnalok

jatamansi: An herb used to darken hair

ji: An honorific, usually placed after a person's name; can also be used as respectful acknowledgment, in the place of "yes"

jootis: Flat shoes with pointed tips

kabzedar: Usurper

kaccha sari: A sari draped in a manner similar to a *dhoti*, for ease of movement; worn with a *choli*

kachori: A round, fried pastry stuffed with a sweet or savory filling

kadhi: A cream-colored gravy, made of yogurt, chickpea flour, spices, and vegetables

kali: A flower bud (pronounced "kuh-lee"); not to be confused with the Hindu goddess Kali (pronounced "kaa-lee")

khichdi: A rice-and-lentil dish

khoba roti: A thick flatbread made with indents on the surface

lathi: A long wooden staff, used as a weapon

levta: A black mudfish

maang-teeka: A hair ornament; worn by women

madira: Alcohol

*makara: A *Pashu* who is part crocodile, part human

mawa: A sweet paste made by simmering milk on the stove

methi bajra puri: A fried flatbread made with spinach and pearl millet

moong dal: Split green gram

*neela chand: Refers to one's mate or soulmate in Svapnalok; literally translates to "blue moon"

pakoda: A vegetable fritter

pallu: The loose ends of a sari

paneer: A type of curd cheese

*Paras: The language of the kingdom of Jwala

*Pashu: A race of part-human, part-animal beings; native to the kingdom of Aman

peepul: A sacred fig tree

*peri: A gold-skinned *Pashu* who is part human, part bird

prasad: Food used as a religious offering, normally consumed after worship

pulao: A rice dish made with spices and vegetables and/or meat

putra: Son; when used as a suffix, it means "son of"

putri: Daughter; when used as a suffix, it means "daughter of"

raag: A melodic framework used for improvisation and composition of Indian classical music

rabdi: A sweet, creamy dish made with condensed milk and nuts

raj darbar: The royal court

raja: King

rajkumar: Prince

rajkumari: Princess

rajnigandha: Tuberose

rajsingha: A *Pashu* who is part lion, part human

rani: Queen

rekha: A magical barrier

rupee: A silver coin

sabzi: Cooked vegetables

sadhvi: A holy woman

samarpan: The act of dedication, submission, and sacrifice to a person or cause

sandhi: A symbiosis

sangemarmar: A white marble; native to the kingdom of Jwala

sant: Saint

Sau aabhaar: A hundred thank-yous

sev: Vermicelli

Shubhdivas: Good day

*Shubhraat: Good night

*Shubhsaver: Good morning

*shvetpanchhi: A large, carnivorous bird with white and black
feathers; native to Svapnalok

*simurgh: A *Pashu* who is part eagle and part peacock with a woman's
face

sohan halwa: A sweet made of *ghee*, milk, flour, and sugar

surma: A black cosmetic, used to line the eyes

*swarna: A gold coin

talwar: A long sword with a curved blade

thanedar: A police officer

thhor: A multistemmed, cactus-like succulent found in the desert

tulsi: Holy basil

*vaid: A magical healer

*Vani: The language of the kingdom of Ambar

*Yudhnatam: A martial art

yuvraj: Heir apparent

zamindar: An aristocratic landowner

Author's Note

The setting described in this book is, as the name suggests, a *svapnalok* or a "dream world"—a brief journey through my twisted imagination.

Having said that, fantasy is usually inspired by reality, and I drew inspiration from two different periods of Indian history while writing this story: the intellectual brilliance of Vedic India and the splendor of the medieval courts. Mythology also plays a role in this series, and I have drawn on both parts of my heritage—Indian and Persian—to conceive my own myths.

I've further been inspired by Indian women—from my mother, grandmothers, aunts, and friends, to historical figures such as Rani Lakshmibai, Nur Jahan, and Razia Sultana, and welfare organizations such as the Gulabi Gang.

That we are capable of magic and wielding weapons should surprise no one.

Acknowledgments

My heartfelt gratitude to:

The Canada Council for the Arts and the Ontario Arts Council for funding this project.

Mom for your endless love and the cups of tea, and Dad for our brainstorming power walks and always asking me: "What happens next?"

Janine O'Malley and Melissa Warten—for your editorial brilliance and patiently talking things through with me as both Gul and I traveled unfamiliar paths in this book.

Eleanor Jackson—for always having my back no matter how much time passes between our conversations. I couldn't have asked for a better agent.

Beth Clark and Shreya Gupta—for your cover designing and map-making excellence.

Tracy Koontz and Mandy Veloso—for keeping me on track with your pertinent copyediting questions.

Kelsey Marrujo, Allegra Green, Katie Halata, Kristen Luby, Gaby Salpeter, and everyone at Macmillan Children's publicity and school and library marketing teams—for your tireless work and support behind the scenes.

Erika David, Bridget Hodder, Laith Khalil, and Carlie Sorosiak—for being amazing early readers. Your advice on this book's prior iterations was invaluable.

Kristen Ciccarelli—for your generosity, kindness, and heart. I'm so glad I know you.

Megan Bannen—fellow Nizami and Ranveer Singh fan, all your "Megan-specific comments" were the very best ones.

Shveta Thakrar—tara prem ane protsahan mate khub khub aabhaar. Your honest feedback helped me tons.

Lynne Missen, Sam Devotta, and Team Penguin Canada—for championing this book on home ground.

Tarini Uppal and Team Penguin India—for your excitement and enthusiasm for all my books, including this kalpanik katha.